FIVE GO TO MYSTERY MOOR
FIVE HAVE PLENTY OF FUN
FIVE ON A SECRET TRAIL

Enid Blyton

The Famous Five

FIVE GO TO MYSTERY MOOR
FIVE HAVE PLENTY OF FUN
FIVE ON A SECRET TRAIL

**Hodder
Children's
Books**

a division of Hodder Headline Limited

Text copyright © Enid Blyton Ltd

Enid Blyton's signature is a Registered Trade Mark of Enid Blyton Ltd

This collection published in 2005
by Hodder Children's Books
For sale in the Indian Sub-continent only.

Five Go To Mystery Moor first published in Great Britain in 1954
Five Have Plenty of Fun first published in Great Britain in 1954
Five On a Secret Trail first published in Great Britain in 1956

The right of Enid Blyton to be identified as the Author of
the Work has been asserted by her in accordance with the
Copyright, Designs and Patents Act 1988.

For further information on Enid Blyton please contact
www.blyton.com

4 6 8 10 9 7 5 3

A Catalogue record for this book is available from the
British Library.

ISBN 0 340 91086 0

Typeset by Hewer Text Ltd, Edinburgh
Printed and bound in India by
Gopsons Papers Ltd., Noida

Hodder Children's Books
a division of Hodder Headline Limited
338 Euston Road
London NW1 3BH

FIVE GO TO MYSTERY MOOR

[1]

At the stables

'We've been here a week and I've been bored every single minute!' said George.

'You haven't,' said Anne. 'You've enjoyed all the rides we've had, and you know you've enjoyed messing about the stables when we haven't been out riding.'

'I tell you, I've been bored every single *minute*,' said George, quite fiercely. 'I ought to know, oughtn't I? That awful girl Henrietta too. Why do we have to put up with her?'

'Oh – Henry!' said Anne, with a laugh. 'I should have thought you'd find a lot in common with another girl like yourself, who would rather be a boy, and tries to act like one!'

The two girls were lying by a haystack eating sandwiches. Round them in a field were many horses, most of which the girls either rode or looked after. Some way off was an old rambling building, and by the front entrance was a great board,

Captain Johnson's Riding School

Anne and George had been staying there for a week, while Julian and Dick had gone to camp with other boys from their school. It had been Anne's idea. She was fond of horses, and had heard so much from her friends at school what fun it was to spend day after day at the stables, that she had made up her mind to go herself.

George hadn't wanted to come. She was sulky because the two boys had gone off somewhere without her and Anne, for a change. Gone to camp! George would have liked that, but girls were not allowed to go camping with the boys from Julian's school, of course. It was a camp just for the boys alone.

'You're silly to keep feeling cross because you couldn't go camping too,' said Anne. 'The boys don't want us girls round them all the time.'

George thought differently. 'Why not? I can do anything that Dick and Julian can do,' she said. 'I can climb, and bike for miles, I can walk as far as they can, I can swim, I can beat a whole lot of boys at most things.'

'That's what Henry says!' said Anne, with a laugh. 'Look, there she is, striding about as usual, hands in her jodhpur pockets, whistling like the stable boy!'

George scowled. Anne had been very much amused to see how Henrietta and George hated one another at sight – and yet both had so very much the same ideas. George's real name was Georgina, but she would only answer to George. Henry's real name was Henrietta, but she would only answer to Henry, or Harry to her *very* best friends!

She was about as old as George, and her hair was short too, but it wasn't curly. 'It's a pity yours is curly,' she said to George, pityingly. 'It looks so *girlish*, doesn't it?'

'Don't be an ass,' George said, curtly. 'Plenty of boys have curly hair.'

The maddening part was that Henrietta was a wonderful rider, and had won all kinds of cups. George hadn't enjoyed herself a bit during that week at the stables, because for once another girl had outshone her. She couldn't bear to see Henrietta striding about, whistling, doing everything so competently and quickly.

Anne had had many a quiet laugh to herself, especially when the two girls had each made up their minds not to call one another Henry and George, but to use their full names, Henrietta and Georgina! This meant that neither of them would answer the other when called, and Captain Johnson, the big burly owner of the riding stables, got very tired of both of them.

'What are you behaving like this for?' he demanded one morning, seeing their sulky looks at one another at breakfast-time. 'Behaving like a couple of idiotic schoolgirls!'

That made Anne laugh! A couple of idiotic school*girls*. My goodness, how annoyed both girls were with Captain Johnson. Anne was a bit scared of him. He was hot-tempered, outspoken, and stood no nonsense at all, but he was a wonder with the horses, and loved a good, hearty laugh. He and his wife took either boys or girls for the holidays, and worked them hard, but the children always enjoyed their stay immensely.

'If it hadn't been for Henry, you'd have been perfectly happy this week,' said Anne, leaning back against the haystack. 'We've had heavenly April weather, the horses are lovely, and I like Captain and Mrs Johnson very much.'

'I wish the boys were here,' said George. 'They would soon put that silly Henrietta in her place. I wish I'd stayed at home now.'

'Well, you had the choice,' said Anne, rather cross. 'You could have stayed at Kirrin Cottage with your father and mother, but you chose to come here with me, till the boys came back from camp. You shouldn't make such a fuss if things aren't exactly to your liking. It spoils things for *me*.'

'Sorry,' said George. 'I'm being a pig, I know, but I do miss the boys. We can only be with them in the hols and it seems funny without them. There's just *one* thing that pleases me here, you'll be glad to know . . .'

'You needn't tell me, I know what it is!' said Anne, with a laugh. 'You're glad that Timmy won't have anything to do with Henry!'

'With Henrietta,' corrected George. She grinned suddenly. 'Yes, old Timmy's got some sense. He just can't stick her. Here, Timmy boy, leave those rabbit holes alone and come and lie down for a bit. You've run for miles this morning when we took the horses out, and you've snuffled down about a hundred rabbit holes. Come and be peaceful.'

Timmy left his latest rabbit hole reluctantly and came to flop down beside Anne and George. He gave George a hearty lick and she patted him.

'We're just saying, Timmy, how sensible you are not to make friends with that awful Henrietta,' said George. She stopped suddenly at a sharp nudge from Anne. A shadow fell across them as someone came round the haystack.

It was Henrietta. By the annoyed look on her face it was clear that she had heard George's remark. She held out an envelope to George.

'A letter for you, Georgina,' she said, stiffly. 'I thought I'd better bring it in case it was important.'

'Oh, thanks, Henrietta,' said George, and took the envelope. She tore it open, read it and groaned.

'Look at that!' she said to Anne and passed it to her. 'It's from Mother.'

Anne took the letter and read it. 'Please stay another week. Your father is not well. Love from Mother.'

'What bad luck!' said George, a familiar scowl on her face. 'Just when I thought we'd be going home in a day or two, and the boys would join us at Kirrin. Now we'll be stuck here by ourselves for ages! What's the matter with Father? I bet he's only got a headache or something, and doesn't want us stamping about in and out of the house and making a noise.'

'We could go to *my* home,' said Anne. 'That's

if you don't mind its being a bit upside-down because of the decorating we're having done.'

'No. I know you want to stay here with the horses,' said George. 'Anyway your father and mother are abroad, we'd only be in the way. Blow, blow, blow! Now we'll have to do without the boys for another week. They'll stay on in camp, of course.'

Captain Johnson said yes, certainly the two girls could stay on. It was possible that they might have to do a bit of camping out if one or two extra children came, but they wouldn't mind that, would they?

'Not a bit,' said George. 'Actually we'd rather like to be on our own, Anne and I. We've got Timmy, you see. So long as we could come in to meals and do a few jobs for you, we'd love to go off on our own.'

Anne smiled to herself. What George really meant was that she wanted to see as little of Henrietta as possible! Still, it *would* be fun to camp out if the weather was fine. They could easily borrow a tent from Captain Johnson.

'Bad luck, Georgina!' said Henry, who was listening to all this. 'Very bad luck! I know you're terribly bored here. It's a pity you don't really like horses. It's a pity that you—'

'Shut up,' said George, rudely, and went out of the room. Captain Johnson glared at Henrietta, who stood whistling at the window, hands in pockets.

'You two girls!' he said. 'Why don't you behave yourselves? Always aping the boys, pretending you're so mannish! Give me Anne here, any day! What you want is your ears boxing. Did you take that bale of straw to the stables?'

'Yes,' said Henrietta, without turning.

Suddenly, a small boy came running in. 'There's a traveller kid outside with a horse, a skewbald, a mangy-looking thing. He says can you help him – the horse has got something wrong with its leg.'

'Those travellers again!' said Captain Johnson. 'All right, I'll come.'

He went out and Anne went with him, not

wanting to be left alone with the angry Henrietta. She found George outside with a traveller boy and a patient little skewbald horse, its brown and white coat looking very flea-bitten.

'What have you done to your horse *this* time?' said Captain Johnson, looking at its leg. 'You'll have to leave it here, and I'll see to it.'

'I can't do that,' said the boy. 'We're off to Mystery Moor again.'

'Well, you'll have to,' said Captain Johnson. 'It's not fit to walk. Your caravan can't go with the others, this horse isn't fit to pull it. I'll get the police to your father if you try to work this horse before it's better.'

'Don't do that!' said the boy. 'It's just that my dad says we've *got* to go tomorrow.'

'What's the hurry?' said Captain Johnson. 'Can't your caravan wait a day or two? Mystery Moor will still be there in two days' time! It beats me why you go there, a desolate place like that, not even a farm or cottage for miles!'

'I'll leave the horse,' said the boy, and

stroked the skewbald's nose. It was clear that he loved the ugly little horse. 'My father will be angry, but the other caravans can go on without us. We'll have to catch them up.'

He gave a kind of half-salute to the captain and disappeared from the stable-yard, a skinny little sunburnt figure. The skewbald stood patiently.

'Take it round to the small stable,' said Captain Johnson to George and Anne. 'I'll come and see to it in a minute.'

The girls led the little horse away. 'Mystery Moor!' said George. 'What an odd name! The boys would like that, they'd be exploring it at once, wouldn't they?'

'Yes. I do wish they were coming here,' said Anne. 'Still, I expect they'll like the chance of staying on in camp. Come on, you funny little creature, here's the stable!'

The girls shut the door on the traveller's pony and turned to go back. William, the boy who had brought the message about the horse, yelled to them.

'Hey, George and Anne! There's *another* letter for you!'

The two hurried into the house at once. 'Oh, I hope Father is better and we can go home and join the boys at Kirrin!' said George. She tore open the envelope and then gave a yell that made Anne jump.

'Look, see what it says. They're coming *here*!' Anne snatched the letter and read it.

'Joining you tomorrow. We'll camp out if no room. Hope you've got a nice juicy adventure ready for us! Julian and Dick.'

'They're coming! They're coming!' said Anne, as excited as George. '*Now* we'll have some fun!'

'It's a pity we've no adventure to offer them,' said George. 'Still, you simply never know!'

[2]
Julian, Dick – and Henry

George was quite a different person now that she knew her two cousins were coming the next day. She was even polite to Henrietta!

Captain Johnson scratched his head when he heard that the boys were arriving. 'We can't have them in the house, except for meals,' he said. 'We're full up. They can either sleep in the stables or have a tent. I don't care which.'

'There will be ten altogether then,' said his wife. 'Julian, Dick, Anne, George, Henry – and John, Susan, Alice, Rita and William. Henry may have to camp out too.'

'Not with us,' said George, at once.

'I think you're rather unkind to Henry,' said Mrs Johnson. 'After all, you and she are very alike, George. You both think you ought to have been boys, and—'

'I'm not a *bit* like Henrietta!' said George, indignantly. 'You wait till my cousins come, Mrs Johnson. *They* won't think she's like me. I don't expect they'll want anything to do with her.'

'Oh well, you'll just have to shake down together somehow, if you want to stay here,' said Mrs Johnson. 'Let me see, I'd better get some rugs out. The boys will want them, whether they sleep in the stables or in a tent. Come and help me to look for them, Anne.'

Anne, George and Henry were a good bit older than the other five children staying at the stables, but all of them, small or big, were excited to hear about the coming of Julian and Dick. For one thing George and Anne had related so many of the adventures they had had with them, that everyone was inclined to think of them as heroes.

Henrietta disappeared after tea that day and could not be found. 'Wherever have you been?' demanded Mrs Johnson when she at last turned up.

'Up in my room,' said Henrietta. 'Cleaning my shoes and my jods, and mending my riding jacket. You keep telling me to, and now I've done it!'

'Aha! Preparing for the heroes!' said Captain Johnson, and Henry immediately put on a scowl very like the one George often wore.

'Nothing of the sort!' she said. 'I've been meaning to do it for a long time. If Georgina's cousins are anything like *her* I shan't be very interested in them.'

'But you might like my brothers,' said Anne, with a laugh. 'If you don't there'll be something wrong with you.'

'Don't be silly,' said Henrietta. 'Georgina's cousins and your brothers are the same people!'

'How clever of you to work that out,' said George. But she felt too happy to keep up the silly bickering for long. She went out with Timmy, whistling softly.

'They're coming tomorrow, Tim,' she said. 'Julian and Dick. We'll all go off together, like we always do, the five of us. You'll like that, won't you, Timmy?'

'Woof,' said Timmy approvingly and waved his plumy tail. He knew quite well what she meant.

Next morning George and Anne looked up the trains that arrived at the station two miles away. 'This is the one they'll come by,' said George, her finger on the timetable. 'It's the only one this morning. It arrives at half past twelve. We'll go and meet them.'

'Right,' said Anne. 'We'll start at ten minutes to twelve – we'll be in plenty of time then. We can help them with their things. They won't bring much.'

'Take the ponies up to Hawthorn Field, will you?' called Captain Johnson. 'Can you manage all four of them?'

'Oh yes,' said Anne, pleased. She loved the walk to Hawthorn Field, up a little narrow lane set with celandines, violets and primroses, and the fresh green of the budding hawthorn bushes. 'Come on, George. Let's catch the ponies and take them now. It's a heavenly morning.'

They set off with the four frisky ponies, Timmy at their heels. He was quite a help with the horses at the stable, especially when any had to be caught.

No sooner had they left the stables and gone on their way to Hawthorn Field than the telephone rang. It was for Anne.

'Oh, I'm sorry, she's not here,' said Mrs Johnson, answering it. 'Who is it speaking? Oh, Julian her brother? Can I give her a message?'

'Yes, please,' said Julian's voice. 'Tell her we are arriving at the bus-stop at Milling Green at half past eleven, and is there a little hand-cart she and George could bring, because we've got our tent with us and other odds and ends?'

'Oh, we'll send the little wagon,' said Mrs Johnson. 'The one that always goes to meet the train or the bus. I'll get George to meet you with Anne, they can drive it in. We're pleased you are coming. The weather's very good and you'll enjoy yourselves!'

'You bet!' said Julian. 'Thanks awfully for

putting us up. We won't be any trouble, in fact we'll help all we can.'

Mrs Johnson said good-bye and put down the receiver. She saw Henrietta passing outside the window, looking much cleaner and tidier than usual. She called to her.

'Henry! Where are George and Anne? Julian and Dick are arriving at the bus-stop at Milling Green at eleven thirty and I've said we'll meet them in the little wagon. Will you tell George and Anne? They can put Winkie into the cart and trot him down to the bus-stop.'

'Right,' said Henry. Then she remembered that George and Anne had been sent up to Hawthorn Field with four ponies.

'I say, they won't be back in time!' she called. 'Shall *I* take the wagon and meet them?'

'Yes, do. That would be kind of you, Henry,' said Mrs Johnson. 'You'd better hurry, though. Time's getting on. Where's Winkie? In the big field?'

'Yes,' said Henry and hurried off to get him. Soon he was in the wagon shafts, and Henry was in the driving-seat. She drove off smartly, grinning to herself to think how cross George and Anne would be to find they had missed meeting the two boys after all.

Julian and Dick had already arrived at the bus-stop when Henry drove up. They looked hopefully at the wagon, thinking that perhaps one of the girls was driving in to meet them.

'No go,' said Dick. 'It's somebody else, driving into the village. I wonder if the girls got our message. I thought they would meet us at the bus-stop here. Well, we'll wait a few minutes more.'

They had just sat down on the bus-stop seat again when the wagon stopped nearby. Henry saluted them.

'Are you Anne's brothers?' she called. 'She didn't get your telephone message, so I've come with the wagon instead. Get in!'

'Oh, jolly nice of you,' said Julian, dragging his things to the wagon. 'Er – I'm Julian – and this is Dick. What's your name?'

'Henry,' said Henrietta, helping Julian with

his things. She heaved them in valiantly, then clicked to Winkie to stand still and not fidget. 'I'm glad you've come. There are rather a lot of small kids at the stables. We'll be glad of you two! I say, Timmy will be pleased to see you, won't he?'

'Good old Tim,' said Dick, heaving his things in. Henry gave them a shove too. She wasn't very fat but she was wiry and strong. She grinned round at the boys. 'All set! Now we'll get back to the stables. Or do you want to have an ice-cream or anything before we start? Dinner's not till one.'

'No. We'll get on, I think,' said Julian. Henry leapt into the driver's seat, took the reins and clicked to Winkie. The boys were behind in the wagon. Winkie set off at a spanking pace.

'Nice boy!' said Dick to Julian, in a low voice, as they drove off. 'Decent of him to meet us.'

Julian nodded. He was disappointed that Anne and George hadn't come with Timmy, but it was good to be met by *someone*! It wouldn't have been very funny to walk the long road to the farm carrying their packs by themselves.

They arrived at the stables and Henry helped them down with their things. Mrs Johnson heard them arriving and came to the door to welcome them.

'Ah, there you are. Come along in. I've a mid-morning snack for you, because I guessed you'd have had breakfast early. Leave the things there, Henry. If the boys sleep in one of the stables, there's no sense in bringing them into the house. Now, are George and Anne still not back? What a pity!'

Henry disappeared to put away the wagon. The boys went into the pleasant house and sat down to lemonade and home-made biscuits. They had hardly taken a bite before Anne came running in. 'Henry told me you'd come! Oh, I'm sorry we didn't meet you! We thought you'd come by train!'

Timmy came racing in, his tail waving madly. He leapt at the two boys, who were just giving Anne a hug each. Then in came George, her face one big beam.

'Julian! Dick! I *am* so glad you've come! It's been dull as ditch-water without you! Did anyone meet you?'

'Yes. An awfully nice boy,' said Dick. 'Gave us quite a welcome and dragged our packs into the wagon, and was very friendly. You never told us about him.'

'Oh, was that William?' said Anne. 'Well, he's only little. We didn't bother about telling you of the juniors here.'

'No, he wasn't little,' said Dick. 'He was quite big, very strong too. You didn't mention him at all.'

'Well, we told you about the other *girl* here,' said George. 'Henrietta, awful creature! Thinks she's like a boy and goes whistling about everywhere. She makes us laugh! You'll laugh too.'

A sudden thought struck Anne. 'Did the – er – boy who met you, tell you his name?' she asked.

'Yes, what was it now, Henry,' said Dick. 'Nice chap. I'm going to like him.'

George stared as if she couldn't believe her ears. '*Henry*! Did *she* meet you?'

'No – not she – *he*,' corrected Julian. 'Fellow with a big grin.'

'But that's *Henrietta*!' cried George, her face flaming red with anger. 'The awful girl I told you about, who tries to act like a boy, and whistles and strides about all over the place. Don't tell me she took you in! She calls herself Henry, instead of Henrietta, and wears her hair short, and—'

'Gosh, she sounds very like *you*, George,' said Dick. 'Well, I never! It never occurred to me that he was a girl. Jolly good show she put up. I must say I liked him – her, I mean.'

'*Oh*!' said George, really furious. 'The beast! She goes and meets you and never says a word to us, and makes you think she's a boy – and – and – spoils everything!'

'Hold your horses, George, old thing,' said Julian, surprised. 'After all, you've often been pleased when people take *you* for a boy, though goodness knows why. I thought you'd grown

out of it a bit. Don't blame us for thinking
Henry was a boy, and liking him – her, I mean.'

George stamped out of the room. Julian
scratched his head and looked at Dick. 'Now
we've put our foot in it,' he said. 'What an ass
George is! I should have thought she'd have
liked someone like Henry, who had exactly the
same ideas as she has. Well, she'll get over it, I
suppose.'

'It's going to be a bit awkward,' said Anne,
soberly.

She was right. It was going to be *very* awkward!

[3]

Sniffer

As soon as George had gone out of the room, a scowl on her face, Henry walked in, hands in jodhpur pockets.

'Hallo!' said Dick, at once. '*Henrietta*!'

Henry grinned. 'Oh, so they've told you, have they? I was tickled pink when you took me for a boy.'

'You've even got your riding jacket buttons buttoning up the wrong way,' said Anne, noticing for the first time. 'You really are an idiot, Henry. You and George are a pair!'

'Well, I look more like a real boy than George does, anyway,' said Henry.

'Only because of your hair,' said Dick. 'It's straight.'

'Don't say that in front of George,' said

Anne. 'She'll immediately have hers cut like a convict or something, all shaven and shorn.'

'Well, anyway, it was jolly decent of Henry to come and meet us and lug our things about,' said Julian. 'Have a biscuit, anyone?'

'No thanks,' said Anne and Henry.

'Are we supposed to leave any for politeness' sake?' said Dick, eyeing the plate. 'They're home-made and quite super. I could wolf the lot.'

'We aren't especially polite here,' said Henry, with a grin. 'We aren't especially clean and tidy, either. We have to change out of our jods at night for supper, which is an awful nuisance, especially as Captain Johnson never bothers to change his.'

'Any news?' asked Julian, drinking the last of the lemonade. 'Anything exciting happened?'

'No, nothing,' said Anne. 'The only excitement is the horses, nothing more. This is quite a lonely place, really, and the only exciting thing we've heard is the name of the big, desolate moor that stretches from here to the coast. Mystery Moor it's called.'

'Why?' asked Dick. 'Some long-ago mystery gave it that name, I suppose?'

'I don't know,' said Anne. 'I think only travellers go there now. A little traveller boy came in with a lame horse yesterday, and said his people had to go to Mystery Moor. Why they wanted to go to such a deserted stretch of land I don't know – no farms there, not even a cottage.'

'Travellers have peculiar ideas sometimes,' said Henry. 'I must say I like the way they leave messages for any traveller following – patrins, they're called.'

'Patrins? Yes, I've heard of those,' said Dick. 'Sticks and leaves arranged in certain patterns, or something, aren't they?'

'Yes,' said Henry. 'I know our gardener at home showed me an arrangement of sticks outside our back gate once, which he said was a message to any traveller following. He told me what it meant, too!'

'What did it mean?' asked Julian.

'It meant "Don't beg here. Mean people. No

good!"' said Henry, with a laugh. 'That's what he *said*, anyway!'

'We might ask the little traveller boy who came with the skewbald horse,' said Anne. 'He'll probably show us some messages. I'd like to learn some. You never know when anything like that could come in useful!'

'Yes. And we'll ask him why the travellers go to Mystery Moor,' said Julian, getting up and dusting the crumbs off his coat. 'They don't go there for nothing, you may be sure!'

'Where's old George gone?' asked Dick. 'I do hope she's not going to be silly.'

George was in one of the stables, grooming a horse so vigorously that it was most surprised. Swish-swish-swish-swish! What a brushing! George was working her intense annoyance out of herself. She mustn't spoil things for the boys and Anne! But oh, that horrible Henrietta, meeting them like that, pretending to be a boy. Heaving their luggage about, playing a joke on them! But surely they might have guessed!

'Oh, there you are, George,' said Dick's voice at the stable door. 'Let me help. Gosh, aren't you brown! Just as many freckles as ever!'

George grinned unwillingly. She tossed Dick the brush. 'Here you are, then! Do you and Ju want to go riding at all? There are plenty of horses to choose from here.'

Dick was relieved to see that George appeared to have got over her rage. 'Yes. It might be fun to go off for the day. What about tomorrow? We might explore a little of Mystery Moor.'

'Right,' said George. She began to heave some straw about. 'But not with That Girl,' she announced, from behind the straw she was carrying.

'What girl?' asked Dick, innocently. 'Oh, Henry, you mean? I keep thinking of her as a boy. No, we won't have her with us. We'll be just the five as usual.'

'That's all right then,' said George happily. 'Oh, here's Julian. Give a hand, Ju!'

It was lovely to have the two boys again, joking, laughing, teasing. They all went out in

the fields that afternoon and heard the tales of
the camp. It was just like old times, and Timmy
was as pleased as anyone else. He went first to
one of the four, then to another, licking each
one as he went, his tail wagging vigorously.

'That's three times you've smacked me in the
face with your tail, Timmy,' said Dick, dodging
it. 'Can't you look behind yourself and see
where my face is?'

'Woof,' said Timmy happily, and turned
round to lick Dick, wagging his tail in Julian's
face this time!

Somebody squeezed through the hedge behind them. George stiffened, feeling sure that it
was Henrietta. Timmy barked sharply.

It wasn't Henrietta. It was the little traveller
boy. He came up to them. There were tear
streaks down his face.

'I've come for the horse,' he said. 'Do you
know where he is?'

'He's not ready for walking yet,' said George.
'Captain Johnson told you he wouldn't be.
What's the matter? Why have you been crying?'

'My father hit me,' said the boy. 'He cuffed me and knocked me right over.'

'Whatever for?' said Anne.

'Because I left the horse,' said the boy. 'My father said all it wanted was a bit of ointment and a bandage. He has to start off with the other caravans today, you see.'

'Well, you really *can't* have the horse yet,' said Anne. 'It isn't fit to walk, let alone drag a caravan. You don't want Captain Johnson to tell the police you're working it when it's not fit, do you? You know he means what he says?'

'Yes. But I must have the horse,' said the small boy. 'I daren't go back without it. My father would half kill me.'

'I suppose he doesn't care to come himself, so he sends you instead,' said Dick, in disgust.

The boy said nothing, and rubbed his sleeve across his face. He sniffed.

'Get your hanky,' said Dick.

'Please let me have my horse,' said the boy. 'I tell you, I'll be half killed if I go back without him.' He began to cry again.

The children felt sorry for him. He was such a thin, skinny misery of a boy, and goodness, how he sniffed all the time!

'What's your name?' asked Anne.

'Sniffer,' said the boy. 'That's what my father calls me.'

It was certainly a good name for him; but what a horrid father he must have!

'Haven't you got a proper name?' asked Anne.

'Yes. But I've forgotten it,' said Sniffer. 'Let me have my horse. I tell you, my father's waiting.'

Julian got up. 'I'll come and see your father and put some sense into him. Where is he?'

'Over there,' said Sniffer with a big sniff, and he pointed over the hedge. 'I'll come too,' said Dick. In the end everyone got up and went with Sniffer. They walked through the gate and saw a dark-faced, surly-looking man standing motionless not far off. His thick, oily hair was curly, and he wore enormous gold rings hanging from his ears. He looked up as the little company came near.

'Your horse isn't fit to walk yet,' said Julian.

'You can have it tomorrow or the next day, the captain says.'

'I'll have it now,' said the man, in a surly tone. 'We're starting off tonight or tomorrow over the moor. I can't wait.'

'But what's the hurry?' said Julian. 'The moor will wait for you!'

The man scowled and shifted from one foot to another. 'Can't you stay for another night or two and then go after the others?' said Dick.

'Listen, Father! You go with the other caravans,' said Sniffer, eagerly. 'Go in Moses' caravan and leave ours here. I can put our horse into the shafts tomorrow, or maybe the next day, and follow after!'

'But how would you know the way?' said George.

Sniffer made a scornful movement with his hand. 'Easy! They'll leave me patrins to follow,' he said.

'Oh yes,' said Dick, remembering. He turned to the silent traveller. 'Well, what about it? It seems that Sniffer here has quite a good idea, and you most certainly can't have the horse today anyway.'

The man turned and said something angry and scornful to poor Sniffer, who shrank away from the words as if they were blows. The four children couldn't understand a word, for it was all poured out in a language that they could not follow. Then the man turned on his heel and, without so much as a look at them, slouched away, his earrings gleaming as he went.

'What did he say?' asked Julian.

Sniffer gave one of his continual sniffs. 'He was very angry. He said he'd go with the others, and I could come on with Clip the horse, and drive our caravan,' he said. 'I'll be all right there tonight with Liz.'

'Who's Liz?' asked Anne, hoping that it was someone who would be kind to this poor little wretch.

'My dog,' said Sniffer, smiling for the first time. 'I left her behind because she sometimes goes for hens, and Captain Johnson doesn't like that.'

'I bet he doesn't,' said Julian. 'All right, that's settled then. You can come for Clip, or Clop, or whatever your horse is called, tomorrow, and we'll see if it's fit to walk.'

'I'm glad,' said Sniffer, rubbing his nose. 'I don't want Clip to go lame, see? But my father's very fierce.'

'So we gather,' said Julian, looking at a bruise on Sniffer's face. 'You come tomorrow and you can show us some of the patrins, the messages, that you use. We'd like to know some.'

'I'll come,' promised Sniffer, nodding his head vigorously. 'And you will come to see my caravan? I shall be all alone there, except for Liz.'

'Well, I suppose it would be something to do,' said Dick. 'Yes, we'll come. I hope it's not too smelly.'

'Smelly?' said Sniffer, surprised. 'I don't know. I will show you patrins there and Liz will show you her tricks. She is very, very clever. Once she belonged to a circus.'

'We must certainly take Timmy to see this clever dog,' said Anne, patting Timmy, who had been hunting for rabbits and had only just come back. 'Timmy, would you like to go and visit a very clever dog called Liz?'

'Woof,' said Timmy, wagging his tail politely.

'Right,' said Dick. 'I'm glad you approve, Tim. We'll all try and come tomorrow, Sniffer, after you've been to see how Clip is getting on. I don't somehow think you'll be able to have him then, though. We'll see!'

[4]
A bed in the stable

The boys slept in one of the stables that night. Captain Johnson said they could either have mattresses sent out, or could sleep in the straw, with rugs.

'Oh, straw and rugs, please,' said Julian. 'That's fine. We'll be as snug as anything with those.'

'I wish Anne and I could sleep in a stable too,' said George, longingly. 'We never have. Can't we, Captain Johnson?'

'No. You've got beds that you're paying for,' said the captain. 'Anyway, girls can't do that sort of thing, not even girls who try to be boys, George!'

'I've *often* slept in a stable,' said Henrietta. 'At home when we've too many visitors, I always turn out and sleep in the straw.'

'Bad luck on the horses!' said George.

'Why?' demanded Henry at once.

'Because you must keep them awake all night with your snoring!' said George.

Henry snorted crossly and went out. It was maddening that she should snore at night, but she simply couldn't help it.

'Never mind!' George called after her. 'It's a nice *manly* snore, Henrietta!'

'Shut up, George,' said Dick, rather shocked at this sudden display of pettiness on George's part.

'Don't tell *me* to shut up,' said George. 'Tell Henrietta!'

'George, don't be an ass,' said Julian. But George didn't like that either, and stalked out of the room in just the same stiff, offended way that Henry had done!

'Oh dear!' said Anne. 'It's been like this all the time. First Henry, then George, then George, then Henry! They really are a couple of idiots!'

She went to see where the boys were to sleep.

They had been told to use a small stable, empty except for the traveller's horse that lay patiently down, its bandaged leg stretched out on the floor. Anne patted it and stroked it. It was an ugly little thing but its patient brown eyes were lovely.

The boys had heaps of straw to burrow into, and some old rugs. Anne thought it all looked lovely. 'You can wash and everything at the house,' she said. 'Then just slip over here to sleep. Doesn't it smell nice? All straw and hay and horse! I hope the horse won't disturb you. He may be a bit restless if his leg hurts him.'

'Nothing will disturb *us* tonight!' said Julian. 'What with camp life and open air and wind-on-the-hills and all that kind of thing, we're sure to sleep like logs. I think we're going to enjoy it here, Anne, very quiet and peaceful!'

George looked in at the door. 'I'll lend you Timmy if you like,' she said, anxious to make up for her display of temper.

'Oh, hallo, George! No thanks. I don't particularly want old Tim climbing over me all night long, trying to find the softest part of me to sleep on!' said Julian. 'I say, look, he's showing me how to make a good old burrow to sleep in! Hey, Tim, come out of my straw!'

Timmy had flung himself into the straw and was turning vigorously round and round in it as if he were making a bed for himself. He stood and looked up at them, his mouth open and his tongue hanging out at one side.

'He's laughing,' said Anne, and it did indeed look as if Timmy was having a good old laugh at them. Anne gave him a hug and he licked her lavishly, and then began to burrow round and round in the straw again.

Someone came up, whistling loudly, and put her head in at the door. 'I've brought you a couple of old pillows. Mrs Johnson said you'd better have something for your heads.'

'Oh thanks awfully, Henry,' said Julian, taking them.

'How kind of you, Henri*etta*,' said George.

'It's a pleasure, Geor*gina*,' said Henry, and the boys burst out laughing. Fortunately the supper-bell went just then and they all went across the yard at once. Somehow everyone was always hungry at the stables!

The girls looked very different in the evening, because they had to change out of their dirty, smelly jodhpurs or breeches and put on dresses. Anne, Henry and George hurried to change before Mrs Johnson rang the supper-bell again. She always gave them ten minutes' grace, knowing that they might sometimes have a job to finish with the horses, but everyone was supposed to be at the table when the second supper-bell had finished ringing.

George looked nice, because her curly hair went with a skirt and blouse quite well, but Henry looked quite wrong, somehow, in her frilly dress.

'You look like a boy dressed up!' said Anne, and this pleased Henry, but not George. The talk at the supper-table was mainly about all the wonderful things that Henry had done in her life. Apparently she had three brothers and did everything with them, and according to her own tales, she was considerably better than they were!

They had sailed a ship up to Norway. They had hiked from London to York.

'Was Dick Turpin with you?' inquired George, sarcastically. 'On his horse, Black Bess? I expect you got there long before *him*, didn't you?'

Henry took no notice. She went on with wonderful tales of her family's exploits, swimming across wide rivers, climbing Snowdon to the top, goodness, there wasn't a single thing she didn't seem to have done!

'You certainly ought to have been a boy, Henry,' said Mrs Johnson, which was exactly what Henry wanted everyone to say!

'Henry, when you've told us the story of how you climbed Mount Everest and got there before anyone else, perhaps you would finish your plateful,' said Captain Johnson, who got very tired of Henry's tongue.

George roared with laughter, not that she thought it was very funny, but because she loved any chance to laugh at Henry. Henry tackled the rest of her food at top speed. How she did love to hold everyone spellbound with her extraordinary tales! George didn't believe a word, but Dick and Julian thought it quite likely that this tall, wiry girl *could* do things just as well as her brothers.

There were a few jobs to be done after supper, and Henry kept well away from George, knowing quite well that she would have a few cutting things to say. Well, *she* didn't care! Everyone else thought she was marvellous! She tore off her frilly dress and put on jodhpurs again, although it would only be a short time before they all went to bed.

George and Anne went with the boys to their stable. They were in pyjamas and dressing-gowns, both yawning as they went. 'Got your torches?' said George. 'We're not allowed to have candles in the stables, because of the straw, you know. Good night! Sleep well! And I hope that that idiot of a Henry doesn't come along early in the morning, whistling like a paper-boy, and wake you up!'

'Nothing will wake me up tonight, nothing at all,' said Julian, with a huge yawn. He lay down in the straw and pulled an old rug over him. 'Oh, what a bed! Give me stable straw every time to sleep in!'

The girls laughed. The boys really *did* look very comfortable. 'Sleep tight,' said Anne, and walked off with George to the house.

Soon all the lights were out everywhere. Henry was asleep and snoring as usual. She had to have a separate room, otherwise she kept everyone awake! But even so, Anne and George could hear her, snoring away – rrrumph – rrrumph! rrrumph – RRRRUMPH!

'Blow Henrietta!' said George, sleepily. 'What a row she makes. Anne, she's not to come with us when we go riding tomorrow. Do you hear, Anne?'

'Not very well,' murmured Anne, trying to open her eyes. 'G'night, George!'

Timmy was on George's feet as usual. He lay snuggled there, eyes shut and ears asleep too. He got as tired as everyone else, running over the hills all day, scrabbling at scores of rabbit holes, chasing dozens of remarkably fleet-footed rabbits. But at night he too slept like a log.

Out in the stable the two boys slept peacefully, covered by the old rug. Nearby the little skewbald horse moved restlessly, but they heard nothing. An owl came swooping over the stable, looking for mice down below. It screeched loudly, hoping to scare a mouse into sudden flight. Then it would swoop down and take it into its talons.

Not even the screech awakened the boys. They slept dreamlessly, tired out.

The door of the stable was shut and latched. Clip, the horse, suddenly stirred and looked round at the door. The latch was moving! Someone was lifting it from the outside. Clip's pricked ears heard the sound of a little shuffle.

He watched the door. Who was coming? He hoped it was Sniffer, the boy he liked so much. Sniffer was always kind to him. He didn't like being away from Sniffer. He listened for the sniff-sniff that always went with the little boy, but he didn't hear it.

The door opened very slowly indeed. It gave no creak. Clip saw the night sky outside, set with stars. He made out a figure outlined against the darkness of the starry night, a black shadow.

Someone came into the stable, and whispered 'Clip!'

The horse gave a little whinny. It wasn't Sniffer's voice. It was his father's. Clip did not like him, he was too free with cuffs and kicks, and slashes with the whip. He lay still, wondering why the traveller had come.

The man had no idea that Dick and Julian were sleeping in the stable. He had come in quietly because he had thought there might be other horses there, and he did not want to startle them and make them stamp about in fright. He had no torch, but his keen eyes made out Clip at once, lying in his straw.

He tiptoed across to him and fell over Julian's feet, sticking out from the straw bed he was lying on. He fell with a thud, and Julian sat up very suddenly indeed, awake at once.

'Who's there! What is it?'

The traveller shrank down beside Clip, keeping silent. Julian began to wonder if he had been dreaming. But his foot distinctly hurt him. Surely somebody had trodden on it, or fallen over it? He woke Dick.

'Where's the torch? Hallo, look, the stable door is open! Quick, Dick, where on earth is the torch?'

They found it at last and Julian clicked it on. At first he saw nothing, for the man was in Clip's stall, lying down behind the horse. Then the torch picked him out.

'Hallo! Look there – it's that traveller, Sniffer's father!' said Julian. 'Get up, you! What on earth are you doing here, in the middle of the night?'

[5]

George gets a headache!

The man got up sullenly. His earrings shone in the light of the torch. 'I came to get Clip,' he said. 'He's my horse, isn't he?'

'You were told he wasn't fit to walk yet,' said Julian. 'Do you want him to go lame for life? You ought to know enough about horses to know when one can be worked or not!'

'I've got my orders,' said the man. 'I've got to take my caravan with the others.'

'Who said so?' said Dick, scornfully.

'Barney Boswell,' said the man. 'He's boss of our lot here. We've got to start off together tomorrow.'

'But why?' said Julian, puzzled. 'What's so urgent about all this? What's the mystery?'

'There isn't any mystery,' said the man, still sullen. 'We're just going to the moor.'

'What are you going to do there?' asked Dick, curiously. 'It doesn't seem to me to be the place to take a lot of caravans to. There's nothing there at all, is there? Or so I've heard.'

The man shrugged his shoulders and said nothing. He turned to Clip as if to get him up. But Julian rapped out at him at once.

'Oh no, you don't! If you don't care about injuring a horse, I do! You've only got to be patient for a day or two more, and he'll be quite all right. You're not to take him tonight. Dick, go and wake Captain Johnson. He'll know what to do.'

'No,' said the man, scowling. 'Don't wake anybody. I'll go. But just see that Clip is given to Sniffer as soon as it's possible, or I'll know the reason why! See?'

He looked at Julian in a threatening way.

'Take that scowl off your face,' said Julian. 'I'm glad you've seen sense. Clear out now. Go off with the others tomorrow and I'll see that Sniffer has the horse in a short time.'

The man moved to the door and slid out like

a shadow. Julian went to watch him across the yard, wondering whether, out of spite, the man might try to steal a hen, or one of the ducks sleeping beside the pond.

But there was no sudden clucking, no loud quack. The man had gone as silently as he had come.

'Most peculiar, all this!' said Julian, latching the door again. He tied a piece of thick string over it his side, so that it could not be lifted from outside. 'There! Now if the traveller comes again, he'll find he can't get in. What a nerve, coming here in the middle of the night like that!'

He got back into the straw. 'He must have fallen right over my foot,' he said, snuggling down. 'He woke me up with an awful jump. Good thing for Clip that we were sleeping out here tonight, or he'd be dragging along a heavy caravan tomorrow, and going lame again. I don't like that fellow!'

He fell asleep again and so did Dick. Clip slept too, his leg feeling easier. How glad he had been that day not to have to drag along the heavy caravan!

The boys told Captain Johnson next morning about the traveller's midnight visit. He nodded. 'Yes, I ought to have warned you that he might come. They're not always very good to their horses. Well, I'm glad you sent him off. I don't reckon Clip's leg will be ready for walking on till the day after tomorrow. There's no harm in giving the poor creature a few days' rest. Sniffer can easily take the caravan on after the others.'

It looked as if that day was going to be fun. After all the horses had been seen to, and many odd jobs done, the four, with Timmy, planned to set out for a day's ride. Captain Johnson said he would let Julian ride his own sturdy cob and Dick took a bonny chestnut horse with four white socks. The girls had the horses they usually rode.

Henry hung about, looking very mournful. The boys felt quite uncomfortable. 'We *really* ought to tell her to come along too,' said Dick to Julian. 'It seems jolly mean to leave her behind with those little kids.'

'Yes, I know. I agree with you,' said Julian. 'Anne, come here! Can't you suggest to George that we take Henry too? She's longing to come, I know.'

'Yes, she is,' said Anne. 'I feel awful about it. But George will be mad if we ask Henry. They really do get on each other's nerves. I simply daren't ask George to let Henry come, Ju.'

'But this is *silly*!' said Julian. 'To think we don't *dare* to ask George to let somebody come! George will have to learn sense. I like Henry. She's boastful, and I don't believe half the tales she tells, but she's a sport and good fun. Hey, Henry!'

'Coming!' yelled Henry, and came running, looking very hopeful.

'Would you like to come with us!' said Julian. 'We're all going off for the day. Have you got any jobs to do, or can you come?'

'Can I *come*! You bet!' said Henry, joyfully. 'But – does George know?'

'I'll soon tell her,' said Julian, and went in search of George. She was helping Mrs Johnson to get saddle-bags ready, full of food.

'George,' said Julian, boldly, 'Henry is coming too. Will there be enough food for everyone?'

'Oh! How *nice* of you to ask her!' said Mrs Johnson, sounding very pleased. 'She's dying to come. She's been so good this week, too, while we've been short-handed. She deserves a treat. Isn't that *nice*, George?'

George muttered something peculiar and went out of the room, her face scarlet. Julian stared after her, his eyebrows cocked in a comical manner.

'I don't somehow feel that George thinks it's nice,' he said. 'I feel as if we are in for an awkward day, Mrs Johnson.'

'Oh, don't take any notice of George when she's silly,' said Mrs Johnson, comfortably, filling another paper bag with delicious-looking sandwiches. 'And don't take any notice of Henry, either, when she's idiotic. There! If you get through all this food, I shall be surprised!'

William, one of the younger ones, came in just then. 'What a lot of food you've given them,' he said. 'Will there be enough left for *us* to have today?'

'Good gracious, yes!' said Mrs Johnson. 'You think of nothing but your tummy, William! Go and find George and tell her the food is ready for her to put into the saddle-bags.'

William disappeared and then came back. 'George says she's got a headache and doesn't think she'll go on the ride,' he announced.

Julian looked startled and upset. 'Now listen to me, Julian,' said Mrs Johnson, beginning to insert the parcels of food carefully into the saddle-bags, 'just leave her to her imaginary headache. Don't go fussing round her, and begging her to come and saying you won't have Henry. Just believe quite firmly in her headache, and go off by yourselves. It's the quickest way to make George see sense, believe *me*!'

'Yes, I think you're right,' said Julian, frowning. To think that George should behave like a sulky little girl, after all the adventures they had been through together! Just because of Henry. It really was absurd.

'Where *is* George?' he said to William.

'Up in her room,' said William, who had been engrossed in picking up and eating all the crumbs he could. Julian went out of the room and into the yard. He knew which window belonged to the room where George and Anne slept. He yelled up.

'George! Sorry about your headache! Sure you don't feel like coming?'

'No!' came back an answering shout, and the window was shut down with a slam.

'OK! Awfully disappointed and all that!' shouted Julian. 'Do hope your head will soon be better! See you later!'

No other reply came from the window, but, as Julian went across the yard to the stables, a very surprised face watched him go, from behind the bedroom curtains. George was extremely astonished to have been taken at her word, shocked at being left behind after all, and angry with Henry and everyone else for putting her into this fix!

Julian told the others that George had a

headache and wasn't coming. Anne was most concerned and wanted to go and comfort her but Julian forbade her to.

'No. She's up in her room. Leave her alone, Anne. That's an order – OK?'

'All right,' said Anne, half-relieved. She felt sure that George's headache was mostly temper, and she didn't at all want to go and argue with her for half an hour. Henry hadn't said a word. She had flushed with surprise when Julian had announced that George was not coming, and she knew at once that there was no real headache! *She* was George's headache, she knew that!

She went up to Julian. 'Look, I guess it's because you've asked *me* to come, that Georgina won't come with us. I don't want to spoil things. You go and tell her I'm not going after all.'

Julian looked at Henry gratefully. 'That's jolly nice of you,' he said. 'But we're taking George at her word. Anyway, we didn't ask you out of politeness. We *wanted* you to come!'

'Thanks,' said Henry. 'Well, let's go before anything else happens! Our horses are ready. I'll fix the saddle-bags.'

Soon all four were on their horses, and were walking over the yard to the gate. George heard the clippity-clop-clippity-clop of the hooves and peeped out of the window again. They were going after all! She hadn't thought they really *would* go without her. She was horrified.

Why did I behave like that? I've put myself in the wrong! thought poor George. Now Henrietta will be with them all day and will be as nice as possible, just to show me up. What an ass I am! 'Timmy, I'm an ass and an idiot, and a great big idiot! Aren't I?'

Timmy didn't think so. He had been puzzled to hear the others going off without him and George, and had gone to the door and whined. Now he came back to George and put his head on her knee. He knew George was not happy.

'*You* don't care how I behave, do you, Tim?' said George, stroking the soft, furry head. 'That's the best thing about a dog! You don't care if I'm in the wrong or not, you just love me all the same, don't you? Well, you shouldn't love me today, Tim. I've been an idiot!'

There was a knock at her door. It was William again. 'George! Mrs Johnson says, if your headache is bad, undress and get into bed. But if it's better, come down and help with Clip, the traveller's horse.'

'I'll come down,' said George, flinging away her sulks at one go. 'Tell Mrs Johnson I'll go to the stable at once.'

'All right,' said the stolid William, and trotted off like a reliable little pony.

George went downstairs with Timmy, and into the yard. She wondered how far the others had gone. She couldn't see them in the distance. Would they have a good day together, with that horrid Henry? Ugh!

The others were almost a mile away, cantering easily. What *fun*! A whole day before them, on Mystery Moor!

[6]
A grand day

'I think it's a jolly good name, Mystery Moor,' said Dick, as the four of them went along. 'Look at it stretching for miles, all blazing with gorse.'

'I don't think it looks at all mysterious,' said Henry, surprised.

'Well, it's got a sort of quietness and broodiness,' said Anne, 'as if something big happened long ago in the past and it's waiting for something to happen again.'

'Quiet and broody? It sounds like one of the farmyard hens sitting on her eggs!' said Henry with a laugh. 'I think it might be a bit frightening and mysterious at night, but it's just an ordinary stretch of country in the daytime, fine for riding over. I can't think why it's called Mystery Moor.'

'We'll have to look it up in some book that tells about this part of the country,' said Dick. 'I expect it was called that because of some strange happening or other, hundreds of years ago, when people believed in witches and things like that.'

They followed no road or path, but rode where they pleased. There were great stretches of wiry grass, masses of heather springing up afresh, and, blazing its gold everywhere on this lovely April day, was the gorse.

Anne sniffed continually as they rode past the gorse bushes. Dick looked at her.

'You sound like Sniffer!' he said. 'Have you got a cold?'

Anne laughed. 'No, of course not. But I do so love the smell of the gorse. What does it smell of? Vanilla? Hot coconut? It's a lovely *warm* smell!'

'Look! What's that moving over there?' said Julian, suddenly reining in his horse. They all strained their eyes to see.

'It's caravans!' said Julian, at last. 'Of course! They were setting out today, weren't they?

Well, they must find it very rough going, that's all I can say. There's no real road anywhere, as far as I can see.'

'Where can they be going?' wondered Anne. 'What's over in that direction?'

'They'll come to the coast if they keep on the way they are going,' said Julian, considering. 'Let's ride over and have a look at them, shall we?'

'Yes. Good idea!' said Dick. So they turned their horses' heads to the right, and rode towards the faraway caravans. These made quite a splash of colour as they went along. There were four of them – two red ones, a blue one and a yellow one. They went very slowly indeed, each pulled by a small, wiry horse.

'They all look like skewbalds, brown and white,' said Dick. 'It's funny that so many travellers have skewbald horses. I wonder why it is?'

They heard shouting as they came near the caravans, and saw one man pointing them out to another. It was Sniffer's father!

'Look, that's the fellow who woke us up in the stable last night,' said Julian to Dick. 'Sniffer's father! What a nasty bit of work he is! Why doesn't he get a hair cut?'

'Good morning!' called Dick, as they rode up to the caravans on their horses. 'Nice day!'

There was no answer. The travellers driving their caravans, and those walking alongside, looked sourly at the four riders.

'Where are you going?' asked Henry. 'To the coast?'

'It's nothing to do with you,' said one of the travellers, an old man with curly grey hair.

'Surly folk, aren't they?' said Dick to Julian. 'I suppose they think we're spying on them, or something. I wonder how they manage about food on this moor, no shops or anything. I suppose they take it all with them.'

'I'll ask them,' said Henry, not at all put off by the surly looks. She rode right up to Sniffer's father.

'How do you manage about food and water?' she asked.

'We've got food there,' said Sniffer's father, jerking his head back towards one of the caravans. 'As for water, we know where the springs are.'

'Are you camping on the moor for a long time?' asked Henry, thinking that a traveller's life might be a fine one, for a time! Fancy living out here on this lovely moor with gorse blazing gold all around, and primroses by the thousand in the sheltered corners!

'That's nothing to do with *you*!' shouted the old man with curly grey hair. 'Clear off and leave us alone!'

'Come on, Henry,' said Julian, swinging round to go off. 'They don't like us asking them questions. They think it's prying, not interest. Maybe they have lots of things to hide, and don't want us poking around – one or two chickens from a farm, a duck or so from the pond. They live from hand to mouth, these folk.'

Some bright-eyed children peered from the vans as they went by. One or two were running outside, but they sheered off like frightened rabbits when Henry cantered towards them.

'Oh well, they simply don't *want* to be friendly,' she said, and went to join the other three. 'What a strange life they lead, in their houses on wheels! Never staying anywhere for long, always on the move. Get up, there, Sultan. Go after the others!'

Her horse obediently followed the other three, taking care not to step into any rabbit holes! What fun it was to be out here in the sunshine, jogging up and down on the horse's back, without a care in the world! Henry was very happy.

The other three were enjoying their day, but they were not quite so happy. They kept wondering about George. They missed Timmy too. He should be trotting beside them, enjoying the day as well!

They lost sight of the caravans after a time. Julian kept track of the way they went, half-afraid of being lost. He had a compass with him, and checked their direction continually. 'It would never do to have to spend a night out here!' he said. 'Nobody would ever find us!'

They had a magnificent lunch about half past twelve. Really, Mrs Johnson had surpassed herself! Egg and sardine sandwiches, tomato and lettuce, ham – there seemed no end to them! Great slices of cherry cake were added too, and a large, juicy pear each.

'I like this kind of cherry cake,' said Dick, looking at his enormous slice. 'The cherries have all gone to the bottom. They make a very nice last mouthful!'

'Any drinks?' said Henry, and was handed a bottle of ginger-beer. She drank it thirstily.

'Why does ginger-beer taste so nice on a picnic?' she said. '*Much* nicer than drinking it sitting down in a shop, even if it's got ice in it!'

'There's a spring or something nearby,' said Julian. 'I can hear it bubbling.'

They all listened. Yes, there was a little bubbling, tinkling noise. Anne got up to trace it. She found it in a few minutes and called the others. There was a round pool, cool and blue, lying two or three feet down, and into it, from one side, fell a crystal-clear spring of water, tinkling as it fell.

'One of the springs that the travellers use, when they come to this deserted moor, I expect,' said Julian. He cupped his hands under the falling water and got his palms full. He carried the water to his mouth and sipped it.

'Delicious! Cool as an ice-box,' he said. 'Taste it, Anne.'

They rode a little farther, but the moor seemed the same everywhere, heather, wiry grass, gorse, a clear spring falling into a pool or tiny stream here and there, and a few trees, mostly silver birch.

Larks sang all the time, soaring high in the air, almost too far up to see.

'Their song falls down like raindrops,' said Anne, holding out her hands as if to catch them. Henry laughed. She liked this family, and was very glad they had asked her to come out with them. She thought George was silly to have stayed at the stables.

'I think we ought to get home,' said Julian at last, looking at his watch. 'We're a good way away. Let me see now. We want to make more or less for the setting sun. Come on!'

He led the way, his horse picking its own path over the heather. The others followed. Dick stopped after a while.

'Are you sure we're quite right, Ju? I don't somehow feel that we are. The moor is different here, rather sandy and not so much gorse.'

Julian stopped his horse and looked round and about. 'Yes, it does look a bit different,' he said. 'But yet we seem to be going in the right direction. Let's go a bit more to the west. If only there was something on the horizon to guide us. But this moor hasn't a thing that stands out anywhere!'

They went on again, and then Henry gave an exclamation. 'I say! What's this? Do come here.'

The two boys and Anne swerved over to Henry. She was now off her horse, and was bending over, scraping away at the heather.

'Look, it seems like rails, or something,' said Henry. 'Very old and rusty. But they can't be surely?'

Everyone was now down on their knees, scraping sand and heather away. Julian sat back and considered.

'Yes, it's rails. Old ones, as you say. But what in the world were rails laid down here for?'

'I can't think,' said Henry. 'I only caught sight of them by chance, they're so overgrown. I couldn't believe my eyes!'

'They must lead from somewhere *to* somewhere!' said Dick. 'Perhaps there was a quarry or something on the moor and they ran little engines with trucks there, to fetch the sand, and take it back to town to sell.'

'That's about it,' said Julian. 'It's very sandy here, as we noticed. Good, fine sand. Maybe there is a quarry on the moor. Well, *that* way, behind us, goes right out on the moor, so *this* way must lead back to some town or village, probably Milling Green or somewhere like that.'

'Yes. You're right,' said Dick. 'In which case, if we follow the lines along, we'll get back to civilisation sooner or later!'

'Well, seeing that we seem to be more or less lost, that would be quite a good idea!' said Henry. She mounted her horse again and rode along the lines.

'They're fairly easy to see!' she called. 'If you ride between them, that is, because they go so straight.'

The lines ran steadily over the moor, sometimes very overgrown, and in about half an hour's time Henry gave a cry and pointed forward. 'Houses! I thought we'd soon come to some place!'

'It *is* Milling Green!' said Julian, as the rails came to a sudden end, and they rode out into a small cart road.

'Well, we haven't far to go now, to get to the stables,' said Henry, pleased. 'I say, wouldn't it be fun to follow those lines all across the moor and see where they really lead to?'

'Yes. We might do that one day,' said Julian.

'Gosh, it's getting late. I wonder how old George has been getting on today!'

They walked quickly along to the stables, thinking of George. Would she have retired to bed? Would she still be cross, or worse still, hurt and grieved? It was anybody's guess!

[7]
George, Sniffer and Liz

George had had quite an interesting day. First she had gone down to help Captain Johnson do Clip's leg again and bandage it up. The little skewbald stood very patiently, and George felt a sudden liking for the ugly little creature.

'Thanks, George,' said Captain Johnson, who, to her relief, had said nothing about her not having gone riding with the others. 'Now would you like to come and put jumps up for the youngsters? They're longing to do some more jumping.'

George found that it was quite amusing to teach the younger ones how to jump. They were so very, very proud of themselves when they went over even a foot-high jump on their little ponies.

After that Sniffer arrived, accompanied by a

peculiar little mongrel called Liz. Liz was a bit
of a spaniel, a bit of a poodle, and odd bits of
something else – and looked rather like a small,
walking hearth-rug of black curly fur.

Timmy was amazed to see this walking mat,
and sat and watched Liz sniffing here and there
for some time, before he came to the conclusion
that it really *was* some kind of dog. He gave a
sharp little bark to see what this comical creature would do when she heard it.

Liz took no notice at all. She had unearthed a
small bone, which smelt extremely interesting.
Timmy considered that all bones within the
radius of at least a mile belonged to him and
him alone. So he ran over to Liz at once and
gave a small, warning growl.

Liz immediately dropped the bone humbly
at his feet, then sat up on her hind-legs
and begged. Timmy eyed her in astonishment. Then Liz stood up on her hind-legs
and walked daintily all round Timmy and
back again.

Timmy was astounded. He had never seen a

dog do that before. *Could* this hearth-rug affair be a dog after all?

Liz saw that Timmy was really impressed, and went on with yet another trick she had learnt during the time she had been with the circus.

She turned head-over-heels, yapping all the time. Timmy retreated a few steps into the bushes. This was going *too* far! What was this animal doing? Trying to stand on its head?

Liz went on turning head-over-heels very rapidly and ended up almost on Timmy's front paws. He had now backed into the bush as far as he could.

Liz remained on her back, paws in the air, tongue hanging out, panting. She gave a very small, beseeching whine.

Timmy bent his head down and sniffed at her paws. Behind him his tail began to move a little, yes, it had a wag in it! He sniffed again. Liz leapt on to her four feet and pranced all round Timmy, yapping as if to say 'Come on and play! Do come!'

And then suddenly Timmy fell upon the absurd little creature and pretended to worry it. Liz gave a delighted volley of yaps and rolled over and over. They had a marvellous game, and when it was all over, Timmy sank down, panting for breath, in a sunny corner of the yard and Liz settled herself between his front paws, as if she had known him all her life!

When George came out of the stable with Sniffer, she could hardly believe her eyes. 'What's that Timmy's got between his paws?' she said. 'It's surely not a *dog*!'

'It's Liz,' said Sniffer. 'She can get round any dog there is, George! Liz! You're a monkey, aren't you! Walk, then, walk!'

Liz left Timmy and ran over to Sniffer, walking daintily on her hind legs. George laughed. 'What a funny little creature, like a bit cut out of a furry hearth-rug!'

'She's clever,' said Sniffer and patted Liz. 'Well, George, when can I have Clip, do you think? My father has gone off with the other caravans and he's left me with ours. So it doesn't matter whether it's today or tomorrow, or even the next day.'

'Well, it won't be today, that's certain,' said George. 'It might perhaps be tomorrow. Haven't you got a hanky, Sniffer? I never in my life heard anyone sniff as often as you do!'

Sniffer rubbed his sleeve across his nose. 'I've never had a hanky,' he said. 'But I've got my sleeve!'

'I think you're quite disgusting,' said George. 'I'm going to give you one of my own hankies, and you're to use it. You're *not* to keep sniffing like that.'

'Didn't know I did,' said Sniffer, half sulkily. 'What does it matter, anyway?'

But George had gone indoors and up the stairs. She chose a large hanky, in red and white stripes. That would do nicely for Sniffer! She took it down to him. He looked at it in surprise.

'That's a scarf for my neck!' he said.

'No, it isn't. It's a hanky for your nose,' said George. 'Haven't you a pocket to put it in?

That's right. Now, use it instead of sniffing, for goodness' sake!'

'Where are the others?' asked Sniffer, putting the hanky carefully into his pocket, almost as if it were made of glass.

'Gone riding,' said George, shortly.

'They said they would come and see my caravan,' said Sniffer. 'They said so!'

'Well, they won't be able to today,' said George. 'They'll be back too late, I expect. I'll come and see it, though. There's nobody in it, is there?'

George was not keen on meeting Sniffer's father or any other of his relations! He shook his head. 'No, it's empty. My father's gone, I told you, and my aunt and my grandma too.'

'What do you *do* on the moor?' asked George, as she followed Sniffer across the field and up the hill to where the caravans had stood. Now only one was left – Sniffer's.

'Play around,' said Sniffer, and gave an enormous sniff. George gave him a shove in the back.

'Sniffer! What did I give you the hanky for? *Don't* do that! It gets on my nerves!'

Sniffer used his sleeve at once, but fortunately George didn't notice. She had now come to the caravan and was staring at it. She thought of Sniffer's answer to her question a minute or two back.

'You said you just played around on the moor. But what does your *father* do, and your uncle and grandad and all the rest of the men? There's nothing to do there at all, as far as I can see, and no farmhouse to beg eggs or milk or anything from.'

Sniffer shut up like a clam. He was just about to sniff and thought better of it. He stared at George, his mouth set in an obstinate line.

George looked at him impatiently. 'Captain Johnson said you and your caravans went there every three months,' she said. 'What for? There must be *some* reason?'

'Well,' said Sniffer, looking away from her, 'we make pegs, and baskets, and—'

'I know that! All travellers make things to

sell,' said George. 'But you don't need to go into the middle of a deserted moor to make them. You can do them just as well in a village, or sitting in a field near a farmhouse. *Why* go to such a lonely place as the moor?'

Sniffer said nothing, but bent over an odd little arrangement of sticks set on the path beside his caravan. George saw them and bent over them too, her question forgotten.

'Oh! Is that a patrin? A traveller message! What does it mean?'

There were two sticks, one long and one short, neatly arranged in the shape of a cross. A little farther up on the path were a few single, straight sticks, all pointing in the same direction.

'Yes,' said Sniffer, very glad to have the subject changed. 'It's our way of telling things to those who may come after us. See the sticks in the shape of the cross? That's a patrin that says we've been along this way and we're going in the direction that the long stick points.'

'I see,' said George. 'How simple! But what

about these four straight sticks, all pointing the same way too. What do *they* mean?'

'They mean that the travellers went in caravans,' said Sniffer, giving a sudden sniff. 'See, four sticks, four caravans, going that way!'

'I *see*,' said George, making up her mind that she herself would evolve quite a few 'patrins' for use at school when they went for walks. 'Are there any more "patrins", Sniffer?'

'Plenty,' said the boy. 'Look, when I leave here, I shall put a patrin like this!' He picked a large leaf from a nearby tree, and then a small one. He placed them side by side, and weighted them down with small stones.

'What in the world does that mean?' said George.

'Well, it's a patrin, a message, to say that me and my little dog have gone in the caravan too,' said Sniffer, picking up the leaves. 'Suppose my father came back to find me, and he saw those leaves there, he'd know I'd gone on with my dog. It's simple. Big leaf for me, little leaf for my dog!'

'Yes. I like it,' said George, pleased. 'Now let's look at the caravan.'

It was an old-fashioned kind of caravan, not very big, and with huge wheels. The door and the steps down were in front. The shafts rested on the ground waiting for Clip to come back. The caravan was black with red designs on it here and there.

George went up the steps. 'I've been inside a few caravans,' she said. 'But never one quite like this.'

She peeped in curiously. It certainly wasn't very clean, but it wasn't as dirty as she expected either.

'It's not smelly, is it?' said Sniffer, quite anxiously. 'I tidied it up today, seeing as how I thought you were all visiting me. That's our bed at the back. We all sleep on it.'

George stared at the big bunk-like bed stretched at the end of the caravan, covered with a bright quilt. She imagined the whole family sleeping there, close together. Well, at least they would be warm in the winter.

'Don't you get hot in the summer, sleeping in this small caravan?' asked George.

'Oh no, only my grandma sleeps here then,' said Sniffer, swallowing a sniff in a hurry, before George could hear it. 'Me and the others sleep under the caravan. Then if it rains it doesn't matter.'

'Well, thanks for showing me so many things,' said George, looking round at the cupboards, the little locker-seats, and the over-big chest of drawers. 'How you all get in here is a miracle.'

She didn't go in. Even though Sniffer had tidied up, there was still a distinctly peculiar smell hanging about!

'Come and see us tomorrow, Sniffer,' she said, going down the steps. 'Clip may be all right by then. And Sniffer, don't you forget you've got a hanky now.'

'I won't forget,' said Sniffer proudly. 'I'll keep it as clean as can be, George!'

[8]

Sniffer makes a promise

George was feeling very lonely by the time the evening came. How had the others got on without her? Had they missed her at all? Perhaps they hadn't even *thought* of her!

'Anyway, they didn't have *you*, Timmy!' said George. 'You wouldn't go off and leave me, would you?'

Timmy pressed against her, glad to see that she was happier again. He wondered where the others were, and where they had gone to all day.

There was suddenly a clattering of hooves in the stable-yard and George flew to the door. Yes, they were back! How should she behave? She felt cross and relieved and rather humble and glad all at once! She stood there, not knowing whether to frown or to smile.

The others made up her mind for her. 'Hallo, George!' shouted Dick. 'We did miss you!'

'How's your head?' called Anne. 'I hope it's better!'

'Hallo!' called Henry. 'You ought to have come. We've had a super day!'

'Come and help us stable the horses, George,' shouted Julian. 'Tell us what you've been doing!'

Timmy had sped over to them, barking in delight. George found her legs running towards them too, a welcoming smile on her face.

'Hallo!' she called. 'Let me help! Did you really miss me? I missed you too.'

The boys were very relieved to see that George was herself again. Nothing more was said about her headache! She busied herself unsaddling the horses and listening to their story of the day. Then she told them about Sniffer and his patrins, and how she had given him a brand-new handkerchief.

'But I'm sure he thinks he's got to keep it spotlessly clean!' she said. 'He never used it once when I was with him. There's the supper-bell, we'll only *just* be in time! Are you hungry?'

'You bet we are!' said Dick. 'Though after Mrs Johnson's sandwiches I never thought I'd be able to eat any supper at all. How's Clip?'

'Never mind now. I'll tell you everything at supper,' said George. 'Do you want any help, Henry?'

Henry was surprised to hear George call her Henry instead of Henrietta. 'No thanks – er – George,' she said. 'I can manage.'

It was a very jolly supper-time that evening. The youngsters were set at a table by themselves, so the older ones talked to their heart's content.

Captain Johnson was very interested to hear about the old railway they had found. 'I never knew there was anything like that on the moors,' he said. 'Though of course, we've only been here about fifteen years, so we don't know a great deal of the local history. You want to go and ask old Ben the blacksmith about that. He's lived here all his life, and a long life it is, for he's over eighty!'

'Well, we've got to take some of the horses to be shod tomorrow, haven't we?' said Henry, eagerly. 'We could ask him then! Why, he might even have helped to make the rails!'

'We saw the caravans, George, when we had got pretty far out on the moor,' said Julian. 'Goodness knows where they were heading for, towards the coast, I should think. What's the coast like beyond the moor, Captain Johnson?'

'Wild,' said the captain. 'Great, unclimbable cliffs, and reefs or rocks stretching out to sea. Only the birds live there. There's no swimming, no boating, no beach.'

'Well, it beats me where those caravans are going,' said Dick. 'It's a mystery. They go every three months, don't they?'

'About that,' said Captain Johnson. 'I've no idea what the attraction of the moor is for the travellers. It just beats me! Usually they won't go anywhere there aren't a few farms, or at least a small village where they can sell their goods.'

'I'd like to go after them and see where they are and what they're doing,' said Julian, eating his third hard-boiled egg.

'All right. Let's,' said George.

'But how? We don't know where they've gone,' said Henry.

'Well, Sniffer's going to join them tomorrow, or as soon as Clip is all right for walking,' said George. 'And he's got to follow the patrins left on the way by the others. He says that he looks at the places where fires have been made on the way, and beside them somewhere he will see the patrins, the sticks that point in the direction he must follow.'

'He's sure to destroy them,' said Dick. '*We* couldn't follow them!'

'We'll ask him to leave his *own* patrins,' said George. 'I think he will. He's not a bad little boy, really. I could ask him to leave *plenty* of patrins, so that we could easily find the way.'

'Well, it might be fun to see if we could read the right road to go, just as easily as the travellers do,' said Julian. 'We could make it a day's ride. It would be interesting!'

Henry gave a most enormous yawn, and that made Anne yawn too, though hers was a very polite one.

'Henry!' said Mrs Johnson.

'Sorry,' said Henry. 'It just came almost like a sneeze does. I don't know why, but I feel almost asleep.'

'Go to bed then,' said Mrs Johnson. 'You've had such a day of air and sunshine! You all look very brown too. The April sun has been as hot as July today.'

The five of them, and Timmy, went out for a last look at the horses, and to do one or two small jobs. Henry yawned again, and that set everyone else off, even George.

'Me for the straw!' said Julian, with a laugh. 'Oh, the thought of that warm, comfy straw bed is too good for words! You girls are welcome to the beds!'

'I hope Sniffer's pa doesn't come in the middle of the night again,' said Dick.

'I shall tie up the latch,' said Julian. 'Well, let's go and say good night to Mrs Johnson.'

It wasn't long before the three girls were in bed and the two boys cuddled down in the straw of the stable. Clip was there still, but he no longer fidgeted. He lay down quietly, and did not once move his bad leg. It was getting much better. He would certainly be able to go after the others the next day!

Julian and Dick fell asleep at once. No one came creeping in at the stable door that night. Nothing disturbed them until the morning, when a cock got into the stable through a window, sat on a rafter just above them, and crowed loudly enough to wake both boys with a jump.

'What's that!' said Dick. 'That awful screeching in my ear! Was it you, Ju?'

The cock crowed again and the boys laughed. 'Blow him!' said Julian, settling down again. 'I could do with another couple of hours' sleep!'

That morning Sniffer came slipping in at the

gate again. He never came boldly in; he slid through the hedge, or crept in at the gate, or appeared round a corner. He saw George and went over to her.

'George,' he called. 'Is Clip better?'

'Yes!' called back George. 'Captain Johnson says you can take him today. But wait a bit, Sniffer, I want to ask you something before you go.'

Sniffer was pleased. He liked this girl who had presented him with such a magnificent handkerchief. He took it carefully out of his pocket, hoping to please her.

'See,' he said. 'How clean it is! I have kept it very carefully.' He sniffed loudly.

'You're an idiot,' said George, exasperated. 'I gave it to you to *use*, not to keep clean in your pocket. It's to stop your *sniffing*. Honestly, you're a bit of a mutt, Sniffer. I shall take that hanky away if you don't use it!'

Sniffer looked alarmed. He shook it out carefully and then lightly touched his nose with it. He then folded it up conscientiously in the right creases and put it back into his pocket again.

'Now, NO sniffing!' commanded George, trying not to laugh. 'Listen, Sniffer, you know those patrins you showed me yesterday?'

'Yes, George,' said Sniffer.

'Well, will the other travellers who have gone in front, leave you patrins to follow, so that you will know the way?' said George.

Sniffer nodded. 'Yes, but not many, because I have been that way twice before. They will only leave them in places where I might go wrong.'

'I see,' said George. 'Now Sniffer, we want to have a sort of game. We want to see which of us can follow patrins, and we want you to lay patrins for us quite often, on your way to your family today. Will you?'

'Oh yes, I will,' said Sniffer, quite proud to have a favour asked of him. 'I will lay the ones I showed you, the cross, the long sticks, and the big and little leaf.'

'Yes, do,' said George. 'That will mean that

you have passed in a certain direction and you are a boy and a dog. That's right, isn't it?'

'Yes,' said Sniffer, nodding his head. 'You have remembered!'

'Right. And we're going to have a kind of game, trying to pretend we are travellers following others who have passed,' said George.

'You must not show yourselves when you come up to our caravans,' said Sniffer, looking suddenly alarmed. 'I should get into trouble for laying patrins for you.'

'All right. We'll be careful,' said George. 'Now let's go and get Clip.'

They fetched the patient little skewbald who came out gladly. He no longer limped, and his rest seemed to have done him good. He went off at a good pace with Sniffer. The last George heard of them was a very loud sniff indeed!

'Sniffer!' she shouted, warningly. He put his hand in his pocket and pulled out the hanky. He waved it gaily in the air, a sudden grin lighting up his face.

George went to find the others. 'Sniffer has

taken Clip,' she said. 'What about going down to the blacksmith, and taking those horses that want shoeing?'

'Good idea,' said Julian. 'We can ask him all about Mystery Moor then, and the strange little railway line, or whatever it is! Come on.'

They took the horses that needed shoeing. There were six of them, so they each rode one, and Julian led the sixth. Timmy ran happily along beside them. He loved the horses, and they regarded him as a real friend, bending their long noses down to sniff at him, whenever he came near.

They went slowly down the long lane to the blacksmith's. 'There it is!' said George. 'A proper old smithy with a lovely fire! And there's the smith!'

Old Ben was a mighty figure of a man, even though he was over eighty. He didn't shoe many horses now, but sat in the sun, watching all that was going on. He had a great mane of white hair, and eyes that were as black as the coal he had so many times heated to a fiery flame.

'Good morning, young masters and Miss,' he said and Julian grinned. That would please George and Henry!

'We've got some questions to ask you,' said George dismounting.

'Ask away!' said the old man. 'If it's about this place, there's nothing much old Ben can't tell you! Give Jim your horses. Now, ask away!'

The blacksmith tells a tale

'Well,' began Julian, 'we went riding on Mystery Moor yesterday, and for one thing we'd like to know if there is any reason for the curious name. *Was* there ever a mystery on that moor?'

'Oh, there were plenty of mysteries away there,' said Old Ben. 'People lost and never come back again, noises that no one could find the reason of . . .'

'What kind of noises?' said Anne, curiously.

'Ah now, when I was a boy, I spent nights up on that moor,' said old Ben, solemnly, 'and the noises that went on there! Screeches and howls and the like, and moans and the sweep of big wings . . .'

'Well, all that might have been owls and foxes and things like that,' said Dick. 'I've heard a barn owl give a screech just over my head which made me nearly jump out of my skin. If I hadn't known it was an owl I'd have run for miles!'

Ben grinned and his face ran into a score of creases and wrinkles.

'Why is it called *Mystery* Moor?' persisted Julian. 'Is it a very old name?'

'When my grandad was a boy it was called *Misty* Moor,' said the old blacksmith, remembering. 'See, *Misty*, not *Mystery*. And that was because of the sea-fogs that came stealing in from the coast, and lay heavy on the moor, so that no man could see his hand in front of his face. Yes, I've been lost in one of those mists, and right scared I was too. It swirled round me like a live thing, and touched me all over with its cold damp fingers.'

'How horrid!' said Anne with a shiver. 'What did you do?'

'Well, first I ran for my life,' said Ben, getting out his pipe and looking into the empty bowl. 'I ran over heather and into gorse. I fell a dozen times, and all the time the mist was feeling me with its damp fingers, trying to get me, that's what the old folk used to say of that mist, it was always trying to get you!'

'Still, it was only a mist,' said George, feeling that the old man was exaggerating. 'Does it still come over the moor?'

'Oh ay,' said Ben, ramming some tobacco into his pipe. 'Autumn's the time, but it comes suddenly at any moment of the year. I've known it come at the end of a fine summer's day, creeping in stealthily, and my, if you don't happen to see it soon enough, it gets you!'

'What do you mean, it *gets* you?' said George.

'Well, it may last for days,' said old Ben. 'And if you're lost on the moors, you're really lost, and you never come back. Ah, smile if you like, young man, but I *know*!' He went off into memories of long ago, looking down at his pipe. 'Let's see now, there was old Mrs Banks, who went bilberry-picking with her basket on a summer's afternoon, and no one ever heard of her again, after the mist came down. And there was young Victor who played truant and went off to the moor, and the mist got him too.'

'I can see we'd better watch out for the mist if we go riding there,' said Dick. 'This is the first I've heard of it.'

'Yes. You keep your eyes skinned,' said old Ben. 'Look away to the coast side and watch there, that's where it comes from. But there aren't many mists nowadays, though I don't know why. No, now I think of it, there hasn't been a mist, not a proper wicked one, for nearly three years.'

'What I'd like to know is why was the name changed to *Mystery* Moor,' said Henry. 'I can understand its being called Misty Moor, but now everyone calls it *Mystery*, not Misty.'

'Well now, that must have been about seventy years ago, when I was a boy,' said Ben, lighting his pipe and puffing hard. He was enjoying himself. He didn't often get such an interested audience as this, five of them, including a dog who sat and listened too!

'That was when the Bartle family built the little railway over the moor,' he began, and stopped at the exclamations of his five listeners.

'Ah! We wanted to know about that!'

'Oh! You know about the railway then?'

'Do go on!'

The blacksmith seemed to get some trouble with his pipe and pulled at it for an exasperatingly long time. George wished she was a horse and could stamp her foot impatiently!

'Well, the Bartle family was a big one,' said Ben at last. 'All boys, but for one ailing little girl. Big strong fellows they were, I remember them well. I was scared of them, they were so free with their fists. Well, one of them, Dan, found a mighty good stretch of sand out there on the moor—'

'Oh yes, we *thought* there might have been a sand-quarry,' said Anne. Ben frowned at the interruption.

'And as there were nine or ten good strong

Bartles, they reckoned to make a fine do of it,' said Ben. 'They got wagons and they went to and from the quarry they dug, and they sold their sand for miles around, good, sharp sand it was . . .'

'We saw some,' said Henry. 'But what about the rails?'

'Don't hurry him,' said Dick, with a frown.

'They made a great deal of money,' said Ben, remembering. 'And they set to work and built a little railway to carry an engine and trucks to the quarry and back, to save labour. My, my, that was a nine days' wonder, that railway! Us youngsters used to follow the little engine, puffing along, and we all longed to drive it. But we never did. Those Bartles kept a big stick, each one of them, and they whipped the hide off any boy that got too near them. Fierce they were, and quarrelsome.'

'Why did the railway fall into ruin?' asked Julian. 'The rails are all overgrown with heather and grass. You can hardly see them.'

'Well, now we come to the Mystery you keep

on about,' said Ben, taking an extra big puff at his pipe. 'Those Bartles fell foul of the travellers up on the moor—'

'Oh, were there travellers on the moor *then*?' said Dick. 'There are some now!'

'Oh ay, there's always been travellers on the moor, long as I can remember,' said the blacksmith. 'Well, it's said those travellers quarrelled with the Bartles, and it wasn't hard to do that, most people did! And the travellers pulled up bits of the line, here and there, and the little engine toppled over and pulled the trucks with it.'

The children could quite well imagine the little engine puffing along, coming to the damaged rails and falling over. What a to-do there must have been up on the moor then!

'The Bartles weren't ones to put up with a thing like that,' said Ben, 'so they set about to drive all the travellers off the moor, and they swore that if so much as one caravan went there, they'd set fire to it and chase the travellers over to the coast and into the sea!'

'They *must* have been a fierce family,' said Anne.

'You're right there,' said Ben. 'All nine or ten of them were big upstanding men, with great shaggy eyebrows that almost hid their eyes, and loud voices. Nobody dared to cross them. If they did, they'd have the whole family on their doorstep with sticks. They ruled this place, they did, and my, they were hated! Us children ran off as soon as we saw one coming round a corner.'

'What about the travellers? Did the Bartles manage to drive them off the moor?' asked George, impatiently.

'Now let me go my own pace,' said Ben, pointing at her with his pipe. 'You want a Bartle after you, young man, that's what you want!' He thought she was a boy, of course. He did something to his pipe and made them all wait a little. Julian winked at the others. He liked this old fellow with his long, long memories.

'Now, you can't cross the travellers for long,'

said Ben, at last. 'That's a fact, you can't. And one day all the Bartles disappeared and never come back home. No, not one of them. All that was left of the family was little lame Agnes, their sister.'

Everyone exclaimed in surprise and old Ben looked round with satisfaction. Ah, he could tell a story, he could!

'But what happened?' said Henry.

'Well, no one rightly knows,' said Ben. 'It happened in a week when the mist came swirling over the moors and blotted everything out. Nobody went up there except the Bartles, and they were safe because all they had to do was to follow their railway lines there and back. They went up to the quarry each day the mist was there, and worked the same as usual. Nothing stopped those Bartles from working!'

He paused and looked round at his listeners. He dropped his voice low, and all five of the children felt little shivers up their backs.

'One night somebody in the village saw twenty or more travellers' caravans slinking through the village at dead of night,' said Ben. 'Up on the moor they went in the thick mist. Maybe they followed the railway; nobody knows. And next morning, up to the quarry went the Bartles as usual, swallowed up in the mist.'

He paused again. 'And they never came back,' he said. 'No, not one of them. Never heard of again!'

'But what *happened*?' said George.

'Search-parties were sent out when the mist cleared,' said old Ben. 'But not one of the Bartles did they find, alive or dead. Not one! And they didn't find any travellers' caravans either. They'd all come creeping back the next night, and passed through the village like sha-dows. I reckon the travellers set upon the Bartles in the mist that day, fought them and defeated them, and took them and threw them over the cliffs into the roaring sea!'

'How horrible!' said Anne, feeling sick.

'Don't worry yourself!' said the blacksmith. 'It all happened a long time ago, and there weren't many that mourned those Bartles, I can tell you. Funny thing was, their weakly little sister, Agnes, she lived to be a hale old woman of ninety-six, and only died a few years ago! And to think those strong fierce brothers of hers went all together like that!'

'It's a most interesting story, Ben,' said Julian. 'So Misty Moor became *Mystery* Moor then, did it? And nobody ever *really* found out what happened, so the mystery was never solved. Didn't anyone work the railway after that, or get the sand?'

'No, not a soul,' said Ben. 'We were all scared, you see, and young Agnes, she said the railway and the trucks and engine could rot, for all she cared. I never dared to go near them after that. It was a long time before anyone but the travellers set foot on Misty Moor again. Now it's all forgotten, the tale of the Bartles, but those travellers still remember, I've no doubt! They've got good memories, they have.'

'Do you know why they come to Mystery Moor every so often?' asked Dick.

'No. They come and they go,' said Ben. 'They've their own funny ways. They don't belong anywhere, those folk. What they do on the moor is their own business, and I wouldn't want to poke *my* nose into it. I'd remember those old Bartles, and keep away!'

A voice came from inside the smithy, where Jim, the blacksmith's grandson, had been shoeing the horses. 'Grandad! Stop jabbering away there, and let the children come and talk to *me*! I've shod nearly all the horses.'

Ben laughed. 'Go along,' he said to the children. 'I know you'd like to be in there and see the sparks fly, and the shoes made. I've wasted your time, I have, telling you long-ago things. Go along into the smithy. And just remember two things – watch out for that mist, and keep away from the travellers on the moor!'

[10]

Sniffer's patrins

It was fun in the smithy, working the bellows, seeing the fire glow, and watching the red-hot shoes being shaped. Jim was quick and clever, and it was a pleasure to watch him.

'Have you been hearing Grandad's old stories?' he said. 'It's all he's got to do now, sit there and remember, though when he wants to he can make a horseshoe as well as I can! There, that's the last one. Stand still, Sultan. That's right!'

The five children were soon on their way back again. It was a lovely morning, and the banks and ditches they passed were bright gold with thousands of celandines.

'All beautifully polished!' said Anne, picking two or three for her button-hole. It *did* look as if someone had polished the inside of each petal, for they gleamed like enamel.

'What a strange tale the old man told,' said Julian. 'He told it well!'

'Yes. He made me feel I don't want to go up on the moor again!' said Anne.

'Don't be feeble!' said George. 'It all happened ages ago. Jolly interesting too. I wonder if the travellers who are there now know the story. Maybe their great-grandparents were the ones who set on the Bartles that misty day!'

'Well, Sniffer's father looked sly enough to carry out a plan like that,' said Henry. 'What about us having a shot at following the way they went, and seeing if we can make out the patrins that Sniffer told George he would leave?'

'Good idea,' said Julian. 'We'll go this afternoon. I say, what's the time? I should think it must be half past lunch-time!'

They looked at their watches. 'Yes, we're late, but we always are when we get back from the blacksmith,' said George. 'Never mind, I bet Mrs Johnson will have an extra special meal for us!'

She had! There was an enormous plate of stew for everyone, complete with carrots, onions, parsnips and turnips, and a date pudding to follow. Good old Mrs Johnson!

'You three girls must wash up for me afterwards,' she said. 'I've such a lot to do today.'

'Why can't the boys help?' said George at once.

'*I'll* do all the washing-up!' said Anne with a sudden grin. 'You four *boys* can go out to the stables!'

Dick gave her a good-natured shove. 'You know we'll help, even if we're not good at it. I'll dry. I hate those bits and pieces that float about in the washing-bowl.'

'Will it be all right if we go up on the moors this afternoon?' asked George.

'Yes, quite all right. But if you want to take your tea, you'll have to pack it yourselves,' said Mrs Johnson. 'I'm taking the small children out for a ride, and there's one on the leading-rein still, as you know.'

They were ready to set off at three o'clock,

their tea packed and everything. The horses were caught in the field and got ready too. They set off happily.

'Now we'll see if we are as clever as we think we are, at reading traveller patrins!' said George. 'Timmy, don't chase *every* rabbit you see, or you'll be left behind!'

They cantered up on to the moor, passing the place where the caravans had stood. They knew the direction they had taken, and here and there they saw wheel-marks. It was fairly easy to follow their trail, because five caravans made quite a path to follow.

'Here's where they camped first,' said Julian, riding up to a blackened spot that showed where a fire had been lit. 'We ought to find a message left somewhere here.'

They searched for one. George found it. 'It's here, behind this tree!' she called. 'Out of the wind.'

They dismounted and came round George. On the ground was the patrin, the shape of a cross, the long stick pointing forwards, in the direction they were going. Other single sticks lay there, to show that a caravan had gone that way, and beside them were the large and the small leaf, weighted with tiny stones.

'What did those leaves show now, oh yes, Sniffer and his dog!' said Dick. 'Well, we're on the right way, though we'd know that anyhow, by the fire!'

They mounted again and went on. It proved quite easy to find and follow the patrins. Only once did they find any difficulty and that was when they came to a place, marked by two trees, where there was no apparent sign in the heather of any caravan marks.

'The heather's so jolly thick here that it's taken the caravans as if it were a feather-bed, springing up when they had gone, and giving no sign of where they had passed,' said Julian. He dismounted and had a good look round. No, there was no sign.

'We'll go on a little way,' he said. 'We may come to a camping place, then we'll know.'

But they came to no old camping place, and

stopped at last in bewilderment. 'We've lost the trail,' said Dick. 'We're not such good travellers after all!'

'Let's go back to those two trees,' said George. 'We can still just see them. If it's so easy to lose the way there, there *might* be a patrin, although there are no camp marks. After all, a patrin is left to show the way, in case the ones following take the wrong route.'

So back they rode to the two trees, and there, sure enough, was Sniffer's patrin! Henry found it set carefully between the trees, so that nothing could disturb it.

'Here's the cross, and the single sticks, and the leaves!' she said. 'But look, the long stick of the cross points to the east and we went off to the north. No wonder we found no signs of the caravans!'

They set off to the east this time, across the thick, springy heather, and almost at once found signs of the passing of caravans: twigs broken off the bushes, a wheel rut on a soft piece of ground.

'We're right now,' said Julian, pleased. 'I was beginning to think it was all too easy for words! But it isn't!'

They rode for two hours, and then decided to have tea. They sat down in a little glade of silver birches, with an unexpected copse of pale primroses behind. Timmy had to make up his mind which to choose, a rabbit chase, or titbits from the children's tea!

He chose both, racing after an imaginary rabbit, and then coming back for a sandwich!

'You know, it's a lot better for us when Mrs Johnson makes sandwiches of tomato or lettuce or something like that,' said Henry. 'We do get them all then, but when we have meat or sardine or egg sandwiches Timmy gets as much as we do!'

'Well, surely you don't mind that, Henrietta,' said George at once. 'You make Timmy sound very greedy. After all, you don't need to give him any of *your* sandwiches!'

'Now, Georgina!' murmured Dick, in her ear.

'Sorry, Georgina,' said Henry, with a grin. 'I just can't *help* giving him a sandwich or two when he comes and sits down and looks at me so longingly.'

'Woof,' said Timmy, and at once sat down in front of Henry, his tongue out, and his eyes fixed unblinkingly on her.

'He sort of *hypnotises* me,' complained Henry. 'Make him go away, George, I shan't be able to keep a single sandwich or bit of cake for myself. Go and stare at someone else, Timmy, for goodness' sake!'

Julian looked at his watch. 'I don't think we ought to spend *too* long over tea,' he said. 'I know we've got summertime now, and the evenings are nice and light, but we haven't reached the travellers' camp yet, and after that we've got to go all the way back. What about starting off again?'

'Right,' said everyone and remounted their horses. They set off through the heather. Soon they found it unexpectedly easy to follow the caravan route, because the soil became sandy, and there were many bare patches on which the marks of the wheels could plainly be seen.

'Goodness, if we go to the east much more, we'll come to the sea!' said Dick.

'No, it's still some miles away,' said Julian. 'Hallo, there's a little hill or something in the distance. First time we've seen anything but complete flatness!'

The wheel-marks led steadily towards the little hill, which, as they came near, seemed to grow considerably bigger. 'I bet the caravans are there,' said George. 'That hill would give a nice bit of shelter from the wind that came from the sea. I believe I can see one!'

George was right. The caravans were there. They showed up well against the hill, in their bright colours.

'They've even got up a washing-line as usual!' said Anne. 'Clothes flapping in the wind!'

'Let's go and ask if Clip is all right,' said Julian. 'It will be a very good excuse for going right up to the camp.'

So they cantered straight up to the little group of five caravans. Four or five men appeared as soon as they heard the sound of hooves. They looked silent and rather forbidding. Sniffer ran out and shouted.

'Hallo! Clip's fine! Quite all right again!'

His father gave him a push and said something sharp to him. He disappeared under the nearest caravan.

Julian rode up to Sniffer's father. 'Did I hear Sniffer say that Clip was quite all right?' he asked. 'Where is he?'

'Over there,' said the man, with a nod of his head. 'No need for you to see him. He's mended fine.'

'All right, all right! I'm not going to take him away from you!' said Julian. 'This is a nice sheltered place you've got, isn't it? How long are you staying?'

'What's that to do with you?' said an old traveller, unpleasantly.

'Nothing,' said Julian, surprised. 'Just a polite question, that's all!'

'How do you get water?' called George. 'Is there a good spring here?'

There was no reply at all. The four or five men had now been joined by others, and there were three mangy-looking dogs growing round. Timmy was beginning to growl back.

'You'd better go before our dogs get you,' said Sniffer's father, sourly.

'Where's Liz?' said George, remembering Sniffer's dog, but before she got an answer the three dogs suddenly made an attack on Timmy! They pounced on him and he had hard work to keep them off. He was far bigger than they were, but they were nippy little things.

'Call off those dogs!' yelled Julian, seeing that George was dismounting to go to Timmy's help. She would get bitten. 'Do you hear me? Call off those dogs.'

Sniffer's father whistled. The three dogs reluctantly left Timmy and went over to the men, their tails down. George had reached Tim and had now got her hand on his collar to stop him from chasing the other three dogs.

'Mount your horse, whistle Timmy, and we'll go,' shouted Julian, not at all liking the silent, sour-looking travellers. George did as she was told. Timmy ran beside her, and they all cantered away from the unpleasant camp.

The men stood watching them in complete silence. 'What's up with them?' said Dick, puzzled. 'Anyone would think they were planning another Bartle affair!'

'Don't!' said Anne. 'They're planning *some*-thing, all alone out here, far away from any-where! I shan't go near them again.'

'They thought we were prying and spying,' said Dick. 'That's all. Poor old Sniffer. What a life he has!'

'We couldn't even tell him that we found his patrins useful,' said George. 'Oh well, there's probably nothing in it, not even an adventure!'

Was she right or wrong? Julian looked at Dick and Dick looked back, his eyebrows raised. They didn't know. Oh well, time would tell!

A nice little plan

The five of them told Captain and Mrs Johnson about their afternoon's experience, as they were having supper.

'Patrins!' said Mrs Johnson. 'So Sniffer told you about those? But I really don't think you should visit the travellers' camp. Those particular travellers are a surly, bad-tempered lot.'

'Did you ever hear the tale of the Big Bartles?' said Henry, getting ready to relate it, and add little bits of her own, here and there!

'No. But it can wait, I'm sure,' said Mrs Johnson, knowing Henry's habit of leaving her food quite uneaten once she began on some marvellous tale. 'Is it one of your tales? You can tell it after supper.'

'It's *not* Henry's tale,' said George, annoyed that Henry should get all the limelight again, and take the blacksmith's tale for her own. 'It's one old Ben told us. Ju, *you* tell it!'

'Nobody is to tell it *now*,' said Captain Johnson. 'You came in late for supper, we waited for you, and the least you can do is to get on with your eating.'

The five juniors at the other table were disappointed. They had hoped to hear another of Henry's marvellous stories. But Captain Johnson was hungry and tired.

'Old Ben is a great age, as you said,' began Henry, after a few mouthfuls. 'He—'

'Not another word, please, Henrietta,' said the captain, curtly. Henry went red and George grinned, kicking at Dick under the table. Unfortunately she kicked Henry instead, and the girl glared at her for a whole minute.

'Oh dear!' thought Anne. 'Just as we'd had such a lovely day! I suppose we're all tired and scratchy.'

'*Why* did you kick me?' began Henry in a cross voice, as soon as she and George left the table with the others.

'Shut up, you two,' said Julian. 'She probably meant to kick me or Dick, not you.'

Henry shut up. She didn't like Julian to tick her off. George looked mutinous and went off with Timmy.

Dick yawned. 'What jobs are there to do, if any?' he said. 'Don't say there's washing-up again. I feel I might break a few things.'

Mrs Johnson heard him and laughed. 'No, there's no washing-up. The woman has come in to do it tonight. Have a look at the horses – and see that Jenny the mare is not with Flash, you know she doesn't like her for some reason, and *will* kick out at her. She must always be kept in another field.'

'That's all right, Mrs Johnson,' said William, suddenly appearing, stolid and competent as ever. 'I've seen to that. I've seen to everything, really.'

'You're better than any stable boy, William,' said Mrs Johnson, smiling at him. 'I wish you'd take a permanent job here!'

'I wish you meant that,' said William, earnestly. There was nothing he would have liked better! He went off looking pleased.

'I think you'd better all go to bed then, as William appears to have done everything necessary,' said Mrs Johnson. 'Any plans for tomorrow?'

'Not yet,' said Julian, trying to stop a yawn. 'So if you want anything done, we'll do it.'

'We'll see what tomorrow brings,' said Mrs Johnson and said good night. The boys said good night to the three girls and went off to the stable.

'Gosh, we've forgotten to undress and wash and everything,' said Julian, half-asleep. 'What's the matter with us at this place? I can't seem to keep my eyes open after half past eight!'

The next day certainly brought a few things. It brought a letter for Henry that filled her with disgust. It brought two letters for Mrs Johnson that made her start fussing and worrying. It brought a letter for Captain Johnson that sent him down to the station at once.

Henrietta's letter was from two of her great-aunts. They announced that as they would be near the stables that day and the following, they would like to fetch her and take her out with them.

'Blow!' said Henrietta, ungratefully. 'Great-Aunts Hannah and Lucy *would* choose this very week to come along and see me! Just when Julian and Dick are here, and everything is such fun. Can't I phone and say I'm too busy, Mrs Johnson?'

'Certainly not,' said Mrs Johnson, shocked. 'That would be very rude, Henry, and you know it. You're having the whole of the Easter holidays here, and yet you think you can't spare two days. As a matter of fact I shall be glad if your aunts *do* take you off my hands for a couple of days.'

'Why?' asked Henry, astonished. 'Have I been a nuisance?'

'Oh no, but I've had two letters this morning telling me that four children are coming un-expectedly,' said Mrs Johnson. 'They were not supposed to come till three of the others left this weekend, but there you are! These things happen. *Where* I am to put them I really don't know!'

'Oh dear!' said Anne. 'Do you think Dick and Julian ought to go home, Mrs Johnson? You didn't plan for them, you know, they just came.'

'Yes, I know,' said Mrs Johnson. 'But we're more or less used to that, and I do like having bigger boys, I must say, they're such a help. Now let me see. What *can* we do?'

Captain Johnson came in, looking hurried. 'I've just had a letter, dear,' he said. 'I've got to go down to the station. Those two new horses have arrived. Two days before I wanted them – what a nuisance!'

'This is one of those *days*!' said Mrs Johnson, desperately. 'Good gracious, how many shall we be in the house? And however many horses shall we have? No, I can't count this morning. I'm all muddle-headed!'

Anne felt that it was a pity that she and George and the boys couldn't immediately pack and go home. After all, poor Mrs Johnson had thought that she and George *would* have gone home three or four days ago, and instead of that they had stayed on and the boys had arrived as well!

Anne hurried to find Julian. He would know what to do. She found him with Dick, carrying straw for the stables.

'Julian! Listen! I want to talk to you,' said Anne. Julian let the load of straw slip to the ground, and turned to Anne.

'What's up?' he said. '*Don't* tell me it's a row between George and Henry again, because I shan't listen!'

'No. Nothing like that,' said Anne. 'It's Mrs Johnson. She's got four children coming unexpectedly, before the others go. She's in a great state about it, and I wondered what we could do to help. You see, she didn't expect any of *us* four to be here this week.'

'No. That's true,' said Julian, sitting down on his straw. 'Let's think hard.'

'It's easy!' said Dick. 'We'll simply take our

tents, some food, and go and camp out on the moor by some spring. WHAT could be nicer?'

'Oh *yes*!' said Anne, her eyes shining. 'Oh Dick that's a *marvellous* idea! Mrs Johnson will get rid of us all and Timmy too, then, and we would have a lovely time all by ourselves!'

'Killing quite a lot of birds with one stone!' said Julian. 'We've got a couple of tents in our kit, Anne. Very small ones, but they'll do. And we can borrow rubber sheets to put on the heather, though it's as dry as a bone, as far as I can see!'

'I'll go and tell George!' said Anne, joyfully. 'Let's go today, Julian, and be out of the way before the new children come. Captain Johnson's got two new horses coming too. He'll be very glad to have a few of us out of the way!'

She flew off to tell George. George was busy polishing some harness, a job she liked very much. She listened to Anne's excited tale. Henry was there too, looking gloomy. She looked gloomier still at the end.

'It's too bad,' she said, when Anne had

finished. 'I could have come with you if it hadn't been for these great-aunts of mine. WHY did they have to come just at this very moment? Don't you think it's maddening?'

Neither Anne nor George thought it was maddening. They were secretly very pleased indeed to think that they could once more go off entirely on their own, with Timmy, as they had so often done before. But they would have *had* to ask Henry if her aunts hadn't written at this very lucky moment!

George didn't like to show how delighted she was to think of going off camping on the moor. She and Anne did a little comforting of poor Henry and then went off to make arrangements with Mrs Johnson.

'Well, that's a very bright idea of Dick's!' she said in delight. 'It solves a whole lot of problems. And I know you don't mind. You're thrilled at the chance, aren't you! It's really very helpful. I only wish poor Henry could go too, but she *must* go out with her old great-aunts. They adore her!'

'Of course she must,' said George, solemnly. She and Anne exchanged a look. Poor Henry! But really, it would be very nice to be without her for a little while.

Everyone began to be suddenly very busy. Dick and Julian undid their packs to find out exactly what was in them. Mrs Johnson looked out rubber sheets and old rugs. She was a wonder at producing things like that!

William wanted to go with them and help to carry the things, but nobody wanted his help. They just wanted to be off and away by themselves, just the Five and nobody else! Timmy caught the excitement too and his tail thumped and wagged the whole morning.

'You'll be pretty well loaded,' said Mrs Johnson, doubtfully. 'It's a good thing that fine weather is forecast, or you'd have to take macs as well. Still, I imagine you won't go very far on the moors, will you? You can easily get back to the stable if you have forgotten anything, or want more food.'

They were ready at last, and went to find

Henry to say good-bye. She stared at them mournfully. She had changed into a smart little coat and dress. She looked completely different and very gloomy.

'What part of the moor are you going to?' she asked eagerly. 'Up the railway?'

'Yes. We thought we would,' said Julian. 'Just to see where it goes to. And it's a nice straight way to follow. We can't lose our way if we keep near the railway!'

'Have a good time, Henry,' said George, with a grin. 'Do they call you Henrietta?'

'Yes,' said poor Henry, putting on a pair of gloves. 'Well, good-bye. For goodness' sake don't stay away too long. Thank goodness you're all such a hungry lot. You'll simply have to come back and get more food in a couple of days!'

They grinned and left her, Timmy at their heels. They made their way to the moor, intending to cut out the part of the railway that ran to Milling Green, and join it some way before that.

'Now we're off,' said George, contentedly. 'Without that chatterbox of a Henry.'

'She's *really* not too bad,' said Dick. 'All the same, it's fine to be on our own, just the Famous Five together!'

[12]
The little railway

It was a very hot day. The five had had their lunch before they started, as Mrs Johnson said it would be easier to carry that inside than outside!

Even Timmy carried something. George said that he ought to do his share, and had neatly fastened a bag of his pet biscuits on his back.

'There now!' she said. 'You've got your load too. No, don't try and sniff the biscuits all the time, Timmy. You can't walk with your head screwing round like that. You ought to be used to the smell of biscuits by this time!'

They set off to the railway line, or where they hoped it would be. It took a little time to discover it running under the heather. Julian was glad. He didn't want to walk right into Milling Green to find the beginning of it and then walk all the way up again!

Anne found it by tripping over it! 'Oh!' she said. 'Here it is! I caught my foot in a bit of rusty line. Look, you can hardly see it!'

'Good,' said Julian, and stepped in between the narrow pair of old, rusty lines. In some places they had rusted away, and there were gaps. In other places the heather had grown completely over the lines, and unless the children had known that they must keep straight forward, they would have lost them completely. As it was they sometimes missed them and once had to do quite a bit of scrabbling about in the heather to see if they could feel them.

It was very hot. Their packs began to feel distinctly heavy. Timmy's biscuits began to slide round his body and eventually hung below his tummy. He didn't like that, and George suddenly spied him sitting down trying to prise open the bag with his teeth!

She put down her own pack and adjusted Timmy's. 'If only you didn't keep chasing rabbits, and making your pack swing about, it wouldn't slip,' she said. 'There now, it's all right again, Tim. Walk to heel and it won't slip any more.'

They went on and on up the railway lines. Sometimes the rails took a curve round an unexpected rock. Soon the soil began to look sandy, and the heather did not grow so thickly. It was easier to see the lines, though in some places the sand had sifted over them and hidden them.

'I really *must* have a rest!' said Anne, sitting down in some heather. 'I feel I want to pant and hang my tongue out like Timmy!'

'I wonder how far these lines go,' said Dick. 'It's so very sandy now underfoot that I feel we must be getting near the quarry!'

They lay back in the heather and felt very sleepy. Julian yawned and sat up.

'This really won't do!' he said. 'If we fall asleep we'll never want to start off with our heavy packs again. Stir yourselves, lazy-bones!'

They all got up again. Timmy's biscuits had slithered round to his tummy once more, and George had to put them right again. Timmy stood quietly, panting, his tongue hanging out. He thought the biscuits were a great nuisance. It would be much easier to eat them!

The sand got deeper and soon there were big sandy patches with no heather or grass at all. The wind blew the sand up in the air, and the five found that they had to shut their eyes against it.

'I say! The lines end here!' said Julian, stopping suddenly. 'Look, they're broken, wrenched out of place, the engine couldn't go any farther.'

'They may appear again a bit farther on,' said Dick, and went to look. But he couldn't find any, and came back to look at the lines again.

'It's funny,' he said. 'We aren't at any quarry yet, are we? I quite thought that the line would run right to the quarry, the trucks would fill up there, and the engine would pull them back to Milling Green. *Where* is the quarry? Why do the lines stop so suddenly here?'

'Yes. The quarry *should* be near here,

shouldn't it?' said Julian. 'Well, there simply must be more lines somewhere! Ones that go to the quarry. Let's look for the quarry first, though. We ought to see that easily enough!'

But it wasn't really very easy to find because it was behind a great mass of thick tall gorse bushes. Dick rounded them and stopped. Behind the enormous spread of bushes was a great pit, a sandy pit quarried and hollowed for its beautiful sand.

'Here it is!' called Dick. 'Come and look! My word, there's been some quarrying here for sand. They must have taken tons and tons out of it!'

The others came to look. It certainly was an enormous pit, deep and wide. They put their packs beside it and leapt down. Their feet sank into the fine sand.

'The sides are pitted with holes,' said Dick. 'I bet hundreds of sand-martins nest here in May!'

'There are even some caves,' said George, in surprise. 'Sand caves! Well, we can easily shelter here if we have rain. Some of these caves seem to go quite a long way back.'

'Yes. But I'd be a bit afraid of the sand falling in and burying me, if I crawled in,' said Anne. 'It's quite loose, look!' She scraped some down with her hand.

'I've found the lines!' called Julian. 'Here, look. The sand has almost covered them. I trod on a rail and it was so rotten it broke beneath my foot!'

The others went to see, Timmy too. He was quite delighted with this place. The rabbit holes in it! What fun he was going to have!

'Let's follow these lines,' said Julian. So they kicked away the sand from the rails and followed them slowly out of the quarry and towards the ends of the other broken lines.

About ten yards from these the lines they were following were wrenched apart. Some were flung into the nearby heather, and could be seen there, bent and rusty.

The children stared at them. 'I guess the travellers did that, when the Bartles were here years ago,' said Dick. 'The day they attacked them perhaps. I say, look, what*ever's* that great lump over there, with gorse growing over it?'

They went to see. Timmy saw the lump and couldn't make it out. He growled warningly at it.

Julian took up a broken piece of rail and forced back the gorse bush that had grown over and around the great lump, almost hiding it.

'See what it is?' he said, startled.

They all stared. 'Why, it's the engine! The little engine old Ben the blacksmith told us about!' said Dick. 'It must have run right off the broken lines and overturned here, and through the years these great gorse bushes grew up and hid it. Poor old engine!'

Julian forced the gorse back a little more. 'What a funny old-fashioned affair!' he said. 'Look at the funnel, and the fat little boiler. And see, there's the small cab. It can't have had much more power, only just enough to puff along with a few trucks!'

'What happened to the trucks?' wondered Anne.

'Well, they would be easy enough to set upright again and put on the rails, and hand-pushed to Milling Green,' said Dick. 'But this engine couldn't be lifted, except by some kind of machinery. Not even a dozen men could lift it and set it on the rails!'

'The travellers must have set on the Bartles in the mist, having first broken up the lines so that the engine would run off and overturn,' said Julian. 'They may even have used the broken rails to attack them with. Anyway, they won the battle, because not one of the Bartles ever returned.'

'Some of the villagers must have gone to see what became of them and have got the trucks back on the lines and pushed them to Milling Green,' said George, trying to reconstruct the long-ago happenings in her mind. 'But they couldn't do anything about the engine.'

'That's about it,' said Julian. 'My word, what a shock for the Bartles when they saw the travellers creeping out at them from the mist, like shadows!'

'I hope we don't dream about this tonight,' said Anne.

They went back to the quarry. 'This wouldn't be a bad place to camp in,' said Dick. 'The sand is so dry and so soft. We could make lovely beds for ourselves. We wouldn't need the tents up, either, because the sides of the quarry shelter us beautifully from the wind.'

'Yes. Let's camp here,' said Anne, pleased. 'There are quite a lot of nice holes to store our things in.'

'What about water?' asked George. 'We want to be fairly near it, don't we? Timmy, find some water! Drink, Timmy, drink! Aren't you thirsty? Your tongue looks as if it is, the way you are hanging it out like a flag!'

Timmy put his head on one side as George talked to him. Water? Drink? He knew what both those words meant! He ran off, sniffing the air. George watched him.

He disappeared round a bush and was away for about half a minute. When he came back George gave a pleased shout.

'He's found some water! Look – his mouth is all wet! Timmy, where is it?'

Timmy wagged his tail vigorously, glad that George was pleased with him. He ran round the bush again and the others followed.

He led them to a little green patch and stopped. A spring bubbled up like a small fountain, dancing a little in the sunshine. The water fell from it into a little channel it had made for itself in the sand, ran away for a short distance, and then disappeared underground again.

'Thank you, Tim,' said George. 'Julian, is the water all right to drink here?'

'Well, I can see some that *is*!' said Julian, pointing to the right. 'The Bartles must have put a pipe in that bank, look, and caught another spring there, a much bigger one. It's as clear as can be. That will do fine for us!'

'Good,' said Anne, pleased. 'It's hardly any way from the quarry. It's as cold as ice, too – feel!'

They felt, and then they drank from their

palms. How cold and pure! The moor must be full of these little bubbling springs, welling up from underground. That explained the brilliant green patches here and there.

'Now let's sit down and have some tea,' said Anne, unpacking the bag she had carried. 'It's too hot to feel really hungry.'

'Oh no, it isn't,' said Dick. 'Speak for yourself, Anne!'

They sat in the sunny quarry, the sand warm to their legs. 'Far away from anybody!' said Anne, pleased. 'Nobody near us for miles!'

But she wasn't quite right. There was somebody much nearer than she thought!

[13]

A noise in the night

It was Timmy who first knew there was somebody not far off. He pricked up his ears and listened. George saw him.

'What is it, Tim?' she said. 'Nobody is coming here, surely?'

Timmy gave a tiny growl, as if he were not quite sure of himself. Then he leapt up, his tail wagging, and tore out of the quarry!

'Where's he gone to?' said George, astonished. 'Gosh, here he is, back again!'

So he was, and with him was a funny little hearth-rug of a dog – yes, Liz! She was not quite sure of her welcome and crawled up to the children on her tummy, looking more like a hearth-rug than ever!

Timmy leapt round her in delight. She might have been his very best friend, he was so delighted! George patted the funny little dog and Julian looked thoughtful.

'I hope this doesn't mean that we are any-where near the travellers' camp,' he said. 'It's quite likely that the lines might end somewhere near them. I've rather lost my sense of direction.'

'Oh goodness, I do HOPE we're not near their camp!' said Anne, in dismay. 'Those old-time travellers must have camped pretty near to the Bartles' quarry before they attacked them, so perhaps the present camp is near too.'

'Well, what's it matter if it is?' said Dick. 'Who's afraid of them? *I'm* not!'

They all sat still, thinking hard, Liz licking Anne's hand. And in the silence they heard an all-too-familiar sound.

Sniff! Sniff!

'Sniffer!' called George. 'Come on out, wher-ever you are hiding. I can hear you!'

A pair of legs stuck out from a great clump of heather at the edge of the quarry, and then the whole of Sniffer's wiry little body slithered out and down into the sand. He sat there, grinning at them, half-afraid to come any nearer in case they were cross with him.

'What are *you* doing here?' said Dick. 'Not spying on us, I hope?'

'No,' said Sniffer. 'Our camp isn't very far away. Liz heard you, I think, and ran off. I followed her.'

'Oh blow. We hoped we weren't near anyone else,' said George. 'Does anyone at your camp know we're here?'

'Not yet,' said Sniffer. 'But they'll find out. They always do. I won't tell, though, if you don't want me to.'

Dick tossed him a biscuit. 'Well, keep your mouth shut if you can,' he said. 'We're not interfering with anyone and we don't want anyone interfering with us. See?'

Sniffer nodded. He suddenly put his hand in his pocket and pulled out the red and white hanky that George had given him. It was still clean and beautifully folded.

'Not dirty yet!' he said to George.

'Well, it ought to be,' said George. 'It's for your sniffs. No, *don't* use your coat-sleeve.'

Sniffer simply could *not* understand why he should use a beautiful clean hanky when he had a dirty coat-sleeve. He put the hanky carefully back into his pocket.

Liz ran to him and fawned on him. Sniffer fondled the peculiar little creature, and then Timmy went over and played with them both. The four finished their tea, threw Sniffer one last biscuit, and got up to put their things away safely. Now that Sniffer was about, and the travellers' camp near, they didn't feel it was terribly safe to leave anything unguarded or unhidden.

'Scoot off, now, Sniffer,' said Julian. 'And no spying on us, mind! Timmy will know immediately you arrive anywhere near, and come hunting for you. If you want to see us, give a whistle when you get near. No creeping or slipping into the quarry. Understand?'

'Yes,' said Sniffer, standing up. He took the hanky from his pocket again, waved it at George, and disappeared with Liz at his heels.

'I'm just going to see exactly how near to the travellers' camp we are,' Julian said. He walked to the entrance of the quarry and up on to the moor. He looked in the direction that Sniffer had gone. Yes, there was the hill in the shelter of which the travellers had their caravans. It wasn't more than a quarter of a mile away. Blow! Still, it was far enough for the travellers not to discover them, unless by chance.

'Or unless Sniffer gives the game away,' thought Julian. 'Well, we'll spend the night here, anyway, and we can move off somewhere else tomorrow if we feel like it.'

They felt rather energetic that evening and played a ball game in the quarry, in which Timmy joined wholeheartedly. But as he always got the ball before anyone else did they had to tie him up in order to get a game themselves. Timmy was very cross. He turned his back on them and sulked.

'He looks like you now, George,' said Dick, grinning, and got the ball bang on the side of his head from an angry George!

Nobody wanted much supper. Julian took a little aluminium jug to the spring and filled it once for everyone. It really was lovely water from that bubbling spring!

'I wonder how Henry's getting on,' said Anne. 'Spoilt to bits by her great-aunts, I expect. Didn't she look odd in proper clothes!'

'Yes, she ought to have been a boy,' said Dick. 'Like you, George,' he added hastily. 'Both of you are real sports, plucky as anything.'

'How do you know Henry's plucky?' said George, scornfully. 'Only by her silly tales! I bet they're all made up and exaggerated.'

Julian changed the subject. 'Shall we want rugs tonight, do you think?' he said.

'You bet! It may be warm now, and the sand is hot with the sun, but it won't be quite so nice when it's gone down,' said Anne. 'Anyway we can always creep into one of those cosy little caves if we feel chilly. They're as warm as toast. I went into one, so I know.'

They settled down quite early to sleep. The

boys took one side of the quarry, the girls the other. Tim, as usual, was on George's feet, much to Anne's discomfort.

'He's on mine too,' she complained to George. 'He's *so long*, he stretches over my feet as well. Move him, George.'

So George moved him, but as soon as Anne was asleep he stretched out again and lay on both girls' legs. He slept with one ear open.

He heard a scurrying hedgehog. He heard all the rabbits out for a night-time game. He heard the frogs in a far-off pool croaking in the night. His sharp ear even heard the tinkle of the little spring outside the pit.

Nobody moved in the quarry. There was a small moon but it gave very little light. The stars that studded the sky seemed to give more light than the moon.

Timmy's one open ear suddenly pricked itself right up. Then the other ear stood up too. Timmy was still asleep but his ears were both listening very hard!

A low, humming sound came slowly over the

night. It came nearer and nearer. Timmy awoke properly and sat up, listening, his eyes wide open now.

The sound was now very loud indeed. Dick awoke and listened. What *was* that noise? An aeroplane? It must be jolly low! Surely it wasn't about to land on the moor in the dark!

He woke Julian and they both got up and went out of the quarry. 'It's an aeroplane all right,' said Dick, in a low voice. 'What's it doing? It doesn't seem to be going to land. It's gone round in a low circle two or three times.'

'Is it in trouble, do you think?' asked Julian. 'Here it comes again.'

'Look, what's that light over there?' suddenly said Dick, pointing to the east. 'See, that sort of glow. It's not very far from the travellers' camp.'

'I don't know,' said Julian, puzzled. 'It's not a fire, is it? We can't see any flames and it doesn't seem to flicker like a fire would.'

'I think it may be some sort of guide to that plane,' said Dick. 'It seems to be circling round and about over the glow. Let's watch it.'

They watched it. Yes, it did seem to be circling round the glow, whatever it was, and then, quite suddenly it rose in the air, circled round once more and made off to the east.

'There it goes,' said Dick, straining his eyes. 'I can't tell what kind it is, except that it's very small.'

'What can it have been doing?' said Julian, puzzled. 'I thought the glow might have been to guide it in landing, though where it could land here in safety I simply don't know. But it didn't land at all, it just circled and made off.'

'Where would it have come from?' said Dick. 'From the coast, I suppose, from over the sea, do you think?'

'I simply don't know,' said Julian. 'It beats me! And why should the travellers have anything to do with it? Travellers and planes don't seem to mix, somehow.'

'Well, we don't know that they do have anything to do with the plane, except that we saw that glow,' said Dick. 'And that's going now, look.'

Even as they watched, the bright glow died completely away. Now the moor lay in darkness again.

'Funny,' said Julian, scratching his head. 'I can't make it out. It's true that the travellers may be up to something, the way they come out here secretly, apparently for no purpose at all, and also they don't want us snooping round, that's clear.'

'I think we'd better try and find out what that glow is,' said Dick. 'We could have a bit of a snoop tomorrow. Or perhaps Sniffer could tell us.'

'He might,' said Julian. 'We'll try him. Come on, let's get back into the quarry. It's cold out here!'

The quarry felt quite warm to them as they went down into it. The girls were sound asleep still. Timmy, who had been with them, did not wake them. He had been as puzzled as Julian and Dick over the low-flying plane, but he had not barked at all. Julian had been glad about that, Timmy's bark might have carried right over to the travellers' camp and warned them that someone was camping near.

They got back under their rug, keeping close to one another for warmth. But they soon lost their shivers, and Dick threw off his share of the rug. In a few minutes they were asleep.

Timmy awoke first and stretched himself out in the warm morning sunshine. Anne sat up with a little scream. 'Oh Timmy, *don't*! You nearly squashed me to bits. Do that to George if you must stretch yourself all over somebody!'

The boys awoke then, and went to the spring to splash their faces and bring back a jugful of water to drink. Anne got the breakfast, and over it the boys told the girls of the aeroplane in the night.

'How strange!' said Anne. 'And that glow too. It must have been a guide of some sort to the plane. Let's go and see where it was. It must have been a fire of *some* kind!'

'Right,' said Dick. 'I vote we go this morning, but we'll take Tim with us in case we meet those travellers!'

[14]

The travellers are not pleased

Julian and Dick went to stand where they had stood the night before, trying to see exactly in what direction the glow had been.

'I *think* it was beyond the travellers' camp, to the left,' said Julian. 'What do you think, Dick?'

'Yes. That's about it,' said Dick. 'Shall we go now?' He raised his voice. 'We're going, George and Anne. Are you coming? We can leave our stuff here, tucked away in the caves because we shan't be very long.'

George called back. 'Julian, I think Timmy's got a thorn in his foot or something. He's limping. Anne and I think we'll stay here with him and try to get it out. You go, but for goodness' sake don't get into trouble with the travellers!'

'We shan't,' said Julian. 'We've as much right

on this moor as they have and they know it. All right, we'll leave you two here then with Timmy. Sure you don't want any help with his paw?'

'Oh no,' said George. 'I can manage, thank you.'

The two boys went off, leaving Anne and George fussing over Timmy's paw. He had leapt into a gorse bush after a rabbit and a thorn had gone right into his left fore-paw. Then it had broken off, leaving the point in poor Timmy's pad. No wonder he limped. George was going to have quite a time trying to ease out the bit of thorn.

Julian and Dick set off over the moor. It was a day like summer, far too warm for April. There was not a single cloud to be seen in the sky, which was as blue as forget-me-nots. The boys felt too hot in their pullovers and longed to take them off. But that would mean carrying them, which would be an awful nuisance.

The travellers' camp was not really far away. They soon came near to the curious hill that stood up from the flatness of the moor. The caravans still stood in its shelter, and the boys saw that a little group of men were sitting together, talking earnestly.

'I bet they're having a jaw about that aeroplane last night,' said Dick. 'And I bet it was they who set the light or fire, or whatever it was, to guide it. I wonder why it didn't land.'

They kept in the shelter of big gorse bushes, as they skirted the camp. They were not particularly anxious to be seen. The dogs, sitting round the group of men, apparently did not see or hear them, which was lucky.

The boys made their way towards the place where they thought they had seen the glow, some way to the left of the camp, and beyond it.

'Doesn't seem to be anything out of the ordinary anywhere,' said Julian, stopping and looking round. 'I was expecting to see a big burnt patch, or something.'

'Wait – what's in that dip over there?' said Dick, pointing to where the ground seemed to dip downwards. 'It looks like another old quarry, rather like the one we're camping in, but smaller, much smaller. I bet that's where the fire was!'

They made their way to the quarry. It was much more overgrown than theirs was, and was evidently one that had been worked at an earlier time. It dipped down to quite a pit in the middle and set there was something unusual. What was it?

The boys scrambled down into the pit-like quarry and made their way to the middle. They stared at the big thing that was set there, pointing to the sky.

'It's a lamp, a powerful lamp of some kind,' said Julian. 'Like those we see making a flare-path at an aerodrome, guiding planes in to land. Fancy seeing one here!'

'How did the travellers get it?' wondered Dick, puzzled. 'And why signal to a plane that doesn't land? It looked as if it wanted to, circling round low like that.'

'Maybe the travellers signalled that it wasn't safe to land for some reason,' said Julian. 'Or perhaps they were going to give something to the pilot and it wasn't ready.'

'Well, it's a puzzle,' said Dick. 'I can't *imagine* what's going on. Something is, that's certain. Let's snoop round a bit.'

They found nothing else, except a trail that led to the lamp and back. Just as they were examining it, a shout came to their ears. They swung round – and saw the figure of a traveller at the edge of the pit.

'What are you doing here?' he shouted, in a harsh voice. He was joined by a few others, and they all looked threateningly at Julian and Dick as they climbed out of the pit.

Julian decided to be honest. 'We're camping out on the moor for a night or two,' he said, 'and we heard a plane last night, circling low. We also saw a glow that appeared to be guiding it, and we came along to see what it was. Did *you* hear the plane?'

'Maybe we did and maybe we didn't,' said the nearest traveller, who was Sniffer's father. 'What of it? Planes fly over this moor any day!'

'We found that powerful lamp,' said Dick, pointing back at it. 'Do you know anything about *that*?'

'Nothing,' said the traveller, scowling. 'What lamp?'

'Well, as far as I can see there's no charge for looking at it,' said Julian. 'Go and have a squint, if you don't know anything about it! But I can't believe that you didn't see the light it gave last night! It's a jolly good place to hide it, I must say.'

'We don't know anything about any lamp,' said another traveller, the old one with grey hair. 'This is our usual camping place. We don't interfere with anything or anybody – unless they interfere with us. Then we make them sorry for it.'

The boys at once thought of the long-ago mystery of the disappearance of the Bartles. They felt quite uncomfortable.

'Well, we're going now, so don't worry,' said Julian. 'We're only camping for a night or two, as I said. We won't come near here again, if you object to us.'

He saw Sniffer creeping up behind the men, with Liz, who for some reason of her own, was walking sedately on her hind-legs. Sniffer pulled at his father's arm.

'They're all right,' he said. 'You know our Clip got his leg made better at the stables. They're all right!'

All he got was a savage cuff that sent him to the ground, where he rolled over and over. Liz dropped down on all fours and went to lick him.

'Hey!' said Julian, shocked. 'Leave that kid alone! You've no right to hit him like that!'

Sniffer set up such a yelling that some of the women left the caravans not far off and came running to see what was up. One of them began to shout at Sniffer's father and he shouted back. Soon there was quite a row going on between the men and the angry women, one of whom had picked up poor Sniffer and was dabbing his head with a wet cloth.

'Come on, it's a good time to go,' said Julian to Dick. 'What an unfriendly lot they are, except poor Sniffer, and he was doing his best for us, poor kid.'

The two boys went off quickly, glad to be away from the men and their dogs. They were puzzled about everything. The men said they knew nothing about the lamp, but they *must* know something about it. Nobody but a traveller could have lit it last night.

They went back to the girls and told them what had happened. 'Let's get back to the stables,' said Anne. 'There's something funny going on. We'll be in the middle of an adventure before we know where we are!'

'We'll stay one more night,' said Julian. 'I want to see if that plane comes again. Those travellers don't know where we're camping and though Sniffer knows, I'm pretty sure he won't tell. It was plucky of him to try and stick up for us to his father.'

'All right. We'll stay,' said George. 'I'm not particularly anxious for Timmy to have that long walk home today. I *think* I've got most of that thorn out of his pad, but he still won't put his foot to the ground.'

'He's jolly clever at running about on three legs,' said Dick, watching Timmy tearing round the quarry, sniffing as usual for rabbits.

'The amount of quarrying that Timmy has done in this pit already is colossal!' said Julian, staring round at the places where Timmy had tried to get in at some rabbit hole and scrabbled out big heaps of sand. 'He would have been a great help to the Bartles when they dug out sand! Poor old Tim – your bad foot has stopped you scraping for rabbits, hasn't it!'

Timmy ran over on three legs. He enjoyed all the fussing he got when anything happened to him. He meant to make the most of his bad foot!

They had a very lazy day indeed. It really was too hot to do anything much. They went to the little spring and sat with their feet in the rivulet it made – it was deliciously cool! They went and had a look at the old engine again, lying on its side, half-buried.

Dick scraped away a lot of the sand that had seeped into the cab. Soon they were all helping. They uncovered the old handles and levers and tried to move them. But they couldn't of course.

'Let's go round to the other side of the gorse bush and see if we can see the funnel again,' said Dick, at last. 'Blow these thorns. I'm getting pricked all over. Timmy's very sensible, sitting there, not attempting to examine this old Puffing Billy!'

They had to cut away some of the gorse before they could examine the funnel properly. Then they exclaimed in wonder.

'Look! It's very like the long funnel that Puffing Billy had, you know, one of the first engines ever made!'

'It's filled with sand,' said Dick, and tried to scrape it out. It was fairly loose, and soon he was able to peer down the funnel quite a long way.

'Funny to think of smoke puffing out of this strange old funnel,' said Dick. 'Poor old engine, lying here for years, quite forgotten. I'd have thought *someone* would rescue it!'

'Well, you know what the blacksmith told us,' said George. 'The Bartle sister that was left wouldn't have anything more to do with the railway or the engine or the quarry. And certainly nobody could move this great thing on their own.'

'I shouldn't be surprised if we're the only people in the world who know where the old engine is,' said Anne. 'It's so overgrown that nobody could see it except by accident!'

'I feel jolly hungry, all of a sudden,' said Dick, stopping his work of getting sand off the engine. 'What about something to eat?'

'We've got enough to last for a day or two more,' said Anne. 'Then we'll have to get something else – or go back to the stables.'

'I *must* spend one more night here,' said Julian. 'I want to see if that plane returns again.'

'Right. We'll all watch this time,' said George. 'It will be fun. Come on, let's go and get something to eat. Don't you think that's a good idea, Timmy?'

Timmy certainly did. He limped off at top speed on three legs, though really his left fore-paw no longer hurt him. Timmy, you're a fraud!

[15]

A startling night

No travellers came near them that day, not even Sniffer. The evening was as lovely as the day had been, and almost as warm.

'It's extraordinary!' said Dick, looking up into the sky. 'What weather for April! The bluebells will be rushing out soon if the sun goes on being as hot as this!'

They lay on the sand in the quarry and watched the evening star shine in the sky. It looked very big and bright and round.

Timmy scrabbled round in the sand. 'His paw is much better,' said George. 'Though I notice that he still sometimes holds it up.'

'Only when he wants you to say "Poor Timmy, does it hurt?"' said Dick. 'He's a baby, likes to be fussed!'

They talked for a while and then Anne

yawned. 'It's early, I know – but I believe I'm going to sleep.'

There was soon a trek to the spring, and everyone sluiced themselves in the cool water. There was only one towel between them, but that did very well. Then they settled down in their sandy beds. The sand was beautifully warm and they did not bother about putting down the rubber sheets. There could not possibly be any dampness in that quarry after it had been baked so much by the hot sun!

'I hope we wake when the plane comes, if it does come,' said Julian to Dick, as they lay without any covering in their soft, sandy bed. 'My goodness, isn't it hot! No wonder Timmy's panting over there!'

They went to sleep at last, but Dick awoke suddenly, feeling much too hot. Phew! What a night! He lay looking up at the brilliant stars, and then shut his eyes again. But it was no use, he couldn't go to sleep.

He sat up cautiously, so as not to awake Julian. I think I'll just go and have a squint to see if that big lamp is lit again, down in that pit by the travellers' camp, he thought.

He went to the edge of the quarry and climbed up. He looked towards the travellers' camp and gave a sudden exclamation. Yes! he thought. It's glowing again! I can't see the lamp, of course, but its light is so powerful that I can easily see the glow it makes. It must be very bright, looked down on from the sky. I wonder if the plane is due to come now that the lamp is lit.

He listened, and yes, he could distinctly hear a low humming noise from the east. It must be the plane coming again! Would it land this time, and if so, who was in it?

He ran to wake Julian and the girls. Timmy was alert at once, wagging his tail excitedly. He was always ready for anything, even in the middle of the night! Anne and George got up too, very thrilled.

'Is the lamp really alight again? And I can hear the plane too now! Oh, I say! This is exciting! George, Timmy won't bark and give us away, will he?'

'No. I've told him to be quiet,' said George. 'He won't make a sound. Listen, the plane is coming nearer!'

The noise was now loud enough for them to search the starry sky for the plane. Julian gave Dick a nudge. 'Look, you can just see it, straight over where the travellers' camp is!'

Dick managed to pick it out. 'It's very small,' he said. 'Smaller even than I thought it was last night. Look, it's coming down!'

But it wasn't. It merely swept low, and then went round in a circle, as it had done the night before. It rose a little again and then came in low once more, almost over the boys' heads.

Then something extraordinary happened. Something fell not far from Julian, something that bounced and then came to rest! It made a thud as it fell, and all four jumped. Timmy gave a startled whine.

Thud! Something else fell. Thud, thud, thud! Anne gave a squeal. 'Are they trying to bomb us or something? Julian, what are they doing?'

Thud! Thud! Julian ducked at the last two

thuds, they sounded so near. He took hold of Anne and pulled her down into the quarry, calling to Dick and George.

'Get down here, quickly! Force yourselves into the caves somewhere! We shall get hit!'

They ran across the quarry as the plane swooped round in a circle once more and then again began dropping the things that went 'thud! thud!'. Some even fell into the quarry this time. Timmy got the shock of his life when one bounced in front of his nose and rolled away. He yelped and tore after George.

Soon they were all safely squeezed into the little caves that lined the sides of the quarry. The plane swept round once more, up and then round, and the thud-thudding began again. The four could hear that some of the thuds were actually in the quarry again and they were thankful they were well sheltered.

'Well, nothing is exploding,' said Dick, thankfully. 'But what on earth is the plane dropping? And why? This is a most peculiar adventure to have.'

'It's probably a dream,' said Julian, and laughed. 'No, not even a dream could be so mad. Here we are, snuggling into sandy caves in a quarry on Mystery Moor, while a plane drops something all round us in the middle of the night! Quite mad.'

'I believe the plane's going away now,' said Dick. 'It's circled round but hasn't dropped anything. Now it's climbing, it's going away! The engine doesn't sound nearly so loud. Goodness, when we were standing out there at the edge of the quarry, I almost thought the plane would take my head off, it was so low!'

'I thought that too,' said Anne, very glad that there was to be no more swooping down and dropping dozens of unknown things. 'Is it safe to go out?'

'Oh yes,' said Julian, scrambling out of the sand. 'Come on. We shall easily hear if the plane comes back again. I want to see what it has dropped!'

In great excitement they ran to get the

parcels. The stars gave so much light on that clear night that the four did not even need a torch.

Julian picked up something first. It was a firm, flattish parcel, done up well, sewn into a canvas covering. He examined it.

'No name. Nothing,' he said. 'This is most exciting. Let's have three guesses what's inside.'

'Bacon for breakfast, I hope!' said Anne at once.

'Idiot,' said Julian, getting out a knife to slit the string threads that sewed up the canvas. 'I guess it's smuggled goods of some sort. That's what that plane was doing, I should think, flying over from France, and dropping smuggled goods in a pre-arranged place, and I suppose the travellers pick them up, and take them away, well hidden in their caravans, to deliver them somewhere. Very clever!'

'Oh Julian, is *that* the explanation?' said Anne. 'What would be in the parcels then, cigarettes?'

'No,' said Julian. 'The parcels wouldn't be so

heavy if they only contained cigarettes. There, I've slit the threads at last!'

The others crowded round to see. George took her torch out of her pocket so that they could see really well. She flashed it on.

Julian ripped off the canvas covering. Next came some strong brown paper. He ripped that off too. Then came strong cardboard, tied round with string. That was undone as well, and the cardboard fell to the ground.

'Now, what have we got?' said Julian, excited. Thin sheets of paper, dozens and dozens of them packed together. Shine your torch nearer, George.'

There was a silence as all the four craned over Julian's hands.

'Whew! I say! Gosh, do you see what they are?' said Julian, in awe. 'American money, dollar notes. But look what they are, *one hundred*-dollar notes! And my word there are scores and scores of them in this one packet.'

The four stared in amazement as Julian rifled

through the packet of notes. However much would they be worth?

'Julian, how much is a hundred-dollar note worth in our money?' asked George.

'About fifty pounds I think,' said Julian. 'Yes, just about that. Gosh, and there are scores in this one packet, and we know they dropped *dozens* of the packets too. Whatever is it all about?'

'Well, there must be thousands and thousands of dollars lying around us, here in the quarry and outside it,' said George. 'I *say*! Surely this *isn't* a dream?'

'Well, I must say it's a very *extravagant* kind of dream, if so,' said Dick. 'A dream worth thousands of pounds isn't very usual. Ju, hadn't we better get busy picking up these parcels?'

'Yes. We certainly had,' said Julian. 'I'm beginning to see it all now. The smugglers come over in a plane from France, say, having previously arranged to drop these packets in a lonely spot on this moor. The travellers are in the plot to the extent that they light the guiding lamp and pick up the parcels.'

'I see, and then they quietly pack them into their caravans, slip off the moor, and deliver them to somebody else, who pays them well for their trouble,' said Dick. 'Very smart!'

'That's about it,' said Julian. 'But I can't for the life of me see why *dollar* notes have to be smuggled here. They can be brought freely enough into the country – why *smuggle* them?'

'Stolen ones, perhaps?' said George. 'Oh well, it's quite beyond *me*. What a thing to do! No wonder the travellers didn't want us around.'

'Better buck up and collect all these parcels and clear off back to the stables with them,' said Julian, picking up one near him. 'The travellers will be after them, there's no doubt about that! We must be gone before they come.'

The four of them went about looking for the parcels. They found about sixty of them, and they made quite a heavy load.

'We'll put them somewhere safe, I think,'

said Julian. 'What about stuffing them into one of the sand caves? I don't very well see how we can carry them like this.'

'We could put them in the rugs and tie up the ends and carry them like that,' said George. 'It would be mad to leave them hidden somewhere in this quarry. It's the first place the travellers would search.'

'All right. We'll follow your idea,' said Julian. 'I think we've about collected all the packets there are. Get the rugs.'

George's idea proved to be a good one. Half the parcels were rolled into one rug, and tied up, and half into the other.

'Good thing the rugs are nice and big,' said Dick, tying his up strongly. 'Now I can just about manage mine nicely on my back. You all right, Ju?'

'Yes, come along, you girls,' said Julian. 'Follow behind us. We'll go down the railway line. Leave everything else here. We can easily get it another time. We *must* leave before the travellers come.'

Timmy began to bark suddenly. 'That must mean the travellers are coming,' said Dick. 'Come on, quick! Yes, I can hear their voices – for goodness' sake, HURRY!'

[16]

The terrible mist

Yes, the travellers were certainly coming! Their dogs were with them, barking. The four children hurried out of the quarry with Timmy at their heels, quite silent.

'Those fellows may not know we were camping in the quarry,' panted Dick. 'They may just be coming to find the parcels, and while they are hunting around, we may be able to get a good start. Buck up!'

They set off to where the lines ended, near where the old engine lay half-buried. The travellers' dogs heard them and set up a yelping and howling. The travellers stopped to see what had excited them.

They spied shadows moving in the distance, the four children slipping away from the quarry. One of the men shouted loudly.

'Hey you – stop! Who are you? Stop, I say!'

But the five didn't stop. They were now stumbling between the railway lines, glad of George's torch and Anne's. The boys could not have held one for it was all they could do to hang on to the heavy-laden rugs.

'Quick, oh quick!' whispered Anne, but it was impossible to go very quickly.

'They must be catching us up,' said Julian, suddenly. 'Look round and see, George.'

George looked round. 'No, I can't see anyone,' she said. 'Julian, everywhere looks peculiar. What's happening? Julian, stop. Something strange is happening!'

Julian stopped and looked round. His eyes had been fixed on his feet, trying to see where he was going without stumbling. Anne had shone her torch down for him but it was still difficult to get along properly. Julian gazed all round, wondering what George meant.

Then he gave a gasp. 'Gosh! How strange! There's a mist come up, look. It's even blotted out the stars. No wonder it seems so jolly dark all of a sudden.'

'A mist!' said Anne, scared. 'Not that *awful* mist that sometimes covers the moor! Oh Julian, is it?'

Julian and Dick watched the swirling mist in astonishment. 'It's come from the sea,' Julian said. 'Can't you smell the salt in it? It's come just as suddenly as we've been told it comes, and look, it's getting thicker every minute!'

'What a good thing we're on the railway lines!' said George. 'What shall we do? Go on?'

Julian stood and thought. 'The travellers won't come after us in this mist,' he said. 'I've a good mind to hide this money somewhere, and then walk back to get the police. If we keep on the lines we can't go wrong. But we must be sure not to leave them, or we'll be completely lost!'

'Yes, let's do that,' said Dick, who was heartily sick already of lugging along his heavy load. 'But where do you propose to hide them, Ju? Not in the quarry! We'd have to walk through this awful mist to do that, and we'd get lost at once.'

'No. I've thought of a fine place,' said Julian, and he lowered his voice. 'Remember that old engine, fallen on its side? Well, what about stuffing these packets all the way down that great long funnel, and then stopping the top of it up with sand? I bet you anything you like that nobody would find the packets there.'

'Grand idea!' said Dick. 'The travellers will be sure we've gone off carrying the money, and they'll not hunt about for it long, once they find the dropped packets are all gone. We'll be halfway home by the time they try to catch us, if they dare to brave this mist.'

Anne and George thought Julian's idea was first-rate, a stroke of genius. 'I'd never, never have thought of the engine funnel!' said Anne.

'Now, there's no need for you two girls and Timmy to walk all the way to the engine with us,' said Julian. 'You sit down here on the lines and wait for us to come back. We shan't be long. We'll walk straight up the railway, find the engine, pack the money into the funnel, and walk back.'

'Right,' said George, squatting down. 'Bring the rugs back with you, though. It's cold now!'

Julian and Dick went off together, with Anne's torch. George kept hers. Timmy pressed close against her, astonished at the thick mist that had so suddenly swirled up and around them.

'That's right. Keep close to us and keep us warm, Tim,' said George. 'It's jolly cold now. This mist is damp!'

Julian stumbled along, keeping a look-out for the travellers. He could see nothing of them, but then, if they had been only two feet away he could not have seen anything of them in the mist! It seemed to get thicker and thicker.

I know what old Ben meant now, when he said that it had damp fingers, thought Julian, feeling little touches like fingers on his face, hands and legs as the mist wreathed itself round him.

Dick nudged him. 'Here we are,' he said.

'The lines are broken here. The engine should be just over there, a few feet away.'

They stepped cautiously away from the lines. The big gorse bush could not be seen, but it could be felt! Julian felt thorns pricking his legs, and knew he was beside it.

'Shine your torch here, Dick,' he whispered. 'That's right. There's the cab of the engine, see? Now let's circle the bush, and we'll come to the funnel.'

'Here it is,' said Dick, in a few moments. 'Look! Now then, let's do a bit of work, shoving these packets down. Gosh, what a lot of them there are! I hope the funnel will take them all.'

They spent ten minutes ramming the packets into the wide funnel. Down they went to the bottom! More and more followed and then, at last, the final one was shoved in and rammed down.

'That's the lot,' said Dick, relieved. 'Now we'll pack some sand in. Gosh, isn't this bush full of prickles! It's really spiteful!'

'The packets *almost* fill the funnel,' said Julian. 'Hardly any room for sand. Still, we can put in enough to hide the money all right. There, that's done. Now pull this gorse branch over the top of the funnel. My word, I never knew a bush so set with spines! I'm scratched to bits!'

'Can you hear anything of the travellers?' asked Dick, in a low voice, as they prepared to go back to the lines.

They listened. 'Not a thing,' said Julian. 'It's my belief they're scared of this mist, and are lying low till it clears.'

'They may be in the quarry,' said Dick. 'Waiting there in safety. Well, long may they be there! They won't get the money now!'

'Come on,' said Julian, and walked round the bush. 'It's just about here that we step out to get to the lines. Take my arm. We mustn't get separated. Did you ever see such a mist in your life? It's the thickest fog I ever knew. We can't even see our feet in the light of the torch now.'

They took a few steps and then felt about for

the rails. They couldn't feel even one. 'A bit farther, I think,' said Julian. 'No, this way.'

But they still couldn't find the railway lines. Where *were* the wretched things? A small feeling of panic came into Julian's mind. Which way should they step now, to find the rails? How had they gone wrong?

Now both boys were on hands and knees, feeling for the broken rails. 'I've got one,' said Dick. 'No, blow, it isn't. It's a bit of wood, or something. For goodness' sake, keep close to me, Ju.'

After ten minutes' search, the two boys sat back on their heels, the little torch between them.

'Somehow we've just missed those two or three correct steps from the gorse bush to the rails,' said Julian. 'Now we're done for! I don't see anything for it but to wait till the mist clears.'

'But what about the two girls?' said Dick, anxiously. 'Let's try a bit longer. Look, the mist is clearing a little there. Let's go forward and hope we'll stumble over the lines soon. If the mist does clear, we shall soon be able to get our bearings.'

So they went forward hopefully, seeing the mist clear a little in front of them, so that the torch made a longer beam for them to see by. Now and again, when their feet knocked against something hard, they felt for the rails. But they could not find even one!

'Let's shout,' said Julian, at last. So they shouted loudly. 'George! Anne! Can you hear us?'

They stood and listened. No answer.

'GEORGE!' yelled Dick. 'TIMMY!'

They thought they heard a far-off bark. 'That was Timmy!' said Julian. 'Over there!'

They stumbled along and then shouted again. But this time there was no bark at all. Not a sound came out of that dreadful mist, which had now closed tightly round them again.

'We'll be walking in it all night long,' said Julian, desperately. 'Why did we leave the girls?

Suppose this frightful fog doesn't clear by to-morrow? Sometimes it lasts for days.'

'What a horrible idea,' said Dick, lightly, sounding much more cheerful than he felt. 'I don't think we need worry about the girls, Ju. Timmy's with them and he can easily take them back to the stables across the moor, in the mist. Dogs don't mind fogs.'

Julian felt most relieved. He hadn't thought of that. 'Oh yes, I'd forgotten old Tim,' he said. 'Well, seeing that the girls will probably be all right with Timmy to guide them, let's sit down somewhere and have a rest. I'm tired out!'

'Here's a good thick bush,' said Dick. 'Let's get into the middle of it if we can, and keep the damp out of us. Thank goodness it's not a gorse bush!'

'I wish I knew if the girls had had the sense not to wait for us any longer, but to try to find their way back down the lines,' said Julian. 'I wonder where they are now?'

*   *   *

Anne and George were no longer where Julian and Dick had left them! They had waited and waited, and then had become very anxious indeed.

'Something's happened,' said George. 'I think we ought to go and get help, Anne. We can easily follow the railway down to where we have to break off for the stable. Timmy will know, anyway. Don't you think we ought to go back and get help?'

'Yes, I do,' said Anne, getting up. 'Come on George. Gosh, this mist is worse than ever! We'll have to be careful we don't lose the lines! Even Timmy might find it hard to smell his way in this fog!'

They got up. Anne followed George and Timmy followed behind, looking puzzled. He couldn't understand this night-time wandering about at all!

Anne and George kept closely to the railway lines, walking slowly along, shining the light of the torch downwards, and following carefully.

After a time George stopped, puzzled. 'This

line's broken here,' she said. 'There's no more of it. That's funny, I don't remember it being as badly broken as this. The lines simply stop. I can't see any more.'

'Oh *George*!' said Anne, peering down. 'Do you know what we've done? We've come all the way *up* the lines again – instead of going down them, homewards! How *could* we have been so mad? Look, this is where they break off, so the old engine must be somewhere near, and the quarry!'

'Blow!' said George, quite in despair. 'What asses we are. It shows how we can lose our sense of direction in a mist like this.'

'I can't see or hear anything of the boys,' said Anne, fearfully. 'George, let's go to the quarry and wait there till daylight comes. I'm cold and tired. We can squeeze into one of those warm sand caves.'

'All right,' said George, very much down in the dumps. 'Come along, and for goodness' sake don't let's lose our way to the quarry!'

[17]

Prisoners together

The two girls and Timmy made their way carefully, hoping to come across the lines that led to the quarry. They were lucky. They went across the gap in the lines where once long ago the travellers had wrenched out the rails, and came to where they began again, and led to the edge of the quarry.

'Here they are!' said George, thankfully. 'Now we're all right. We've only just got to follow these and we'll be in the quarry. I hope it will be warmer than here. Brrr! This mist is terribly cold and clammy.'

'It came up so *suddenly*,' said Anne, shining her torch downwards. 'I couldn't believe my eyes when I looked round and saw it creeping up on us. I—'

She stopped suddenly. Timmy had given a

low growl. 'What's up, Tim?' whispered George. He stood quite still, his hackles up and his tail motionless. He looked steadfastly into the mist.

'Oh dear. What can be the matter now?' whispered Anne. 'I can't hear a thing, can you?'

They listened. No, there was nothing to hear at all. They went on into the quarry, thinking that Timmy might have heard a rabbit or hedgehog, and growled at it as he sometimes did.

Timmy heard a sound and ran to the side, lost in the mist at once. He suddenly yelped loudly, then there was a heavy thud, and no more sound from Timmy!

'Timmy! What's happened? Timmy, come here!' shouted George, at the top of her voice. But no Timmy came. The girls heard the sound of something heavy being dragged away, and George ran after the sound.

'Timmy! Oh Timmy, what's happened!' she cried. 'Where are you? Are you hurt?'

The mist swirled round, and she tried to beat against it with her fists, angry that she could not see. 'Tim! Tim!'

Then a pair of hands took her arms from behind and a voice said, 'Now you come with me! You were warned not to snoop about on the moor!'

George struggled violently, less concerned for herself than for Timmy.

'Where's my dog?' she cried. 'What have you done to him?'

'I knocked him on the head,' said the voice, which sounded very like Sniffer's father. 'He's all right, but he won't feel himself for a bit! You can have him back if you're sensible.'

George wasn't sensible. She kicked and fought and wriggled and struggled. It was no use. She was held in a grip like iron. She heard Anne scream once and knew that she had been caught too.

When George was too tired to struggle any more, she was led firmly out of the quarry with Anne.

'Where's my dog?' she sobbed. 'What have you done with him?'

'He's all right,' said the man behind her. 'But if you make any more fuss I'll give him another blow on the head. NOW will you be quiet.'

George was quiet at once. She was taken with Anne across the moor for what seemed like miles, but was really only the fairly short distance between the quarry and the travellers' camp.

'Are you bringing my dog?' asked George, unable to contain her fears about Timmy.

'Yes. Somebody's got him,' said her captor. 'You shall have him back safe and sound, if you do what you're told!'

George had to be content with that. What a night! The boys gone, Timmy hurt, she and Anne captured, and this horrible, wreathing mist all the time!

The mist cleared a little as they came near to the travellers' camp. The hill behind seemed to keep it off. George and Anne saw the light of a fire, and of a few lanterns here and there. More

men were gathered together, waiting. Anne
thought she could see Sniffer and Liz in the
background but she couldn't be sure.

If only I could get hold of Sniffer, she
thought. He would soon find out if Timmy is
really hurt. Oh Sniffer, do come nearer if it's
you!

Their captors took them to the little fire, and
made both girls sit down. One of the men there
exclaimed in surprise.

'But these are not those two boys! This is a
boy and a girl, not as tall as the others were!'

'We're two girls,' said Anne, thinking that
the men might treat George less roughly if they
knew she was not a boy. 'I'm a girl and so is
she.'

She got a scowl from George, but took no
notice. This was not the time to pretend anything. These men were ruthless, and very angry. They thought their plans had gone wrong,
all because of two boys. Perhaps when they
found they had got two girls, they would let
them go.

The men began to question them. 'Where are the boys then?'

'We've no idea! Lost in the mist,' said Anne. 'We all went out to go back home, and got separated, so George, I mean Georgina, and I went back to the quarry.'

'Did you hear the plane?'

'Of course!'

'Did you see or hear it dropping anything?'

'We didn't *see* anything drop, we heard it,' said Anne. George stared at her furiously. Why was Anne giving all this away? Perhaps she thought that Timmy would be given back to them if they proved helpful? George immediately changed her mind about feeling cross with Anne. If only Timmy were all right!

'Did you pick up what the plane dropped?' The man rapped out the question so sharply that Anne jumped. What should she say?

'Oh yes,' she heard herself saying. 'We picked up a few strange parcels. What was in them, do you know?'

'Never you mind,' said the man. 'What did you do with the parcels?'

George stared at Anne, wondering what she was going to say? Surely, surely she wouldn't give *that* secret away?

'I didn't do anything with them,' said Anne, in an innocent voice. 'The boys said they would hide them. So they went off into the mist with them, but they didn't come, back. So George and I went to the quarry again. That's when you caught us.'

The men talked among themselves in low voices. Then Sniffer's father turned to the girls again.

'Where did the boys hide these packets?'

'How do I know?' said Anne. 'I didn't go with them. I didn't see what they did with them.'

'Do you think they will still have got them with them?' asked the man.

'Why don't you go and *find* the boys and ask them?' said Anne. 'I haven't seen or heard of the boys since they left us and went into the mist. I don't know *what* became of them or the parcels!'

'They're probably lost somewhere on the moors,' said the old, grey-haired traveller. 'With the packets! We'll look for the boys tomorrow. They won't get home in this! We'll fetch them back here.'

'They wouldn't come,' said George. 'As soon as they saw you, they'd run. You'd never catch them. Anyway they'd get back home as soon as the mist cleared.'

'Take these girls away,' said the old traveller, sounding tired of them. 'Put them in the far cave, and tie them up.'

'Where's my dog?' shouted George, suddenly. 'You bring me my dog!'

'You haven't been very helpful,' said the old traveller. 'We'll question you again tomorrow, and if you are *more* helpful, you shall have your dog.'

Two men took the girls away from the fire and over to the hill. A large opening led into the strange hill. One of the men had a lantern and led the way, the other man walking behind.

A passage led straight into the hill. There was

sand underfoot, and it seemed to Anne as if
even the walls were made of sand. How
strange!

The hill was honeycombed with passages.
They criss-crossed and forked like burrows in
a rabbit warren. Anne wondered however the
men could find their way!

They came at last to a cave that must have
been right in the heart of the hill, a cave with a
sandy floor, and a post that was driven deeply
into the ground.

Ropes were fastened firmly to it. The two
girls looked at them in dismay. Surely they were
not going to be tied up like prisoners!

But they were! The ropes were fastened
firmly round their waists and knotted at the
back. The knots were travellers' knots, firm,
tight and complicated. It would take the girls
hours to unpick those, even supposing they
could manage to reach right round to their
backs!

'There you are,' said the men, grinning at
the two angry girls. 'Maybe in the morning

you will remember where those packets were put!'

'You go and get my dog,' ordered George. But they only laughed loudly and went out of the cave.

It was stuffy and hot in there. George was worried to death about Timmy, but Anne was almost too tired to think.

She fell asleep, sitting up uncomfortably with the ropes round her waist, and the knots digging into her back. George sat brooding. Timmy – where was he? Was he badly hurt? George was very miserable indeed.

She didn't go to sleep. She sat there, worrying, wide awake. She made an attempt to get at the knots behind her, but it was no use, she couldn't.

Suddenly she thought she heard a noise. Was that someone creeping up the passage to the cave? She felt frightened. Oh, if only Timmy were here!

Sniff! Sniff!

'Gracious goodness, it must be Sniffer!'

thought George, and at that moment she almost loved the dirty little traveller boy!

'Sniffer!' she called quietly, and put on her torch. Sniffer's head appeared and then his body. He was crawling quietly up the passage on all fours.

He came right into the cave, and stared at her and the sleeping Anne. 'I've sometimes been tied up here too,' he said.

'Sniffer, how is Timmy?' asked George, anxiously. 'Tell me, quickly!'

'He's all right,' said Sniffer. 'He's just got a bad cut on his head. I bathed it for him. *He's* tied up too, and he's mad about it!'

'Sniffer, listen, go and get Timmy and bring him to me,' said George, breathlessly. 'And bring me a knife too, to cut these ropes. Will you? Can you?'

'Oooh, I dunno,' said Sniffer, looking frightened. 'My father would half kill me!'

'Sniffer, is there anything you want, anything you've *always* wanted?' said George. 'I'll give it to you if you do this for me, I promise you!'

'I want a bike,' said Sniffer, surprisingly. 'And I want to live in a house, and ride my bike to school.'

'I'll see that you have what you want, Sniffer,' said George, wildly. 'Only, do, do go and get Timmy, and a knife! You got here without being seen, you can surely get back again safely with Timmy. Think of that bike!'

Sniffer thought of it. Then he nodded and disappeared down the passage as silently as he had come.

George waited and waited. Would he bring dear old Timmy to her, or would he be caught?

[18]

George's trick

George sat in the darkness of the cave, hearing Anne's peaceful breathing nearby, waiting for Sniffer to come back. She was longing to see Timmy again. Was the cut on his head *very* bad?

A thought came into her mind. She would send Timmy back to the stables with a note! He was very clever, he knew what to do when he had a note tied to his collar. Then help would come very quickly indeed. Timmy would know his way all right out of this hill, once he had been in it!

Ah, here was Sniffer coming back again. Was Timmy with him? She heard Sniffer's sniff-sniff-sniff, but no sound of Timmy. Her heart sank.

Sniffer appeared cautiously in the cave.

'I didn't dare to take Timmy,' he said. 'My father has him tied up too near to him, and I'd have woken him. But I've brought you a knife, look.'

'Thank you, Sniffer,' said George, taking the knife and putting it into her pocket. 'Listen, there's something important I'm going to do and you've got to help.'

'I'm scared,' said Sniffer. 'I'm really scared.'

'Think of that bicycle,' said George. 'A red one, perhaps with silver handles?'

Sniffer thought of it. 'All right,' he said. 'What are you going to do?'

'I'm going to write a note,' said George, feeling in her pocket for her notebook and pencil. 'And I want you to tie it on to Timmy's collar, under his chin, and set him free somehow. Will you do that? He'll run off back to the stables with the note, and then Anne and I will be rescued, and you will get the most beautiful bicycle in the world!'

'And a house to live in,' said Sniffer, at once. 'So that I can ride my bike to school?'

'All right,' said George, hoping that somehow he could have that too. 'Now, wait a minute.'

She scribbled the note, but she had hardly written more than a few words, when a sound came up the passage. Someone was coughing.

'It's my father!' said Sniffer, in fright. 'Listen, if you cut your ropes and escape, can you find your way out from here? It's very twisty and turny.'

'I don't know. I don't think I can!' whispered George, in a panic.

'I'll leave patrins for you!' said Sniffer. 'Look out for them! Now I'm going to slip into the cave next door, and wait till my father's finished talking to you. Then I'll go back to Timmy.'

He slipped out just in time. The lantern shone into George's cave and Sniffer's father stood there.

'Have you seen Sniffer?' he asked. 'I missed him when I woke just now. If I catch him in here I'll whip him till he squeals.'

'Sniffer? He's not here,' said George, trying to sound surprised. 'Look round the cave and see!'

The man caught sight of the notebook and pencil in George's hand. 'What's that you're writing?' he said suspiciously and took it from her.

'So you're writing for help, are you!' he said. 'And how do you think you're going to get help, I'd like to know? Who's going to take this note home for you? Sniffer?'

'No,' said George, truthfully.

The man frowned as he looked again at the note. 'Look here,' he said, 'you can write another note, to those two boys. And I'll tell you what to say.'

'No,' said George.

'Oh yes, you will,' said the man. 'I'm not going to hurt those boys. I'm just going to get back those packets from wherever they are hidden. Do you want your dog back safely?'

'Yes,' said George, with a gulp.

'Well, if you don't write this note you won't see him again,' said the man. 'Now then, take your pencil and write in that notebook of yours.'

George took up her pencil. 'This is what you must write,' said the man, frowning as he thought hard.

'Wait a minute,' said George. 'How are you going to get this note to the boys? You don't know where they are! You won't be able to find them if this mist still goes on.'

The man scratched his head and thought.

'The only way to get the note to them is to tie it on my dog's collar and send him to find them,' said George. 'If you bring him here to me I can make him understand. He always does what I tell him.'

'You mean he'll take the note to whoever you tell him to take it?' said the man, his eyes gleaming. 'Well, write it then. Say this:

' "We are prisoners. Follow Timmy and he will bring you to us and you can save us." Then sign your name, whatever it is.'

'It's Georgina,' said George, firmly. 'You go and get my dog while I write the note.'

The man turned and went. George looked after him, her eyes bright. *He* thought he was making her play a trick on Julian and Dick, to bring them here so that they could be threatened and questioned about the packets, and where they were hidden!

But *I'm* going to play a trick on him, thought George. I'm going to tell Timmy to take the note to *Henry*, and she'll be suspicious and get Captain Johnson to follow Tim back here, and that will give the travellers an *awful* shock! I expect the captain will be sensible enough to get the police as well. Aha, *I'm* playing a trick too!

In ten minutes' time Sniffer's father returned with Timmy. It was a rather subdued Timmy, with a very bad cut on his head, which really needed stitching. He pattered soberly across to George, and she flung her arms round his neck and cried into his thick hair.

'Does your head hurt you?' she said. 'I'll take you to the vet when I get back, Tim.'

'You can get back as soon as we've got those two boys here and they've told us where those packets are hidden,' said the man.

Timmy was licking George as if he would never stop, and his tail waved to and fro, to and fro. He couldn't understand what was happening at all! Why was George here? Never mind, he was with her again. He settled down on the floor with a thump and put his head on her knee.

'Write the note,' said the man, 'and tie it on to his collar, on the top, so that it can easily be seen.'

'I've written it,' said George. The traveller held out a dirty hand for it and read it.

'*We are prisoners. Follow Timmy and he will bring you to us and you can save us.*
                                    GEORGINA.'

'Is that really your name, Georgina?' asked the man. George nodded. It was one of the few times she ever owned to a girl's name!

She tied the note firmly to Timmy's collar, on the top of his neck. It was quite plainly to be seen. Then she gave him a hug and spoke urgently to him.

'Go to Henry, Tim, go to HENRY. Do you understand, Timmy dear, take this note to HENRY.' She tapped the paper on his collar as he listened to her. Then she gave him a push. 'Go along. Don't stay here any longer. Go and find HENRY.'

'Hadn't you better tell him the other boy's name too?' said the man.

'Oh no, I don't want to *muddle* Timmy,' said George hastily. 'Henry, Henry, HENRY!'

'Woof,' said Timmy, and George knew that he understood. She gave him another push.

'Go, then,' she said. 'Hurry!'

Timmy gave her rather a reproachful look as if to say, 'You haven't let me stay with you very long!' Then he padded off down the passage, the note showing clearly on his collar.

'I'll bring the boys up here as soon as they come with the dog,' said the man, and he turned

on his heel, and went out. George wondered if
Sniffer was still about and she called him. But
there was no answer. He must have slipped
away down the passages back to his caravan.

Anne woke up then, and wondered where
she was. George switched on her torch again
and explained all that had happened.

'You should have woken me,' said Anne. 'Oh
blow these ropes. They're *so* uncomfortable.'

'I've got a knife now,' said George. 'Sniffer
gave it to me. Shall I cut our ropes?'

'Oh yes!' said Anne, in delight. 'But don't
let's try and escape yet. It's still night-time and if
that mist is about, we'll only get lost. We can
pretend we're still tied up if anyone comes.'

George cut her own ropes with Sniffer's
exceedingly blunt knife. Then she cut Anne's.
Oh, what a relief to lie down properly, and not
to have to sit up all the time and feel the knots
at the back!

'Now do remember, if we hear anyone coming, we must tie the ropes loosely round us,' she
said. 'We will stay here till we know it's day,

and perhaps we can find out if the mist is still about, or if it's gone. If it's gone, we'll go.'

They fell asleep on the sandy floor, both glad to lie down flat. Nobody came to disturb them, and they slept on and on, tired out.

Where were the boys? Still under the bush, half-sleeping, half waking, for they were cold and uncomfortable. They hoped the girls were now safely at home. They must have gone right down the railway, and made their way back to the stables, thought Julian, every time he awoke. I do hope they are safe, and Timmy too. Thank goodness he is with them.

But Timmy wasn't with them, of course. He was padding across the misty moor all by himself, puzzled, and with a badly aching head. Why had George sent him to Henry? He didn't like Henry. He didn't think that George did, either. And yet she had sent him to find her. Very strange!

Still, George had given him his orders, and he loved her and always obeyed her. He padded over the heather and grass. He didn't bother about keeping to the railway line. He knew the way back without even thinking about it!

It was still night, though soon the dawn would come. But the mist was so thick that even the dawn would not be able to break through it. The sun would have to remain hidden behind the thick swathes of mist.

Timmy came to the stables. He paused to remember which was Henry's bedroom. Ah yes, it was upstairs, next to the room that Anne and George had had.

Timmy leapt into the kitchen through a window left open for the cat. He padded upstairs and came to Henry's room. He pushed at the door and it opened.

In he went and put his paws on her bed. 'Woof,' he said in her ear. 'Woof! Woof! Woof!'

[19]

Good old Tim!

Henry had been fast asleep and snoring. She awoke with a tremendous jump when she felt Timmy's paw on her arm and heard his sharp little bark.

'Oooh! What is it?' she said, sitting up straight in bed and fumbling for her torch. She was quite panic-stricken. She switched on the torch with trembling fingers and then saw Timmy, his big brown eyes looking at her beseechingly.

'Why, Timmy!' said Henry, in amazement. '*Timmy!* Whatever are you doing here? Have the others come back? No, they couldn't have, not in the middle of the night! Why have *you* come then, Timmy?'

'Woof,' said Timmy, trying to make her understand that he was bringing a message.

Henry put out her hand to pat his head, and suddenly caught sight of the paper tied to his collar at the back.

'What's this on your collar?' she said, and reached out for it. 'Why, it's paper. Tied on, too. It must be a message!'

She untied the piece of paper and unrolled it. She read it.

'*We are prisoners. Follow Timmy and he will bring you to us and you can save us.*

SODALL GEORGINA.'

Henry was astounded. She looked at Timmy and he looked back, wagging his tail. He pawed at her arm impatiently. Henry read the note again. Then she pinched herself to make sure she was not dreaming.

'Oooh, no I'm awake all right,' she said. 'Timmy, is this note true? *Are* they prisoners? And who does "we" mean? George and Anne, or the whole four? Oh, Timmy I *do* wish you could speak!'

Timmy wished the same! He pawed energetically at Henry. She suddenly saw the cut on his head and was horrified.

'You're hurt, Timmy! Oh, you poor, poor thing. Who did that to you? You ought to have that wound seen to!'

Timmy certainly had a very outsize headache, but he couldn't bother to think about that. He gave a little whine and ran to the door and back.

'Yes, I know you want me to follow you, but I've got to *think*,' said Henry. 'If Captain Johnson was here I'd go and fetch him. But he's away for the night, Timmy. And I'm sure Mrs Johnson would have the fright of her life if I fetched her. I simply don't know what to do.'

'Woof,' said Timmy, scornfully.

'It's all very well to say "Woof" like that,' said Henry, 'but I'm not as brave as you are. I *pretend* I am, Timmy, but I'm not really. I'm afraid of following you! I'm afraid of going to find the others. I might be caught too. And there's a terrible mist, Timmy, you know.'

Henry slid out of bed, and Timmy looked suddenly hopeful. Was this silly girl going to make up her mind at last?

'Timmy, there's no grown-up here tonight except Mrs Johnson, and I really *can't* wake her,' said Henry. 'She's had such a very hard, busy day. I'm going to dress, and then get William. He's only eleven, I know, but he's very sensible.'

She dressed quickly in her riding things and then set off to William's room. He slept by himself across the landing. Henry walked in and switched on her torch.

William awoke at once. 'Who's there?' he demanded, sitting up at once. 'What do you want?'

'It's me. Henry,' said Henry. 'William, a most extraordinary thing has happened. Timmy has arrived in my room with a note on his collar. Read it!'

William took the note and read it. He was most astonished. 'Look,' he said, 'George has signed herself *Georgina*. She wouldn't do that unless things were very urgent. She never, never lets herself be called anything but George. We'll have to follow Tim and go, at once, too!'

'But I can't walk miles in a mist over the moor,' said Henry, in a panic.

'We don't need to. We'll saddle our horses and go on those,' said William, beginning to dress, and sounding very sensible indeed. 'Timmy will lead the way. You go and get the horses out. *Do* buck up, Henry. The others may be in danger. You're acting like a Henrietta!'

That made Henry cross. She went out of the room at once and down into the yard. What a pity Captain Johnson happened to be away just that night. He would have decided everything at once.

Courage came to her when she got the horses. They were surprised but quite willing to go for a night-time ride, even in this thick mist! William came up in a very short time with Timmy behind him. Timmy was delighted to have William with him. He liked him, but he was not very fond of Henry.

He ran forward, just in front of the horses, and they followed behind. Both Henry and William had excellent torches, and kept them shining downwards, so that they should not miss Timmy. He did go out of sight once or twice, but came back immediately, when he heard the horses stopping.

Over the moor they rode. They didn't follow the railway, of course. Timmy didn't need to. He knew the way perfectly!

Once he stopped and sniffed the air. What had he smelt? Henry and William had no idea, but Timmy was puzzled by what he had smelt on the misty air.

Surely he had smelt the smell of the two boys, Julian and Dick? It had come on the air for a moment or two, and Timmy was half-inclined to follow it and see if the smell was right. Then he remembered George and Anne and went on through the swirling mist.

The boys were actually not very far away when Timmy smelt them. They were still in the middle of the bush, trying to keep warm, and sleep. If only they had known that Timmy was near, with Henry and William! But they didn't.

Timmy led the way. Soon they came to the quarry, but did not see it because of the mist. They went round it, led by Timmy, and rode towards the travellers' camp. Timmy slowed down, and they took warning.

'He's getting near wherever he wants to take us,' whispered William. 'Had we better dismount and tie the horses up, do you think? Their hooves may give a warning that we are near.'

'Yes. Yes, William,' said Henry, thinking that the boy was really very sensible. They dismounted quietly and tied the horses to a nearby birch tree.

They were quite near the hill in front of which was the travellers' camp. The mist was not so thick here, and the two suddenly caught sight of a dark, shadowy caravan, outlined against a camp-fire, left burning nearby. 'We'll have to be very quiet,' whispered William. 'Timmy's brought us to the travellers' camp on the moor. I had an idea that he would. The others must be held prisoner somewhere near – be as quiet as you can.'

Timmy watched them dismount. He hung his head, panting, his tail down. His head was hurting him very much, and he felt decidedly strange and giddy. But he must get to George, he must!

He led the way to the opening in the hill. William and Henry were most astonished. They followed Timmy through the maze of passages, wondering how he knew the way so surely. But Timmy didn't falter. He only needed to go somewhere once, and after that he never forgot the way!

He was going very slowly now, and his legs felt peculiar and shaky. He wanted to lie down and put his aching head on his paws. But no, he must find George. He must find George.

George and Anne were lying in the little cave, asleep. They were uncomfortable, and the cave was hot, so they were restless, waking up every few minutes. But both were asleep when Timmy walked slowly into the cave, and flopped down beside George.

George awoke when she heard William and Henry come into the cave. She thought it might be Sniffer's father coming back, and she hastily put the ropes round her waist so that she would look as if she were still tied up. Then she heard Timmy panting, and switched on her torch eagerly.

It showed her Timmy, and Henry and William! Henry was full of amazement when she saw George and Anne with ropes round their waists. She gaped at them.

'Oh Timmy darling, you fetched help!' said George, putting her arms round his neck. 'Oh Henry, I'm *so* glad you've come. But didn't you bring Captain Johnson too?'

'No. He's away,' said Henry. 'But William's here. We rode, and Timmy guided us. What-*ever's* happened, George?'

Anne awoke just then, and couldn't believe her eyes when she saw the visitors! There was a hasty discussion, and then William spoke firmly.

'If you want to escape, you'd better come now, while the travellers' camp is asleep. Timmy can guide us out of this rabbit-warren of a hill. We'd never be able to find our way out alone. Come on!'

'Come on, Tim,' said George, shaking him gently. But poor old Timmy was feeling very peculiar. He couldn't see things properly. George's voice sounded blurred to him. His head felt as heavy as lead, and somehow his legs wouldn't carry him. The blow on his head was taking real effect now, and the hurried journey over the moor and back was making it worse.

'He's ill!' said George, in a panic. 'He can't get up! Oh Timmy, what's the matter?'

'It's that cut on his head,' said William. 'It's pretty bad, and he's worn out with coming to fetch us and running all the way back again. He can't possibly guide us back, George. We'll have to do the best we can by ourselves.'

'Oh, poor, poor Timmy!' said Anne, horrified at seeing the dog stretched out quite limp on the floor of the cave. 'George, can you carry him?'

'I think so,' said George, and she lugged him up in her arms. 'He's awfully heavy, but I think I can just manage him. Perhaps the fresh air will revive him when we get outside.'

'But George, we don't know our way out of here,' said Anne, fearfully. 'If Timmy can't lead us, we're lost! We'd end up by wandering miles and miles inside the hill and never getting out!'

'Well, we'll simply *have* to make a shot at it,' said William. 'Come on, I'll lead the way. We really MUST go!'

He went out of the cave and down a passage; the others followed, George carrying the limp Timmy. But very soon William came to a fork and stopped.

'Oh dear – do we go to the left or the right?' he wondered.

Nobody knew. George shone her torch here and there, trying to remember. The beam of light picked up something on the ground near-by.

It was two sticks, one short and one long, in the shape of a cross! George gave an exclamation.

'Look – a patrin! Left by Sniffer to show us the way out. We have to take the passage that the long stick points to! Oh, I hope that Sniffer has left patrins at every corner and every fork!'

They took the right-hand way and went on, their torches making long beams in the darkness, and at every place where they might go wrong, they saw a patrin, a message left by Sniffer to show them the right way to go.

'Another cross, we go *this* way,' said Anne.

'Here's a patrin again, we take *this* fork!' said George. And so it went on until they came safely to the entrance of the hill. How thankful they were to see the mist. At least it meant that they were in the open air!

'Now to get to the horses,' said William. 'They will each have to carry two of us at once, I'm afraid.'

And then, just as they were making their way

to where they had left the horses, the travellers' dogs began to bark the place down!

'They've heard us!' said William, desperately. 'Buck up! We'll be stopped if we don't get off at once!'

Then a voice shouted loudly. 'I can see you over there, with your torches! Stop at once! Do you hear me? STOP!'

[20]

Excitement in the morning

The dawn was coming now. The mist was no longer full of darkness, but was white, and thinning rapidly. The four children hurried to the horses, which were stamping impatiently by the trees. George couldn't go very fast because of Timmy. He really was very heavy.

Suddenly he began to struggle. The fresh, cool air had revived him and he wanted to be set down. George put him down thankfully, and he began to bark defiantly at the travellers who were now coming out of their caravans, their dogs with them.

The four children mounted hurriedly and the horses were surprised at the double weight. William swung his horse's head round and set off with George sitting behind him. Henry took Anne. Timmy, feeling much

better, ran after them, his legs no longer
feeling so shaky.

The travellers ran too, shaking their fists and
shouting. Sniffer's father was amazed beyond
measure. Why, there were the two girls he had
tied up – and that dog he had sent off to trick
the other two boys on the moor.

Then who were these on horseback, and how
had they found their way to the hill? How had
the prisoners been able to find their way *out* of
the hill, too? That was a real puzzle to Sniffer's
father.

The travellers tore after the horses, but the
dogs contented themselves with excited barks.
Not one of them dared to go after Timmy. They
were afraid of him.

The horses went off as fast as they dared in
the mist, Timmy running in front. He seemed
very much better, though George was afraid it
was only the excitement that now kept him
going. She glanced back at the travellers. They
would never catch up now, thank goodness!

Somewhere behind the mist the sun was

shining. Soon it would disperse the strange fog that had come up so suddenly from the sea. She glanced down at her watch. Good gracious, could it really be almost six o'clock in the morning. It was tomorrow now!

She wondered what had happened to Julian and Dick. She thought of Sniffer gratefully, and all those patrins he had left in the hill. They would never have got out but for those. She thought of Henry and William, and gave William a sudden tight hug round the waist for coming out in the middle of the night and rescuing them!

'Where are Julian and Dick, do you suppose?' she said to William. 'Do you think they are still lost on the moor? Ought we to shout, and look for them?'

'No,' called back William over his shoulder. 'We're going straight back to the stables. They can look after themselves!'

Dick and Julian had certainly tried to look after themselves, that cold, misty night, but not very successfully. By the time that their torch showed them that it was a quarter to five by their watches, they had had enough of the bush they were in. If only they had known it, Henry and William, with Timmy, were just then riding over the moor, not a great distance from where they were!

They got out of the bush, damp and stiff. They stretched themselves and looked into the dark night, still full of mist.

'Let's walk,' said Julian. 'I can't bear keeping still in this mist. I've got my compass. If we walk due west we should surely come to the edge of the moor, not far from Milling Green.'

They set off, stumbling in the now dim light of the torch, whose battery was getting low. 'It will give out soon,' groaned Dick, giving it a shake. 'Blow the thing! It hardly gives us any light now, and we simply must keep looking at the compass.'

Julian tripped against something hard and almost fell. He snatched the torch from Dick. 'Quick, let me have it!'

He shone it on what had tripped him and gave a delighted exclamation. 'Look, it's a rail! We're on the railway line again. What a bit of luck!'

'I should *think* so!' said Dick, relieved. 'This torch is just about finished. Now, for GOOD-NESS' sake don't let's lose this railway line. Stop at once if you can't feel it with your foot.'

'To think we were so jolly near the line after all, and didn't know it!' groaned Julian. 'We could have been back at the stables ages ago. I do hope the girls got back safely and didn't alarm anyone about us. They'd know we would come back as soon as it was daylight, anyhow, if we could follow the lines!'

They stumbled in at the stables' entrance about six o'clock, tired out. Nobody was yet up, it seemed. They found the garden door open, left ajar by William and Henry, and went up to the girls' room, hoping to find them in bed.

But the beds were empty of course. They went to Henry's room, to ask her if she had heard anything of the girls, but her bed, though slept in, was empty too!

They went across the landing to William's room. '*He's* gone as well!' said Dick, in great astonishment. 'Where are they all?'

'Let's wake Captain Johnson,' said Julian, who had no idea that the captain was away for the night. So they awakened a very startled Mrs Johnson, and almost scared the life out of her, for she thought they were far away, camping on the moor!

She was even more startled when she heard their tale and realised that George and Anne were missing. 'Where *are* the girls, then!' she said, flinging on a dressing-gown. 'This is serious, Julian. They might be completely lost on the moor, or those travellers might have got them! I must telephone my husband, and the police too. Oh dear, oh dear, why did I ever let you go camping out!'

She was in the middle of telephoning, with Julian and Dick beside her, looking very anxious indeed, when the sound of horses' hooves came in the yard below.

'Now goodness me! Who's that?' said

Mrs Johnson. 'Horses! Who's riding them at this time of the morning?'

They all went to the window and looked down into the yard. Dick gave a yell that almost made Mrs Johnson fall out of the window!

'Anne! George! Look, there they are, and Timmy too. And gosh, there's Henry, and William! What is all this?'

Anne heard the yell and looked up. Tired as she was, she gave a cheerful wave and a grin. George gave a shout.

'Oh Julian! Oh Dick, you're back then! We did hope you would be. After you left us we went back up the lines the wrong way and arrived at the quarry again!'

'And the travellers took us prisoner!' yelled Anne.

'But – but – how do Henry and William come into this?' said poor Mrs Johnson, thinking she must really still be asleep. 'And what's the matter with Timmy?'

Timmy had suddenly flopped on the ground. The excitement was over, they were home, now he could put his poor aching head on his paws and sleep!

George was off her horse immediately. 'Timmy! Darling Timmy! *Brave* Timmy! Help me, William. I'll take him upstairs to my room and see to that cut.'

By this time all the other children were awake and there was such a pandemonium going on that Mrs Johnson couldn't make herself heard.

Children in dressing-gowns and without, children shouting and yelling, children pouring into the yard and asking questions; William trying to quiet the two horses which were getting very excited at all this sudden clamour; and all the cocks round about crowing their heads off! *What* an excitement!

The sun suddenly shone out brilliantly, and the last wisps of mist disappeared. 'Hurrah! That mist has gone!' shouted George. 'The sun's out. Cheer up, Timmy. We'll all be all right now!'

Timmy was half-carried, half-dragged up the stairs by William and George. George and

Mrs Johnson examined his cut head carefully, and bathed it.

'It really should have been stitched up,' said Mrs Johnson, 'but it seems to be healing already. How wicked to hit a dog like that!'

Soon there was the sound of horse's hooves again in the yard, and Captain Johnson arrived, looking very anxious. At almost the same moment a car slid in at the gates, a police car, with two policemen who had been sent to inquire about the missing girls! Mrs Johnson had forgotten to telephone again to say they had arrived.

'Oh dear, I'm so sorry to have bothered you,' said Mrs Johnson to the police sergeant. 'The girls have just arrived back, but I still don't know what has really happened. Still, they're safe, so please don't bother any more.'

'Wait!' said Julian, who was in the room, too. 'I think we *shall* need the police! Something very peculiar has been happening up on the moor.'

'Really? What's that?' said the sergeant, taking out a notebook.

'We were camping there,' said Julian. 'And a plane came over, very low, guided by a lamp set in a sandpit by the travellers.'

'A lamp set by the *travellers*!' said the sergeant, surprised. 'But why should they need to guide a plane? I suppose it landed?'

'No. It didn't,' said Julian. 'It came again the next night, and did exactly the same thing, swooping low and circling. But this time it dropped packages!'

'Oh, it did, did it?' said the sergeant, more interested. 'For the travellers to pick up, by any chance?'

'Yes,' said Julian. 'But the plane's aim wasn't very good, and the packets fell all round *us* and almost hit us. We ran for shelter, because we didn't know if there were any explosives or not!'

'Did you pick up any of the packages?' asked the sergeant. Julian nodded.

'Yes, we did, and I opened one.'

'What was in it?'

'Paper money, dollars!' said Julian. 'In one packet alone there were scores of notes and each note was for a hundred dollars, about fifty pounds a time! Thousands of pounds' worth thrown all around us!'

The sergeant looked at his companion. 'Ha! Now we know! This explains a lot that has been puzzling us, doesn't it, Wilkins?'

Wilkins, the other policeman, nodded grimly. 'It certainly does. So that's what happens! That's how the gang get the dollars over here, from that printing-press in North France. Just a nice little run in a plane!'

'But why do they throw the packets down for the *travellers* to collect?' asked Julian. 'Is it so that they can give them to someone else? Why don't they bring them openly into the country? Surely anyone can bring *dollars* here?'

'Not *forged* ones, my lad,' said the sergeant. 'These will all be forged, you mark my words. The gang have got a headquarters near London, and as soon as those packets are handed over to them by one of the travellers, they will set to work passing them off as real ones, paying hotel bills with them, buying all kinds of goods and paying for them in notes that aren't worth a penny!'

'Whew!' said Julian. 'I never thought of them being forged!'

'Oh yes. We've known of this gang for some time, but all we knew was that they had a printing-press to print the notes in North France, and that somehow the rest of the gang here, near London, received them and passed them off as real ones,' said the sergeant. 'But we didn't know how they were brought here, nor who took them to the gang near London.'

'But now we know all right!' said Wilkins. 'My word, this is a pretty scoop, Sergeant. Good kids these, finding out what we've been months trying to discover!'

'Where are these packages?' said the sergeant. 'Did you hide them? Did the travellers get them?'

'No, we hid them,' said Julian. 'But I guess

the travellers will be hunting all over the place
for them today, so we'd better get on the moors
quick, Sergeant.'

'Where did you hide them?' said the sergeant.
'In a safe place, I hope!'

'Oh very!' said Julian. 'I'll call my brother,
Sergeant. He'll come with us. Hey, Dick! Come
on in here, and you'll hear a very interesting bit
of news!'

[21]
The end of the mystery

Mrs Johnson was amazed to hear that the police wanted Julian and Dick to go out on the moors again.

'But they're tired out!' she said. 'They need something to eat. Can't it wait?'

'I'm afraid not,' said the sergeant. 'You needn't worry, Mrs Johnson. These boys are tough!'

'Well actually I don't think that the travellers can *possibly* find the packets,' said Julian. 'So it wouldn't matter if we had a bite to eat. I'm ravenous!'

'All right,' said the big policeman, putting away his notebook. 'Have a snack and we'll go afterwards.'

Well, of course, George, Anne and Henry all wanted to go too, as soon as they heard about the proposed jaunt over the moors!

'What! Leave us out of *that*!' said George, indignantly. 'What a hope! Anne wants to come too.'

'So does Henry,' said Anne, looking at George, 'even though she didn't help to find the packages of notes.'

'Of *course* Henry must come,' said George at once, and Henry beamed. George had been very struck indeed with Henry's courage in coming with William to rescue her and Anne, and very pleased that she hadn't boasted about it! But Henry knew that William was the one mostly to praise, and she had been unexpectedly modest about the whole affair.

It was quite a large party that set off after everyone had a very good breakfast. Mrs Johnson had set to work cooking huge platefuls of bacon and egg, exclaiming every now and again when she thought of all that had happened up on the moors.

'Those travellers! And fancy that plane com-

ing like that – dropping money all over the place! And the travellers tying up Anne and George in that hill. I never heard anything like it in my life!'

Captain Johnson went with the party too. He could hardly believe the extraordinary tale that the four had to tell, five, with old Timmy! Timmy now had a beautiful patch on his head, and was feeling extremely important. Wait till Liz saw that!

Ten people set out, including Timmy, for William had been included in the party too. He tried to guess where Julian had hidden the notes, but he couldn't, of course. Julian firmly refused to tell anyone. He wanted it to be a real surprise.

They came to the quarry at last, having walked all the way up the old railway line. Julian stood on the edge of the quarry and pointed out the travellers' camp.

'Look, they're leaving,' he said. 'I bet they were afraid we'd spread the news of their behaviour, after the girls escaped.'

Sure enough, the caravans were moving slowly away.

'Wilkins, as soon as you get back, give word to have every traveller watched if he leaves the caravans,' said the sergeant. 'One of them is sure to have arranged a meeting place to give the gang the packets dropped from the plane, and if we watch those caravans, and every traveller in them, we'll soon be able to put our hands on the gang that spends the forged notes.'

'I bet it's Sniffer's father,' said Dick. 'He's the ringleader, anyway.'

They watched the caravans move away one by one. Anne wondered about Sniffer. So did George. What had she promised him last night, if he would help them? A bicycle, and to live in a house so that he could ride it to school! Well, it wasn't likely she would ever see the little boy again, but if she did she would certainly have to keep her word!

'Now, where's this wonderful hiding-place?' asked the sergeant, as Julian turned from

watching the caravans. He had tried to make out Sniffer and Liz, but the vans were too far away.

'Follow me!' said Julian, with a sudden grin, and led the way back up the lines to where they broke off. The gorse bush was there, and the old engine lay on its side as before, almost hidden.

'Whatever's that?' said the sergeant, surprised.

'It's the old Puffing Billy that used to pull the trucks of sand from the quarry,' said Dick. 'Apparently there was a quarrel long ago between the owners of the quarry and the travellers, and the travellers pulled up the lines and the engine ran off and fell over. There it's been ever since, as far as I can see!'

Julian went round to the funnel end, and bent back the prickly gorse branch that hid it. The sergeant looked on in surprise. Dick scraped the sand out of the top of the funnel and then pulled out one of the packages. He had been afraid they would not be there.

'Here you are!' he said, and tossed the packet to the sergeant. 'There are plenty more. I'll come to the one we opened in a minute – yes – here it is.'

The sergeant and Wilkins were amazed to see the packages hauled up from such a peculiar hiding-place. No wonder the travellers hadn't found them. Nobody would ever have looked down the funnel of the old engine, even if they had spotted it, half-buried as it was.

The sergeant looked at the hundred-dollar notes in the opened parcel and whistled. 'My word, this is it! We've seen these before, beautiful forgeries they are! If the gang had got rid of *this* lot, a great many people would have suffered. The money is worth nothing! How many packets did you say there were?'

'Dozens!' said Dick, and pulled more of them out of the funnel. 'Gosh, I can't reach the ones at the bottom.'

'Never mind,' said the sergeant. 'Put some sand in to hide them and I'll send a man to poke the rest out with a stick. The travellers have gone and they are the only people likely to hunt for them. This is a wonderful scoop! You kids have certainly put us on to something.'

'I'm glad,' said Julian. 'I say, we'd better collect all the things we left here yesterday, hadn't we? We went off in rather a hurry, you see, Sergeant, and left our things in the quarry.'

He and George went into the quarry to collect the things they had left there. Timmy went with them. He suddenly growled, and George stopped, her hand on his collar.

'What's up, Tim? Ju, there must be somebody here! Is it one of the travellers, do you think?'

Then Timmy stopped growling and wagged his tail. He dragged away from George's hand and ran over to one of the little caves in the sandy walls. He looked most peculiar with the patch on his head.

Out of the cave came Liz! As soon as she saw Timmy she began to turn head-over-heels as fast as she could. Timmy stared in wonder –

what a dog! How could she turn somersaults like that?

'Sniffer!' called George. 'Come on out. I know you're there!'

A pale, worried face looked out of the cave. Then Sniffer's thin, wiry little body followed, and soon he was standing in the quarry, looking scared.

'I got away from them,' he said, nodding his head towards where the travellers' camp had been. He went up to George, and gave a sniff.

'You said I could have a bike,' he said.

'I know,' said George. 'You *shall* have one, Sniffer. If you hadn't left us patrins in that hill, we'd never have escaped!'

'And you said I could live in a house and ride my bike to school,' said Sniffer urgently. 'I can't go back to my father, he'd half-kill me now. He saw those patrins I left in the hill and he chased me all over the moor for miles. But he didn't catch me. I hid.'

'We'll do the best we can for you,' promised Julian, sorry for this little waif. Sniffer sniffed.

'Where's that hanky?' demanded George. He pulled it out of his pocket, still clean and folded. He beamed at her.

'You're quite hopeless,' said George. 'Listen, if you want to go to school, you'll *have* to stop that awful sniff and use your hanky. See?'

Sniffer nodded, but put the hanky carefully back into his pocket. Then the sergeant came into the quarry and Sniffer fled at the sight of him!

'Funny little thing,' said Julian. 'Well, I should imagine that his father will be sent to prison for his share in this affair, so Sniffer will be able to get his wish and leave the caravan life to live in a house. We might be able to get him into a good home.'

'And I shall keep my word, and take some money out of my savings-bank and buy him a bicycle,' said George. 'He deserves it! Oh, do look at Liz – simply *adoring* Timmy and his patch. Don't look so important, Tim – it's only a patch on your cut!'

'Sniffer!' called Julian. 'Come back. You

needn't be afraid of this policeman. He is a friend of ours. He'll help us to choose a bicycle for you.'

The sergeant looked extremely surprised at this remark, but at any rate it brought Sniffer back at once!

'Well, we'll go back now,' said the sergeant. 'We've got what we want, and Wilkins has already started back to get somebody on to watching the travellers. Once we find out who they have to report to about this forged money we shall feel happy.'

'I hope Wilkins went along down the railway,' said Julian. 'It's so easy to get lost on this moor.'

'Yes. He had the sense to do that, after hearing how *you* got lost!' said the sergeant. 'It's wonderful up here, isn't it, so peaceful and quiet and calm.'

'Yes, you'd never think that mysteries could happen up here, would you?' said Dick. 'Old ones, and new ones! Well, I'm glad we happened to be mixed up in the newest one. It was quite an adventure!'

They all went back to the stables, to find that it was now almost lunch-time and that everyone had a large appetite to match the very large lunch that Mrs Johnson had got ready. The girls went upstairs to wash. George went into Henry's room.

'Henry,' she said, 'thanks most awfully. You're as good as a boy any day!'

'Thanks, George,' said Henry, surprised. 'You're *better* than a boy!'

Dick was passing the door and heard all this. He laughed, and stuck his head in at the door.

'I say, do let me share in these compliments!' he said. 'Just tell me I'm as good as a girl, will you?'

But all he got was a well-aimed hairbrush and a shoe, and he fled away, laughing.

Anne gazed out of her bedroom window over the moor. It looked so peaceful and serene under the April sun. No mystery about it now!

'All the same, it's a good name for you,' said Anne. 'You're full of mystery and adventure,

and your last adventure waited for *us* to come
and share it. I really think I'd call this adventure
"Five Go To Mystery Moor".'

It's a good name, Anne. We'll call it that too!

FIVE HAVE PLENTY OF FUN

[1]

At Kirrin Cottage

'I feel as if we've been at Kirrin for about a month already!' said Anne, stretching herself out on the warm sand, and digging her toes in. 'And we've only just come!'

'Yes – it's funny how we settle down at Kirrin so quickly,' said Dick. 'We only came yesterday, and I agree with you, Anne – it seems as if we've been here ages. I love Kirrin.'

'I hope this weather lasts out the three weeks we've got left of the holiday,' said Julian, rolling away from Timmy, who was pawing at him, trying to make him play. 'Go away, Timmy. You're too energetic. We've swum, had a run, played ball – and that's quite enough for a little while. Go and play with the crabs!'

'Woof!' said Timmy, disgusted. Then he

pricked up his ears as he heard a tinkling noise from the promenade. He barked again.

'Trust old Timmy to hear the ice-cream man,' said Dick. 'Anyone want an ice-cream?'

Everyone did, so Anne collected the money and went off to get the ice-creams, Timmy close at her heels. She came back with five tubs of ice-cream, Timmy jumping up at her all the way.

'I can't think of anything nicer than lying down on hot sand with the sun on every part of my body, eating an ice-cream, and knowing there are still three weeks' holiday in front of us – at Kirrin too!' said Dick.

'Yes. It's heaven,' said Anne. 'It's a pity your father has visitors today, George. Who are they? Have we got to dress up for them?'

'I don't think so,' said George. 'Timmy, you've eaten your ice-cream in one gulp. What a frightful waste!'

'When are these people coming?' asked Dick.

'About half past twelve,' said George. 'They're coming to lunch – but thank goodness Father told Mother he didn't want a pack of children gobbling all round him and his friends at lunch, so Mother said we could go in at half past twelve, say how-do-you-do and then clear off again with a picnic basket.'

'I must say I think your father has some good ideas at times,' said Dick. 'I suppose they are some scientist friends of his?'

'Yes. Father's working on some great scheme with these two men,' said George. 'One of them's a genius, apparently, and has hit on an idea that's too wonderful for words.'

'What kind of modern idea is it?' said Julian, lazily, holding out his fingertips for Timmy to lick off smears of ice-cream. 'Some spaceship to take us on day trips to the moon – or some new bomb to set off – or . . .'

'No, I *think* it's something that will give us heat, light and power for almost nothing!' said George. 'I heard Father say that it's the simplest and best idea anyone had ever worked out, and he's awfully excited about it. He called it a "gift to mankind" and said he was proud to have anything to do with it.'

'Uncle Quentin is very clever, isn't he?' said Anne. George's father was the uncle of Julian, Dick and Anne, and they were cousins to George – short for Georgina. Once more they had all come down to Kirrin for part of their holiday, the last three weeks.

George's father was certainly clever. All the same, George sometimes wished that he was a more *ordinary* parent, one who would play cricket or tennis with children, and not be so horrified at shouting and laughter and silly jokes. He always made a fuss when George's mother insisted that George should have her cousins to stay.

'Noisy, rowdy, yelling kids!' he said. 'I shall lock myself in my study and stay there!'

'All right, dear,' said his wife. 'You do that. But you know perfectly well that they will be out practically all day long. George *must* have other children to stay sometimes, and her three cousins are the nicest ones I know. George loves having them here.'

The four cousins were very careful not to

upset George's father. He had a very hot temper and shouted at the top of his voice when he was angry. Still, as Julian said, he really couldn't *help* being a genius, and geniuses weren't ordinary people.

'Especially *scientific* geniuses who might easily blow up the whole world in a fit of temper,' said Julian, solemnly.

'Well, I wish he wouldn't keep blowing *me* up if I let a door bang, or set Timmy barking,' said George.

'That's only to keep his hand in,' said Dick. 'Just a bit of practice at blowing up!'

'Don't be an ass,' said George. 'Does anyone feel like another swim?'

'No. But I don't mind going and lying in the very edge of the sea, and letting the waves there just curl over me,' said Dick. 'I'm absolutely baked lying here.'

'It *sounds* lovely,' said Anne. 'But the hotter you are the colder the water feels.'

'Come on!' said Dick, getting up. 'I shall hang my tongue out and pant like Timmy soon.'

They all went down to the edge of the water and lay down flat in the tiny curling waves there. Anne gave a little shriek.

'It feels icy! I knew it would. I can't lie down in it yet – I can only sit up!'

However they were soon all lying full-length in the shallow waves at the edge of the sea, sliding down the sand a little every now and again as the tide ebbed farther from them. It was lovely to feel the cool fingers of the sea on every part of them.

Suddenly Timmy barked. He was not in the water with them, but was just at the edge. He thought that lying down in the sea was quite unnecessary! George raised her head.

'What's the matter?' she said. 'There's nobody coming.'

But Dick had heard something too. He sat up hurriedly. 'Gosh, I believe that's someone ringing a bell for us. It sounds like the bell from Kirrin Cottage!'

'But it *can't* be dinner-time yet!' said Anne in dismay.

'It must be,' said Julian, leaping up. 'Blow! This is what comes of leaving my watch in my anorak pocket! I ought to have remembered that time at Kirrin goes more quickly than anywhere else!'

He ran up the beach to his anorak and took his wristwatch from the pocket. 'It's one o'clock!' he yelled. 'In fact, it's a minute past. Buck up, we'll be awfully late!'

'Blow!' said George. 'Mother won't be at all pleased with us, because those two scientist people will be there!'

They collected their anoraks and tore up the beach. It was not very far to Kirrin Cottage, fortunately, and they were soon running in at the front gate. There was a very large car outside, one of the latest American models. But there was no time to examine it!

They trailed in quietly at the garden door. George's mother met them, looking rather cross.

'Sorry, Aunt Fanny,' said Julian. 'Please forgive us. It was my fault entirely. I'm the only one with a watch.'

'Are we *awfully* late?' asked Anne. 'Have you begun lunch yet? Would you like us just to take our picnic basket and slip off without interrupting?'

'No,' said her aunt. 'Fortunately your uncle is still shut up in his study with his friends. I've sounded the gong once but I don't expect they've even *heard* it! I rang the bell for you because I thought that any moment they might come out, and your uncle would be cross if you weren't there just to say how-do-you-do!'

'But Father's friends don't *usually* want to see us,' said George, surprised.

'Well, one of them has a girl a bit younger than you, George – younger than Anne too, I think,' said her mother. 'And he specially asked to see you all, because his daughter is going to your school next term.'

'We'd better buck up and have a bit of a wash then,' said Julian – but at that very moment the study door opened, and his Uncle Quentin came out with two men.

'Hallo – are these your kids?' said one of the men, stopping.

'They've just come in from the beach,' said Aunt Fanny hurriedly. 'I'm afraid they are not really fit to be seen. I—'

'Great snakes!' said the man. 'Don't you dare to apologise for kids like these! I never saw such a fine lot in my life – they're wunnerful!'

He spoke with an American accent, and beamed all over his face. The children warmed to him at once. He turned to George's father. 'These all yours?' he asked. 'I bet you're proud of them! How did they get that tan – they're so dark! My, my – wish my Berta looked like that!'

'They're not all mine,' said Uncle Quentin, looking quite horrified at the thought. 'Only this one is mine,' and he put his hand on George's shoulder. 'The others are nephews and a niece.'

'Well, I must say you've got a fine boy,' said the American, ruffling George's short curls. As a rule she hated people who did that, but because he mistook her for a boy, she grinned happily!

'My girl's going to your school,' he said to Anne. 'Give her a bit of help, will you? She'll be scared stiff at first.'

'Of course I will,' said Anne, taking a liking to the huge loud-voiced American. He didn't look a bit like a scientist. The other man did, though. He was round-shouldered and wore owl-like glasses, and, as Uncle Quentin often did, he stared into the distance as if he was not hearing a single word that anyone said.

Uncle Quentin thought this gossiping had lasted long enough. He waved the children away.

'Come and have lunch,' he said to the other men. The second man followed him at once, but the big American stayed behind. He thrust his hand into his pocket and brought out a pound coin. He gave it to Anne.

'Spend that on yourselves,' he said. 'And be kind to my Berta, won't you?'

He disappeared into the dining-room and

shut the door with a loud bang. 'Goodness –
what will Father say to a bang like *that*!' said
George, with a sudden giggle. 'I like him, don't
you? That must be *his* car outside. I can't
imagine the other man even riding a bicycle,
let alone driving a car!'

'Children – take your picnic basket and *go*!'
said Aunt Fanny, urgently. 'I *must* run and see
that everything is all right!'

She thrust a big basket into Julian's hands,
and disappeared into the dining-room. Julian
grinned as he felt the weight of the basket.

'Come along,' he said. 'This feels good! Back
to the beach, everyone!'

[2]

A visitor in the night

The Five were on the beach in two minutes, and Julian undid the basket. It was full of neatly packed sandwiches, and packets of biscuits and chocolate. A bag contained ripe plums, and there were two bottles of lemonade.

'Home-made!' said Dick, taking it out. 'And icy-cold. And what's this? A fruit cake – a *whole* fruit cake – we're in luck.'

'Woof,' said Timmy, approvingly, and sniffed inside the basket.

Wrapped in brown paper were some biscuits and a bone, together with a small pot of paste. George undid the packet. '*I* packed these for you, Timmy,' she said. 'Say thank you!'

Timmy licked her so lavishly that she cried out for mercy. 'Pass me the towel, Ju!' she said.

'Timmy's made my face all wet. Get away now, Timmy – you've thanked me quite enough! Get *away*, I said. How can I spread paste on your biscuits if you stick your nose into the pot all the time?'

'You spoil Timmy dreadfully,' said Anne. 'All right, all right – you needn't scowl at me, George! I agree that he's *worth* spoiling. Take your bone a *bit* farther away from me, Tim – it's smelly!'

They were soon eating sardine sandwiches with tomatoes, and egg-and-lettuce sandwiches after that. Then they started on the fruit cake and the lemonade.

'I can't think why people ever have table-meals when they can have picnics,' said Dick. 'Think of Uncle and Aunt and those two men tucking into a hot meal indoors on a day like this. Phew!'

'I liked that big American,' said George.

'Aha! We all know why,' said Dick, annoyingly. 'He thought you were a boy. Will you ever grow out of that, George?'

'Timmy's trying to get at the cake!' said Anne. 'Quick, George, stop him!'

They all lay back on the sand after their picnic, and Julian began a long story of some trick that he and Dick had played on their form-master at school. He was most annoyed because nobody laughed at the funny part, and sat up to see why.

'All asleep!' he said, in disgust. Then he cocked his head just as Timmy pricked up his ears. A loud roaring noise came to him.

'Just the American revving up his car, do you think, Tim?' said Julian. The boy stood up and saw the great car tearing down the sea road.

The day was too hot to do anything but laze. The Five were quite content to do that on their first day together again. Soon they would want to plan all kinds of things, but the first day at Kirrin was a day for picking up old threads, teasing Timmy, getting into the 'feel' of things again, as Dick said.

Dick and Julian had been abroad for four weeks, and Anne had been away to camp and had had a school friend to stay with her at home afterwards. George had been alone at Kirrin so it was wonderful to all the Five to meet together once more for three whole summer weeks. At Kirrin too, Kirrin by the sea, with its lovely beach, its fine boating – and its exciting little island across Kirrin Bay!

As usual the first day or two passed in a kind of dream, and then the children began to plan exciting things to do.

'We'll go to Kirrin Island again,' said Dick. 'We haven't been there for ages.'

'We'll go fishing in Lobster Cove,' said Julian.

'We'll go and explore some of the caves in the cliffs,' said George. 'I meant to do that these hols, but somehow it's no fun going alone.'

On the third day, just as they were finishing making their beds, the telephone rang.

'I'll go!' yelled Julian to his aunt, and went to answer it. An urgent voice spoke at the other end.

'Who's that? Oh, you, Julian – you're Quentin's nephew, aren't you? Listen, tell your uncle I'm coming over tonight – yes, tonight. Latish, say. Tell him to wait up for me. It's important.'

'But, won't you speak to him yourself?' said Julian, surprised. 'I'll fetch him, if you'll—'

But the line had gone dead. Julian was puzzled. The man hadn't even given his name – but Julian had recognised the voice. It was the big, cheery American who had come to see his uncle two days before! What had happened? What was all the excitement about?

He went to find his uncle but he was not in his study. So he found his aunt instead.

'Aunt Fanny,' he said, 'I *think* that was the big American on the phone – the one who came to lunch the other day. He said I was to tell Uncle Quentin that he was coming here tonight – late, he said – and that Uncle was to wait up for him, because it was important.'

'Dear me!' said his aunt, startled. 'Is he going to stay the night then? We've no bedroom free now you and the others are here.'

'He didn't say, Aunt Fanny,' said Julian. 'I'm

awfully sorry not to be able to tell you any details – but just as I was saying I'd fetch Uncle Quentin, he rang off – in the very middle of what I was saying.'

'How mysterious!' said his aunt. 'And how annoying. *How* can I put him up, if he wants to stay? I suppose he'll come roaring down at midnight in that enormous car of his. I only hope nothing's gone wrong with this latest work your uncle is doing. I know it's tremendously important.'

'Perhaps Uncle will know the American's telephone number and he can ring him up to find out a bit more,' said Julian, helpfully. 'Where is Uncle?'

'He's gone down to the post office, I think,' said his aunt. 'I'll tell him when he gets back.'

Julian told the others about the mysterious phone call. Dick was pleased.

'I didn't have a chance of getting a good look at that enormous car the other day,' he said. 'I think I'll keep awake tonight till the American comes and then nip down and have a look at it.

I bet it's got more gadgets on the dashboard than any car I've ever seen!'

Uncle Quentin appeared to be as surprised as anyone else at the phone call, and was inclined to blame Julian for not finding out more details.

'What's he want now?' he demanded, almost as if Julian ought to know! 'I fixed everything up with him the other day. *Every*thing! Each of us three has his own part to do. Mine's the least important, as it happens – and his is the most important. He took all the papers away with him; he can't have left any behind. Coming down in the middle of the night like this – quite extraordinary!'

None of the children except Dick meant to stay awake and listen for the American's coming. Dick put on his bedside light and took up a book to read. He knew he would fall asleep and not wake up for any noise, if he didn't somehow keep himself wide awake!

He listened as he read, his ear alert to hear the coming of any car. Eleven o'clock came – then midnight struck. He listened to the twelve dongs from the big grandfather clock in the hall. Goodness – Uncle Quentin wouldn't be at all pleased that his visitor was so late!

He yawned, and turned over his page. He read on and on. Half past twelve. One o'clock. Then he thought he heard a sound downstairs and opened his door. Yes – it was Uncle Quentin in his study. Dick could hear his voice.

'Poor old Aunt Fanny must be up too,' he thought. 'I can hear their voices. Gosh, I shall soon fall asleep over my book. I'll slip down and out into the garden for a breath of fresh air. I shall keep awake then.'

He put on his dressing-gown and went quietly down the stairs. He undid the bolt of the garden door and slipped out. He stood listening for a moment, wondering if he would hear the roar of the American's car in the stillness of the night.

But all he heard was the sound of the tyres of a bicycle on the road outside. A bicycle! Who was riding about at this time of night? Perhaps it was the village policeman?

Dick stood in the shadows and watched. A man was on the bicycle. Dick could just make him out dimly, a big black shadow in the starlit night. To the boy's enormous surprise, he heard the sound of the man dismounting, then the swish of the leaves in the hedge as the bicycle was slung there.

Then someone came quietly up the path and went round to the window of the study. It was the only room in the house that was lit. Dick heard a tapping on the window, and then it was opened cautiously. His uncle's head appeared.

'Who is it?' he said, in a low tone. 'Is it you, Elbur?'

It apparently was. Dick saw that it was the big American who had visited his uncle two days before. 'I'll open the door,' said his aunt, but Elbur was already putting his leg across the window-sill!

Dick went back to bed, puzzled. How strange! Why should the American come so secretly in the night, why should he ride a bicycle instead of driving his car? He fell asleep still wondering.

He did not know whether the American rode away again, or whether his aunt made a bed for him on a couch downstairs. In fact, when he awoke the next morning, he really wondered if it had all been a dream.

He asked his aunt, when he went down to breakfast. 'Did that man who telephoned come last night?' he said.

His aunt nodded her head. 'Yes. But please say nothing about it. I don't want anyone to know. He's gone now.'

'Was it important?' asked Dick. 'Julian seemed to think it was, when he answered the phone.'

'Yes – it was important,' said Aunt Fanny. 'But not in the way you think. Don't ask me anything now, Dick. And keep out of your uncle's way. He's rather cross this morning.'

'Then something must have gone wrong with this new work he's doing,' thought Dick, and went to warn the others.

'It sounds rather exciting,' said Julian. 'I wonder what's up?'

They kept out of Uncle Quentin's way. They heard him grumbling loudly to his wife about something, they heard him slam down his desk-lid as he always did when he was bad-tempered, and then he settled down to his morning's work.

Anne came running to the others after a time, looking surprised. 'George! I've just been into our room and what do you think! Aunt Fanny's put a camp-bed over in the corner – a camp-bed made up with blankets and everything! It looks an awful squash with two other beds as well in the room – mine and yours!'

'Gosh – someone else is coming to stay then – a girl,' said Dick. 'Or a woman. Aha! I expect it's a governess engaged to look after you and Anne, George, to see that you behave like little ladies!'

'Don't be an idiot,' said George, surprised and cross at the news. 'I'm going to ask Mother what it's all about. I won't have anyone else in our room. I just will *not*!'

But just as she was marching off to tell her

mother this, the study door downstairs opened and her father bellowed into the hall, calling his wife.

'Fanny! Tell the children I want them. Tell them to come to my study AT ONCE!'

'Gracious – he does sound cross. Whatever can we have done?' said Anne, scared.

[3]

Annoying news

The four children and Timmy trooped down the stairs together. George's mother was in the hall, just going to call them.

'Oh, there you are,' she said. 'Well, I suppose you heard that you're wanted in the study. I'm coming too. And listen – *please* don't make any more fuss than you can help. I've had quite enough fuss made by Quentin!'

This was very mysterious! What had Aunt Fanny to do with whatever trouble there was? Into the study went the Five, Timmy too, and saw Uncle Quentin standing on the hearthrug looking as black as thunder.

'Quentin, *I* could have told the children,' began his wife, but he silenced her with a scowl exactly like the one George sometimes put on.

'I've got something to say to you,' he began.

'You remember those two friends of mine – scientists working on a scheme with me – you remember the big American?'

'Yes,' said everyone.

'He gave us a whole pound,' said Anne.

Uncle Quentin took no notice of that remark. 'Well,' he said, 'he's got a daughter – let's see now – she's got some silly name . . .'

'Berta,' said his wife.

'Don't interrupt me,' said Uncle Quentin. 'Yes, Berta. Well, Elbur, her father, has been warned that she's going to be kidnapped.'

'Whatever for?' said Julian, amazed.

'Because it so happens that her father knows more secrets about a new scheme we're planning than anyone else in the world,' said his uncle. 'And he says, quite frankly, that if this girl – what's her name now . . .'

'Berta,' said everyone, obligingly.

'That if this Berta is kidnapped, he will give away every single secret he knows to get her back,' said Uncle Quentin. 'Pah! What's he made of? Traitor to us all! How can he even *think* of giving away secrets for the sake of a silly girl?'

'Quentin, she's his only child and he adores her,' said Aunt Fanny. 'I should feel the same about George.'

'Women are always soft and silly,' said her husband, in a tone of great disgust. 'It's a good thing *you* don't know any secrets – you'd give them away to the milkman!'

This was so ridiculous that the children laughed. Uncle Quentin glared at them.

'This is no laughing matter. It has been a great shock to me to be told by one of the leading scientists of the world that he feels certain he might give all our secrets to the enemy if this – this . . .'

'Berta,' said everyone again, at once.

'If this Berta was kidnapped,' went on Uncle Quentin. 'So he came to ask if we'd take this – this Berta into our own home for three weeks. By that time the scheme will be finished and launched, and our secrets will be safe.'

There was a silence. Nobody looked very

pleased. In fact, George looked furious. She burst out at last.

'So *that's* who the bed is for in our room! Mother, have we *got* to be squashed up with nowhere to move about the room, for three whole weeks? It's too bad.'

'For once you and I agree, George,' said her father. 'But I'm afraid you'll have to put up with it. Elbur is in such a state about this kidnapping warning that he couldn't be reasoned with. In fact he threatened to tear up all his figures and diagrams and burn them, if I didn't agree to this. That would mean we couldn't get on with the scheme.'

'But why has she got to come *here*?' said George, fiercely. 'Why put her on to *us*? Hasn't she any relations or friends she can go to?'

'George, don't be so fierce,' said her mother. 'Apparently Berta has no mother, and has been everywhere with her father. They have no relations in this country – and no friends they can trust. He won't send her back to America because he has been warned by the police that she might be followed there – and at the moment he can't leave this country himself to go with her.'

'But why choose *us*?' said George again. 'He doesn't know a thing about us!'

'Well,' said her mother, with a small smile, 'he met you all the other day, you know – and he was apparently very struck with you – and especially with *you*, George, though I can't imagine why. He said he'd rather his Berta was with you four than with any other family in the world.'

She paused and looked at the four, a harassed expression on her face. Julian went over to her.

'Don't you worry!' he said. 'We'll look after Berta! I won't pretend I'm pleased at having a strange girl to join us these last three precious weeks – but I can see her father's point of view – he's scared for Berta, and he's scared he might find himself spilling the beans if anything happened to her! It might be the only way he could get her back.'

'To think of such a thing!' burst out Uncle Quentin. 'All the work of the last two years! The man must be mad!'

'Now Quentin, don't think any more about it,' said his wife. 'I'm glad to have the child here. I would hate George to be kidnapped, and I know exactly how he feels. You won't even notice she's here. One more will make no difference.'

'So you say,' grumbled her husband. 'Anyway, it's settled.'

'When is she coming?' asked Dick.

'Tonight. By boat,' said his uncle. 'We'll have to let Joanna the cook into the secret – but nobody else. That's understood, isn't it?'

'Of course,' said the four at once. Then Uncle Quentin sat down firmly at his desk, and the children went hurriedly out of the room, Aunt Fanny behind them, and Timmy pushing between their ankles.

'It's such a pity, and I'm so sorry,' said Aunt Fanny. 'But I do feel we can't do anything else.'

'I bet Timmy will hate her,' said George.

'Now don't you go and make things difficult, George, old thing,' said Julian. 'We're all agreed it can't be helped, so we might as well make the best of it.'

'I hate making the best of things,' said George, obstinately.

'Well,' said Dick, amiably, 'Julian and Anne and I could go back home and take Berta with us if you hate everything so much. I don't particularly want to stay here for three weeks if you're going to put on a Hate all the time.'

'All right, I won't,' said George. 'I'm only letting off steam. You know that.'

'I'm never sure, with you,' said Dick, with a grin. 'Well, look – let's not spoil this one day when we *will* be by ourselves!'

They all tried valiantly to have as good a time as possible, and went out in George's boat for a long row to Lobster Cove. They didn't do any fishing there, but swum from the boat instead, in water as green and clear as in an open-air pool. Timmy didn't approve of swimming from boats. It was quite easy to jump out of the boat into the water – but he found it extremely difficult to jump in again!

Aunt Fanny had again packed them a wonderful lunch. 'An extra good one to make up for disappointment,' she said, smiling. Anne had given her a hug for that. Here they had all been making such a fuss about having someone extra – and Aunt Fanny had been the only one to feel a real kindness for a child in danger.

They had enough food for tea too, and did not get home until the evening. The sea was calm and blue, and the children could see almost to the bottom of the water, when they leaned over the side of the boat. The sky was the colour of harebells as they rowed into the bay and up to the beach.

'Will Berta be there yet, do you suppose?' said George, mentioning the girl for the first time since they had set out that morning.

'I shouldn't think so,' said Julian. 'Your father said she would be coming tonight – and I imagine that as she's coming by boat, it will be dark – so that she won't be seen.'

'I expect she'll be feeling very scared,' said Anne. 'It must be horrid to be sent away to a strange place, to strange people. I should hate it!'

They beached the boat and left it high and dry. Then they made their way to Kirrin Cottage. Aunt Fanny was pleased to see them.

'You *are* in nice time for supper,' she said. 'Though if you ate all I gave you today for your picnics, you'll surely find it difficult to eat very much supper.'

'Oh, I'm *terribly* hungry,' said Dick. He sniffed, holding his nose up in the air just as Timmy often did. 'I believe you've been making your special tomato soup, with real tomatoes, Aunt Fanny!'

'You're too good at guessing,' said his aunt with a laugh. 'It was meant to be a surprise! Now go and wash and make yourselves tidy.'

'Berta hasn't come yet, I suppose, has she?' asked Julian.

'No,' said his aunt. 'And we'll have to think of another name for her, Julian. It would never do to call her Berta now.'

Uncle Quentin didn't appear for supper. 'He is having his in the study by himself,' said Aunt Fanny.

There was a sigh of relief. Nobody had looked forward to seeing Uncle Quentin that night. It took him quite a long time to get over any annoyance!

'How sunburnt you all are!' said Aunt Fanny, looking round the table. 'George, your nose is beginning to peel.'

'I know,' said George. 'I wish it didn't. Anne's never does. Gosh, I'm sleepy!'

'Well, go to bed as soon as you've finished your supper,' said her mother.

'I'd like to. But what about this Berta?' said George. 'What time is she coming? It would be rather mean to be in bed when she arrives.'

'I've no idea what time she will come,' said her mother. 'But I shall wait up, of course. There's no need for anyone else to. I expect she'll be tired and scared, so I shall give her something to eat – some of the tomato soup, if you've left any! – and then pop her into bed. I expect she would be quite glad not to have to meet any of you tonight.'

'Well – *I* shall go to bed,' said Dick. 'I heard Mr Elbur arriving last night, Aunt Fanny, and it was pretty late, wasn't it? I can hardly keep my eyes open tonight.'

'Come on, then – let's all go up,' said Julian. 'We can read if we can't sleep. Good night, Aunt Fanny. Thank you for that lovely picnic food again!'

All the four went upstairs, Anne and Dick yawning loudly, and setting the others off too. Timmy padded behind them, quite glad that George was going to bed so early.

They were all asleep in ten minutes. The boys slept like logs and didn't stir at all. The girls fell fast asleep for about four hours – and then George was awakened by hearing Timmy growl. She sat up at once.

'What is it?' she said. 'Oh – is it Berta arriving, Tim? Let's keep quiet and see what she's like!'

After a minute Timmy growled again.

George heard the sound of quiet footsteps on the stairs. Then the bedroom door was slid softly open, and two people stood in the light of the landing lamp. One was Aunt Fanny.

The other, of course, was Berta.

[4]
Berta

George sat up in bed and stared at Berta. She
looked very peculiar indeed. For one thing she
was so bundled up in coats and wraps that it
was difficult to see if she was fat or thin, tall or
short, and for another thing she was crying so
bitterly that her face was all screwed up.

Anne didn't wake up. Timmy was so astonished that, like George, he simply sat and stared.

'Tell Timmy not to make a sound,' whispered
George's mother, afraid that the dog might
bark the house down, once he began.

George laid a warning hand on Timmy. Her
mother gave Berta a little push farther into the
room.

'She's been terribly seasick, poor child,' she
told George. 'And she's scared and upset. I
want her to get into bed as soon as possible.'

Berta was still sobbing, but the sobs grew quieter as she began to feel less sick. George's mother was so kind and sensible that she felt comforted.

'Let's take these things off,' she said to Berta. 'My word, you *are* bundled up! But if you came in an open motorboat I expect you needed them.'

'What am I to call you?' asked Berta, with one last sniff.

'You'd better call me Aunt Fanny, as the others do, I think,' said George's mother. 'I expect you know why you've come to stay with us for a while, don't you?'

'Yes,' said Berta. 'I didn't want to come. I wanted to stay with my father. I'm not afraid of being kidnapped. I've got Sally to look after me.'

'Who's Sally, dear?' asked Aunt Fanny, taking a coat or two off Berta.

'My dog,' said Berta. 'She's downstairs in the basket I was carrying.'

George pricked up her ears at *that* bit of

news! 'A dog!' she said. 'We can't have a dog
here. Mine would never allow that. Would you,
Timmy?'

Timmy gave a small wuff. He was watching
this night arrival with great interest. Who was
she? He was longing to get down from George's
bed and go to sniff at her, but George had her
hand on his collar.

'Well, I've brought my dog, and I just reckon
she'll have to stay now,' said Berta. 'The boat's
gone back. Anyway, I wouldn't go anywhere
without Sally. I told my father that, and he said
all right then, take her with you! So I did.'

'Mother, tell her how fierce Timmy is and
that he would fight any other dog who came
here,' said George, urgently. 'I won't have anybody else's dog at Kirrin Cottage.'

To George's annoyance her mother took not
the slightest notice. She went on helping Berta
take off scarves, thick socks and goodness
knows what. George wondered how anyone
could possibly exist in all those clothes on a
warm summer's night.

At last Berta stood in a simple jersey and skirt, a slim, pretty little girl with large blue eyes and wavy golden hair. She shook back her hair and rubbed her face with a hanky.

'Thank you,' she said. 'Can I get Sally my dog now?'

'Not tonight,' said Aunt Fanny. 'You see, you are to sleep in that little camp-bed over in the corner – and I can't let you have your dog here too, because she and Timmy might fight unless we introduce them to one another properly. And there is no time to bother about that tonight. Do you feel hungry now? Would you like some tomato soup and biscuits?'

'Yes, please. I do feel a bit hungry,' said Berta. 'I've been so sick on that awful bumpy boat that I don't expect there's anything left inside me at all!'

'Well, look – you unpack your little night-case, and have a wash in the bathroom if you want to, and then get into your pyjamas,' said Aunt Fanny. 'Then hop into bed and I'll bring you up some soup.'

But one look at the scowling George made her change her mind. Better not leave poor Berta with an angry George on her very first night!

'I think perhaps I won't get the soup myself,' she said. 'George, you go and get it, will you? It's warming up in the saucepan on the stove downstairs. You'll see the little soup-cup on the table, and some biscuits too.'

George got out of bed, still looking very mutinous. She watched Berta shake out a night-dress from her night-case and pursed up her lips.

'She doesn't even wear pyjamas!' she thought. 'What a ninny! And she's had the nerve to bring her own dog, too – spoilt little thing! I wonder where it is? I've a good mind to have a look at it when I'm down-stairs.'

But her mother had an idea that George might do that and she went to the door after her. 'George!' she said, warningly, 'I don't want you to open the dog's basket downstairs. I'm not having any dog-fights tonight. I shall put him in Timmy's kennel outside before I go to bed.'

George said nothing but went on downstairs. The soup was just about to boil and she whipped it off the stove at once. She poured it into the little soup-cup, placed it on the saucer, and put some biscuits on the side.

She heard a small whimpering sound, and turned round. It came from a fairly large basket over in the corner. George was terribly tempted to go and undo it – but she knew perfectly well that if the new dog ran upstairs to find its mistress, Timmy would bark and wake everybody up! It wasn't worth risking.

She took up the soup. Berta was now in the camp-bed and looked very cosy. Anne was still sleeping peacefully, quite undisturbed by all that was going on. Timmy had taken the opportunity of jumping off George's bed and had gone to examine this newcomer. He sniffed her delicately, and Berta put out her hand and stroked his head.

'What lovely eyes he's got,' she said. 'But he's a mongrel, isn't he? A sort of mixture-dog.'

'Don't you say anything like that to George,' said Aunt Fanny. 'She adores Timmy. Now – do you feel better? I hope you'll be happy with us, Berta, dear – I am sure you didn't want to come – but your father was so worried. And it will be nice for you to get to know Anne and Georgina before you go to their school next term.'

'Oh – was that Georgina – the one you called George?' said Berta in surprise. 'I wasn't really sure if she was a boy or not. My father told me there were three boys here and one girl – and that's the girl, isn't it – in bed there?'

She pointed to Anne. Aunt Fanny nodded. 'Yes, that's Anne. Your father thought George was a boy, that's why he told you there were three boys and only one girl here, I suppose. The two boys are in the next room.'

'I don't like George very much,' said Berta. 'She doesn't want me here, does she – or my dog?'

'Oh, you'll find George great fun when you get to know her,' said Aunt Fanny. 'Here she comes now with your soup.'

George came in with the soup, and was not at all pleased to see Timmy standing by the camp-bed, being petted by Berta. She set the soup down sharply and pushed Timmy away.

'Thank you,' said Berta, and took the soup-cup eagerly into her hands. 'What *lovely* soup!' she said. George got into bed and turned over on her side. She knew she was behaving badly, but the thought of someone daring to bring another *dog* to live at Kirrin Cottage was more than she could bear.

Timmy leapt up to lie at her feet as usual. Berta looked at this with much approval.

'I'll have Sally on *my* feet tomorrow!' she said. 'That's an awfully good idea. Pops – that's my father – always let me have Sally in my room, but she had to be in her basket, not on my bed. Tomorrow night she can sleep on my feet, like Timmy does on George's.'

'She will not,' said George, in a fierce voice. 'No dog sleeps in my bedroom except Timmy.'

'Now don't talk any more,' said Aunt Fanny, hurriedly. 'We can settle everything tomorrow when you're not so tired. I'll look after Sally tonight for you, I promise. Lie down now and go to sleep. You look as if you're half-asleep already!'

Berta was suddenly overcome with sleep and flopped down into bed. Her eyes closed, but she managed to force them open and look up at George's mother.

'Good night, Aunt Fanny,' she said, sleepily. 'That's what I was to call you, wasn't it? Thank you for being so kind to me.'

She was asleep almost before she had finished speaking. Aunt Fanny took up the soup-cup and went to the door. 'Are you awake, George?' she said.

George lay absolutely still. She knew that her mother was not pleased with her. It would be better to pretend to be fast asleep!

'I am sure you are awake,' said her mother.

'And I hope you are ashamed of yourself. I shall expect you to make up for this silly behaviour in the morning. It is a pity to behave in such a childish manner!'

She went out of the room, closing the door softly. George put out her hand to Timmy. She *was* ashamed of herself, but she wasn't at all certain that she would behave better in the morning. That silly, soppy girl! Her dog would be as silly as herself, she was sure! And Timmy would simply *hate* having another dog in the house. He would probably growl and snarl to such a degree that Berta would be forced to send her dog away.

'And a good thing too,' murmured George, as Timmy licked her fingers lovingly. '*You* don't want another girl in the house or another dog either, do you, Timmy? Especially a girl like that!'

Aunt Fanny saw to Berta's dog, and put her safely into Timmy's kennel outside. It had a little door to it, which could be shut, so the dog was safe there, and would not be able to run out.

She went back into the house, cleared up
Berta's belongings a little, for they had been
thrown higgledy-piggledy into the room, and
then turned out the light.

She went upstairs to bed. Her husband had
slept soundly all through Berta's late arrival. He
had been very sure that he would wake up and
welcome the girl as well as his wife, but he
hadn't even stirred!

Aunt Fanny was glad. It was much easier for
her to deal with a seasick, frightened girl by
herself. She climbed thankfully into bed and lay
down with a sigh. 'Oh dear – I don't look
forward to the morning! What will happen
then, with George in this mood, and two dogs
to sort out? Berta seems a nice little thing. Well
– perhaps they will all get on better than I
think!'

Yes – things wouldn't be too easy in the
morning. That was quite certain!

[5]

In the morning

George was the first to wake up in the morning. She at once remembered the events of the night before and looked across at Berta in the camp-bed. The girl was asleep, her wavy golden hair spread over the pillow. George leaned across Anne's bed and gave her a sharp nudge.

Anne woke up at once and gazed sleepily at George. 'What's the matter, George? Is it time to get up?'

'Look over there,' whispered George, nodding her head towards Berta. Anne turned over and looked. Unlike George she liked the look of Berta. Her sleeping face was pleasant and open, and her mouth turned up, not down. Anne couldn't bear people whose mouths turned down.

'She looks all right,' whispered back Anne. George frowned.

'She howled like anything when she came,' she told Anne. 'She's a real baby. *And* she's brought a dog!'

'Goodness – Timmy won't like that,' said Anne, startled. 'Where is it?'

'Down in Timmy's kennel,' said George, still whispering. 'I haven't seen it. It was in a closed basket last night and I didn't dare open it in case it tore upstairs and had a fight with Tim. But it can't be very big. I expect it's a horrible Peke, or some silly little lap-dog.'

'Pekes aren't horrible,' said Anne. 'They may be small and have funny little pug-noses, but they're awfully brave. Fancy having another dog! I can't *think* what Timmy will say!'

'It's a pity Berta isn't our kind,' said George. 'Look at her pale face – not a scrap of sun-tan! And she looks *weedy*, doesn't she? I'm sure she couldn't climb a tree or row a boat, or . . .'

'Sh! She's waking up,' said Anne warningly.

Berta yawned and stretched herself. Then she opened her eyes and looked round. At first she had no idea where she was, and then she suddenly remembered. She sat up.

'Hallo!' said Anne, and smiled at her. 'You weren't there when I came to bed last night. I was surprised to see you this morning.'

Berta took an immediate liking to Anne. She's got kind eyes, she thought. She's not like the other girl. I like this one!

She smiled back at Anne. 'Yes – I came in the middle of the night,' she said. 'I came by motor-boat and the sea was so bumpy that I was frightfully sick. My father didn't come with me but a friend of his did and he carried me from the boat to Kirrin Cottage. Even my legs felt seasick!'

'Bad luck!' said Anne. 'You didn't really enjoy the adventure then!'

'No. I can do without adventures!' said Berta. 'I'm not keen on them. Especially when Pops gets all excited and worried about me – he fusses round me like a hen, dear old Pops. I shall hate being away from him.'

George was listening to all this. Not keen on

adventures! Well, a girl like that wouldn't be, of course!

'*I'm* not very keen on adventures either,' said Anne. 'We've had plenty. I prefer adventures when they're all over!'

George exploded. 'Anne! How *can* you talk like that! We've had some *smashing* adventures, and we've enjoyed every one of them. If you feel like that we'll leave you out of the next one.'

Anne laughed. 'You won't! An adventure comes up all of a sudden, like a wind blowing up in the sky, and we're all in it, whether we like it or not. And you know that I like sharing things with you. I say – isn't it time we got up?'

'Yes,' said George, looking at the clock on the mantelpiece. 'Unless Berta wants to have her breakfast in bed? I bet she always does at home.'

'No, I don't. I hate meals in bed,' said Berta. 'I'm going to get up.'

She leapt out of bed and went to the window. Immediately she saw the wide sweep of the bay, sparkling in the morning sun, as blue as corn-flowers. The sea-sparkle was reflected into the bedroom, and made it very bright indeed.

'Oh. I *wondered* why our room was so full of brilliant light,' said Berta. 'Now I know! What a view! Oh, how lovely the sea looks this morning! And what's that little island out there? What a lovely place it looks.'

'That's Kirrin Island,' said George, proudly. 'It belongs to *me.*'

Berta laughed, thinking that George was joking. 'Belongs to *you*! I bet you wish it did. It's really wunnerful!'

'*Wunnerful*!' said George imitating her. 'Can't you say "wonderful"? It's got a D in the middle, you know.'

'Yes. I'm always being told things like that,' said Berta, still staring out of the window. 'I had an English governess and she tried to make me speak like you do. I do try, because I've got to go to an English school. My, my – I wish that island belonged to *me*. I wonder if my pops could buy it.'

George exploded again. '*Buy* it! You donkey, I *told* you it was mine, didn't I?'

Berta turned round in surprise. 'But – you didn't *mean* it, did you?' she said. '*Yours*? But how could it be?'

'It *is* George's,' said Anne. 'It has always belonged to the Kirrin family. That's Kirrin Island. George's father gave it to her, after an adventure we once had.'

Berta stared at George in awe. 'Great snakes! So it *is* yours! Aren't you the lucky one! Will you take me to visit it?'

'I'll see,' said George gruffly, glad to have impressed this American girl so much. Getting her 'Pops' to buy the island indeed! George snorted to herself. What next!

A shout came from the next room. It was Julian. 'Hey, you girls! Are you getting up? We're all too late for a swim before breakfast this morning. Dick and I have only just woken up.'

'Berta's here!' shouted back Anne. 'We'll get dressed, all of us, and then we'll introduce Berta to you.'

'Are they your brothers?' asked Berta. 'I haven't got any. Or sisters either. I shall be pretty scared of them.'

'You won't be scared of Julian and Dick,' said Anne, proudly. 'You'll wish you had brothers like them. Won't she, George?'

'Yes,' said George, shortly. She was feeling rather annoyed just then because Timmy was standing by Berta, wagging his plumy tail. 'Come here, Timmy. Don't make a nuisance of yourself.'

'Oh, he's not,' said Berta, and patted his big head. 'I like him. He seems simply ENOR-MOUS after my Sally. But you'll love Sally, George, you really will. Everyone says how sweet she is – and I've trained her beautifully.'

George took no interest in these remarks at all. She flounced off to wash in the bathroom, but Julian and Dick were there, and there was a lot of yelling and shouting as George tried to make them hurry up and get out. Berta laughed.

'That sounds nice and family-like,' she said.

'You don't get that sort of thing if you're an only child. What do I wear here?'

'Oh – something very simple,' said Anne, looking at the suitcase open on the floor, showing a collection of Berta's clothes. 'That shirt and those jeans will do.'

They were ready just as the gong rang for breakfast. A delicious smell of frying bacon and tomatoes came up the stairs, and Berta sniffed in delight.

'I do like English breakfast,' she said. 'We haven't gotten around to a proper breakfast in America yet! That's bacon and tomatoes I smell, isn't it? My English governess always said that bacon and eggs made the best breakfast in the world, but I guess the one we're going to have will taste pretty good.'

Uncle Quentin was at the table when the children came down. He looked most surprised to see Berta, having quite forgotten that she was coming. 'Who's this?' he said.

'Now Quentin – don't pretend you don't know!' said his wife. 'It's Elbur's girl – your friend Elbur. She came in the middle of the night, but I didn't wake you, you were so sound asleep.'

'Ah yes,' said Uncle Quentin, and he shook hands with the rather scared Berta. 'Glad to have you here, er – let me see now – what's your name?'

'Berta,' said everyone in a chorus.

'Yes, yes – Berta. Sit down, my dear. I know your father well. He's doing some wonderful work.'

Berta beamed. 'He's always at work!' she said. 'He works all through the night sometimes.'

'Does he? Well, what a thing to do!' said Uncle Quentin.

'It's a thing you often do yourself, Quentin,' said his wife, pouring out coffee. 'Though I don't suppose you even realise it.'

Uncle Quentin looked surprised. 'Do I really? Bless us all! Don't I go to bed some nights then?'

Berta laughed. 'You're like my pops! Sometimes he doesn't know what day of the week it is, even! And yet he's supposed to be one of the cleverest guys in the world!'

'Guy?' said Uncle Quentin, surprised, immediately thinking of Firework Night. Everyone laughed. Anne patted her uncle's knee. 'It's all right, Uncle,' she said, 'he's not going to sit on the top of a bonfire!'

But Uncle Quentin was not listening. He had suddenly seen a letter marked 'IMPORTANT' on the top of his pile of correspondence, and he picked it up.

'Well, unless I'm much mistaken, here's a letter from your father,' he said to Berta. 'I'll see what it says.'

He opened the letter and read it to himself. Then he looked up. 'It's all about you – er . . .'

'Her name's Berta,' said Aunt Fanny, patiently.

'About you, Berta,' said Uncle Quentin. 'But I must say your father has some very strange ideas. Yes, very strange.'

'What are they?' asked his wife.

'Well – he says she must be disguised – in case anyone comes to find her here,' said Uncle Quentin. 'And he wants her name changed – and, bless us all, he wants us to buy her boys' clothes – and cut her hair short – and dress her up as a boy!'

Everyone listened in surprise. Berta gave a little squeal.

'I won't! I WON'T be dressed up as a boy! I *won't* have my hair cut off. Don't you dare to make me! I WON'T!'

[6]
A few upsets

Berta looked so upset that Aunt Fanny acted quickly and firmly. 'Don't bother about that letter now, Quentin,' she said. 'We'll go through it afterwards and decide what to do. Let's have our breakfast in peace.'

'I *won't* have my hair cut off,' said Berta, again. Uncle Quentin was not used to being defied openly like this, and he scowled. He looked at his wife.

'Surely you are not going to let this – er what's her name now – Bertha . . .'

'Berta,' said everyone automatically.

'I said that we would not discuss this till after breakfast,' said Aunt Fanny, in the kind of voice that made everyone, including Uncle Quentin, quite certain that she meant what she said. Her husband folded up the letter and opened the next one, frowning. The children looked at one another.

Berta to be a boy! Goodness! If ever anyone looked less like a boy it was Berta! George was most annoyed. She loved to dress like a boy, but she didn't feel inclined to urge anyone else to! She looked at Berta, who was eating her breakfast with tears in her eyes. What a baby! She wouldn't even *look* like a boy, if she was dressed in boys' clothes. She would just look absolutely silly.

Julian began a conversation with his aunt about the garden. She was grateful to him for breaking up the sudden awkwardness caused by the letter. She was very fond of Julian. I can always depend on him, she thought, and talked gladly of the garden fruit, and who would pick the raspberries for lunch and whether the wasps would eat *all* the plums or not!

Dick joined in, and Anne, and soon Berta did too. Only George and her father remained gloomy. They both looked so exactly alike with solemn, rather frowning expressions that Julian nudged Dick and nodded towards them.

Dick grinned. 'Like father, like daughter!' he said. 'Cheer up, George. Don't you like your breakfast?'

George was just about to answer crossly when Anne gave an exclamation. 'Oh, *look* at Uncle Quentin! He's putting mustard on his toast – Aunt Fanny, stop him – he's just going to eat it!'

Everyone roared with laughter. Aunt Fanny managed to smack her husband's hand down from his mouth, just as he was putting his toast and mustard up to it, reading a letter at the same time.

'Hey – what's the matter?' he said, startled.

'*Quentin* – that's the second time this month you've spread your toast with mustard instead of marmalade,' said his wife. 'Do have a little sense.'

After that everyone became very cheerful. Uncle Quentin laughed at himself, and George saw the funny side and laughed loudly too, which made Timmy bark, and Berta giggled. Aunt Fanny was quite relieved that her husband had done such a silly thing.

'Do you remember when Father poured custard all over his fried fish once?' George said, entering into the talk for the first time. 'And he said it was the best egg-sauce he had ever tasted?'

The conversation was very animated after that, and Aunt Fanny felt happier. 'You children can clear away and wash up the breakfast things for Joanna,' she said. 'Or two of you can and the others can make the beds with me.'

'What about my little dog?' said Berta, suddenly remembering her again. 'I haven't seen her yet, because I was only just in time for breakfast. Where is she?'

'You can go and get her now,' said Aunt Fanny. 'We've all finished. Are you going to start your work, Quentin?'

'Yes, I am,' said her husband. 'So I don't want any yelling or shouting or barking outside my study door.'

He got up and went out of the room. Berta stood up too. 'Where's the kennel?' she said.

'I'll show you,' said Anne. 'We'll go and get your dog and introduce it to Timmy. Coming, George?'

'You can bring the dog in here, and we'll see what Timmy says,' said George, going all gloomy again. 'If he doesn't like the dog – and he won't – it will have to live out in the kennel.'

'Oh *no*,' said Berta, at once.

'Well, you don't want Timmy to *eat* it, do you?' said George. 'He's very jealous of other dogs in the house. He might go for yours and savage it.'

'Oh *no*!' said Berta, again, looking upset. 'Timmy's nice. He's not a fierce dog.'

'That's all *you* know!' said George. 'We'll, I've warned you.'

'Come on,' said Anne, pulling at Berta's sleeve. 'Let's go and fetch Sally. She must be wondering why nobody bothers about her. I bet Timmy won't mind *terribly*.'

As soon as the two had gone out, George spoke in Timmy's ear. 'You don't like strange dogs who want to come and live here, do you, Tim? You'll growl and snarl like anything, won't you? Growl your very fiercest! I know you won't bite but if you could just growl your loudest, that will be enough. Berta will make that Sally-dog live out of doors then!'

Soon she heard footsteps returning, and Anne's voice exclaiming in delight.

'Oh, she's sweet! Oh, what a darling! Sally, you're a pet! Julian, Dick, Aunt Fanny – do come and see Berta's dog!'

Everyone came into the room, led by Berta and Anne. Berta held the dog in her arms.

It was a tiny black poodle, whose woolly fur was cut away here and there to give it a very funny look. Sally was certainly an attractive little thing! Her sharp little nose sniffed all the time she was carried into the room, and her quick little eyes looked everywhere.

Berta put her down, and the little poodle stood there, poised on her dainty feet like a

ballet dancer about to perform. Everyone but
George exclaimed in delight.

'She's a poppet!'

'Sally! Sally, you're a pet!'

'Oh, a poodle! I do love poodles! They look
so knowing.'

Timmy stood by George, sniffing hard to get
the smell of this new dog. George had her hand
on his collar in case he sprang. His tail was as
stiff as a ramrod.

The poodle suddenly saw him. She stared at
him out of bright little eyes, quite unafraid.
Then she pulled away from Berta's hand and
trotted right over to Timmy, her funny little tail
wagging merrily.

Timmy backed a little in surprise. The poodle
danced all round him on her toes, and gave a
little whimpering bark, which said as plainly as
possible, I want to play with you!

Timmy sprang. He leapt in the air and came
down with a thud on his big paws, and the little
poodle dodged. Timmy's tail began to wag
wildly. He sprang again in play, and almost

knocked the little poodle over. He barked as if to say 'Sorry, I didn't mean that!'

Then he and the poodle played a most ridiculous game of dodge and run, and although one or two chairs went flying nobody minded – they were all laughing so much at the sight of the quick little poodle leading Timmy such a dance.

At last Sally was tired and sat down in a corner. Timmy pranced about in front of her, showing off. Then he went up to her and sniffed her nose. He licked it gently, and then lay down in front of her, gazing at her adoringly.

Anne gave a little squeal of laughter. 'He's gazing at Sally exactly as he gazes at you, George!' she cried.

But George was not at all pleased. In fact she was quite astounded. To think that Timmy should *welcome* another dog! To think that he should behave like this when she had told him to do the opposite!

'Aren't they sweet together?' said Berta, pleased. 'I *thought* Timmy would like Sally. Of course Sally is a pedigree dog, and cost a lot of money – and Timmy's only a mongrel. I expect he thinks she's *wunnerful*.'

'Oh, Tim may be a mongrel, but he's absolutely wunnerful too,' said Dick, hastily, pronouncing the word like Berta, to try and get a laugh. He saw George's scowl, and knew how cross she felt at hearing her beloved Timmy compared with a pedigree dog. 'He's a magnificent fellow, aren't you, Timmy?' went on Dick. 'Sally may be a darling, but you're worth more than a *hundred* darlings, aren't you?'

'I think he's beautiful,' said Berta, looking down at Timmy. 'He's got the loveliest eyes I ever did see.'

George began to feel a little better. She called Timmy. 'You're making rather a fool of yourself,' she said to him.

'Now that Timmy and Sally are going to be friends, can I have Sally to sleep on my bed at night, like George has Timmy?' said Berta. 'Please say yes, Aunt Fanny.'

'No,' said George at once. 'Mother, I won't have that. I won't!'

'Well, we'll see what we can do about it,' said her mother. 'Sally was quite happy in the kennel last night, I must say.'

'I'm going to have her sleep with me,' said Berta, scowling at George. 'My father will pay you a lot of money to make me happy. He told me he would.'

'Don't be silly, Berta,' said Aunt Fanny, firmly. 'This isn't a question of money. Now, leave this for a little while, please, and go and do your jobs, all of you. And then we must consider your father's letter, Berta, and see exactly what he wants done. We must certainly try to follow his advice about you.'

'But I don't want to—' began Berta, and then felt a firm hand on her arm. It was Julian.

'Come on, kid,' he said. 'Be your age! Remember you're a guest here and put on a few of your best manners. We like American children – but not *spoilt* ones!'

Berta had quite a shock to hear Julian speaking like this. She looked up at him and he grinned down at her. She felt near tears, but she smiled back.

'You haven't any brothers to keep you in your place,' said Julian, linking his arm in hers. 'Well, from now on, while you're here, Dick and I are your brothers, and you've got to toe the line, just like Anne. See? What about it?'

Berta felt that there was nothing in the world she would like better than having Julian for a brother! He was big and tall and had twinkling kindly eyes that made Berta feel he was as responsible and trustable as her father.

Aunt Fanny smiled to herself. Julian always knew the best thing to say and do. Now he would take Berta in hand and see that she didn't upset the household too much. She was glad. It wasn't easy to run a big family like this, with a scientist husband to cope with, unless everyone pulled together!

'You go and help Aunt Fanny with the beds,' said Julian to Berta. 'And take your Sally-dog with you. She's great! But so is Timmy, and don't you forget it!'

[7]
A little conference

Peace reigned in the house for a little while. George and Anne went to help the cook with the washing-up. Joanna was pleased, because with eight people in the house, including herself, there was a lot to do.

She had been very astonished that morning to find a fifth child added to the household, but had been told that after breakfast she could go into the sitting-room and hear an explanation! Joanna must certainly be in the secret too!

Upstairs Berta was helping with the beds – not very successfully because she was not used to doing things for herself. But she was very willing to learn and Aunt Fanny was quite pleased with her. Timmy and Sally darted about together and made things rather more difficult than they need have been, popping under beds and out again at top speed.

'I'm glad Timmy likes Sally,' said Berta. 'I knew he would. I can't think why George thought he wouldn't. George is funny, I think.'

'Not really,' said Aunt Fanny. 'She hasn't any brothers or sisters to rub off her corners, and she didn't even know her three cousins till a few years ago, or go to school. Lonely people aren't so easy to get on with as others – but she is great fun now, as you will soon find out.'

'I'm an only child too,' said Berta. 'But I've always had plenty of other children to play with. My pop saw to that. He's wunnerful – I mean wonDERful. I'll say that word "won-DERful" twenty times, then maybe, I'll get it right.'

'Well, say the word "twenty" as well!' said Aunt Fanny. 'It has a letter T at the end as well as at the beginning, you know. It's "twenTY" not "twenny". But don't make yourself *too* English. It's nice to have a change!'

'WonDERful,   wonDERful,   wonDERful!

TwenTY, twenTY!' chanted Berta, as she made the beds. Dick looked into the room and chuckled.

'Great snakes!' he said, with a grin, and an American accent. 'You shore are wunnerful, baby!'

'Don't be so silly, Dick,' said his aunt, laughing. 'Now – I think we've finished all we have to do, Berta. We'll go downstairs and have a conference. Tell the others, will you?'

Berta, followed closely by Sally, who was also followed closely by an adoring Timmy, went to tell Dick and Julian, and then George and Anne. George was not too pleased with Timmy.

'Where have you been?' she said. 'Can't you stop running about after Sally? She'll get very very tired of you!'

'Wuff!' said Sally, in a high little bark, not at all like Timmy's deep 'Woof!'

Soon all five children and the two dogs, and also Joanna, were in the sitting-room with Aunt Fanny. Berta began to look a little nervous.

Aunt Fanny had the letter that Berta's father had sent. She did not read it out to the children, but told them what was in it. She also explained to Joanna about Berta.

'Joanna, you have always known what important work my husband does,' she said. 'Well, Berta's father does the same kind of work in America, and he and Quentin are working on a great new scheme together.'

'Oh yes,' said Joanna, very much interested.

'Berta's father has been warned by the police that it is possible Berta may be kidnapped and held to ransom, not for money, but for the scientific secrets that he knows,' went on Aunt Fanny. 'So she has been sent to us to be kept safe for three weeks. By that time the scheme will be finished and made public. Berta is going to the same school as Anne and George, and it is a good idea to let them know one another first.'

Joanna nodded. 'I understand that,' she said. 'I think we can keep Berta safe, don't you?'

'Yes,' said Aunt Fanny. 'But her father has

now put up some further ideas that he wants us to follow. He says it would be best to disguise her as a boy—'

'Jolly good idea,' interrupted Dick.

'And to give her another name – a boy's name,' said Aunt Fanny. 'He wants her to have her hair cut short and—'

'Oh please not that!' begged Berta, shaking back her fair, wavy hair. 'I'd hate it. Girls with short hair like boys look so silly, they—'

Anne nudged her and frowned. Berta stopped hurriedly, remembering that George had curly hair cut as short as any boy.

'I think we'll have to do what your father says,' said Aunt Fanny. 'This is very important, Berta. You see, if anyone *should* come here looking for you, thinking of kidnapping, they would never recognise you if you were looking exactly like a boy.'

'But my hair,' said Berta, almost in tears. 'How *could* Pops says I'm to have my hair off? He always said it was wunnerful!'

Nobody liked to point out that there was a D

in wonderful just then! Berta was really so very upset about her hair.

'Your hair will grow quickly enough,' said Aunt Fanny.

'Her *head's* a good shape,' said Julian, looking at it consideringly. 'She should look nice with short hair.'

Berta cheered up. If Julian thought that, then it wouldn't be so bad.

'But what about clothes?' she said, remembering this point with a look of horror. 'Girls look frightful in boys' clothes. Pops always said so till now.'

'You won't look any worse than George does,' said Dick. 'She's got on a boy's jersey, boy's jeans and boy's shoes this very minute!'

'I think she looks awful,' said Berta, obstinately, and George scowled.

'Well, I think *you'd* look horrible,' she said. 'You wouldn't even *look* like a boy, you'd look little-girlish, like a silly little sissy-boy. *I* think it's a stupid idea to put you into boys' clothes!'

'Aha! Our George wants to be the only one!'

said Dick, slyly, and quickly got out of the way of a punch from the furious George.

'Well,' said Julian. 'I'll go out and buy some things for Berta this morning, so that's settled. What about her hair? Shall *I* cut it short?'

Aunt Fanny was amused at Julian's high-handed way of dealing with Berta and her troubles, and even more amused to see that Berta did not even argue with Julian.

'You can certainly go shopping for Berta if you like,' she said. 'But I'd rather you didn't cut her hair. You'd make her look a scarecrow!'

'I don't mind if Julian cuts it,' said Berta, surprisingly meek all at once.

'I shall cut it for you myself,' said Aunt Fanny. 'Now – what about a boy's name? We can't call you Berta any more, that's certain.'

'I'd rather not have a boy's name,' said Berta. 'It's silly for a girl to be called by a boy's name, like George.'

'If you *mean* to be rude to me, I'll—' began George, but got no farther. Julian and Dick had burst into laughter.

'Oh George – you and Berta will be the death of us!' said Julian. 'Here are you doing all you can to *pretend* to be a boy – and here is Berta doing all she can to get *out* of it! For goodness' sake, let's settle the matter without any more bickering. We'll call Berta Robert.'

'No – that's too like Berta,' said Dick. 'It ought to be a completely different name. We'll call her a good plain boy's name like Jim or Tom or John.'

'No,' said Berta. 'I don't like any of them. Let me have my second name, please.'

'What's that? Another girl's name?' asked Julian.

'Yes. But it's used for a boy too, only then it's spelt differently,' said Berta. 'It's Lesley. It's a nice name, I think.'

'Lesley. Yes – it rather suits you,' said Julian. 'It suits you better than Berta. We'll call you Lesley – and people will think it's Leslie spelt l-i-e at the end, and not l-e-y. All right. Everything's settled.'

'Not quite,' said his aunt. 'I just want to say

that you mustn't let Berta – I mean Lesley – out of your sight at all. And you must report at once any mysterious happening or any stranger you see. The local police here know that we have Lesley with us, and why – and anything can be reported to them at once. They also are keeping a good look-out, of course.'

'This almost sounds as if we're in the middle of an adventure!' said Dick, looking pleased.

'I hope not,' said his aunt. 'I don't imagine that anyone will ever guess Berta – I mean Lesley – is anything more than she will appear to be – a boy friend of yours and Julian's, come to stay for a while. Dear me, it's going to be difficult to refer to her as him all the time!'

'It certainly is,' said Julian, standing up. 'If you'll give me some money, Aunt Fanny, I'll go and do a little shopping for Lesley. What size do you think HE needs?'

Everyone laughed. 'HE wears size three shoes,' said Joanna smiling. 'I noticed that this morning.'

'And HE will have to get used to doing his

coat buttons up on the right-hand side instead of on the left,' said Anne, joining in the fun.

'SHE will soon get used to that,' said George. 'Won't SHE, Timmy?'

'Don't spoil it all now, George,' said Julian. 'A slip of the tongue, saying SHE instead of HE, might lead to danger for Ber – I mean Lesley.'

'Yes, I know,' said George. 'It's just that she'll never look like a boy, and—'

'I don't *want* to look like a boy,' said Berta. 'I think *you* look—'

'Here we go again!' said Julian. 'Stop it, Lesley, stop it, George. George, you'd better come out and help me to get the things for Lesley. Come on. And take that scowl off your face. You look like a sulky girl!'

That made George alter her face at once. She couldn't help grinning at the artful Julian.

'I'm coming,' she said. 'Good-bye, Berta. When we come back, you'll be Leslie, haircut and all!'

She and Julian went off. Anne fetched her aunt's sharpest scissors and draped a big towel round Berta's shoulders. Berta looked as if she was going to cry.

'Cheer up,' said Dick. 'You're going to look angelic with short hair! Begin, Aunt Fanny. Let's see what she's like with shorn locks.'

'Sit quite still,' said Aunt Fanny and began. Clip-clip-clip! The wavy golden hair fell to the floor in big strands and Berta began to weep in earnest. 'My hair! I can't bear this. Oh, my hair!'

Soon most of it was on the floor, and Aunt Fanny began to clip what was left as best she could, to make it look as boyish as possible. She made a very good job of it indeed. Dick and Anne watched with the greatest interest.

'There! It's done!' said Aunt Fanny at last. 'Stop crying, Lesley – and let's have a look at you!'

[8]

A transformation

Berta stood in the middle of the floor, blinking her tears away. Anne gave a gasp.

'You know – it's *very* odd – but she does look rather like a boy – a very, very good-looking boy!'

'An angelic boy,' said Dick. 'A choirboy or something. She looks smashing! Who would have thought it?'

Aunt Fanny was very struck with Berta's appearance too. 'It's certainly very odd,' she said. 'But there's no doubt about it – when she's – I mean he's – dressed in boys' clothes, he'll make a fine boy. Better than George, actually, because her hair's *really* too curly for a boy.'

Berta went to the mirror on the wall. She gave a wail. 'I took awful! I don't know myself! Nobody would EVER recognise me!'

'Splendid!' said Dick, at once. 'You've hit the

nail right on the head. Nobody *would* recognise you now. Your father was quite right to say cut your hair off and dress up as a boy. Any prowling kidnapper would never think *you* were Berta, the pretty little girl.'

'I'd rather be kidnapped than look like this,' wept Berta. 'What will the girls at your school say, Anne, when they see me?'

'They don't say anything to George about her short hair, and they won't say anything to you,' said Anne.

'Stop crying, Bert – er – Lesley,' said Aunt Fanny. 'You make me feel quite miserable. You've been very good to sit so still all that time. Now I really must think of a little reward for you.'

Berta stopped crying at once. 'Please,' she said, 'there's only one thing I want now. I want Sally-dog to sleep with me.'

'Oh dear, Ber – er Lesley – I really *can't* have another dog in that little bedroom,' said poor Aunt Fanny. 'And George would make things most unpleasant if I did.'

'Aunt Fanny – Sally is a very very good guard for me,' said Berta. 'She barks at the very slightest sound. I'd feel safe with her in the bedroom.'

'I'd like you to have her,' said Aunt Fanny, 'but . . .'

Joanna had come into the room to put away some things and had heard the conversation. She stared in admiration at Berta's neat golden head, and then made a suggestion.

'Berta could have her camp-bed in *my* room,' she said. 'I don't mind the dog a bit, she can have her and welcome, she's a pet, that little poodle. It's very crowded in the girls' room now, with three beds in it, and my room's a nice big one. So, if Berta doesn't mind sharing it, she's welcome.'

'Oh Joanna – that's good of you,' said Aunt Fanny, relieved at such a simple solution. 'Also, your room is up in the attic – it would be *very* difficult for kidnappers to find their way there – and nobody would think of looking into your room for one of the children.'

'*Thank* you, Joanna, you're just *wunnerful*!'

said Berta in delight. 'Sally, do you hear that? You'll be sleeping on my feet tonight, like Timmy does on George's.'

'I don't really approve of that, you know, Berta,' said Aunt Fanny. 'Oh dear – I called you Berta again. Lesley, I mean. What a muddle I'm going to get into! Anne, get the dustpan and sweep up the hair on the floor.'

When Julian and George came back there was no sign of the golden hair on the floor. They put their parcels down on the table and shouted for Aunt Fanny. 'Mother!' called George. 'Aunt Fanny!' shouted Julian.

She came running downstairs with Berta and Anne and Dick. Julian and George looked at Berta, thunderstruck. 'Gosh – is it *really* you, Berta?' said Julian. 'I simply didn't recognise you!'

'Why – you *do* look like a boy!' said George. 'I never thought you would.'

'A jolly good-looking boy,' said Julian. 'Well, your father was right. It's the best disguise you could have!'

'Where are the clothes?' asked Berta, rather pleased at all the interest in her looks. They opened the parcels and pulled out the things.

They were not really very exciting – a boy's anorak in navy blue, two pairs of boy's jeans, two grey jerseys, a few shirts, a tie and a pull-over without sleeves.

'And shoes and socks,' said George. 'But we decided you'd got plenty of socks that would do, so we only bought one pair of those. Oh – and here's a boy's cap! We bought it just for fun.'

Berta put on the cap at once. There were squeals of laughter from everyone. 'It suits her! She's got it on at just the right angle. She looks a real boy!'

'*You* put it on, George,' said Berta, and George took it, eager to share in the admiration. But it looked ridiculous on her curls, and wouldn't sit down flat as it should. Everyone hooted.

'It makes you look a girl! Take it off!'

George took it off in disappointment. How

very aggravating that this girl Berta should make a better boy than she did! She threw the cap on the table, half-cross that they had bought it.

'Go upstairs and put some of the things on,' said Aunt Fanny, amused at all these goings-on. Up went Berta obediently, and soon came down again, neatly arrayed in jeans, grey shirt and blue tie.

Everyone roared with laughter. Berta was now quite enjoying herself and paraded round the room, her cap tilted on one side of her head.

'She looks like a very tidy, neat little boy, a good and most angelic child!' said Julian. 'Dear Lesley, you must get yourself just a little dirty – you look too good to be true.'

'I don't like getting dirty,' said Berta. 'I think—'

But what she thought nobody knew because at that moment the door opened and Uncle Quentin came into the room.

'I'd like to know how you think I can do my work with all this hooting and cackling going on,' he began, and then he suddenly saw Berta, and stopped.

'Who's this?' he said, looking Berta up and down.

'Don't you know, Father?' said George.

'Of course not. Never seen him in my life before!' said her father. 'Don't tell me it's somebody else come to stay.'

'It's Berta,' said Anne, with a giggle.

'Berta – now who's Berta?' said Uncle Quentin, frowning. 'I seem to have heard that name before.'

'The girl you thought might be kidnapped,' explained Dick.

'Oh *Berta* – Elbur's girl!' said Uncle Quentin. 'I remember *her* all right. But who's *this*? This boy? I've never seen *him* before. What's your name, boy?'

'Lesley,' said Berta. 'But I was Berta when you saw me at breakfast.'

'Good heavens!' said Uncle Quentin, amazed. 'What a – what a transformation! Why, your own father wouldn't know you. I hope I remember who you are. Keep reminding me, if I don't.'

Off he went, back to his study. The children laughed, and Aunt Fanny had to laugh too.

'By the way,' she said, 'I want you all to have lunch at home today, because it's really too late now to start making sandwiches for a picnic; it's only cold ham and salad, so don't get *too* hungry, will you?'

'Is there time for a swim?' asked Julian, looking at his watch.

'Yes – if you'll come in about twelve o'clock and pick the fruit for a pudding for lunch,' said his aunt. 'It takes ages to pick enough for eight people, and Joanna and I have a lot to do today.'

'Right. We'll go for a swim now, and then we'll ALL pick fruit,' said Julian. 'Bags I pick the plums. The raspberries are such fiddly little things.'

'Have you a swimsuit, Berta, I mean Lesley?' asked George.

'Yes. It's an absolutely plain one, so I'll be all

right in it,' said Berta. 'Hurray, I shan't need to wear a cap. Boys never do.'

Berta's cases were now all in Joanna's big room and she ran to get into her swimsuit.

'Bring your anorak and a towel,' yelled George, and went into her own room with Anne.

'I bet Berta can't swim,' she said. 'That will be a pity. We'll have to teach her.'

'Well, don't duck her too often!' said Anne, seeing a look in George's eye that was not too kindly. 'Blow – my swimsuit isn't here – I'm sure I brought it in from the clothes-line.'

It took quite a while to find it, and the boys and Berta had already gone down to the beach with Sally by the time Anne and George were ready to follow with the impatient Timmy.

They were down on the beach at last, and there was Sally-dog guarding the anoraks belonging to Julian, Dick and Berta. She was lying on them, and she even dared to growl at Timmy when he came near.

George laughed. 'Growl back, Timmy! Don't

let a little snippet like that cheek you. Growl back!'

But Timmy wouldn't. He just sat down out of reach of Sally, and looked at her sadly. Wasn't she friends with him any more?

'Where are the others?' said Anne, shading her eyes from the glare of the sun and looking out to sea. 'Goodness, how far out they've swum! That *can't* be Berta with them, surely!'

George looked out over the stretch of blue sea at once. She saw three heads bobbing. Yes, Berta *was* out there!

'She must be a jolly good swimmer,' said Anne, admiringly. 'I couldn't swim out as far as that. We were wrong about Berta. She swims like a fish!'

George said nothing. She ran to the waves, plunged through a big one just as it was curling over, and swam out strongly. She couldn't *believe* that it was Berta out there! And if it was, the boys must be helping her!

But it *was* Berta. Her golden head glistened

wet in the water, and she shouted in glee as she swam.

'This is great! This is wunnerful! Gee, I'm enjoying this! Hi there, George – isn't the water warm?'

Julian and Dick grinned at the panting George. 'Lesley's a fine swimmer,' said Dick. 'Gosh, I thought she was going to race me at one time. She'd beat *you*, George!'

'She wouldn't,' said George, but all the same she didn't challenge Berta to race!

It was fun to be five, fun to chase one another in the sea, to swim under the water and grab somebody's leg. And Anne laughed till she choked when she saw somebody heave themselves out of the water right on to George's back, and duck her well and truly.

It was Berta! And what was more, the angry George couldn't catch her afterwards. Berta could swim much too fast!

[9]

A sudden telephone call

Berta soon settled down happily with the Five. George couldn't bear to think that the girl had to be dressed like a boy, but her jealousy wore off a little as the days went by – though she couldn't help feeling annoyed that Berta proved to be such a good swimmer!

She could dive well too, and swim under water even longer than the boys could, much to their surprise.

'Oh well, you see, back home, we've got a pool in our garden,' she said. 'A wonDERful pool, gee, you should see it. And I learnt to swim in it when I was two. Pops always called me a water-baby.'

Berta ate just as much as the others, although she was not so sturdy and well built. She was loud in her praise of the meals, and this pleased Aunt Fanny and Joanna very much.

'You're getting fatter, Lesley,' said Aunt Fanny a week later, looking at her as she sat eating her lunch with the others. 'And what is better still – you're getting out in the open air. You're almost as tanned as the others!'

'Yes. I thought so too,' said Berta, pleased.

'It's a good thing you caught the sun so easily,' said Aunt Fanny. 'Now, if any kidnappers come round looking for a long-haired pale-faced American girl, they would take one look at the lot of you and off they would go! Nobody would guess you were Berta!'

'All the same, I'd much rather *be* Berta,' said Berta. 'I still don't like pretending to be a boy. It's silly, and it makes me *feel* silly. Anyway, thank goodness my hair's growing a bit longer. I don't look *quite* so much like a boy now!'

'Dear me, you're right,' said Aunt Fanny, and everyone looked at Berta. 'I shall have to cut it short again.'

'Gosh!' said Berta. 'Why did I say that? You

wouldn't have noticed if I hadn't mentioned it. Let it grow again, please, Aunt Fanny. I've been here a week and there isn't even a *smell* of a kidnapper – and I reckon there won't be either!'

But Aunt Fanny was firm about the hair, and after the meal she made Berta sit still while she clipped it a little shorter. It was not a bit curly like George's, and now that it was short, the wave had almost gone from it. She really did look like a good clean little boy!

'Rather a wishy-washy one!' said George, unkindly, but everyone knew what she meant.

Sally the poodle was a great success. Even George couldn't go on disliking the happy, dancing little dog. She trotted and capered about on her slim little legs, and Timmy was her adoring slave.

'She always looks as if she's running about on tip-toe,' said Anne, and so she did. She made friends with everyone, even the paper-boy, who was really scared of dogs.

Uncle Quentin was the only one who didn't get used to Berta and Sally. When he met them together, Berta so like a small boy, Sally at her heels, he stopped and stared.

'Now let me see – who are you?' he said. 'Yes – you're Berta!'

'No – he's LESLEY!' everyone would say.

'You must *not* call her Berta, dear,' said his wife. 'You really must not. It's a funny thing that you never could remember she was Berta, and now that we've made her into Lesley, you immediately remember she's Berta!'

'Well, I must say you've made her look exactly like a boy,' said Uncle Quentin, much to George's annoyance. George was beginning to be afraid that Berta looked more boyish than she did! 'Well, I hope you're having a good time with the others, er – er . . .'

'*Lesley* is the name,' said Aunt Fanny with a little laugh. 'Quentin, do try and remember.'

Another day passed peacefully by, and the five children and two dogs were out of doors all day long, swimming, boating, exploring, really enjoying themselves.

Berta wanted to go over to Kirrin Island, but

George kept making excuses not to go. 'Don't be mean,' said Dick. 'We *all* want to go. It's ages since we went. It's just that you don't want to let Lesley do something she'd like to do!'

'It isn't,' said George. 'Perhaps we'll go to-morrow.'

But when tomorrow came something happened that upset their plans for going to Kirrin Island. A telephone call came for Uncle Quentin, and immediately he was in a panic.

'Fanny! Fanny, where are you?' he called. 'Pack my bag at once. At once, do you hear?'

His wife came running down the stairs at top speed. 'Quentin, why? What's happened?'

'Elbur's found a mistake in our calculations,' said Uncle Quentin. 'What nonsense! There's no mistake. None at all.'

'But why can't he come *here* and work it out with you?' asked his wife. 'Why have *you* got to rush off like this? Tell him to come here, Quentin. I'll find him a bed somehow.'

'He says he doesn't want to, while his daughter – his daughter – what's her name now?'

'*Lesley*,' said his wife. 'All right, don't bother to explain. I see now that it would be foolish for him to come while Lesley's here – she'd be calling him Pops, and—'

'Pops?' said her husband, startled. 'What do you mean – Pops?'

'It's what she calls her father, dear,' said Aunt Fanny, patiently. 'Anyway, he's quite right. It would be foolish to hide Lesley here so well, and then have everyone hear her calling him Pops, and him calling her Berta – if any kidnappers followed him, they would soon find out where his daughter was – here, with our four!'

'Yes – that's what I was trying to tell you,' said her husband, impatiently. 'Anyway I must go to Elbur straight away. So pack my bag, please. I'll be back in two days' time.'

'In that case I'll go with you, Quentin,' said his wife. 'I could do with a quiet two days – and you're not much good when you're alone, are you – losing your socks, and forgetting to have your shoes cleaned, and . . .'

Her husband gave a sudden smile that lit up

his face and made him seem quite young. 'Will you really come with me? I thought you'd hate to leave the children.'

'It's only for two days,' said his wife. 'And Joanna is very good with them. I'll arrange that they shall go out on all-day picnics in the boat – they'll be quite safe then. If any kidnappers *were* around they'd find it difficult to snatch Lesley out of a boat! But I'm beginning not to believe that tale of Elbur's. He just got into a panic when he heard the rumour, I expect.'

The children were told of the sudden decision when they got back to lunch that day. Joanna had to tell them, because Aunt Fanny and her husband had already departed, complete with two suitcases, one containing precious papers and the other clothes for two days.

'Gosh!' said Julian, surprised. 'I hope nothing horrid's happened.'

'Oh no – it was just a sudden telephone call from Lesley's father,' said Joanna, smiling at Berta. 'He had to see your uncle in a hurry – about some figures.'

'Why didn't Pops come down here – then he could have seen *me*?' demanded Berta at once.

'Because everyone would have known who you are, then,' said Dick. 'We're *hiding* you, don't forget!'

'Oh yes – well I do believe I *had* forgotten,' said Berta, rather surprised at herself. 'It's so *lovely* down here in Kirrin with you all. The days seem to *swim* by!'

'Your mother said you had better go off on all-day picnics in the boat,' said Joanna to George. 'That was to make things easy for me, of course. But I don't mind what you do – you can come back to lunch each day, if you like.'

'I do so like you, Joanna!' said Berta, giving the surprised cook a sudden hug. 'You're a real honey!'

'In fact, she's quite wunnerful!' said Dick. 'It's all right, Joanna – we'll go out for the midday meal, *and* for tea, till my aunt comes back. And we'll make the sandwiches and pack up everything ourselves.'

'Well, that's nice of you,' said Joanna. 'Why don't you go across to Kirrin Island for the day? Lesley keeps wanting to go.'

Berta grinned at Joanna.

'We'll go if the boat is ready,' said George, rather reluctantly. 'You know Alf is mending one of the rowlocks. We'll go and see if it's finished.'

They all went to see, but Alf was not there. His father was working on another boat, over by the jetty, and he called to them.

'Do you want my Alf? He's gone off in his uncle's boat for a day's fishing. He said to tell you the rowlock's not mended yet, but he'll do it for certain tonight when he comes back.'

'Right. Thank you,' called back Julian. Berta looked very disappointed. 'Cheer up,' he said. 'We'll be able to go tomorrow.'

'We shan't,' said Berta, mournfully. 'Something else will happen to prevent us – or George will think of another excuse not to go. Gee, if I had a wunnerful – wonDERful – island like that, I'd go and *live* on it.'

They went back to Kirrin Cottage and

packed up a very good lunch for themselves. Berta's father had sent down a parcel of American goodies three days before, and they meant to try them.

'Snick-snacks!' said Dick, reading the name on a tin. 'Shrimp, lobster, crab and a dozen other things all in one tin. Sounds good. We'll make sandwiches with this!'

'Gorgies,' said Anne, reading the name on another tin. 'What a peculiar name! Oh – I suppose it's something you *gorge* yourself with. Let's open it.'

They opened half a dozen tins with most exciting names and made themselves so many sandwiches that Joanna exclaimed in amazement. 'How ever many have you made for each of you?'

'Twenny each – I mean twenTY,' said Berta. 'But we won't be back to lunch *or* tea, Joanna. I guess we'll be plenny hungry.'

'PlenTY!' chorused everyone, and Berta obediently repeated the word, a grin on her suntanned face.

What a day they had! They walked for miles and picnicked in a shady wood near a little stream that bubbled along nearby, sounding very cool and enticing. They decided to sit with their feet in it as they ate, and Anne gave continual little squeals because she said the water tickled the soles of her feet.

They were so tired when they got home that night that it was all they could do to eat their supper and stagger upstairs to bed.

'I shan't wake till half past eleven tomorrow morning,' yawned Dick. 'Oh my poor feet! Gosh, I'm so tired I shall probably fall asleep cleaning my teeth.'

'What a peaceful night!' said Anne, looking out of her window. 'Well – sleep tight, every-one. I don't expect any of us will open an eye till late tomorrow morning. I know I shan't!'

But she did. She opened both eyes very wide indeed in the middle of the night.

[10]

A puzzling thing

All was quiet at Kirrin Cottage. The two boys slept soundly in their room, and George and Anne slept without stirring in theirs. Berta was up in Joanna's attic room, and hadn't moved since she had flopped into bed.

Timmy was on George's feet, as usual, and Sally the poodle was curled up in the crook of Berta's knees, looking like a ball of black wool! Nobody stirred.

A black cloud crept up the sky and blotted out the stars one by one. Then a low roll of thunder came. It was far off, and only a rumble, but it woke both the dogs, and it woke Anne too.

She opened her eyes, wondering what the noise was. Then she knew – it was thunder.

'Oh, I hope a storm won't come and break up

this wonderful weather!' she thought, as she lay and listened. She turned towards the open window and looked for the stars, but there were none to see.

'Well, if a storm's coming, I'll go and watch it at the window,' thought Anne. 'It should be a magnificent sight over Kirrin Bay. I'm so hot too – I'd like a breath of fresh air at the window!'

She got quietly out of bed and padded over to the open window. She leaned out, sniffing the cool air outside. The night was very dark indeed, because of the great black cloud.

The thunder came again, but not very near – just a low growl. Timmy jumped off George's bed and went to join Anne. He put his great paws up on the window-sill and looked out solemnly over the bay.

And then both he and Anne heard another sound – a faraway chug-chug-chug-chug-chug.

'It's a motorboat,' said Anne, listening. 'Isn't it Timmy? Someone's having a very late trip! Can you see any ship-lights, Tim? I can't.'

The engine of the motorboat cut out just then, and there was complete silence except for the swish-swash-swish of the waves on the beach. Anne strained her eyes to see if she could spot any light anywhere to show where the motorboat was. It sounded quite far out in the bay. Why had it stopped on the water? Why hadn't it gone to the jetty?

Then she did see a light, but a very faint one, right out at the entrance of the bay, about the middle. It shone for a while, moved here and there, and then disappeared. Anne was puzzled.

'Surely that's just about where Kirrin Island is?' she whispered to Timmy. 'Is anyone there? Has the motorboat gone there, do you suppose? Well, we'll listen to see if it leaves again and goes away.'

But no further sound came from across the bay, and no light shone either. 'Perhaps the motorboat is *behind* Kirrin Island,' thought Anne, suddenly. 'And then I wouldn't be able to see any lights on it – the island would hide the boat *and* its lights. But what was that *moving* light I saw? *Was* it someone on the island? Oh dear, my eyes are getting so sleepy again that I can hardly keep them open. Perhaps I didn't hear or see anything after all!'

There was no more thunder, and no lightning at all. The big black cloud began to thin out and one or two stars appeared in the gaps. Anne yawned and crawled into bed. Timmy jumped back on George's bed and curled himself up with a little sigh.

In the morning Anne had almost forgotten her watch at the open window the night before. It was only when Joanna mentioned that a big storm had burst over a town fifty miles away that Anne remembered the thunder she had heard.

'Oh!' she said, suddenly. 'Yes – *I* heard thunder too, and I got out of bed, hoping to watch a storm. But it didn't come. And I heard a motorboat far out in the bay, but I couldn't see any lights – except for a faint, moving one I thought was on Kirrin Island.'

George sat up in her chair as if she had had

an electric shock. 'On Kirrin Island! Whatever
do you mean? Nobody's there. *Nobody's* allowed there!'

'Well – I may have been mistaken,' said
Anne. 'I was so very sleepy. I didn't hear the
motorboat go away. I just went back to bed.'

'You *might* have woken me, if you thought
you saw a light on my island,' said George.
'You really might!'

'Oh, Anne – it wouldn't be kidnappers,
would it?' said Joanna, at once.

Julian laughed. 'No, Joanna. What would be
the use of them going to Kirrin Island? They
couldn't do any kidnapping there, in full view
of all the houses round the bay!'

'I guess it was only a dream, Anne,' said
Berta. 'I guess you heard the thunder in your
sleep, and it turned into the sound of a motorboat chugging – dreams *do* that sort of thing. I
know once I left the tap running in my basin
when I went to sleep, and I dreamed all night
long I was riding over the Niagara Falls!'

Everyone laughed. Berta could be very droll

at times. 'If the boat's ready, we'll certainly go over to Kirrin Island today,' said George. 'If any trippers are there I'll send Timmy after them!'

'There will only be the rabbits,' said Dick. 'I wonder if there are still hundreds there – my word, last time we went they were so tame that we nearly fell over them!'

'Yes – but we didn't have Timmy with us,' said Anne. 'George, it *will* be nice to go to Kirrin Island again. We'll have to tell Lesley about the adventures we've had there.'

They washed up after breakfast, made the beds and did their rooms. Joanna put her head round Julian's bedroom door.

'Will you want a packed lunch for a picnic again, Julian?' she said. 'If you don't, I can get you a nice bit of cold ham for lunch. The grocer's just rung up.'

'If the boat's mended, we're going over to the island, Joanna,' said Julian. 'And then we'd like a packed lunch. But if we don't go, we'll stay for lunch. It will be easier for you in a way, won't it? We all got up so late this morning that there's not much time to make sandwiches and pick fruit and so on.'

'Well, you tell me, as soon as you know about the boat,' said Joanna, and disappeared.

George came in. 'I'm going to see if the boat is mended,' she said. 'I'll only be gone a minute. Joanna wants to know.'

She was back almost at once. 'It's not ready,' she said, disappointed. 'But it will be ready at two o'clock this afternoon. So we'll have lunch here, shall we, and then go over to the island afterwards? We'll pack up a picnic tea.'

'Right,' said Julian. 'I vote we swim from the beach this morning, then. The tide will be nice and high and we can have some fun with the big breakers.'

'And also keep an eye on Alf to see that he keeps his word about the boat,' said Dick.

So, when all their jobs were finished – and they were very conscientious about them – the five children and the two dogs went off down to the beach. It was a little cooler after the thunder, but not much, and they were quite warm enough in their swimsuits, with jackets to wear after a swim.

'There's nothing nicer than to feel hot and go into the sea and get cool, and then come out and get hot in the sun again, and then go back into the sea,' began Berta.

'You say that every single day!' said George. 'It's like a record! Still, I must say that I agree with you! Come on – let's have a jolly good swim!'

They all plunged through the big, curling breakers, squealing as the water dashed over their bodies, cold and stinging. They chased one another, swam under water and grabbed at the legs swimming there, floated on their backs, and wished they hadn't forgotten to bring the big red rubber ball with them. But nobody wanted to go and fetch it so they had to do without it.

Timmy and Sally raced about in the shallow waves at the edge of the sea. Timmy was a fine swimmer, but Sally didn't much like the water,

so they always played together at the edge.
They really were most amusing to watch.

The dogs were glad when the children came
panting out of the water. They lay down on the
warm beach and Timmy flopped down beside
George. She pushed him away.

'You smell of seaweed,' she said. 'Pooh!'

After a while Dick sat up to pull on his
anorak. He gazed over the bay to where Kirrin
Island lay basking in the sun and gave a sudden
exclamation.

'I say! Look, all of you!'

Everyone sat up. 'There's someone on Kirrin
Island, though I can't see them,' said Dick.
'Someone lying down, looking through binoculars at our beach. Can you see the sun glitter-
ing on the glasses?'

'Yes!' said Julian. 'You're right! Someone
must be using binoculars to examine this beach.
We can't see them as you say – but it's easy
enough to see the sunlight glinting on the
glasses. Gosh, what cheek!'

'Cheek!' said George, her face crimson with

rage. 'It's a lot more than cheek! How *dare* people go on my island and use it to spy on people on the beach? Let's spy on *them*! Let's get our own field-glasses and look through them. We'll see who it is, then!'

'I'll get them,' said Dick and ran off to Kirrin Cottage. He felt worried. It seemed a strange thing to do – to spy on people sitting on the beach round the bay, using binoculars on Kirrin Island. What was the reason?

He came back with the binoculars, and handed them to Julian. 'I think they're gone now, whoever it was,' said Julian. 'I don't mean gone off the island, but gone somewhere else on it. We can't see the glint of the sun on their glasses any more.'

'Well, buck up and see if you can spy anyone through *our* glasses,' said George, impatiently.

Julian adjusted them, and gazed through them earnestly. The island seemed very near indeed when seen through the powerful glasses. Everyone watched him anxiously.

'See anyone?' asked Dick.

'Not a soul,' said Julian, disappointed. He handed the glasses to the impatient George, who put them to her eyes at once. 'Blow!' she said. 'There's not a thing to be seen, not a thing. Whoever it was has gone into hiding somewhere. If it's trippers having a picnic there I'll be absolutely furious. If we see smoke rising we'll know it *is* trippers!'

But no smoke arose. Dick had a turn at looking through the glasses, and he looked puzzled. He took them down from his eyes and turned to the others.

'We ought to be able to see the rabbits running about,' he said. 'But I can't see a single one. Did either of you, Julian and George?'

'Well – now I come to think of it – no, I didn't,' said Julian, and George said the same.

'They were frightened by whoever was there, of course,' said Dick. 'I suppose it will be all right to take Lesley with us when we go to the island this afternoon? I mean – it's just a bit *odd* that anyone should be using the island to spy from.'

'Yes. I see what you mean,' said Julian. 'If it occurred to the kidnappers, whoever they are, that Berta *might* be down here with us, it would be quite a good idea on their part to land on the island and use it as a place from which to spy on the beach. They would guess we would come down to swim every day.'

'Yes. And they would see five children instead of four and would begin to make enquiries about the fifth!' said Dick. 'They would hope actually to *see* Berta on the beach – they've probably got a photograph of her – and they would be looking for a girl with long wavy hair.'

'And there isn't one!' said Anne. 'Mine's not wavy and it's not right down to my shoulders as Lesley's was. How muddled they would be!'

'There's one thing that would tell them that Berta was here though,' said Julian, suddenly. He pointed to Sally.

'Good gracious, yes!' said Dick. 'Sally would give the game away all right! Whew! We'll have to think about all this!'

[11]

On Kirrin Island again

George wanted to get her boat and go across to the island immediately. She was so furious at the thought of anyone else being there without permission that all she wanted to do was to chase them away.

But Julian said no. 'For one thing the boat won't be ready till two,' he said. 'For another thing we've got to consider whether it's a sensible thing to do, to go to the island *if* possible kidnappers are here, on the lookout for Berta – Lesley, I mean.'

'We could go without her,' said George. 'We could leave her safely with Joanna.'

'That would be a foolish thing to do,' said Dick. 'Anyone watching us coming across in the boat would see that one of the five was missing, and would guess at once it was Berta. If we go, *all* of us must go.'

'Actually I think it might be a good thing to do,' said Julian. 'Carry the war right into the enemy's camp, so to speak – if there *are* enemies! It would be a most useful thing if we could see what they are like and give a description to the police. I rather vote we go.'

'Oh *yes*!' said Dick. 'Anyway, we'll have Tim with us. He can deal with any bad behaviour on the part of the intruders!'

'I don't really think it's anybody but trippers,' said Julian. 'I think we're making too much of the whole thing just because someone gazed at the beach through glasses!'

'Remember that I think I saw a light on the island last night,' Anne reminded him.

'Yes, I'd forgotten that,' said Julian, looking at his watch. 'It's almost lunch-time. Let's go and have something to eat, and then fetch the boat. Alf is working on it now. We'll give him a shout to see if it will be ready at two.'

Alf was hailed, and he shouted back. 'Yes! Be

ready sharp at two o'clock, if you want her. I've done one or two little jobs on her besides the rowlock.'

'That's good,' said Dick, and they walked back to Kirrin Cottage. 'Well, we'll soon find out who's on your island, George – and if they are obstinate about leaving, we'll have a little fun with Timmy! He can round them up all right, can't you, Tim!'

'So could Sally,' said Berta. 'Sally's teeth aren't very big, but they're sharp. She once went for a man who accidentally pushed into me, and you should have seen the nips she gave him, all down his leg!'

'Yes. Sally would come in useful,' said Dick. George looked rather scornful. That silly little poodle! she thought. A fat lot of good *she* would be! Timmy's worth a hundred of her!

Joanna had a fine lunch ready for them – ham and salad and new potatoes piled high in a big dish. There were firm red tomatoes from the greenhouse, and lettuces with enormous yellow-green hearts, crisp radishes, and a whole cucumber ready for anyone to cut as they liked. Slices of hard-boiled egg were mixed in with the salad, and Joanna had put in tiny boiled carrots and peas as well.

'What a salad!' said Dick. 'Fit for a king!'

'And big enough for *several* kings!' said Anne. 'How many potatoes, Ju? Small or large ones?'

Julian looked at the piled-up dish. 'Ha – I can really go for these potatoes!' he said. 'I'll have three large and four small.'

'What's for pudding?' asked Berta. 'I like this kind of salad so much that I might not have room for a stodgy sort of pudding.'

'It's fresh raspberries from the garden, sugar and home-made ice-cream,' said Joanna. 'I didn't think you'd want a hot pudding. My sister came to see me this morning, so I got her to pick the raspberries for me.'

'I can't think of a nicer meal than this,' said Berta, helping herself to the salad. 'I really can't. I like your meals better than the ones we have at home in America.'

'We'll turn you into a proper little English

boy before you know where you are!' said Dick.

They told Joanna about what they had seen that morning on the island. She took a grave view of it at once.

'Now you know what your aunt said, Julian,' she said. 'The police have got to have a report of anything suspicious. You'd better ring them up.'

'I will when we've been over to the island and back,' said Julian. 'I don't want to look an ass, Joanna. If it's only harmless trippers who don't know any better there's no need to bother the police. I *promise* to ring the police if we find anything suspicious.'

'I think you ought to ring them *now*,' said Joanna. 'And what's more I don't think you ought to go over to the island if you're suspicious of the people there.'

'We'll have Timmy with us,' said Dick. 'Don't worry.'

'And Sally too,' added Berta at once.

Joanna said no more, but went out to get the raspberries and ice-cream, looking worried. She brought in an enormous glass dish of fresh red raspberries and another dish of creamy-looking ice-cream blocks from the refrigerator.

A sigh of admiration went up from everyone. 'Who could want anything better?' said Dick. 'And that ice-cream – how do you get it like that, Joanna – not too frozen and not too melty? Just how I like it. I do hope some American doesn't get hold of you and whisk you away across the ocean – you're worth your weight in gold!'

Joanna laughed. 'You say such extravagant things, Dick – and all because of an ordinary dish like raspberries and ice-cream. Get along with you! Lesley will tell you there's nothing clever about raspberries and ice-cream.'

'I agree with every word the others say,' said Berta fervently. 'You're wunnerful, you're a honey, you're . . .'

But Joanna had run out of the room, laughing, very pleased. She didn't mind what she did for children like these!

After they had finished lunch, they went

down to the beach. Alf was still with the boat.

'She's finished!' he called. 'You going out in her now? I'll give you a hand down with her, then.'

Soon all five children and the dogs as well were in George's boat. The boys took the oars and began to pull hard towards the island. Timmy stood at the prow as he loved to do, fore-paws on the edge of the boat, looking out across the water.

'He fancies himself as a figurehead,' said Dick. 'Ah, here comes Sally – she wants to be one too. Mind you don't fall overboard, Sally, and get your pretty feet wet. You'll have to learn to swim if you do!'

Sally stood close beside Timmy, and both dogs looked eagerly towards the island – Timmy because he knew there were hundreds of rabbits there, and Sally because for her it was still quite an adventure to go out in a boat like this.

Berta, too, gazed eagerly at the little island as they drew near. She had heard so many tales about it now! She looked especially at the old castle rising up from it. It was in ruins, and Berta thought it must be very old indeed. Like so many Americans, she loved old buildings and old customs. How lucky George was to own an island like this!

Rocks guarded the island, and the sea ran strongly over them, sending up spray and foam.

'How ever are we going to get safely to the shore of the island?' said Berta, rather alarmed at the array of fierce-looking rocks that guarded it.

'There's a little cove we always use,' said George. She was at the tiller, and she steered the boat cleverly in and out of the rocks.

They rounded a low wall of very sharp rocks and Berta suddenly saw the little cove.

'Oh – is that the cove you mean?' she said. 'Why, it's like a little harbour going right up to that stretch of sand!'

There was a smooth inlet of water running between rocks, making a natural little harbour, as Berta said. The boat slid smoothly into the inlet and up to the beach of sand.

Dick leapt out and pulled it up the shore. 'She's safe here,' he told Berta. 'Welcome to Kirrin Island!'

Berta laughed. She felt very happy. What a truly wonderful place to come to!

George led the way up the sandy beach to the rocks behind, and they climbed over them. They stopped at the top, and Berta exclaimed in amazement.

'Rabbits! Thousands of them! Simply thousands. My, my, I never saw such tame ones in my life. Will they let me pick them up?'

'No,' said George. 'They're not as tame as that! They'll run away when we go near – but they will probably not go into their holes. They know us – we've so often been here.'

Sally the poodle was amazed at the rabbits. She couldn't believe her eyes. She stood close beside Berta, staring at the scuttling rabbits, her nose twitching as she tried to get their smell. She simply couldn't understand why Timmy didn't run at them.

Timmy stood quite still beside George, his

tail down, looking very mournful. A visit to Kirrin Island was not such a pleasure to him as to the children, because he wasn't allowed to hunt the rabbits. *What* a waste of rabbits!

'Poor old Tim! Look at him!' said Julian. 'He looks the picture of misery. Look at Sally, too – she's longing to go after the rabbits, but she doesn't think it's good manners to chase them till Timmy does!'

Good manners or not, little Sally could bear it no longer! She suddenly made a dart at a rabbit who had come temptingly near, and it leapt into the air in fright.

'Sally!' called George, in a most peremptory manner. 'NO! You're not to chase my rabbits! Tim – go and fetch her here!'

Timmy went off to Sally and gave a tiny little growl. Sally looked at him in amazement. Could her friend Timmy *really* be growling at her? Timmy began to push himself against her and she found herself shepherded over to George.

'Good dog, Timmy,' said George, pleased to

have shown everyone how obedient he was. 'Sally, you mustn't chase these rabbits, because they are too tame! They haven't learnt to run away properly yet, because not many people come here and frighten them.'

'Whoever was here this morning scared them all right,' said Julian, remembering. 'Gosh, don't let's forget there may be people here. Well – I can't see anyone so far!'

They went cautiously forward, towards the old castle, Timmy running ahead. Then Julian stopped and pointed to the ground.

'Cigarette ends – look! Fresh ones, too. There *are* people here, that's certain. Walk ahead of us, Tim.'

But at that moment there came the sound that Anne had heard the night before – the sound of a motorboat's engine. R-r-r-r-r-r-r!

'They're escaping!' cried Dick. 'Quick, run to the other side of the island! We may see them then!'

[12]

Very suspicious

The children, with the two dogs barking excitedly, ran to the other, seaward side of the island. Great rocks lay out there, and the sea splashed over them.

'There it is – a motorboat!' cried Dick. They all stood and watched the boat riding over the sea at a very fast speed.

'Where are the glasses – did we bring them with us?' said Julian. 'I'd like to focus them on the boat and see if I can read the name – or even see the men in it!'

But the glasses had been left behind at Kirrin Cottage – what a pity!

'They must have anchored their motorboat out there, and somehow clambered inshore over the rocks,' said George. 'It's a dangerous thing to do if you don't know the best way.'

'Yes – and if they came last night, as I think they must have done, because I'm sure now it was the engine of the motorboat that I heard,' said Anne, 'if they came last night, they must have clambered to the shore in the dark. I wonder they managed it!'

'It must have been the light of a lantern or a torch you saw on the island in the night,' said Julian. 'They probably didn't want to be seen arriving on the island, and that's why they went to the other side, the seaward side. I wonder if they *were* men spying to find out if Berta is with us or not.'

'Let's snoop around a bit more and see if we can find anything else,' said Anne. 'The motorboat is almost out of sight now.'

They went back to the other side of the island. Berta looked with awe at the old castle in the middle. Jackdaws circled round a tower, calling loudly. 'Chack-chack-chack!'

'Once upon a time my castle had strong walls all round it,' said George. 'And there were two great towers. One's almost in ruins, as you can see, but the other is fairly good. Come right into the castle.'

Berta followed the others in, struck dumb with awe. To think that this island, and this wonderful old ruined castle, belonged to George! How very, very lucky she was!

She went through a great doorway, and found herself in a dark room, with stone walls enclosing it. Two narrow, slit-like windows brought in all the light there was.

'It's strange and old and mysterious,' said Berta, half to herself. 'It's asleep and dreaming of the old days when people lived here. It doesn't like us being here!'

'Wake up!' said Dick. 'You look quite dopey!'

Berta shook herself and looked round again. Then she went on through the castle and looked at other rooms, some without roofs, some without one or two of their walls. 'It's a honey of a castle!' she said to George. 'A real honey. Wunnerful. WonDERful.'

They wandered all round, showing the awe-struck Berta everything. 'We'll show you the dungeons too,' said George, very pleased to be impressing Berta so much.

'Dungeons! You've got dungeons too – oh, of course, you told me about them,' said Berta. '*Dungeons*! You don't say! My my, I'll never forget this afternoon.'

As they walked over the old courtyard Timmy suddenly growled and stood still, his tail down, the hackles on his neck rising. Everyone automatically stood still too.

'What is it, Tim?' asked George, in a whisper. Timmy's nose was pointing towards the little harbour where they had left their boat.

'There must be someone there,' said Dick. 'Don't say they're going off with our boat!'

George gave a scream. Her boat! Her precious boat! She set off at top speed with Timmy bounding in front.

'Come back, George – there may be danger!' shouted Julian, but George didn't listen. She ran over the rocks that led down to the little harbour beach, and then stopped still in surprise.

Two policemen were walking up the sandy beach! Their boat was drawn up beside George's. They saluted her and grinned.

'Afternoon, George!'

'What are you doing on my island?' demanded George, recognising them. 'Why have you come here?'

'Someone reported suspicious people on the island,' said the first policeman.

'*Who* did?' said George. 'Nobody knew about it but us!'

'I bet I know who reported it,' said Dick suddenly. 'Joanna did! She didn't like us going off by ourselves; she said we ought to telephone the police.'

'That's right,' said the policeman. 'So we came to see for ourselves. Found anyone?'

Julian took command then, and related how they had first seen the cigarette ends, and then heard the motorboat starting up, and had gone to see it roaring away from the island.

'Ah,' said the policeman, profoundly. 'Ah!'

'What do you mean – "AH"?' asked Dick.

'Fred here heard a motorboat somewhere in the bay in the night,' said the first man. 'What was it doing there, I'd like to know?'

'So would we,' said Julian. '*We* saw someone on the island looking through binoculars at the beach this morning.'

This brought forth two more 'Ah's, and the policemen exchanged glances.

'Good thing you've got a couple of dogs with you,' said the one called Fred. 'Well – we'll just have a bit of a look round, and then we'll go back on our beats again. And mind you ring us up next time anything turns up, George, see?'

Off they went together, looking closely at the ground. They found the cigarette ends and picked them up. Then on they went again.

'Let's go back,' said George, in a low voice. 'It spoils things if other people are on the island. I don't want to have a picnic here now. We'll go off in the boat somewhere and have a picnic tea in a cove.'

So they dragged the boat down to the water and jumped in. Sally was very pleased to be back in the boat and ran from end to end wagging her stiff tail in delight. Timmy followed her up and down and got in everyone's way.

'How can I row if you keep on jumping over me, Timmy?' complained Dick. 'Sally, you're just as bad. Berta, are you all right? You look a bit green.'

'It's only excitement and the bumpy bit past the rocks,' said Berta, anxious not to appear seasick in front of the others. 'I'll be all right as soon as we get on to calm waters.'

But she wasn't, so it was regretfully decided that they must row to the shore. They had a lazy tea on the beach, and Berta recovered enough to join in heartily.

'Anyone got room for an ice-cream?' asked Anne. 'Because if so I'll stroll down to the shops and get some. I want to buy a new pair of shoelaces too. One of mine broke this morning.'

Everyone appeared to have room for an ice-cream, so Anne set off with Sally, who wanted to come with her. She went to the draper's and got the laces, and then went to the tea-shop that sold ices.

'Seven, please,' she said. The girl in the shop smiled.

'Seven! You used to ask for five.'

'Yes, I know. But we've got someone staying with us – and another dog,' explained Anne. 'And both dogs like ice-creams.'

'That reminds me – someone was in my shop yesterday asking about your uncle,' said the girl. 'He said he knew him. He wanted to know how many children were staying at Kirrin Cottage, and I thought only the four of you were there – and Timmy, of course. He seemed surprised, and said, surely there was another girl?'

'Good gracious!' said Anne, startled. 'Did he really? How inquisitive! What did you say then?'

'I just said there were two boys and a girl, and a girl who liked to dress as a boy,' said the girl.

Anne was glad to think the shop-girl hadn't

known about Berta. 'What was the man like?' she asked.

'Quite ordinary,' said the girl, trying to remember. 'He wore dark glasses like so many visitors do in the bright sun. I noticed he had a large gold ring on his finger when he paid my bill. That's all I can remember.'

'Well, if anyone else asks you about us, just say we've got a friend staying with us called Lesley,' said Anne. 'Good-bye.'

She went off at top speed, anxious to tell the others. The man in the tea-shop must have been one of those who had gone to the island to watch the beach – he might have been staring at the five of them as they had played together. He must be one of the men now in the motorboat. Anne didn't like it, and it made her feel very uneasy.

She told the others what the shop-girl had said as they sat in the sand and ate their ice-creams. Timmy gobbled his almost at once, and sat patiently watching Sally deal with hers, hoping that she would leave some.

All the four listened intently to Anne's little story. 'That settles it,' said Dick. 'Those men are certainly snooping round trying to find out if Lesley is here.'

'They are getting uncomfortably close,' said Julian.

'Still, your uncle and aunt come back tomorrow,' said Berta. 'We'll tell them, and maybe they'll have some good plan.'

'I hope those men don't know that they are away,' said Dick, uneasily. 'I think we'll have to keep a pretty close watch from now on. I wonder if Berta ought to stay on here with us.'

'See what Father says tomorrow,' said George. So it was decided that nothing should be done except to keep a sharp look-out until George's parents came back. They all went back rather soberly to Kirrin Cottage and told Joanna what had happened on the island.

'You telephoned the police, Joanna!' said Dick, shaking his finger at her.

'I did. And I was right to,' said Joanna. 'And what's more, Lesley's bed is going to be moved away from the window tonight *and* the window's going to be fastened even if we melt, *and* the door will be locked.'

'I'll lend you Timmy, too, if you like,' said George. 'He can sleep in the room with Sally. You ought to be safe then!'

She really only meant it as a joke, but to her surprise Joanna accepted at once. 'Thank you,' she said. 'I'd be glad of Timmy. I feel all of a dither, left on my own like this, and kidnappers closing in on us!'

Julian laughed. 'Oh, it's not so bad as that, Joanna. Only one more night and Uncle Quentin and Aunt Fanny will be back.'

'Oh – I quite forgot to tell you,' said Joanna. 'A letter's arrived. They're staying away a whole week! That's why I feel so scared. A week – well, a lot can happen in a week!'

[13]

A horrid shock

Julian was not very happy to hear that his aunt and uncle were staying away for a week. He picked up the letter. It was addressed to George, but Joanna had opened it.

'Not returning for a week,' it said. 'Complications have arisen. Hope all goes well. Love from Mother.'

There was no address. How annoying! Now Julian couldn't even let them *know* that he was feeling uneasy. He made up his mind to guard Berta every minute! Thank goodness they had Timmy. Nobody would dare to do any kidnapping under Timmy's eye!

He thought it was a good idea to put Timmy in Joanna's room that night with Berta. In fact, if George would agree, it would be best to do that each night. He thought it would not be wise to ask George now, though, because he could see that she was half sorry she had made the offer to Joanna!

Julian was quite fussy that evening. He insisted on the blinds being drawn when they sat down to play cards after their supper. He would not let Berta take Sally out for a run, but took her himself, watching for any strange person as he went down the lane.

'You're making me feel quite scared!' said Anne with a laugh. 'Oh Ju, it's so hot in this room. Do, do let's have the blind up for a few minutes and let some air in. I shall begin to sizzle if we don't. Timmy would soon growl if there was anyone outside.'

'All right,' said Julian and drew up the blind. It was dark outside now, and the light streamed out.

'That's better,' said Anne, mopping her wet forehead. 'Now, whose turn is it? Yours, George.'

They sat round the table, playing. Julian and Berta sat side by side, as Julian was helping her in a new game of cards. She looked exactly like a very earnest little boy, with her straight close-cut fair hair. George sat opposite the window with Dick on one side of her and Anne on the other.

'Your turn, Dick,' said George. 'Do buck up, you're slow tonight.' She sat and waited, looking out of the window into the darkness.

Then suddenly she slammed down her cards and leapt up, shouting. Everyone jumped almost out of their skins.

'What is it, what is it, George?' cried Julian.

'Out there – look – a face! I saw a face peeping in at us – the light of the window just caught it! Timmy, Timmy! Quick, go after him!'

But Timmy wasn't there! Nor was Sally. George called frantically again. 'TIMMY! Come here, quickly. Oh, blow him, that fellow will get away. TIM!'

Timmy came bounding up the hall and into the sitting-room, barking. Sally followed behind.

'Where were you! Idiot!' cried George furiously. 'Jump out of the window – go on – chase him, find him!'

Timmy leapt out of the window and Sally tried to do the same, but couldn't. She barked and yelped, trying again and again to jump out. Joanna came running in, panic-stricken, wondering what was happening.

'*Listen*,' said Julian, suddenly. 'Shut up, Sally. *Listen*!'

They were all suddenly quiet, Sally too. There was the sound of a car being revved up down the lane, and then the sound died down as the car sped away.

'He's got away, whoever he was,' said Dick, and sat down suddenly. 'Gosh, I feel as if I'd been running a mile. You nearly scared the life out of me when you slammed down your cards like that, George, and yelled in my ear.'

Timmy leapt in at the window at that moment and Dick almost jumped out of his skin again. So did everyone else, including Sally, who fled behind the sofa in panic.

'*What's* all this about?' said Joanna, quite fiercely. 'Really!'

George was in a tearing rage – with Timmy of all things! She shouted at the surprised dog and he put his tail down at once.

'Where were you? Why did you slink out of the room into the kitchen? How dare you leave me and go off like that? Just when we needed you! I'm ashamed of you, Timmy – you could have caught that fellow easily!'

'Oh don't,' said Berta, almost in tears. 'Poor Timmy! Don't, George!'

Then George turned on Berta. 'You just let me scold my own dog if he needs it! And you go and scold yours too. I bet Timmy followed your horrid little woolly pet out into the kitchen – it was *her* fault, not his!'

'Shut up, George,' said Julian. 'Your temper gets us nowhere. Calm down and let's hear what you saw. CALM DOWN, I say.'

George stared at him, about to retort with something defiant. Then Timmy gave a small whimper – his heart was almost broken to hear

George – George, his beloved mistress – rave at him in such anger. He had no idea what he had done to displease her.

The whimper brought George to her senses. 'Oh Timmy!' she said, and knelt down and flung her arms round his neck. 'I didn't mean to shout at you. I was so angry because we missed our chance of getting that man who was peeping in at us. Oh Timmy, it's all right, it really is.'

Timmy was extremely glad to hear it. He licked George lavishly, and then lay down by her very soberly. He wished he knew what all the excitement was about.

So did Joanna. She thumped on the table to get everyone's attention, and at last got Julian to explain everything to her. She stared out of the window, half-thinking that she could see faces in the darkness outside. She drew the blind down sharply.

'We'll go to bed,' she said. 'All of us. I don't like this. I shall ring up the police and warn them. Lesley, you come with me straight away now.'

'I think perhaps you're right, Joanna,' said Julian. 'I'll lock up everywhere. Come on, girls.'

Timmy was astonished and upset to find himself handed over to Joanna and Berta. Was George still cross with him then? It was a very, very long time since he had slept away from her at night. He cheered up a little when he saw that Sally was going to be with him, and trotted rather mournfully up the attic stairs to Joanna's room.

Joanna soon got Berta into bed, and then undressed herself. She fastened the window and locked the door. She gave Timmy a rug in a corner, and Sally jumped up on Berta's bed as usual.

'Now we ought to be quite safe!' said Joanna, and settled creakingly into her bed.

On the floor below the two boys followed the same procedure, and so did Anne and George. Doors were locked and windows fastened, though it was a hot night and they were all sure they would be melted by the morning. George couldn't bear to think of Timmy with

Berta and Joanna – especially as she had been so very cross with him. She lay in bed, full of remorse. Dear, kind, faithful Timmy – how *could* she have shouted at him like that?

'Do you suppose Timmy is feeling very upset?' she said, when she and Anne were in bed.

'A bit, perhaps,' said Anne. 'But dogs are very forgiving.'

'I know. That somehow makes it worse,' said George.

'Well, you really *shouldn't* get into such tempers,' said Anne, seizing the opportunity to tell George a few home truths. 'I thought you were getting over the tantrums you used to have. But these hols you've been pretty bad. Because of Berta, I suppose.'

'I wish I could go up and say good night to Timmy,' George began again, after a few minutes' silence.

'Oh for goodness' sake, George!' said Anne, sleepily. 'Do be sensible. You *can't* go and bang on Joanna's door and ask for Timmy – you'd scare them to death!'

Anne fell asleep, but George didn't. Then suddenly she heard the sound of a door being unlocked, and sat up. It sounded as if it came from the attic. Was it Joanna unlocking her door? What did she want?

A cautious little knock came at George's door. 'Who is it?' said George.

'Me. Joanna,' said Joanna's voice. 'I've brought Sally down, George. Timmy keeps trying to get up on Berta's bed to be with Sally, and she simply *can't* go to sleep, her camp-bed is too small to hold all three of them. So will you have Sally, please?'

'Oh blow!' said George, and went to open her door. 'How's Timmy?' she said, in a low voice.

'All right,' said Joanna. 'He'll be annoyed I've taken Sally away. I'm glad to have him up there tonight with all these goings on!'

'Is he – is he happy, Joanna?' asked George, but Joanna had turned away and didn't hear. George sighed. *Why* had she offered to let Joanna and Berta have Timmy tonight of all nights, when she had scolded him so unfairly? Now she had to have this silly little Sally instead!

Sally whimpered. She didn't like being away from Berta, and she was not fond of George. She wriggled out of George's arms and ran round the room, still whimpering.

Anne woke up with a jump. 'Whatever's going on?' she said. 'Why – it's Sally in the room! How did *she* get here?'

George told her, sounding very cross. 'Well, I hope she'll settle down,' said Anne. 'I don't want her to whimper and run round the bedroom all night long.'

But Sally wouldn't settle down. Her whimpering became louder, and when she took a flying jump on to George's bed and landed right on George's middle, the girl had had enough of it. She sat up and spoke in a fierce whisper.

'You little idiot! I'm jolly well going to take you downstairs and put you into Timmy's kennel!'

'Good idea,' said Anne, sleepily. George

picked up the lively little poodle and went out of the room, shutting the door softly. Anne promptly went to sleep again.

George crept down the stairs and went to the garden door. She undid it and walked out in dressing-gown and pyjamas, her curly hair all tousled, carrying the whimpering little dog.

Suddenly she felt Sally stiffen in her arms, and growl. Grrrrrr! George stood quite still. What had Sally heard?

Then things happened very suddenly indeed. A torch was flashed in her face, and before she could cry out, a cloth was thrown over her head so that she could not make a sound.

'This is the one!' said a low voice. 'The one with curly hair! And this is her dog, the poodle. Put him in that kennel, quick, before he barks the place down.'

Sally, too scared even to growl, was pushed into the kennel and the door shut on her. George, struggling and trying vainly to call out, was lifted off her feet and carried swiftly down to the front gate.

The garden door swung creaking to and fro in the night wind. Sally whimpered in her kennel. But no one heard either door or dog. Everyone in Kirrin Cottage was sound asleep!

[14]
Where is George?

Next morning, about half past seven, Joanna went downstairs as usual. Berta was awake and decided to fetch Sally from George's bedroom. She put on her dressing-gown and padded downstairs with Timmy behind her, to George's room on the floor below. The door was shut, and she knocked gently.

'Come in,' said Anne's sleepy voice. 'Oh, it's you, Berta.'

'Yes. I've come for Sally,' said Berta. 'Hallo – where's George?'

Anne looked at the empty bed beside hers. 'I don't know. The last thing I heard of her was in the middle of the night when we got cross because Sally wouldn't settle down, and George said she would take her down to the kennel.'

'Oh. Well, probably George has gone down

to fetch her back,' said Berta. 'I'll go up and dress. It's a heavenly morning again. Are you going to swim before breakfast, because if so I'll just put on my swimsuit.'

'Yes. I think we might today – we're nice and early,' said Anne, scrambling out of bed. 'Go and wake the boys. Timmy, go down and find George.'

Dick and Julian were awake, and quite ready for a before-breakfast swim. Anne joined them as they went downstairs. Berta had already gone down and had discovered Sally in the kennel, most excited to see her. She pranced round barking happily.

Timmy came up to the children, looking puzzled. He had hunted everywhere for George and hadn't found her. 'Woof,' he said to Anne. 'Woof, woof!' It was just as if he were saying, 'Please, where is George?'

'Haven't you found George yet?' said Anne in surprise. She called to Joanna. 'Joanna, where's George? Has she gone down to swim already?'

'I haven't seen her,' said Joanna. 'But I expect she has because the garden door was open when I came down, and I guessed one of you had gone for an early swim.'

'Well, George must be down on the beach, then,' said Anne, feeling rather puzzled. Why hadn't George woken her and told her to come too?

Soon all four were on the beach with the two dogs, Sally very happy to be with Berta again, and Timmy very downcast and puzzled. He stood staring up the beach and down, looking quite lost.

'I can't see George anywhere,' said Dick, suddenly feeling scared. 'She's not in the sea.'

They all gazed over the water, but no one was swimming that morning. Anne turned to Julian in sudden panic.

'Ju! Where is she?'

'I wish I knew,' said Julian, anxiously. 'She's not here. And she hasn't gone out in her boat – it's over there. Let's go back to the house.'

'I don't think George would have gone for an

early swim without telling me,' said Anne. 'And I also think I would surely have woken up just for a moment when she came back after taking Sally down – oh Julian, I think something happened when she went downstairs with Sally late last night!'

'I've been thinking that too,' said Julian soberly. 'We know that there was someone about last night, because George saw a face outside the window. Let's go back to the house and see if we can spot anything to help us near the garden door or the kennel.'

They went back, looking very anxious. As soon as they began to look about near the kennel, Anne gave an exclamation and bent down. She picked up something and held it out to the others without a word.

'What is it – gosh, it's the cord off George's dressing-gown!' said Dick, startled. 'That proves it! George was caught when she came down to put Sally into her kennel!'

'They must have thought she was *me*,' said Berta, in tears. 'You see – she was carrying Sally and they know Sally belongs to me – and she has short hair too and dresses like a boy in the daytime.'

'That's it!' said Julian. 'Actually you *look* like a boy in your boys' things, but George doesn't – and the kidnappers are looking for a girl dressed as a boy – and George fitted the bill nicely, especially as she had the poodle with her. She's been kidnapped!'

'And will my father get the usual note to say his daughter will not be harmed if he does what the kidnappers want, and hands over this new secret?' said Berta.

'Sure to,' said Julian.

'What will they say when they know they've got George, not me?' asked Berta.

'Well . . .' said Julian, considering. 'I really don't know. They might try the same thing with Uncle Quentin, but of course, he hasn't got the figures they want.'

'What about *Berta* now?' asked Dick. 'Once those men find they've got the wrong girl, they'll be after Berta in a trice!'

'George won't tell them,' said Anne, at once. 'She'll know that Berta would be in immediate danger if she did tell them – so she'll say nothing as long as she can.'

'Would she really?' said Berta, wonderingly. 'She's brave, isn't she? She could get herself set free at once if she said she wasn't me, and proved it. Gee, she's wunnerful if she could do a thing like that!'

'George is brave all right,' said Dick. 'As brave as anything when she's in a fix! Julian, let's go and tell Joanna. We've GOT to make up our minds what we are going to do about this – and also, we *must* safeguard Berta somehow. She can't possibly wander round with us any more.'

Berta all at once began to feel scared. George's sudden disappearance had brought home to her the very real danger she was in. She had not really believed in it before. She looked over her shoulder and all round and about as if she expected someone to pounce on her.

'It's all right, Berta – there's no one here at

present!' said Dick, comfortingly. 'But you'd better get indoors, all the same. I don't *think* George would give away the fact that she wasn't you, but the men might find out some other way – and back they would come, hot-foot!'

Berta raced indoors as if someone was chasing her! Julian shut and locked the garden door and called Joanna.

They had a very serious conference indeed. Joanna was horrified. She wept when she heard that George must have been kidnapped in the middle of the night. She wiped her eyes with her apron.

'I *said* we must lock the doors and the windows, I *said* we must tell the police – and then George has to go down all by herself into the garden!' she said. 'If only she hadn't had the poodle with her! No wonder they thought she was Berta, with Sally in her arms.'

'Listen, Joanna,' said Julian. 'There are a lot of things to do. First we must tell the police. Then somehow we must contact Aunt Fanny and Uncle Quentin – it's so like them not to give us an address! Then we must most certainly decide about Berta. She must be well hidden away somewhere.'

'Yes. That's certain,' said Joanna wiping her eyes again. She sat and thought for a minute, and then her face lightened.

'I know where we could hide her!' she said. 'You remember Jo – the little traveller girl you've had one or two adventures with?'

'Yes,' said Julian. 'She lives with your cousin now, doesn't she?'

'She does,' said Joanna. 'And my cousin would have Berta straight away if she knew about this. She lives in a quiet little village where nothing ever happens, and nobody would think anything of my cousin having a child to stay with Jo. She often does.'

'It really seems an idea,' said Dick. 'Doesn't it, Julian? We've simply *got* to get Berta away at once. We could trust Jo to look after her, too – Jo's as sharp as a packet of needles!'

'The police would know, too,' said Julian,

'and would keep an eye on her as well. Joanna, can you ring up and get a taxi and take Berta now, this very minute?'

'It'll be a surprise for my cousin, my arriving this time of the morning,' said Joanna, standing up and taking off her apron, 'but she's quick on the uptake, and she'll do it, I know. Lesley, get a few things together – nothing posh, mind, like your silver hairbrush.'

Berta looked extremely scared by now, and was inclined to refuse to go. Julian put his arm round her.

'Look,' he said, 'I bet George is holding her tongue so that we can get you away in safety before the men tumble to the fact that they've got the wrong boy – so you can play up, too, can't you, and be brave?'

'Yes,' said Berta, looking up at Julian's kind, serious face. 'I'll do what you say – but what's this Jo like? Joanna said she was a little traveller girl. I might not like her.'

'You'll like this one all right,' said Julian. 'She's a pickle and a scamp and a scallywag –

but her heart's in the right place – isn't it, Joanna?'

Joanna nodded. She had always been fond of the reckless, cheeky little Jo, and it was she who had found a home for her when Jo's father had had to go to prison. 'Come on, Lesley,' she said. 'We must hurry. Julian, is she to go as a girl or a boy now – we've got to decide that too.'

'A girl, please, please, a girl!' said Berta, at once.

Julian considered. 'Yes, I think you're right,' he said. 'You'd better be a girl now – but for goodness' sake don't call yourself Berta yet.'

'She can be Jane,' said Joanna, firmly. 'That's a nice name, but quite ordinary enough for nobody to notice. Berta is too noticeable a name. Come along, now – we'll have to pick out your simplest clothes!'

'Now I'll ring up the police,' said Julian, 'and also ring for a taxi.'

'No, don't get a taxi for us,' said Joanna. 'I don't want to arrive at my cousin's little cottage in a taxi, and make everyone stare! Jane and I will catch the market bus and people will think I'm going off to market. We can get another bus there, that will take us almost all the way to my cousin's. We've only to walk down the lane then.'

'Good idea,' said Julian, and went to the telephone. He got hold of the police sergeant, and told his tale. The man showed not the least excitement but took down quickly all that Julian told him. 'I'll be up in ten minutes,' he said. 'Wait in till I come.'

Julian put down the receiver. Dick and Anne were watching him with troubled eyes. What was happening to George? Was she frightened – or furious – or perhaps hurt?

Timmy was absolutely miserable. He knew by now that something had happened to George. He had gone a dozen times to the place where her dressing-gown cord had been found, and had sniffed round disconsolately.

Sally knew he was unhappy and trotted after him soberly. When he lay down she lay down beside him. When he got up, she got up too. It would have been amusing to watch if anyone had felt like being amused. But nobody felt that way!

Footsteps came up the path. 'The police!' said Julian. 'They've not been long!'

[15]

Discoveries in the wood

The sergeant had come and also a constable. Anne felt comforted when she saw the big, solid, responsible looking men. Julian took them into the sitting-room, and began to tell all that had happened.

In the middle of it there came the sound of footsteps racing down the stairs, and up the hall. 'We're just off!' shouted Joanna's voice. 'Can't stop to say good-bye, or we shall miss the bus!'

Down the garden path rushed Joanna, carrying a small suitcase of her own, which she had lent Berta, because Berta's was too grand. In it she had packed the very simplest of Berta's clothes, but secretly she had thought that she would tell her cousin to dress Berta in some of Jo's things.

Berta ran behind her – a different Berta now, wearing a dress instead of jeans and jumper. She waved to the others as she went, trying to smile.

'Good old Berta!' said Dick. 'She's got quite a lot in her, that kid.'

'In fact, she's quite a honey!' said Julian, trying to make Anne smile.

'What's all that?' said the sergeant, in surprise, nodding his head towards the front path, down which Joanna and Berta had just rushed.

Julian explained. The sergeant frowned. 'You shouldn't have arranged about that till you'd consulted us,' he said. Julian was quite taken aback.

'Well, you see,' he said, 'it seemed to me that I must get Berta out of the house and hidden away at once in case the kidnappers realised quickly that they'd got the wrong girl.'

'That's so,' said the sergeant. 'Still, you *should* have consulted us. It seems quite a good idea to put her in that quiet village, with Jo to see to her – she's sharp, that Jo. I wouldn't put it past her to hoodwink the kidnappers any day!

But this is a very serious business, you realise, Julian — it can't be dealt with by children.'

'Can you get George back?' asked Anne, breaking in with the question she had been longing to ask ever since the police came.

'Maybe,' said the sergeant. 'Now I'll get in touch with your aunt and uncle, Julian, and with Mr Elbur Wright, and—'

The telephone rang just then and Anne answered it. 'It's for you, Sergeant,' she said, and he took the receiver from her.

'Ha. Hm. Just so. Yes, yes. Right. Ha. Hm.' The sergeant replaced the receiver and went back to Julian and the others. 'News has just come in that the kidnappers have contacted Mr Elbur Wright, and told him they've got his daughter Berta,' he said.

'Oh! And have they demanded that he shall tell them the secret figures he knows?' asked Julian.

The sergeant nodded. 'Yes. He's almost off his head with shock! He's promised to give them all they want. Very foolish!'

'Gosh – you'd better tell him it's *not* Berta they've got, but George,' said Dick. 'Then he'll sit tight!'

The sergeant frowned. 'Now, you leave this to *us*,' he said, ponderously. 'You'll only hinder us if you interfere or try meddling on your own. You just sit back and take things easy.'

'What! With George kidnapped and in danger?' exploded Dick. 'What are *you* going to do to get her back?'

'Now, now!' said the sergeant, annoyed. 'She is in no danger – she's not the person they want. They will free her as soon as they realise that.'

'They won't,' said Dick. 'They'll get on to her father and make *him* give up a few secrets!'

'Well, that will give us a little more time to find these men,' said the irritating sergeant, and he stood up, big and burly in his navy blue uniform. 'Let me know *at once* if you have any other news, and please do not try to meddle. I assure you that we know the right things to do.'

He went out with the constable. Julian groaned. 'He doesn't see that this is *urgent*. It's so complicated too – the wrong girl kidnapped, the wrong father informed, the right one not at all inclined to give up powerful secrets – and poor old George not knowing what is happening!'

'Well, thank goodness we got *Berta* out of the way,' said Dick. 'Anne, you look funny – are you all right?'

'Yes. I think I'm just shocked – and oh dear, I feel awfully *empty*!' said Anne, pressing her tummy.

'Gosh – we forgot all about breakfast!' said Dick, staring at the clock. 'And it's almost ten o'clock now! What *have* we been doing all this time? Come on, Anne – get us some food, there's a dear. We shall all feel better then.'

'I'm so sorry for poor old Timmy and little Sally,' said Anne, going into the kitchen. 'Timmy, darling, don't look at me like that! I don't know *where* your beloved George is, or I'd take you to her straight away! And Sally, you will have to put up with me for a little while, because although I do know where Berta is, I can't possibly take you there!'

They were soon sitting down to a plain breakfast of boiled eggs, toast and butter. It seemed strange only to be three. Dick tried to make conversation, but the other two were very quiet. Timmy sat under the table with his head on Anne's foot, and Sally stood beside her, paws on her knee. Anne comforted both the mournful dogs as best she could!

After breakfast Anne went to wash up and make the beds, and the boys went outside to have another look at the place where George's dressing-gown cord had been found. Sally and Timmy came with them.

Timmy sniffed around a good bit, and then, nose to ground went down the garden path to the front gate, and then pushed it open and went through it. Nose to ground he went down the lane and turned off into a little path.

'Dick – he's following some kind of trail,' said Julian. 'I'm certain it's George's. Even if somebody *carried* her away, Timmy is clever enough to know George might be with him – he might just get a whiff of her.'

'Come on – let's follow Timmy,' said Dick, and the boys and Sally went along the little path, hot on Timmy's track. Timmy began to run, and Dick called to him.

'Not so fast, old boy! We're coming too.'

But Timmy did not slow down. Whatever it was he smelt, the scent was quite strong. The boys ran after him, beginning to feel excited.

But soon Timmy came to a full stop, in a little clearing in the wood. Dick and Julian panted up to where he was nosing round. He looked up at them forlornly. Evidently the scent came to an end there.

'Car-tracks!' said Dick, pointing down to where the dampish grass under a great oak tree had been rutted with big tyre-marks. 'See? The men brought a car here and hid it, then crept through the woods to Kirrin Cottage, and waited for a chance to get Berta. They got George instead – but they wouldn't have got *anyone* if only George hadn't been ass enough to take Sally to the kennel! The house was well and truly locked and bolted!'

Julian was looking at the wheel-tracks. 'These tracks were made by very big tyres,' he said. 'It was a car – and I rather think these are *American* tyre-marks. I can check that when I get back – I'll go and ask Jim at the local garage – he'll know. I'll just sketch one quickly.'

He took out a notebook and pencil and began to sketch. Dick bent down and looked more carefully at the tracks. 'There is quite a lot of criss-crossing of tracks,' he said. 'I think the men came here and waited. Then, when they got George, they must have pushed her into the car, and turned it to go back the way they came – see, the tracks lead down that wide path over there. They made a mess of the turning, though – bumped into this tree, look – there's a mark right across it.'

'Where?' said Julian at once. 'Yes – a bright blue mark – the car was that colour – or the wings were, at any rate. Well, that's something we've learnt! A big blue car, probably American. Surely the police could trace that?'

'Timmy's still nosing round, the picture of misery,' said Dick. 'Poor old Tim. I expect he knows George was pushed into a car just there. Hallo – he's scraping at something!'

They ran to see what it was. Timmy was trying to get at some small object embedded in a car-rut. Evidently, in turning, the car had run over whatever it was.

Dick saw something broken in half – something green. He picked up the halves. 'A comb! Did George have a little green comb like this?'

'Yes. She did,' said Julian. 'She must have thrown it down when she got near to the car – to show us she was taken here – hoping we would find it. And look, what's that?'

It was a handkerchief hanging on a gorse bush. Julian ran to it. It had the initial G on it in blue.

'Yes, it's George's,' he said. 'She's got six of these, all with different-coloured initials. She must have thrown this out too. Quick, Dick, look for anything else she might have thrown out of the car, while they were trying to turn it.

They would probably put her in the back, and she would just have had a chance to throw out anything she had in her dressing-gown pocket, to let us know she was here if we came along this way.'

They searched for a long time. Timmy found one more thing, again embedded in a car-rut – a boiled sweet wrapped in cellophane paper.

'Look!' said Dick, picking it up. 'One of the sweets we all had the other night! George must have had one in her dressing-gown pocket! If only she had had a pencil and bit of paper – she might have had time to write a note too!'

'That's an idea!' said Julian. 'We'll hunt even more carefully!'

But although they searched every bit of ground and every bush, there was no note to be found. It was too much to hope for!

'Let's just follow the car-tracks and make sure they reached the road,' said Julian. So they followed them down the wide woodland path.

At the side a little way along, a piece of paper blew in the wind, hopping an inch or two each

time the breeze flapped it. Dick picked it up –
and then looked at Julian excitedly.

'She *did* have time to write a note! This is her
writing. But there's only one word, look –
whatever does it mean?'

Julian and Dick frowned over the piece of
paper. Yes, it was George's writing – the G was
exactly like the way she always wrote the big G
at the beginning of her signature.

'Gringo,' read Julian. 'Just that one word.
Gringo! What *does* it mean? It's something she
heard them say, I suppose – and she just had
time to write it and throw out the paper.
Gringo! Timmy, what does *Gringo* mean?'

[16]
Jo!

Dick and Julian went back to Kirrin Cottage with the two disconsolate dogs. They showed Anne the things they had found, and she too puzzled over the word Gringo.

'We'll have to tell the police what you have discovered,' she said. 'They might trace the car, and they might know who or what Gringo is.'

'I'll telephone them now,' said Julian. 'Dick, you go down to the garage with this sketch of the tyre-mark, and see if it's an American design.'

The police were interested but not helpful. The sergeant said he would send his constable up to examine the place where the car had stood in the clearing, and gave it as his opinion that the bit of paper wasn't much use, as the boys had found it some way from the turning place of the car.

'Your cousin wouldn't be able to throw it out of the window once the car was going,' he said. 'There would be sure to be someone in the back with her. The only reason she could throw things out at the clearing would be because the second fellow – and there would certainly be two – would be guiding the other man in the turning of the car.'

'The wind might have blown the note along the path,' said Julian. 'Anyway, I've given you the information.'

It was a very miserable day, although the sun shone down warmly, and the sea was blue and most inviting. But nobody wanted to swim, nobody really wanted to do anything but talk and talk about George and what had happened, and where she could be at that moment!

Joanna came back in time to get their lunch, and was pleased to find that Anne had done the potatoes and prepared a salad, and that Dick had managed to pick some raspberries. They were very glad to see Joanna. She was someone sensible and comforting and matter-of-fact.

'Well, Jane is now safely in my cousin's cottage,' she said. 'She was very miserable but I told her she must smile and play about, else the neighbours would wonder about her. I put her into some of Jo's clothes – they fitted her all right. Hers are too expensive-looking, and would make people talk!'

They told Joanna what they had discovered in the clearing that morning. She took the note and looked at it. 'Gringo!' she said. 'That's a funny word – sounds like a traveller word to me. It's a pity Jo isn't here – she might tell us what it means!'

'Did you see Jo?' asked Dick.

'No. She was out shopping,' said Joanna, lifting the lid to look at the potatoes. 'I only hope she gets on with Jane all right. Really, it's getting very difficult to remember that child's change of names!'

The only fresh news that day was a worried telephone call from Aunt Fanny. She was shocked and amazed at the news she had heard. 'Your uncle has collapsed!' she said. 'He has been working very hard, you know, and now this news of George has been quite the last straw. He's very ill. I can't leave him at the moment – but anyway we couldn't *do* anything! Only the police can help now. To think those horrible men took George by mistake!'

'Don't worry too much, Aunt Fanny,' said Julian. 'We've hidden Berta away safely, and I expect the men will free George as soon as she tells them she's the wrong girl.'

'If she *does* tell them!' said Dick, under his breath. 'She might not, for Berta's sake, for a few days at any rate!'

Everyone went miserable to bed that night. Anne took Timmy and Sally with her, for both were so forlorn that she couldn't bear to do anything else. Timmy wouldn't eat anything at all, and Anne was worried about him.

Julian could not go to sleep. He tossed and turned, thinking about George. Hot-tempered, courageous, impatient, independent George! He worried and worried about her, wishing he could *do* something!

A small stone suddenly rattled against his window! He sat up, alert at once. Then something fell right into the room, and rolled over the floor. Julian was at the window in a trice. Who was throwing pebbles at his window?

He leaned out. A voice came up to him at once. 'Is it you, Dick?'

'Jo! What *are* you doing here?' said Julian, startled. 'It's Julian speaking. Dick's asleep. I'll wake him, and let you in.'

But he did not need to go down and let Jo in. She was up a tree outside the window and across some ivy and on his window-sill before he had even shaken Dick awake!

She slid into the room. Julian switched on his light. There was Jo, sitting at the end of Dick's bed, the familiar cheeky grin on her face! She was very brown, but still showed her freckles, and her hair was as short and curly as ever.

'I *had* to come,' she said. 'When I got home from shopping, there was this girl Jane. She told me all about how George had been captured in mistake for her – and when I said to her, "You go straight away and say you're safe and sound, and it's all a mistake, and George has got to be set free!" she wouldn't! She just wouldn't! All she did was to sit and cry. Little coward!'

'No, no, Jo,' said Dick, and tried to explain everything to the indignant girl. But he could not convince her.

'If I was that girl Jane I wouldn't let someone stay kidnapped because of *me*,' she said. 'I don't like her, she's silly. And I'm supposed to keep an eye on her! Phoo! Not me! I'd *like* her to be kidnapped, the way she's behaving about George.'

Julian looked at Jo. She was very, very loyal to the Five, and proud of being their friend. She had been in two adventures with them now, a crafty little traveller girl, but a very loyal friend. Her father was in prison, and she was living with a cousin of Joanna's, and, for the first time in her life, going to school to learn lessons!

'Listen, Jo – we've found out a few more things since Berta – I mean Lesley – no, I don't, I mean Jane . . .'

'What *do* you mean?' said Jo, puzzled.

'I mean Jane,' said Julian. 'We've found out something else since Joanna parked Jane with her cousin this morning.'

'Go on, tell me,' said Jo. 'Have you found out where George is? I'll go and break in and get her out, if you have!'

'Oh Jo – it's no use just being fierce,' said Dick. 'Things are not so easy as all that!'

'George threw out a bit of paper with this written on it,' said Julian, and he put it before Jo. 'See? Just that one word – "Gringo". Does it mean anything to you?'

'Gringo?' said Jo. 'That rings a bell! Let's see now – *Gringo*!'

She frowned as she thought hard. Then she nodded. 'Oh yes, I remember now. A fair came to the town a few weeks back – the big town not far from our village. It was called Gringo's Great Fair.'

'Where did it go?' asked Dick, eagerly.

'It was going to Fallenwick, then to Granton,' said Jo. 'I made friends with the boy whose father owned the roundabout, and gosh, I had about a hundred free rides.'

'You *would*!' said both boys together, and Jo grinned.

'Do you suppose this Gringo, who runs the Fair, could be anything to do with the name Gringo that George wrote on this paper?' said Julian.

'*I* dunno!' said Jo. 'But if you like I can go and find the fair and get hold of Spiky – that's the roundabout boy – and see if I can find out anything. I know Spiky said Gringo was a real horror to work for, and thought himself as good as a lord!'

'Had he a car – a big car?' asked Dick, suddenly.

'I dunno that either,' said Jo. 'I can find out. Here – I'll go *now*! You lend me a bike and I'll bike to Granton!'

'Certainly not,' said Julian, startled at the idea of Jo biking the twelve miles to Granton in the middle of the night.

'All right,' said Jo, rather sulkily. 'I just

thought you'd like me to help. It might be that this Gringo has got George somewhere. He was the kind of fellow who was a go-between, if you know what I mean.'

'How?' asked Dick.

'Well, Spiky said that if anyone wanted something dirty done, this Gringo just held out his hand, and if a wad of notes was put into it, he'd do it, and nothing said!' said Jo.

'I see,' said Julian. 'Hm – it sounds as if kidnapping would be right up his street, then.'

Jo laughed scornfully. 'That would be nothing to him – chicken-feed. Come on, Julian – let me have a lend of your bike.'

'NO,' said Julian. 'Thanks very, very much, but I'm not letting anyone ride to a fair in the middle of the night to find out if a fellow called Gringo has anything to do with George. I can't believe he has, either – it's too far-fetched.'

'All right. But you *asked* me if the name meant anything to me,' said Jo, sounding offended. 'Anyway, it's a common enough nickname in the circus world and the fair world too. There's probably a thousand Gringos about!'

'It's time you went back home,' said Julian, looking at his watch. 'And be decent to Berta – I mean Jane – *please*, Jo. You can come over tomorrow to see if there's any more news. How did you get here tonight, by the way?'

'Walked,' said Jo. 'Well – ran, I mean. Not by the roads, though – they take too long. I go like the birds do – as straight as I can, and it's *much* shorter!'

Dick had a sudden picture of the valiant little Jo speeding through woods and fields, over hills and through valleys, as straight as a crow flying homewards. How did she find her way like that? He knew *he* would never be able to!

Jo slipped out over the window-sill, and down the tree, as easily as a cat. 'Bye!' she said. 'See you soon.'

'Give our love to Jane,' whispered Dick.

'Shan't!' said Jo, much too loudly, and disappeared.

Julian switched out the light. 'Whew!' he

said, 'I always feel as if I've been blown about by a strong, fresh wind when I see Jo. What a girl! Fancy wanting to ride all the way to Granton tonight, after running all the way here from Berta's!'

'Yes. I'm jolly glad you wouldn't let her take your bike,' said Dick. 'It's a good thing she wouldn't dare to disobey you!'

He got into bed – and just at that very moment the two boys heard a loud ringing noise. Dick sat up straight away.

'Well I'm blowed!' he said. 'The little wretch!'

'What's up?' said Julian, and then he too realised what the ringing was – a bicycle bell. Yes, a bell rung loudly and defiantly by someone cycling swiftly along the sea-road towards Granton!

'It's *Jo!*' said Dick. 'And she's taken *my* bike! I know its bell. Gosh, won't I rub her face in the mud when I get hold of her!'

Julian gave a loud guffaw. 'She's a monkey, a gallant, plucky, loyal, aggravating *monkey*.

What a cheek she's got! She didn't dare to take *my* bike when I'd said no – so she took yours. Well – we can't do a thing about it now. What that roundabout boy is going to think when he's woken in the middle of the night by Jo, I cannot imagine.'

'He's probably used to her,' said Dick. 'Well, let's go to sleep. I wonder if George is asleep or awake? I hate to think of her a prisoner somewhere.'

'I bet Timmy hates it more than we do,' said Dick, hearing a long-drawn whimper from the next room. 'Poor old Tim. He can't go to sleep either!'

Dick and Julian managed to go to sleep at last, both thinking of a speedy little figure on a bicycle, racing through the night to ask questions of a roundabout boy called Spiky!

[17]
To Gringo's Fair

At half past seven next morning Joanna came running upstairs to Julian's bedroom, a piece of paper in her hand. She knocked on the door.

'Julian! A dirty little note was on the front door mat when I got down this morning. It's folded over with your name on the outside.'

Julian was out of bed in a trice. A note from the kidnappers perhaps? No – it couldn't be. They wouldn't write to *him*!

It was from Jo! She had scribbled it so badly that Julian could hardly read it.

'Julian, I saw Spiky, he's coming to the beach at eleven. I took Dick's bike to go home on. I will bring it back at eleven, don't be too cross. Jo.'

'Little scallywag,' said Dick. 'I hope she hasn't damaged my bike in any way.'

Jo hadn't. She had actually managed to find time to clean it before she left home, and arrived with it so bright and gleaming that Dick hadn't the heart to scold her!

She was early so she came to the house instead of the beach. She rode through the gate and up the front path and Timmy ran to greet her with a volley of delighted barks. He liked Jo – in fact he really loved the little girl. She certainly had a way with animals! Sally followed, dancing on her tiptoes as usual, ready to welcome as a friend anyone that Timmy liked.

Dick hailed Jo from the front door as she came up. 'Hallo, bicycle-stealer! My word, what's happened to my bike – have you spring-cleaned it?'

Jo grinned, looking at Dick warily. 'Yes. I'm sorry I took it, Dick.'

'You're not a bit sorry – but I'll forgive you,' said Dick, grinning too. 'So you got to the fair safely after all?'

'Oh yes – and I woke up Spiky – he wasn't half surprised,' said Jo. 'But his pa was sleeping in the same caravan as he was, so I couldn't say much. I just told him to be on Kirrin Beach at eleven. Then I rode back home. I ought to have left your bike on the way back, but I was a bit tired, so I rode home, instead of walking.'

'You can't have had much sleep last night,' said Julian, looking at the sunburnt girl with her untidy curly hair. 'Hallo – who's that?'

A short, plump boy was hurrying past the gate. He had a mop of black hair which stuck up into curious spikes of hair at the crown.

'Oh – that's Spiky!' said Jo. 'He's on time, isn't he? He's called Spiky because of his hair. You won't believe it, but he spends a fortune on hair-oil, trying to make those spiky bits go flat. But they won't.' She called loudly.

'Spiky! Hey, SPIKY!'

Spiky turned at once. He had a pleasant, rather lop-sided face, and eyes as black as currants. He stood staring at Jo and the boys. 'I'm just off to the beach,' he said.

'Right. We're coming too,' said Jo, and she

and the boys went to join him. They met the ice-cream man on the way and Julian bought an ice-cream for each of them.

'Coo – thanks,' said Spiky, pleased. He was rather shy of Dick and Julian, and wondered very much why he had been asked to come.

They sat down on the beach. 'I wasn't half scared when you came tapping at the window last night,' he said to Jo, licking his ice-cream with a very pink tongue. 'What's it all about?'

'Well,' said Julian, cautiously, 'we're interested in somebody called Gringo.'

'Old Gringo?' said Spiky. 'A lot of people're interested in Gringo. Do you know what we say at the fair? We say Gringo ought to put up a notice. "All dirty work done here!" He's a bad lot, Gringo is – but he pays us well, even if he makes us work like slaves.'

'He owns the fair, doesn't he?' said Julian, and Spiky nodded. 'I expect he uses it as a cover for all his other, bigger jobs,' Julian said to Dick. He looked at the plump, black-eyed boy, wondering how far he could trust him. Jo saw the look and knew what it meant.

'He's all right,' she said, nodding towards Spiky. 'You can say what you like. He's an oyster, he is. Aren't you, Spiky?'

Spiky grinned his lop-sided grin. Julian decided to trust him, and speaking in a low voice that really thrilled Spiky, he told him about the kidnapping of George. Spiky's eyes nearly fell out of his head.

'Coo!' he said. 'I bet old Gringo's at the bottom of that. Last week he went off up to London – he told my pa he was on to a big job – an American job, he said it was.'

'Yes – it sounds as if it all fits,' said Julian. 'Spiky, this kidnapping happened the night before last. Did anything unusual occur in the fair camp, do you know? It must have happened in the middle of the night.'

Spiky considered. He shook his head. 'No – I don't think so. Gringo's big double-caravan is still there – so he can't have gone. He had it moved right away from the camp yesterday morning – said there was too much noise for his old ma, who lives in his posh caravan and looks after him. We was all glad it was moved – now he can't spy on us so easily!'

'I suppose you—' began Julian, and then stopped as Dick gave an exclamation.

'I've got an idea!' he said. 'Suppose that caravan was moved for *another* reason – suppose someone was making a row inside the van – someone shouting for help, say! Gringo would have to move it away from the rest of the camp in case that someone was heard.'

There was a pause, and then Spiky nodded. 'Yes. It could be,' he said. 'I've never known Gringo move his caravan away from the camp before. Shall I do a bit of snooping for you?'

'Yes,' said Julian, excited. 'My word – it *would* be a bit of luck if we could find George so quickly – and so near us too! A fair camp would be a fine place to hide her, of course. Thank goodness we found that bit of paper with "Gringo" written on it!'

'Let's all go to the fair this afternoon,' said

Dick. 'Timmy too. He'd smell out George at once.'

'Hadn't we better tell the police first?' said Julian. At once Spiky and Jo got up in alarm. Spiky looked as if he were going to run away immediately!

'Don't you get the police, Julian!' said Jo urgently. 'You won't get anything more out of Spiky, if you do. Not a thing.'

'I'm going,' said Spiky, still looking terrified.

'No you're not,' said Dick, and caught hold of him. 'We shan't go to the police. They might frighten off Gringo and make him smuggle George away at once. I've no doubt he has plans to do so at any minute. We shan't say a word, so sit down and be sensible.'

'You can believe him,' Jo told Spiky. 'He's straight, see?'

Spiky sat down, still looking wary. 'If you're coming to the fair, come at four,' he said. 'It's half-day closing today for the towns around, and the place will be packed. If you want to do any snooping, you won't be noticed in that crowd.'

'Right,' said Julian. 'We'll be there. Look out for us, Spiky, in case you've got any news.'

Spiky then left, and the boys couldn't help smiling at his back view – the spikes of hair at the top of his head were so very noticeable!

'You'd better stay to lunch with us, Jo,' said Dick, and the delighted girl beamed all over her face.

'Will Joanna's cousin mind you not being back to dinner?' asked Julian.

'No. I said I wouldn't be back all day,' said Jo. 'It's still school holidays, you see. Anyway, I can't stand that Jane – she moons about all the time – and she's got some of my clothes on, too.'

Jo sounded so indignant about Berta that the boys had to laugh. They all went back to Kirrin Cottage, and found Joanna and Anne hard at work in the house.

'Well, you monkey!' said Joanna to Jo. 'Up to tricks as usual, I hear. Throwing stones at people's windows in the middle of the night. You just try that on *my* window and see what happens to you! Now, put on that apron, and help round a bit. How's Jane?'

Joanna was most excited to hear about the boys' latest ideas as to where George might be. Julian gave her a warning.

'But no ringing up the police behind our backs *this* time, Joanna,' he said. 'This is something best done by Dick and me.'

'Can't I come with Sally?' asked Anne.

'We can't *possibly* take Sally,' said Dick, 'in case Gringo's about and recognises her. So you'd better stay and look after her, and we'll take Timmy. He would be sure to smell where George is, if she's hidden anywhere in the camp. But I think she's probably in Gringo's own caravan.'

Timmy pricked up his ears every time he heard George's name mentioned. He was a very miserable dog indeed, and kept running to the front gate, hoping to see George coming along. Whenever they missed him, they knew where to find him – lying mournfully on George's empty bed – probably with an equally mournful Sally beside him!

The boys and Jo set off to the fair about half past three, on their bicycles. Jo rode Anne's this time, and Timmy ran valiantly beside them. Jo glanced at Dick's bicycle from time to time, proud of its brilliant look – how well she had cleaned it that morning!

They came to the fair. 'You can put your bikes up against Spiky's caravan,' said Jo. 'They'll be safe there. Will you pay, and then we'll get in straightaway? You needn't pay for me – I'm going through the gap in the hedge. I'm Spiky's friend, so it's all right.'

She gave Dick her bicycle and disappeared. Julian paid and went in at the gate. They saw Jo waving wildly to them from the side of the big field and wheeled the three bicycles over to her. Timmy followed closely at their heels.

'Hallo!' said Spiky, appearing suddenly. 'See you soon!' I've got to go and tend to the round-about. I've got a bit of news, but not much. That's Gringo's caravan over there, the double one, big van in front, little van behind.'

He nodded his head to where a most magnificent caravan stood, right away from the rest of the camp. There were people milling about all round the other vans, but there was nobody at all by Gringo's. Evidently no one dared to go too near.

'I vote we buy a ball at one of the stands, and then go and play near Gringo's caravan,' said Dick, in a low voice. 'Then one of us will throw the ball too hard and it will go near the van – and we'll somehow manage to get a peep inside. Timmy can go sniffing round while we play. If George is there he'll bark the place down.'

'Jolly good idea!' said Julian. 'Come on, Jo! And keep your eyes open all the time in case you've got to warn us of danger.'

[18]

Spiky is very helpful

The two boys and Jo, with Timmy at their heels, wandered round the fair to find somewhere to buy a ball. There seemed to be none for sale, so they had a go at a Hoopla stall, and Julian managed to get a ring round a small red ball. Just the thing!

It was a big and noisy fair, and hundreds of people from the nearby towns had come on this shops' early-closing day to enjoy the fun. The roundabout played its loud, raucous music all the time, swings went to and fro, the dodgem cars banged and bumped one another as usual, and men went round shouting their wares.

'Balloons! Giant balloons! Fifty pence each!'

'Ice-cream! All flavours.'

'Tell your fortune, lady? I'll tell it true as can be!'

Jo was very much at home in the fair. She had been brought up in one, and knew all the tricks of the trade. Timmy was rather amazed at the noise, and kept close to the boys, his tail still down because he could not forget that George was missing.

'Now let's play our little game of ball,' said Julian. 'Come on, Tim – and if we get into any trouble, just growl and show your teeth, see?'

The three of them, with Timmy, went to the clear space of field that separated the magnificent caravan from the rest of the camp. A man at a nearby stall called to them.

'Hey! You'll get into trouble if you play there!' But they took no notice and he shrugged his shoulders and began to shout his wares.

They threw the ball to one another, and then Julian flung it so wildly that it ran right up to the wheels of the front caravan of the pair. In a trice Dick and Jo were after it. Jo leapt up on a wheel and looked in at the big window, while Dick ran to the small van that was attached behind the big one.

A quick glance assured Jo that the big caravan was empty. The interior was furnished in a most luxurious way and looked like a very fine bed-sitting-room. She leapt down.

Dick peered into the window of the smaller van. At first he thought there was no one there – and then he saw a pair of very fierce, angry eyes looking at him – the eyes of a small, bent old woman with untidy hair. She looked rather like a witch, Dick thought. She was sitting sewing on a bunk, and, as he looked in, she shook her fist at him and called out something he couldn't hear.

He jumped down and joined the others. 'No one at all in the big van,' said Jo.

'Only a witch-like old woman in the other,' reported Dick, in deep disappointment. 'Unless George is pushed under a bunk or squashed into a cupboard, she's certainly not there!'

'Timmy doesn't seem interested in the caravans at all, does he?' said Julian. 'I'm sure if George really *was* in one of those caravans, he'd bark and try to get inside.'

'Yes – I think he would,' said Dick. 'Hallo, there's somebody coming out of the second van. It's the old lady! She's in a fine old temper!'

So she was! She came down the steps to the van, shouting and shaking her fist at them. 'Tim – go and find, go and find – in that van!' said Julian, suddenly, as the old woman came towards them.

The three of them stood their ground as the old woman came right up. They couldn't understand a word she said, partly because she had no teeth, and partly because she spoke a mixture of many languages. Anyway, it was quite obvious that she was ticking them off for daring to play near the two vans.

Timmy had understood what Julian had said, and had slipped inside the second van. He was there for half a minute, and then he barked. The boys jumped, and Dick made a move towards the van.

Then Timmy appeared, dragging something behind him with his teeth. He tried to bark at the same time, but he couldn't. He dragged the coat-like thing right down to the ground before the old woman was on him, screaming in a high voice, and hitting him. She pulled the garment away and went up the steps, kicking out at the surprised Timmy as he tried to pull it away. The door slammed.

'If that old woman hadn't been old, Timmy would have soon shown her he was top dog!' said Dick. 'Whatever was he pulling out of the van?'

'Come over here, out of sight of the van,' said Julian, urgently. 'Didn't you recognise it, Dick? It was *George's dressing-gown*!'

'My word!' said Dick, stopping in surprise. 'Yes, you're right – it was. Whew! What does that mean exactly? George certainly isn't in those vans, or Timmy would have found her.'

'I sent him in to see if he could *smell* that George had been hidden there,' said Julian. 'I thought he would bark excitedly if he smelt her scent anywhere – on the bunk, perhaps. I never guessed he'd find her *dressing-gown* and drag it out to show us!'

'Good old Timmy! Clever old Timmy!' said Dick, patting the dog, whose tail was now at half-mast instead of right down. He had at least found George's dressing-gown – but how surprising to find it in that caravan!

'Why on earth didn't they take the dressing-gown with them, when they took George off?' wondered Julian. 'There's no doubt that she has *been* in that caravan – she was taken straight there the night before last, I expect. Where is she now?'

'She must have been dressed differently,' said Dick. 'They must have had to dress her properly, when they took her somewhere else. After all, she was only in pyjamas and dressing-gown.'

Jo was listening to all this, puzzled and worried. She nudged Dick. 'Spiky's beckoning to us,' she said. They went over to the round-about boy, whose father was now in charge of the noisy machine.

Spiky took them into his caravan, a small and rather dirty one, in which he lived with his father.

'I saw Gringo's old ma chasing you!' he said with his lop-sided grin. 'What was your dog dragging out of the van?'

They told him. He nodded. 'I've been asking round a bit, cautiously,' he said, 'just to see if anyone had heard anything from Gringo's caravan – and the fellow whose caravan is nearest told me he heard shouts and yells two nights ago. He reckoned it was someone in Gringo's van – but he's too scared of Gringo to go and interfere, of course.'

'That would be George yelling,' said Dick.

'Well, then Gringo's vans were moved the next day right away from the other vans,' said Spiky. 'And this afternoon, before the fair opened, Gringo got his car and towed the little van – the second one – out of the field, and set off with it. We all wondered why, but he told somebody it needed repairing.'

'Whew! And George was inside!' said Dick. 'What a cunning way of moving her off to another hiding place.'

'When did the van come back?' asked Julian.

'Just before you came,' said Spiky. 'I don't know where it went. It was gone an hour, I should think.'

'An hour,' said Dick. 'Well, suppose it goes at an average of 25 miles an hour – you can't go very fast if you are towing something – that would mean he had gone somewhere about 12 miles or so away, and come back the same distance – making about an hour's drive, allowing for a stop when they arrived at the place they had to leave her at.'

'Yes,' said Julian. 'But there are lots of places within the radius of 12 miles!'

'Where's Gringo's *car*?' said Dick suddenly.

'Over there, under that big tarpaulin,' said Spiky. 'It's a silver-grey one – American and very striking. He thinks the world of it, Gringo does.'

'I'm going to have a peep at it,' said Julian, and strode off. He came to the tarpaulin, which covered the car right to the ground. He lifted it and was just about to look under it when a man ran up, shouting.

'Here, you! Leave that alone! You'll be turned out of the fair if you mess about with things that don't concern you!'

But Timmy was with Julian, and he turned and growled so fiercely that the man stopped in a hurry. Julian had plenty of time to take a good look under the tarpaulin!

Yes – the car was silver-grey, a big American one – and the wings were bright blue! Julian took a quick look at the two left-hand ones and saw a deep scratch on one of them. Before he dropped the tarpaulin he had time to glance at the tyres. He was sure they had the same pattern as those shown in the wheel-tracks he had sketched! He had checked the sketch with Jim, at Kirrin Garage, who had told him they were an American design.

Yes – this was the car that had hidden in the clearing the night before last – the car that had turned with difficulty and made those deep ruts – the car that had taken George away, and this afternoon had towed away the caravan with her inside, to hide her somewhere else.

He dropped the tarpaulin and walked back to the others, excited, taking no notice of the rude things that the nearby man called out to him.

'It's the car, all right,' said Julian. 'Now – WHERE did it go this afternoon? If only we could find out!'

'It's such a very striking car that anyone would notice it – especially as it was towing a rather nice little caravan,' said Dick.

'Yes – but we can't go round the countryside asking everyone we meet if they've noticed a silver-grey car with blue wings,' said Julian.

'Let's go back home and get a map and see the lie of the country round about,' said Dick. 'Spiky, which way did the car turn when it went out of the field gate?'

'Towards the east,' said Spiky. 'On the road to Big Twillingham.'

'Well, that's something to know,' said Dick. 'Come on, let's get our bikes. Thanks a lot, Spiky. You've been a terrific help. We'll let you know what happens.'

'Call on me if ever you want more help,' said Spiky, proudly, and gave them a smart little salute, bobbing his head so that his spikes of hair shook comically.

The three of them rode off, with Timmy running beside them again. As soon as they got home they told Anne and Joanna all they had found out. Joanna was for ringing up the police at once again, but Julian stopped her.

'I think perhaps we can do this next bit of work better than they can,' he said. 'We're going to try and find out where the car went, Joanna. Now – where are the maps of the district?'

They found them and began to pore over them. Jo was quite lost when it came to map-reading. She could find her way anywhere, day or night – but not with a map!

'Now – here's the road to Big Twillingham and Little Twillingham,' Julian said. 'Let's list carefully all the roads the car could take from there. My word – it's a job!'

[19]
An exciting plan

After fifteen minutes they had six towns on their list, all of which could have been reached in about half an hour from Big Twillingham, which was two miles away from the fair.

'And *now* what do you propose to do, Ju?' asked Dick. 'Bike over to all the towns and ask if anyone has seen the car?'

'No. We can't possibly do that,' said Julian. 'I'm going down to the garage to see our friend Jim, and get *his* help! I'm going to ask him to ring up any friends he has in the garages in those towns, and ask if they've seen the car passing through.'

'Won't he think it's a bit funny?' asked Anne.

'Yes. But he won't mind how funny it is if we pay for the telephone calls and give him some money for his trouble!' said Julian, folding up the map. 'And what's more he won't ask any questions either. He'll probably think it's some silly bet we've got on with one another.'

Jim was quite willing to ring up the garages for them. He knew boys working in main garages in four of the towns, and he knew the hall porter of a hotel in the fifth town. But he knew no one in the sixth.

'That doesn't matter!' he said. 'We'll ring up the garage in the High Street there, and just ask whoever comes to the phone.'

Jim rang up the garage in Hillingford, and had a rather cheeky conversation with his friend there. He put the receiver down. 'No go,' he said. 'He says no car like that came through Hillingford, or he'd have noticed it that time of day. I'll ring up Jake at Green's Garage in Lowington now.'

'That's no go, either,' he said, after a minute's telephone conversation. 'I'll try my hall porter now. He's a cousin of mine.'

The hall porter had some news. 'Yes!' Jim kept saying. 'Yes, that's the one! Yes, yes!

You heard him say that, did you? Thanks a lot.'

'What is it?' asked Dick, eagerly, when Jim at last put down the receiver.

'Pat – that's the hall porter – says he was off duty this afternoon, and went to buy some cigarettes at a little shop in the main street of Graysfield, where his hotel is – and as he stood talking to the fellow in the shop an enormous car drew up at the kerb – silver-grey, with blue wings – an American car, left-hand drive and all.'

'Yes – what next?' said Julian, eagerly.

'Well, the driver got out to get some cigarettes at the shop. He had dark glasses on, and a big gold ring on his finger – Pat noticed that . . .'

'That must be the man who asked about us at the tea-shop in Kirrin!' said Julian, remembering. 'Go on, Jim – this is wonderful!'

'Well, Pat's interested in big cars, so he went out and had a good look at it,' said Jim. 'He said the car had its blinds drawn down at the back, so he couldn't see inside. The fellow with the dark glasses came out and got into the driver's seat again. He called out to whoever was behind and said "Which way now?" '

'Yes, yes – did he hear the answer?' said Julian.

'Somebody called back and said, "Not far now. Into Twining, turn to the left, and it's the house on the hill." '

'*Well*! Of all the luck!' said Dick. 'Would that be where G—' He stopped at a sharp nudge from Julian, and remembered that he mustn't give too much away to the helpful Jim.

Julian passed over a pound to the pleased garage boy, who pocketed it at once, grinning. 'Now, you just come along to me if you want to know about any more cars,' he said. 'I'll phone all over the place for you! Thanks a lot!'

They sped back to Kirrin Cottage, too excited even to talk. They flung their bicycles against the wall and ran in to tell Anne and Joanna. Timmy and Sally sensed their excitement and danced round, barking loudly.

'We know where George is!' cried Dick. 'We know, we know!'

Joanna and Anne listened eagerly. 'Well, Julian,' said Joanna, in admiration, 'it was really smart of you to make Jim phone up like that. The police couldn't have done better. What are you going to do now? Ring up that sergeant?'

'No,' said Julian. 'I'm so afraid that if the police get moving on this now, they'll alarm Gringo and he'll spirit George away somewhere else. Dick and I will go to this place tonight, and see if we can't get hold of George and bring her back! After all – it's only an ordinary house, I imagine – and as Gringo doesn't suspect that anyone knows where George is, he won't be on the look-out!'

'Good!' said Dick. 'Good, good, good!'

'I'm coming too,' said Jo.

'You are not,' said Julian, at once. 'That's flat – you are NOT COMING, Jo. But I shall take Timmy, of course.'

Jo said no more, but looked so sulky that

Anne laughed. 'Cheer up, Jo. You can keep me and Sally company. Oh Julian – wouldn't it be *wonderful* to find George and rescue her!'

There was more map-reading as the boys decided which was the best way to bicycle over to Graysfield. 'Look out the best torches we've got, Anne, will you?' said Dick. 'And let me see – how can we bring George back once we've got her? On my bike-step, I think, though I know it's not allowed. But this is very urgent. We can't very well take a third bike with us. Gosh, isn't this exciting!'

'We really ought to ring up the police,' said Joanna, who kept saying this at intervals.

'Joanna, you sound like a parrot!' said Julian. 'If we're not back by morning you can ring up all the police in the country if you want to!'

'There's been another phone call from your aunt today, Julian – I nearly forgot to tell you,' said Joanna. 'Your uncle is better and they are coming home as soon as possible.'

'Not this evening, I hope,' said Julian, in

alarm. 'Did they tell you anything about Mr Elbur Wright – Berta's father?'

'Oh, he's hanging on to his secrets quite happily now that he knows it isn't Berta who is kidnapped,' said Joanna. 'I don't know if the kidnappers even know they've got the wrong girl yet. It's all very hush-hush. Even your uncle and aunt are having to obey the police. Your poor aunt is so terribly upset about George.'

'Yes. She must be frightfully worried,' said Julian, soberly. 'We've had so much excitement today that I've almost forgotten to worry. And anyway when you're able to *do* something, things don't seem so bad.'

'Be careful you don't go and do too much and land yourself in trouble,' said Joanna, darkly.

'I'll be careful!' said Julian, winking at Dick. 'I say – isn't it nearly supper-time? I feel awfully hungry.'

'Well, we haven't had any tea. No wonder we're hungry.'

'Would you like bacon and eggs for a treat?'

said Joanna, and there was a chorus of approval at once. Timmy and Sally wagged their tails as if Joanna's question applied to them too!

'We'll set off as soon as it's dark,' said Julian. 'Jo, you'd better go home after supper. They'll be worrying about you.'

'All right,' said Jo, pleased to have been asked to supper, but still sulky at being forbidden to go with Julian and Dick that night.

Jo disappeared after supper, with many messages to Berta from Dick, Julian, Anne and Sally.

'And I bet she doesn't give a single one of them!' said Dick. 'Now, let's have a game before we set off, Julian. Just to take our minds off the excitement. I'm getting all worked up!'

Joanna went up to bed at ten because she was tired. Anne stayed up to see the boys off. 'You *will* be careful,' she kept saying. 'You *will* be careful, won't you? Oh dear, I think it's almost worse to stay behind and wonder what's happening to you, than to go with you and find out!'

At last the time came for the boys to go. It was a quarter to twelve and, except for a small moon, was a dark night, with great clouds looming up, often hiding the moon.

'Come on, Timmy,' said Dick. 'We're going to find George.'

'Woof!' said Timmy, delighted. Sally wuffed too, and was most disappointed at being left behind. The boys wheeled their bicycles to the front gate.

'So long, Anne!' said Dick. 'Go to bed – and hope to see George when you wake up!'

They set off on their bicycles, with Timmy loping along beside them. They soon arrived at the field where the fair was, and went swinging away to the east, following the road the silver-grey car had gone that afternoon.

They knew the way by heart, for they had studied the map so well. As they passed the signposts they felt their excitement beginning to mount. 'Graysfield next,' said Dick at last. 'Soon be there, Timmy! You're not getting tired, are you?'

They came into Graysfield silently. The town was asleep, and not a single light showed in any window. A policeman suddenly loomed up out of the shadows, but when he saw two boys cycling, he did not stop them.

'Now – into Twining village, turn to the left – and look for the house on the hill!' said Dick.

They rode through the tiny, silent village of Twining, and took the lane to the left. It led up a steep, narrow lane. The boys had to get off and walk because the hill was too much for them.

'There's the house!' said Julian, suddenly whispering. 'Look – through those trees. My word, it looks a dark and lonely one!'

They came to some enormous iron gates, but when they tried to open them, they found them locked. A great wall ran completely round the grounds. They followed it a little way, leaving their bicycles against a tree by the gate, but it was soon certain that nobody could climb a wall like that!

'Blow!' said Julian. 'Blow!'

'What about the gates?' whispered Dick. Then he glanced round him nervously, hearing a twig crack. 'Did you hear that? There's nobody following us, is there?'

'No! Don't get the jitters, for goodness' sake!' said Julian. 'What was it you were saying?'

'I said "What about the gates?"' said Dick. 'I don't see why we can't climb over them, do you? Nobody would do that in the daytime, they'd be seen – but I can't see why we can't do it *now* – they didn't look too difficult – just ordinary wrought-iron ones.'

'Yes! Of course!' said Julian. 'That's a brainwave. Come on!'

[20]

A thrilling time

The two boys went back to the gates. Dick turned round and looked behind him two or three times. 'I do hope nobody *is* shadowing us!' he said. 'I keep on feeling somebody's watching us all the time.'

'Oh, stuff!' said Julian, impatiently. 'Look – here are the gates. Give me a leg-up and I'll be over in a jiffy.'

Dick gave him a shove, and Julian climbed over the gates without much difficulty. They were bolted, not locked. He slid the great bolts carefully, and opened one gate a little for Dick and Timmy. 'Timmy can't be left behind!' he said. 'And he certainly couldn't climb this gate!'

They kept to the shadowed side of the drive as they walked up towards the house. The small moon came out from behind a cloud as they came near. It was an old house, with high chimneys, an ugly house with narrow windows that seemed like watching eyes.

Dick glanced behind him suddenly and Julian saw him. 'Got the jitters again?' he said, impatiently. 'Dick, don't be an ass. You know perfectly well that if anyone was shadowing us, Timmy would hear them and go for them at once.'

'Yes, I know,' said Dick. 'I'm an idiot – but I've just got that feeling tonight – the feeling that someone else *is* there!'

They came right up to the house. 'How shall we get in?' whispered Julian. 'The doors are all sure to be locked. We'll have to try the windows.'

They tiptoed silently round the big house. As Julian had said, the doors were all locked. The windows were all fastened too – well and truly fastened. Not one was open or could be opened.

'If this is a house belonging to Gringo he must be able to hide plenty of things in absolute safety – bolted gates, high walls, locked doors, fastened windows!' said Dick. 'No burglar could possibly get in.'

'And neither can we,' said Julian, desperately. 'We've been all round the house three times now! There's no door, no window we can get in. No balcony to climb up to – no ivy to hang on to – nothing!'

'Let's go round once more,' said Dick. 'We *might* have missed something.'

So once more they went round – and discovered something curious when they got to the kitchen quarters. The moon came out, and showed them a round black hole in the ground! Whatever could it be?

They tiptoed to it just as the moon went in again. They shone their torches on it briefly.

'It's a coal-hole!' said Dick, astonished. '*Why* didn't we see it before? Look, there's the lid just beside it. It's been left open. I suppose the moon was in last time we came by this part of the house. I can't think how we didn't notice it.'

Julian was uneasy. 'I didn't see it before,

certainly. It's strange. Could it be a trap, do you think?'

'I don't see how it could be,' said Dick. 'Come on – let's get down. At least it's a way in.' He shone his torch into the hole. 'Yes, look – there's a whole lot of coke down there – we can easily jump on to it. Tim, you go first and spy out the land.'

Timmy jumped down at once, the coke slithering away from beneath his four paws. 'He's down all right,' said Julian. 'I'll go next. Then you.'

Down they jumped, and the coke slithered away again, making what seemed to be a very loud noise in the silent night. Julian shone his torch around.

They were standing on a very large heap of coke in the middle of a big cellar. At the end was a door.

'Hope it's not locked,' said Dick, in a whisper. 'Now, Tim, keep to heel, for goodness' sake, and don't make a sound!'

They went to the door, treading on gritty bits

of coke. Julian turned the dirty handle – and the door opened inwards! 'It's not locked!' said Julian, thankfully.

They crept through it, Timmy treading on their heels, and found themselves in another cellar, set with stone shelves on which were piled tins and boxes and crates. 'Enough food here to stand a siege!' whispered Dick. 'Where are the cellar steps? We've got to get out.'

'Over there,' said Julian. Then he stopped and put out his torch. He had heard something.

'Did you hear that?' he whispered. 'It sounded like somebody treading on the coke in the coal-cellar! Gosh, I hope nobody *is* shadowing us. We'll soon be prisoners if so.'

They listened but heard nothing further. Up the stone steps they went and undid the door at the top. A big kitchen lay beyond, lit by the dim moon. A shadow rose suddenly in front of them and Timmy growled. Dick's heart almost stopped beating. What in the world was that, crawling silently over the floor and disappearing in the shadows? He clutched at Julian and made him jump.

'Don't do that, ass! That was only the kitchen cat you saw,' whispered Julian. 'Gosh, you made me jump. Wasn't it a good thing that Timmy didn't go for the cat? There would have been an awful yowling!'

'Where do you suppose George will be?' asked Dick. 'Somewhere at the top of the house?'

'I've no idea. We'll just have to look into every room,' said Julian. So they looked into every room on the ground floor, but they were empty. They were huge rooms, ugly and over-furnished.

'Come on – up the stairs!' said Dick, and up they went. They came to an enormous landing, hung with tapestry curtains at the windows. Timmy suddenly gave a small growl and in a trice both boys had hidden themselves in the folds of the long window-curtains. Timmy went with them, feeling surprised. Dick peeped out after a minute.

'I think it was that cat again,' he whispered. 'Look, there it is, up on that chest. It's following us, wondering what on earth we're doing, I expect!'

'Blow it!' said Julian. '*I'm* getting the jitters now, being watched by a shadowy cat. I suppose it *is* real?'

'Timmy thinks so!' said Dick. 'Come on – there are any amount of bedroom doors on this landing.'

They tiptoed into the ones whose doors were open, but no one was sleeping in the beds there. They came to a closed door and listened. Someone was snoring inside!

'That's not George,' said Dick. 'Anyway, she'd be locked in, and the key is in this door.'

They went to the next door, which was also shut. They listened and could hear someone breathing heavily.

'Not George,' said Dick, and they went on up to the next flight of stairs. There were four more rooms there, two of them not even furnished. The doors of the other two were ajar, and it was clear that people were sleeping in them, because once more there was loud breathing to be heard.

'There don't seem to be any more rooms,' said Dick, in dismay, as they flashed their torches carefully round the top landing. 'Blow! Where's George then?'

'Look – there's a little wooden door there,' said Julian, in Dick's ear. 'A door leading into the cistern room, I should think.'

'She wouldn't be there,' said Dick. 'But wait – look, there's a strong bolt on the door! And cistern rooms don't have bolts on their doors, or even locks. This one hasn't a lock, but it *has* a bolt.'

'Sh! Not so loud!' said Julian. 'Yes, that's funny, I must say. How can we get the door open without waking the people in those other two rooms?'

'We'll shut their doors very quietly, and we'll lock them!' said Dick, excited. 'I'll go and do it.'

He drew the doors gently to, and then locked first one and then the other, having taken the

keys from the other side of the doors to do so.
Except that one made a slight click as he locked
it, there was no noise. Nobody stirred in the
two rooms, and the boys breathed freely again.

They went to the little wooden door opposite. They pulled gently at the bolt, afraid that it
might squeak. But it didn't. It was obviously
quite new, and ran easily. The door opened
outwards with a small creak. There was pitch
darkness inside, and the sound of trickling
water from the cistern.

Dick flashed his torch on and off quickly. In
that second he saw something that made his
heart jump!

There was a small mattress on the floor of
the little cistern room, and someone was lying
on it, rolled so completely in blankets that even
the head was covered! Julian had seen it too,
and he put his arm on Dick's, afraid that it
might not be George, afraid that it might be
someone who would give the alarm, perhaps
another prisoner.

But Timmy knew who it was! Timmy ran

straight in with a small, loving whimper and flung himself on the sleeping figure!

Dick shut the cistern room door at once, afraid of the noise being heard. Timmy might bark with joy in a moment, or George might shout!

The figure gave a grunt and sat up. The blanket fell away from the head – and there was George's curly mop, and her startled face.

'Sh!' said Dick, raising his finger warningly. 'SH!' Timmy was licking George from head to foot, wild with delight, but extraordinarily silent – clever old Timmy knew that this was one of the times when joy must be dumb!

'Oh!' said George, hugging Timmy anywhere she could. 'Oh, Timmy! I missed you so! Darling, darling, Tim! Oh Timmy!'

Dick stood by the closed door, listening to find out if anyone was stirring in the other rooms. He heard nothing at all. Julian went to George.

'Are you all right, George?' he asked. 'Have you been treated well?'

'Not very,' said George. 'But then I didn't behave very well! I did quite a lot of kicking and biting – so they locked me in here!'

'Poor old George!' said Julian. 'Well, we'll hear everything when we've got out of here. So far, we've been jolly lucky. Can you come now?'

'Yes,' said George and got off the mattress. She was dressed in an odd selection of clothes, and looked rather peculiar. 'That awful old woman – Gringo's mother – found these for me when I was taken to the caravan,' she said. 'Gosh, I've got a lot to tell you!'

'Sh!' said Dick, at the door. 'Not a sound, now! I'm going to open the door!'

He opened it slowly. All was quiet. 'Now we'll go down the stairs,' he said. 'Not a sound!'

They went down the first flight of stairs and on to the enormous landing. Then, just as Dick put his foot on to the next stair down, he trod on something soft that yowled, spat and scratched. It was that cat!

Dick fell halfway down the stairs, and Timmy could not stop himself from chasing the cat up the landing and up the top stairs to the cistern room. Nor could he stop himself from barking!

Shouts came from two of the nearby bedrooms and two men appeared in pyjamas. One switched on the landing light, and then both of them tore down the stairs after the three children. Dick picked himself up, but he had ricked his ankle and could not even walk!

'Run, George – I'll see to Dick!' yelled Julian. But George stopped too – and in a trice the two men were on to them, catching hold of Dick and Julian, and jerking them into a nearby room.

'Tim! TIM!' shouted George. 'Help, Timmy!'

But before Timmy could come pelting down the stairs from the attic George was shoved into the room too, and the door locked.

'Look out for the dog!' shouted one of the men. 'He's dangerous!'

Timmy certainly was! He came tearing

towards the men, snarling, his eyes blazing, showing all his teeth.

The men darted into the room next to the one into which they had locked the children, and banged the door. Timmy flung himself against it in rage, snarling and growling in a most terrifying manner. If only he could get at those men! If only he could!

[21]

Most unexpected!

Soon there was real pandemonium in the old house! The sleepers in the rooms on the top landing awoke suddenly and found their doors locked, and began to bang on them and shout. The three children in the locked room on the ground floor shouted and banged too – and Timmy nearly went mad!

Only the men in the room next to the children were silent. They were terrified at Timmy's growling and snarling. They would have liked to lock themselves in, but the key was on the other side of the door – and they certainly didn't dare to open it to get the key!

Soon the children quietened down. Dick sat on a chair, exhausted. 'That cat! That wretched, prowling, sly old cat! Gosh, I stepped on it and it scratched me to the bone – to say nothing of pitching me headlong down the stairs and making me wrench my ankle!'

'We so *nearly* managed to escape!' groaned Julian.

'I can't *think* what will happen now!' said George. 'Timmy's out there and can't get in to us, and we can't possibly get out to him because the door's locked – and those men won't dare to set a foot outside *their* door while Tim's there!'

'And we've locked the people into their rooms upstairs!' said Julian. 'Well, it's certain that nobody can get out of their rooms to help anyone else – so it looks as if we'll all be here till Doomsday!'

It certainly did seem a very poor look-out. The only people who were not behind locked doors were the two men, whoever they were – and they simply dared not put a foot outside their room. Timmy roamed about, occasionally whimpering and scratching outside the children's door, but more often growling outside the next door, sometimes flinging his heavy body against it as if he would break it down.

'I bet the men are shaking with fright,' said Dick. 'They won't even dare to try and get out of a window in case they meet Timmy outside somewhere!'

'Serve them right,' said George. 'Gosh, I'm glad you came! Wasn't I an absolute ass to take Sally down to the kennel that night?'

'You were,' said Julian, 'I agree wholeheartedly. The men were waiting for a chance to get Berta, of course, and they saw you, complete with Berta's dog, and thought you were the girl they wanted!'

'Yes. They flung something all over my head so that I couldn't make a sound,' said George. 'I fought like anything, and my dressing-gown cord must have slipped off – did you find it?'

'Yes,' said Dick. 'We were jolly glad to find a few other things too – the comb – the hanky – the sweet – and of course the note!'

'They carried me quite a way to somewhere in the wood,' said George. 'Then they plonked me down in the back of the car. But they had to turn it and it was difficult – and I had the bright thought of throwing out all the things in my dressing-gown pocket just in *case* you came along and saw them.'

'What about that note – with the word Gringo on?' asked Julian. 'That was a terrific help. We wouldn't be here tonight if it hadn't been for that.'

'Well, I heard one of the men call the other Gringo,' said George. 'And it was such an unusual name I thought I'd scribble it on a bit of paper and throw that out too – it was just on chance I did it.'

'A jolly good chance!' said Dick. 'Good thing you had a notebook and pencil with you!'

'I hadn't,' said George. 'But one of the men had left his coat in the back of the car and there was a notebook with a pencil in the breast-pocket. I just used that!'

'Jolly good!' said Julian.

'Well, they whizzed me off in the car to some fairground or other,' said George. 'I heard the roundabout music next day. There was a horrid old witch-like woman in the caravan; she didn't seem at all pleased to see me. I had to sleep in a chair that night, and I got so wild that I yelled and shouted and threw things about and smashed quite a lot of cups and saucers. I enjoyed that.'

The boys couldn't help laughing. 'Yes – I bet you did,' said Dick. 'They had to move the caravan away from the fair itself, because they were afraid people would hear you. In fact, I expect that's why Gringo decided to hide you here!'

'Yes. I suddenly felt a jolt, and found the caravan we were in was being towed away!' said George. 'I was awfully surprised. I waved at the windows and shouted as we drove through the streets, but nobody seemed to notice anything wrong – in fact some people waved back to me! Then we swung in through some gates, and came here – and, as I told you, they put me up here because I made such a nuisance of myself!'

'Did you tell them you weren't Berta?' asked Dick.

'No,' said George. 'Of course not. For two reasons – I knew there would be no fear of Berta's father giving those secrets away, because he'd be told by you that *I* had been kidnapped, not his precious Berta. So he'd hang on to them. And also I thought *Berta* would be safe, so long as I didn't tell the men they'd got the wrong person.'

'You're a good kid, George,' said Julian, and slapped her gently on the back. 'A – very – good – kid. I'm jolly proud of you. There's nobody like our George!'

'Don't be an idiot,' said George, but she was very pleased all the same.

'Well, there's no more to tell,' she said, 'except that the cistern room was most frightfully draughty, and I had to wrap my head up as well as my body when I lay down. And the cistern made awful noises – sort of *rude* noises, that made me want to say "I beg your pardon!" all the time! Of course I knew you'd rescue me, so I wasn't awfully worried!'

'And we *haven't* rescued you!' said Julian.

'All we've done is to get ourselves locked up as well as you!'

'Tell me how you found out I was here,' said George. So the boys told her everything and she listened, thrilled.

'So Berta went to stay with Jo!' she said. 'I bet Jo didn't like that.'

'She didn't,' said Julian. 'But she's been quite a help. I only wish she were here now, and could do one of her ivy-climbing stunts, or something!'

'I say – Timmy's very quiet all of a sudden!' said George, listening. 'What's happened?'

They listened. Timmy was not barking or whimpering. There was no sound from him at all. What was happening? George's heart sank – perhaps those men had managed to do something to him?

But suddenly they heard him again, whimpering – but whimpering gladly and excitedly. And then a familiar voice came to their ears.

'Dick! Julian! Where are you?'

'Gosh – it's JO!' said Dick, astounded. He

limped to the door. 'We're in here, Jo. Unlock the door!'

Jo unlocked it and looked in, grinning, Timmy tore in like a whirlwind and flung himself on George, almost knocking her over. Dick limped out of the room immediately Jo rushed in, much to everyone's astonishment. Then he returned, looking rather pleased with himself.

'Let's go while the going's good,' he said.

'Yes – but, be careful, those men will be out, now that Timmy isn't there to guard them!' cried Julian, suddenly realising that the two angry fellows could easily escape while Timmy was in with them – and might lock the door on the lot of them, Timmy too!

'It's all right – there's no desperate hurry!' said Dick. 'I thought of that. I slipped out and locked their door on *them*, as soon as Jo rushed in to us. And there they can stay till the police arrive in the morning. They can then collect the whole lot – the men upstairs too.'

'And I'm sure the police will be quite pleased to search the house and the cellars,' said Julian.

'There will be plenty of stuff here that they will be interested in! Well, let's go at once.'

They called a cheery good-bye to the two men. 'We're off!' shouted Dick. 'You'd better look out for the dog in case he gets you!' They all went down the hall, Dick hobbling, for his ankle was still painful.

'We might as well leave in style,' said Julian, and unbolted and unlocked the front door. 'Also it would be as well to leave this door open for the police to come in by – I don't expect *they* will want to come in through the coal-hole! It was a good idea of yours to let the men think we were leaving Tim behind to guard them, Dick – they won't dare even to climb out of the windows in case he's waiting for them!'

'We've left a good many lights on,' said George, looking back. 'Never mind – we're not paying the bill! Come on, Timmy, out into the dark, dark night!'

They went down the front steps and into the dark drive. Everyone felt safe with Timmy running ahead.

'Jo – exactly how did you get here?' said Dick, suddenly. 'You were forbidden to come.'

'I know,' said Jo. 'Well, I just took Anne's bike and followed you, that's all. And I walked in through the front gates when you'd left them open, of course. That was easy.'

'Gosh – I kept *feeling* there was someone behind me!' said Dick. 'And there was – it was *you*, you little horror! No wonder Timmy didn't bother to bark or growl.'

'Yes, it was me,' said Jo. 'And I followed you round and round the house, while you were trying to get in – and I thought you never *would* see that coal-hole – so I took the lid off and put it on the ground, hoping you'd see it then. And you did!'

'So *you* did that!' said Dick. 'I must say I was astonished to see it. I knew we must have passed it before. So that was you too! You want a good telling off, you disobedient, cheeky little wretch!'

Jo laughed. 'I couldn't bear you to go off without me,' she said. 'It's a good thing I *did* come! I waited and waited inside that coal-hole for you to come back with George – and when you didn't, I left the coal-hole and got into the house. And Timmy heard me and came running down the stairs. He nearly knocked me over, he was that pleased!'

'Here are the gates at last,' said George. 'What are we going to do about bikes? There isn't one for me.'

'Jo can stand behind on my step and hold on to my shoulder,' said Julian. 'You take Anne's bike, George. We'll leave these gates open. The police ought to be pleased with us for saving them so much trouble!'

Off they went down the steep hill, Timmy running behind, his tail wagging happily. He had got George back again. All was well again in his doggy world!

[22]

'These kids sure are wunnerful!'

What shrieks and shouts there were from Joanna and Anne when the four arrived at Kirrin Cottage at last, at half past three in the morning! Joanna was awake, but Anne had just gone to sleep. She was sleeping in Joanna's room for company and Sally was there too.

The stories had to be told again and again. First Dick, then Julian, then George, then Jo – they all talked without stopping, excited and happy. Sally ran from one to the other, and followed Timmy about – but sometimes her little stiff tail drooped when she remembered that Berta was not there.

'I *say*,' said Dick, suddenly drawing back the sitting-room curtains '– it's daylight! The sun's up! And all the time I've been thinking it was still night!'

'No use going to bed, then,' said Jo, at once. She was so much enjoying this that she felt as if she never wanted it to stop!

'Well, I suppose it isn't,' said Joanna. 'I know what we'll do – we'll have a big breakfast now, a very big one to celebrate – and then we'll all go back to bed and sleep till lunch-time. We're tired out really – just look at our black-rimmed eyes and pale cheeks!'

'Joanna! We're all as sunburnt as can be, you're just making that up!' said George. 'Come on – let's get this celebration breakfast going! Bacon – eggs – tomatoes – fried bread. Oh, and mushrooms too – have you any mushrooms, Joanna? And lots and lots of hot coffee, and toast and marmalade. I'm ravenous.'

They discovered that they all were, and twenty minutes later they sat at the table tucking in as if they had eaten nothing for a month.

'I can't eat a thing more,' said Dick, 'and I

don't know what's happened to my eyes – they keep closing!'

'So do mine,' said George, with an enormous yawn. 'Joanna – don't say we've got to do the washing-up, will you?'

'Of course not!' said Joanna. 'Go on up to your beds now – don't even bother to undress.'

'I feel as if there's something I ought to do – but I can't remember it,' said Julian, sleepily, staggering upstairs. 'I – just – can't remember!'

He flopped on his bed and was asleep as soon as his head fell on the pillow. In two minutes everyone but Joanna was asleep too. Joanna stopped to give Timmy a drink, and then he bounded up to George and curled up in the crook of her knees as usual.

Joanna went to lie down too, thinking she would just have a rest, but not go to sleep. But in half a second she slept too.

The sun rose higher in the sky. The milkman came whistling up the path and left four bottles of milk on the step. The gulls in the bay circled and soared and called loudly. But nobody stirred in Kirrin Cottage.

A car came up to the front gate, and another one followed. Out of the first stepped Uncle Quentin, Aunt Fanny, Mr Elbur Wright – and Berta! Out of the second car stepped the sergeant and his constable.

Berta flew to the front door, but it was shut. She raced round to the garden door. That was locked too – and so was the kitchen door!

'Pops! We'll have to ring – all the doors are locked!' she called. And then, from up above came a sound of excited barking, and Sally's head appeared at a bedroom window. When she saw it really was Berta down below, she tore down the stairs and scraped at the front door.

'What's happened? Where *is* everyone?' said Aunt Fanny in amazement. '*All* the doors locked? But it's ten o'clock in the morning. Where are the children?'

'I've got my key,' said Uncle Quentin, and he put it into the front door lock. He opened the door and Sally leapt straight into Berta's arms, licking her face from forehead to chin!

Aunt Fanny went into the hall and called, 'Anyone at home?'

No answer. Timmy heard her call, but as George did not stir, he didn't either. He was not going to leave George for a minute, not even to go downstairs!

Aunt Fanny walked into all the rooms on the ground floor. Nobody there! She marvelled at the remains of the meal spread all over the dining-room table, and even more at the dirty pans and dishes in the kitchen. What was Joanna thinking of? WHERE was everybody? She did not expect George to be there, because she knew George had been kidnapped – but where in the world were all the others?

She went upstairs and her husband followed with Berta and her father. They were all feeling most astonished now. They went into Julian's room – good gracious he *was* there, then! And Dick too – lying floppily on their beds, absolutely sound asleep! Aunt Fanny couldn't understand it.

And then she went into the girls' room – and there was Anne fast asleep too – and GOOD GRACIOUS, could that be *George*? But surely George was kidnapped – then how – why – where . . .

Her mother suddenly put her arms round the sleeping George and kissed her and hugged her. She had worried so much about her – and now here she was, safe and sound after all!

George awoke at once. She sat up and gazed at her mother and father in astonishment.

'Oh – you're back! Oh, how lovely! When did you come?'

'Just now,' said her mother. 'But George – why is everyone asleep – and how did *you* get here – we thought you were . . .'

'Oh, Mother – yes, of course you don't know half the story, do you?' said George. 'Gosh, there's Berta here too – and your pops, Berta! Hallo, everyone.'

She was still so sleepy that she was not quite

sure whether this was a dream or not. But then Anne woke up and squealed, and that woke Julian and Dick. They came into the very crowded bedroom, and soon there was such a noise that Joanna and Jo, in the room above, awoke too.

Down they came, looking very dishevelled, Joanna full of apologies. She rushed downstairs to put some coffee on and bumped into the two policemen in the hall. She screamed.

'Excuse me,' said the sergeant to Joanna. 'Isn't anyone ever coming down again? We're supposed to be guarding Berta.'

'Oh my – you don't need to do that now!' said Joanna. 'Didn't Julian telephone you last night – this morning, I mean – I thought he was going to.'

'What about?' said the sergeant.

'About the kidnappers. Everything's all right,' explained Joanna to the two astonished policemen. 'We've got George back – and oh, bless us all, there's those kidnappers – you haven't been told they're all locked up and waiting for you, have you?'

'Look here, what *are* you talking about?' said the sergeant, bewildered. 'This is too bad – what do you *mean* – kidnappers locked up and waiting!'

'Julian!' called Joanna, 'the police are here – and you forgot to telephone and tell them what happened last night. They'd better go to that house and get the men, hadn't they?'

'I *knew* there was something I'd forgotten,' said Julian, running down the stairs. 'I did mean to telephone, but I was so tired that I forgot.'

Everyone then came downstairs and went into the sitting-room. Jo was shy with so many people there, and wouldn't sit anywhere near the two policemen.

'I've just been told, Mr Wright, that there's no need to guard your daughter now,' said the sergeant, rather stiffly. 'Seems as if the police are the last to hear about anything!'

'Well, the fact of the matter is that we found out that Gringo, who owns the fair called Gringo's Fair, was paid to kidnap Berta,' said

Julian. 'He kidnapped George instead, by mistake. We found out where Gringo had taken
her and went to rescue her last night. You go
on, Dick.'

'And we left Gringo and somebody else
locked up in a room on the ground floor,
and two other people locked up in a top-floor
room – and we've left the front door open for
you and the drive gates open too,' said Dick.
'So don't be too annoyed about it, Sergeant,
because we really have tried to make things
easy for you! We've rescued George, as you see
– and now *you* can get the men.'

The sergeant looked as if he found it difficult
to believe a single word! Uncle Quentin tapped
him sharply on the shoulder.

'Well, look alive, man – they'll escape before
you can get them if you don't hurry.'

'What's the address?' said the sergeant, stolidly.

'I don't know the name of the house, or the
lane it's in,' said Julian. 'But you go through the
village of Twining, turn to the left, and it's the
house up on the hill.'

'How did you find out all this?' said the sergeant.

'It's too long to tell you now!' said Dick. 'We'll write it all down in a book, and send you a copy. We'll call it – er – we'll call it – what *shall* we call it, you others? It's a peculiar adventure really – it ended with everyone fast asleep in bed!'

'I want some coffee,' announced Uncle Quentin. 'I think we've talked enough. Do go and catch your kidnappers, my good men.'

The policemen disappeared. Mr Elbur Wright beamed round happily, Berta on his knee.

'Well, this is a very happy ending!' he said. 'And I can take my little Berta back with me after all!'

'Oh no!' wailed Berta, much to her father's surprise.

'What do you mean?' he asked.

'Gee, Pops, be a honey and let me stay on here,' begged Berta. 'These kids sure are wunnerful.'

'WonDERful, wonDERful, wonDERful!' chanted the others.

'Of course let her stay on if she'd like to,' said Aunt Fanny. 'But as a girl this time, not a boy!'

George heaved a sigh of relief. That was all right then. She wouldn't mind Berta as a girl, even though she was a *silly* girl!

'Woof!' said Timmy suddenly, and made everyone jump.

'He says he's jolly pleased you're staying, Berta, because now Sally-dog will have to stay too,' said Dick. 'So *he'll* have someone to play with as well!'

'Shall we really send the sergeant a book about this adventure?' said Anne. 'Did you *really* mean it, Dick?'

'Rather!' said Dick. 'Our fourteenth adventure – and may we have many more! What shall we call the book?'

'I know!' said George, at once. 'I know! Let's call it "FIVE HAVE PLENTY OF FUN".'

Well, they did – and they hope you like it!

FIVE ON A SECRET TRAIL

[1]

George is rather difficult

'Mother! Mother, where are you?' shouted George, rushing into the house. 'Mother, quick!'

There was no answer. George's mother was out in the garden at the back of Kirrin Cottage, picking flowers. George yelled again, this time at the top of her very strong voice.

'MOTHER! MOTHER! Where are you? IT'S URGENT.'

A door was flung open nearby and George's father stood there, glaring at her.

'George! What's this row about? Here am I in the middle of some very difficult—'

'Oh Father! Timmy's hurt!' said George. 'He went—'

Her father looked down at Timmy, standing

meekly behind George. He gave a little snort.

'Hurt! He seems all right to me. I suppose he's got a thorn in his paw again – and you think it's the end of the world or something, and come yelling in here and—'

'Timmy *is* hurt!' said George, with tears in her voice. 'Look!'

But her father had gone back into his study again, and the door slammed. George glared at it, looking exactly like her hot-tempered father.

'You're unkind!' she shouted, 'and . . . oh there's MOTHER. MOTHER!'

'Dear me, George, whatever *is* the matter?' said her mother, putting down the flowers. 'I heard your father shouting, and then you.'

'Mother – Timmy's hurt!' said George. 'Look!'

She knelt down by the dog, and gently pulled forward one ear. Behind it was a big cut. Timmy whined. Tears came into George's eyes, and she looked up at her mother.

'Now don't be silly, George,' said Mrs Kirrin. 'It's only a cut. How did he do it?'

'He tried to jump over a ditch, and he didn't see some old barbed wire there,' said George. 'And a rusty piece caught his ear, and ripped that awful cut. I can't stop it bleeding.'

Her mother looked at it. It certainly was quite deep. 'Take him to the vet, George,' she said. 'Perhaps it ought to be stitched. It does look rather deep. Poor old Timmy-boy – well, it's a good thing it wasn't his eye, George.'

'I'll take him to the vet at once,' said George, getting up. 'Will he be in, Mother?'

'Oh yes – it's his surgery hour,' said her mother. 'Take him along now.'

So Timmy was hurried along the country lanes to the pretty little house where the vet lived. George, very anxious indeed, was most relieved to see that the vet seemed quite unconcerned.

'A couple of stitches and that cut will heal well,' he said. 'Hold him, will you, while I do the job? He'll hardly feel it. There, old boy – stand still – that's right.'

In five minutes' time George was thanking the vet wholeheartedly. 'Thank you! I *was* worried! Will he be all right now?'

'Good gracious, yes – but you mustn't let him scratch that wound,' said the vet, washing his hands. 'If he does, it may go wrong.'

'Oh. But how can I stop him?' asked George anxiously. 'Look – he's trying to scratch it now.'

'Well, you must make him a big cardboard collar,' said the vet. 'One that sticks out right round his neck, so that his paw can't get near that cut, however much he tries to reach it.'

'But – but Timmy won't like that a bit,' said George. 'Dogs look silly wearing cardboard collars like great ruffs round their necks. I've seen them. He'll hate one.'

'Well, it's the only way of stopping him from scratching that wound,' said the vet. 'Get along now, George – I've more patients waiting.'

George went home with Timmy. He padded along quietly, pleased at the fuss that George was making of him. When he was nearly home, he suddenly sat down and put up his hind leg to scratch his bad ear.

'No, Timmy! NO!' cried George, in alarm. 'You must NOT scratch. You'll get the plaster off in no time, and break the stitches. NO, Timmy!'

Timmy looked up in surprise. Very well. If scratching was suddenly upsetting George, he would wait till he was alone.

But George could read Timmy's thoughts as easily as he could read hers! She frowned.

'Blow! I'll *have* to make him that cardboard collar. Perhaps Mother will help me.'

Her mother was quite willing to help. George was not good at things of that sort, and she watched her mother cutting out a big cardboard collar, fitting it round the surprised Timmy's head, and then lacing the edges together with thread so that he could not get it off. Timmy was most surprised, but he stood very patiently.

As soon as the collar was finished, and safely round his neck, he walked away. Then he raised his hind leg to scratch at his smarting ear – but, of course, he couldn't get it over the collar, and merely scratched the cardboard.

'Never mind, Timmy,' said George. 'It will only be for a few days.'

The study door nearby opened and her father came out. He saw Timmy in his collar and stopped in surprise. Then he roared with laughter.

'Hey, Timmy – you look like Queen Elizabeth the First in a fine big ruff!' he said.

'Don't laugh at him, Father,' said George. 'You know that dogs can't bear being laughed at.'

Timmy certainly looked offended. He turned his back on George's father and stalked off to the kitchen. A little squeal of laughter came

from there and then a loud guffaw from someone at the kitchen door – the milkman.

'Oh Timmy – whatever have you got that
collar on for?' said the cook's voice. 'You do
look peculiar!'

George was angry. She remained angry all
that day and made everyone most uncomfortable. How *mean* of people to jeer at poor
Timmy! Didn't they realise how terribly uncomfortable a collar like that was – and Timmy
had to wear it night and day! He couldn't even
lie down comfortably. George mooned about
looking so angry and miserable that her mother
felt worried.

'George dear, don't be silly about this. You
will make your father cross. Timmy will have to
wear that collar for at least a week, you know,
and he *does* look a bit comical when you first
see him. He's getting used to it, he soon won't
notice it.'

'Everybody laughs at him,' said George, in
an angry voice. 'He went into the garden and

a lot of kids hung over the wall and laughed like anything. And the postman told me it was cruel. And Father thinks it's funny. And—'

'Oh dear, George, don't get into one of your moods,' said her mother. 'Remember, Anne is coming soon. She won't enjoy things much if you behave like this.'

George bore it for one day more. Then, after two upsets with her father over Timmy, another with a couple of boys who laughed at him, and one with the paper-boy, she decided she wouldn't stay at Kirrin Cottage for one day longer!

'We'll take my little tent, and go off by ourselves somewhere,' she told Timmy. 'Some place where nobody can see you till your ear is better and that hateful collar is off. Don't you think that's a good idea, Timmy?'

'Woof,' said Timmy. He thought that any of George's ideas were good, though the collar puzzled him very much.

'You know the *dogs* laugh at you too, Timmy,' said George, earnestly. 'Did you see how that silly little poodle belonging to Mrs Janes up the lane stood and stared at you? He looked *exactly* as if he was laughing. I won't have you laughed at. I know you hate it.'

Timmy certainly didn't like it, but he really was not as upset about the collar as George seemed to be. He followed her as she went up to her bedroom and watched her as she began to put a few things into a small bag.

'We'll go to that lonely little spot on the common,' she said to him. 'We'll pitch our tent near a little stream, and we'll jolly well stay there till your ear's better. We'll go tonight. I'll take my bike, and strap everything on to the back.'

So, in the middle of the night, when Kirrin Cottage was dark and quiet, George stole downstairs with Timmy. She left a note on the dining-room table, and then went to get her bicycle. She strapped her little tent on it, and the bag containing food and other odds and ends.

'Come on!' she whispered to the surprised Timmy. 'We'll go. I'll ride slowly and you can run beside me. Don't bark for goodness' sake!'

They disappeared into the darkness, Timmy running like a black shadow beside the bicycle. Nobody guessed they were gone. Kirrin Cottage was quiet and undisturbed – except for the creaking of the kitchen door, which George had forgotten to shut.

But in the morning, what a disturbance! Joanna the cook found George's note first and wondered what a letter in George's writing was doing on the dining-room table. She ran straight up to George's room and looked inside.

The bed was empty. There was no George and Timmy's basket was empty. Joanna went to take the note to Mrs Kirrin.

'Oh *dear*! How silly George is!' she said, when she had read it. 'Look, Quentin – such a fuss about Timmy! Now George has gone off with him, goodness knows where!'

Her husband took the note and read it out loud. 'Dear Mother, I'm going off for a few days with Timmy till his ear is better. I've taken my tent and a few things. Don't worry, please. Tell Anne if she wants to join me, to come to the end of Carters Lane on the common and I will show her where I'm camping. Tell her to come at twelve. Love from George.'

'Well, I'm blessed!' said George's father. 'All right, let her stay away if she wants to – I'm tired of her sulky face and Timmy's hang-dog looks. Tell Anne to join George, and maybe I shall have peace for a few days!'

'George should be all right,' said his wife. 'She's quite sensible really – and she's got Timmy. I'll tell Anne to join her when she arrives this morning.'

When Anne arrived at Kirrin Station, and looked out for George and Timmy, they weren't there – only her aunt was there, smiling as usual.

'What's happened?' said Anne. 'Where's George – and Timmy?'

'Oh, George has gone off by herself,' said her Aunt Fanny. 'Come along, and I'll tell you!'

[2]

Anne joins the little camp

Aunt Fanny soon told Anne about Timmy's ear
and the big collar of cardboard that had caused
all the trouble. Anne couldn't help smiling.

'Oh Aunt Fanny – George is quite crazy
about old Tim, isn't she? I'll go and meet her
at twelve, and of course I'll camp with her for a
day or two. It's lovely weather and I'd like to. I
expect Uncle Quentin will be glad to have us
out of the house!'

'How are Julian and Dick?' asked her aunt.
She was very fond of Anne's two brothers,
George's cousins. 'Will they be coming down
here at all these holidays?'

'I don't know,' said Anne. 'They're still in
France, you know, on a schoolboys' tour. I feel
funny without them! George will be cross to

hear they probably won't be coming to Kirrin. She'll just have to put up with *me*!'

At twelve o'clock Anne was standing patiently at the end of Carters Lane. It ran to the common and then ended in a small, winding path that led to nowhere in particular. Big gorse bushes grew here and there, and slender birch trees. Anne, her belongings strapped to her back, and a bag in her hand, looked over the common to see if she could spy George coming.

There was no sign of her. 'Blow!' said Anne. 'I suppose she's changed her mind or something. Perhaps her watch has stopped and she doesn't know the time. She ought to, though, by looking at the sun! How long shall I wait?'

She sat down by a big gorse bush, out of the hot sun. She hadn't been there for more than a minute when she heard a hissing sound.

'Pssssst!'

Anne sat up at once. The sound came from

the other side of the bush, and she got up and walked round it. Half-hidden under a prickly branch were George and Timmy!

'Hallo!' said Anne, surprised. 'Didn't you see me when I arrived? Hallo, Tim darling! How's your poor old ear? Oh, doesn't he look a quaint old dear in that collar, George?'

George scrambled out of the bush. 'I hid here just in case Father or Mother should come with you and try to make me come back,' she said. 'I wanted to make quite sure they weren't waiting somewhere a little way away. I'm glad you've come, Anne.'

'Of course I've come,' said Anne. 'I wouldn't stay alone at Kirrin Cottage while you were camping out. Besides, I understand how you feel about Timmy. The collar's a jolly good idea, of course – but it does make him look comical. I think he looks rather a dear in it, I do really.'

George was almost relieved that Anne had not laughed at Timmy as most people had. She smiled at her cousin, and Timmy licked her till Anne really had to push him away.

'Let's go,' said George, scrambling up. 'I've got a lovely camping place, Anne. You'll like it. It's near a little spring too, so there's plenty of water for Timmy to drink – and us too. Did you bring any more food? I didn't really bring much.'

'Yes. I've brought heaps,' said Anne. 'Aunt Fanny made me. She's not cross with you, George. I didn't see your father. He was shut up in his study.'

George's spirits suddenly rose. She gave Anne a friendly punch. 'This is going to be fun! Timmy's ear will soon be better, and he loves camping out as much as we do. I've really found a good place – about the loneliest on the common! Nobody near us for miles!'

They set off together, Timmy at their heels, darting off every now and again when he smelt rabbit.

'When are Julian and Dick coming down?'

asked George. 'In a few days? Timmy's ear will be all right then and we can go back to Kirrin Cottage to welcome the boys, and have some fun there.'

'They may not be coming down at all these hols,' said Anne, and George's face fell at once. She stopped and stared at Anne in dismay.

'Not coming! But they *always* come in the hols – or we go away somewhere together!' she said. 'They *must* come! I shall be miserable without Ju and Dick.'

'Well – they're still in France, on a tour or something,' said Anne. 'We shall hear if they're staying on there or coming down to Kirrin when we get back to the cottage. Don't look so woebegone, George!'

But George felt woebegone. The holidays stretched before her, suddenly seeming long and dreary. Her two boy cousins were always such fun – they had had such wonderful adventures together. And now – now they weren't coming!

'We shan't have any adventures at all if the boys don't come,' she said, in a small voice.

'I shan't mind that,' said Anne. 'I'm the peaceful one, not always on the look-out for something to happen, like you and the boys! Perhaps these holidays will be quite unexciting without even the *smell* of an adventure! Oh George – cheer up! *Don't* look so mournful. You'd better send a letter to Julian and Dick if you feel so badly about it.'

'I've a good mind to!' said George. 'I can't *imagine* hols without the boys. Why – we shan't be the Five – the Famous Five – if they don't come!'

'Woof!' said Timmy, quite agreeing. He sat down and tried to scratch his ear, but the big collar prevented him. He didn't seem to mind and ran off after a rabbit quite happily.

'I think *you* are more upset about that collar than Timmy,' said Anne, as they walked along. 'Are we getting near this place of yours, George? It's a jolly long way.'

'We go up this hill in front of us – and then drop down to a little copse,' said George. 'There's a funny old cottage nearby – quite ruined and empty. At first I thought perhaps people lived there, but when I went nearer I saw that it was ruined. There's a big old rose-rambler climbing all over it, even inside. I suppose the people who used to live there planted it.'

They walked up the little hill and down again, following curving rabbit paths. 'Better look out for adders,' said Anne. 'This is just the kind of place for them. My word, it's hot, George. Is there anywhere to swim near here – a pool or anything?'

'I don't know. We could explore and see,' said George. 'I did bring my swimsuit just in case. Look, you can see part of the old cottage now. My camp is fairly near there. I thought I'd better camp near the spring.'

They were soon at George's rough little camp. Her tent was up, and she had made a

bed inside of the springy heather. A mug, a bag
of dog biscuits, a few tins, and a loaf of bread
were at one end of the tent. It didn't seem to
Anne as if George had brought very much, and
she felt glad that she had managed to pack such
a lot of things.

'Aunt Fanny cut dozens and dozens of sandwiches,' said Anne. 'She said if we kept them in
this tin they wouldn't go stale, and would last
us a day or two till we went back. I'm hungry.
Shall we have some now?'

They sat out in the sun, munching the ham
sandwiches. Anne had brought tomatoes too,
and they took a bite at a sandwich and then a
bite at a tomato. Timmy had to make do with a
handful of dog biscuits and half a sandwich
every now and again. After a bit he got up and
wandered off.

'Where's he going?' asked Anne. 'To look for
a rabbit?'

'No. Probably to get a drink,' said George.
'The spring is in the direction he's gone. I'm

thirsty too – let's take the mug and get a drink ourselves.'

They went off with the mug, Anne following George through the thick heather. The little spring was a lovely one. It had evidently been used by the people who had once lived in the old cottage, and was built round with big white stones, so that the spring ran through a little stony channel, as clear as crystal.

'Oooh – it's as cold as ice!' said Anne. 'Simply delicious! I could drink gallons of this!'

They lay on the heather out in the sun, talking, when they came back from the spring. Timmy wandered off by himself again.

'It's so peaceful here,' said Anne. 'Nobody near us for miles. Just the birds and the rabbits. This is what I like!'

'There's hardly a sound,' said George, yawning.

And then, just as she said that, there came a noise in the distance. A sharp sound, like metal on stone. It came again and again and then stopped.

'What's that, do you suppose?' said George, sitting up.

'I can't imagine,' said Anne. 'Anyway, it's a long way away – everything is so still that sounds carry from quite a distance.'

The sharp noises began again in a little while and then stopped. The girls shut their eyes, and slept. There wasn't a sound now except the pop-pop-pop of gorse pods exploding in the sun and sending out their little black seeds.

George woke up when Timmy came back. He sat down heavily on her feet and she woke up with a jump.

'Timmy! Don't!' she said. 'Get off my feet, you made me jump!' Timmy obligingly removed himself and then picked up something he had dropped, lay down and began gnawing it. George looked to see what it was.

'Timmy! That's a bone! Where did you get it?' she said. 'Anne, did you bring a bone for Tim?'

'What? What did you say?' said Anne, half asleep. 'A bone. No, I didn't. Why?'

'Because Timmy's found one,' said George, 'and it's a bone that has had cooked meat on it, so it's not a rabbit or anything Timmy's caught. Timmy, where did you get it?'

'Woof,' said Timmy, offering the bone to George, thinking that she too might like a gnaw, as she seemed so interested in it.

'Do you suppose anyone else is camping near us?' asked Anne, sitting up and yawning. 'After all, bones don't grow in the heather. That's quite a good meaty one, too. Timmy, have you stolen it from another dog?'

Timmy thumped his tail on the ground and went on with his bone. He looked pleased with himself.

'It's rather an old bone,' said George. 'It's smelly. Go away, Tim – take it further off.'

The sharp metallic noises suddenly began again and George frowned. 'I believe there *is* someone camping near us, Anne. Come on –

let's do a bit of exploring and find out. I vote we move our camp if there are other people near. Come on, Timmy – that's right, bury that horrible bone! This way Anne!'

[3]

The old cottage – and a surprise

The two girls, with Timmy at their heels, left their camping place and set off in the hot sun. Anne caught sight of the ruined cottage and stopped.

'Let's have a look at it,' she said. 'It must be awfully old, George.'

They went in at the wide doorway. There was no door left, only the stone archway. Inside was a big room, whose floor had once been paved with slabs of white stone. Now grass and other weeds had grown between the cracks, and had actually lifted up some of the slabs so that the whole floor was uneven.

Here and there parts of the walls had fallen

away and the daylight came through. One window was still more or less intact, but the others had fallen out. A small crooked stairway of stone led upwards in one corner.

'To rooms above, I suppose,' said Anne. 'Oh, here's another doorway, leading into a second room – a small one. It's got an old sink in it, look – and this must be the remains of a pump.'

'There's not much to see, really,' said George, looking round. 'The top rooms must be quite ruined, because half the roof is off. Hallo, here's another door – a back door. It's actually a *door* too, not just a doorway.'

She gave a push at the stout wood – and the old door promptly fell off its hinges and crashed outwards into an overgrown yard.

'Goodness!' said George, startled. 'I didn't know it was quite so rotten. It made poor Tim jump almost out of his skin!'

'There are outhouses here – or the remains of

them,' said Anne, exploring the back-yard. 'They must have kept pigs and hens and ducks. Here's a dried-up pond, look.'

Everything was falling to pieces. The best preserved corner of the old place was what must have been a small stable. Rusted mangers were still there and the floor was of stone. An old, old piece of harness hung on a big nail.

'It's got quite a nice "*feel*" about it, this old place,' said Anne. 'Sometimes I don't like the feel of places – they give me an uneasy feeling, a feeling that horrid things may have happened there. But this is quite different. I think people have been happy here, and led peaceful lives. I can almost hear hens clucking and ducks quacking, and pigs gr—'

'Quack, quack, quack! Quack!'

'*Cuck*-cuk-cuk-cuk-cuk! *Cuck*-cuk-cuk-cuk-cuk!'

Anne clutched George and the two girls looked extremely startled to hear the sudden loud noise of quacking and clucking. They stood and listened.

'What was it?' said Anne. 'It *sounded* like hens and ducks – though I'm not quite sure. But there aren't any here, surely. We shall hear a horse whinnying next!'

They didn't hear a whinny – but they heard the snorting of a horse at once. 'Hrrrrr-umph! Hrrrrr-umph!'

Both girls were now quite alarmed. They looked for Timmy. He was nowhere to be seen! Wherever could he have got to?

'*Cuck*-cuk-cuk-cuk-cuk!'

'This is silly,' said George. 'Are we imagining things? Anne, there *must* be hens near. Come round the back of these stables and look. Timmy, where are you? TIMMY!'

She whistled shrilly – and immediately an echo came – or so it seemed!

'Phee-phee-phee-phee-phee!'

'TIMMY!' yelled George, beginning to feel as if she was in a dream.

Timmy appeared, looking rather sheepish. He wagged his tail – and to the girls' enormous amazement, they saw that he had a ribbon tied on it. A ribbon – a bright blue one at that!

'Timmy! Your tail – the ribbon – Timmy, what's all this about?' said George, really startled.

Timmy went to her, still looking sheepish, and George tore the ribbon off his tail. 'Who tied it there?' she demanded. 'Who's here? Timmy, where have you been?'

The two girls searched the old buildings thoroughly, and found nothing and nobody. Not a hen, not a duck, not a pig – and certainly not a horse. Then – what was the explanation? They stared at one another in bewilderment.

'And where did Timmy get that silly ribbon?' said George, exasperated. '*Someone* must have tied it on.'

'Perhaps it was a hiker passing by – perhaps he heard us here and saw Timmy and played a joke,' said Anne. 'But it's strange that old Tim *let* him tie on the ribbon. I mean – Timmy's not overfriendly with strangers, is he?'

The girls gave up the idea of exploring any further and went back to their little camp. Timmy went with them. He lay down – and then suddenly got up again, making for a thick gorse bush. He tried to squirm underneath.

'*Now* what's he after?' said George. 'Really, I think Timmy's gone mad. Timmy, you *can't* get under there with that great collar on. TIMMY, do you hear me!'

Timmy backed out reluctantly, the collar all crooked. After him came a peculiar little mongrel dog with one blind eye and one exceedingly bright and lively one. He was half-white and half-black, and had a ridiculously long thin tail, which he waved about merrily.

'*Well*!' said George, amazed. 'What's that dog doing there? And how did Timmy get so friendly with him? Timmy, I can't make you out.'

'Woof,' said Timmy, and brought the mongrel dog over to Anne and George. He then proceeded to dig up the smelly bone he had buried, and actually offered it to the little dog, who looked away and took no interest in it at all.

'This is all very peculiar,' said Anne. 'I shall expect to see Timmy bring a cat to us next!'

At once there came a pathetic mewing.

'Mee-ew! Mee-ew-ee-ew-ee-ew!'

Both dogs pricked up their ears, and rushed to the bush. Timmy was once again kept back by his big collar and barked furiously.

George got up and marched to the bush. 'If there's a cat there, it won't have much chance against two dogs,' she called to Anne. 'Come away, Tim. Hey, you little dog, come away, too.'

Timmy backed out, and George pulled out the small dog very firmly indeed. 'Hold him, Anne!' she called. 'He's quite friendly. He won't bite. I'm going to find that cat.'

Anne held on to the small mongrel, who gazed at her excitedly with his one good eye and wagged his tail violently. He was a most friendly little fellow. George began to crawl into the bare hollow space under the big gorse bush.

She looked into it, not able to see anything at first, because it was dark there after the bright sunlight. Then she got a tremendous shock.

A round, grinning face stared back at her, a face with very bright eyes and tousled hair falling on to the forehead. The mouth was set in a wide smile, showing very white teeth.

'Mee-ew-ee-ew-ee-ew!' said the face.

George scrambled back at top speed, her heart thumping. 'What is it?' called Anne.

'There's somebody hiding there,' said George. 'Not a cat. An idiot of a boy who is doing the mewing.'

'Mew-ee-ew-ee-ew!'

'Come out!' called Anne. 'Come out and let's see you. You must be crazy.'

There was a scrambling noise and a boy came head first from the hollow space under the bush. He was about twelve or thirteen, short, sturdily built, and with the cheekiest face Anne had ever seen.

Timmy rushed at him and licked him lovingly. George stared in amazement.

'How does my dog know you?' she demanded.

'Well, he came growling at me yesterday when I was in my own camp,' said the boy. 'And I offered him a nice meaty bone. Then he saw my little dog Jet – short for jet-propelled, you know – and made friends with him – and with me too.'

'I see,' said George, still not at all friendly. 'Well, I don't like my dog to take food from strangers.'

'Oh, I couldn't agree more,' said the boy. 'But I thought I'd rather he ate the bone than ate *me*. He's a nice dog, yours. He feels a bit of an idiot wearing that collar, doesn't he? You should have heard Jet laugh when he first saw it!'

George frowned. 'I came here to be alone so that Timmy shouldn't be jeered at,' she said. 'He's got a bad ear. I suppose *you* were the fathead who tied a blue ribbon on his tail?'

'Just for a joke,' said the boy. '*You* like frowning and glaring, I can see. Well, *I* like joking and tricking! Your Timmy didn't mind a bit. He took to my dog right away. But everyone likes Jet! I wanted to find out who owned Timmy – because, like you, *I* don't like strangers messing about when I'm camping out. So I came along.'

'I see. And you did all the clucking and quacking and hrrr-umphing?' said Anne. She liked this idiot of a boy, with his broad friendly grin. 'What are you doing – just camping – or hiking – or botanising?'

'I'm digging,' said the boy. 'My father's an archaeologist – he loves old buildings more than anything else in the world. I take after him, I suppose. There was once an old Roman camp on this common, you know – and I've found a place where part of it must have been, so I'm digging for anything I can find – pottery, weapons, anything like that. See, I found this yesterday – look at the date on it!'

He suddenly thrust an old coin at them – a strange, uneven one, rather heavy to hold.

'Its date is 292,' he said. 'At least, as far as I can make out. So the camp's pretty old, isn't it?'

'We'll come and see it,' said Anne, excited.

'No, don't,' said the boy. 'I don't like people messing round me when I'm doing something serious. Please don't come. I won't bother you again. I promise.'

'All right. We won't come,' said Anne, quite understanding. 'But don't you play any more silly tricks on us, see?'

'I promise,' said the boy. 'I tell you, I won't come near you again. I only wanted to see whose dog this was. Well, I'm off. So long!'

And, whistling to Jet, he set off at a furious pace. George turned to Anne.

'What a peculiar boy!' she said. 'Actually – I'd rather *like* to see him again. Wouldn't you?'

[4]

That night

It was now tea-time, according to Anne's watch and also according to everyone's feelings, including Timmy's. Timmy felt the heat very much and was always wandering off to the little spring to lap the crystal-cold water. Anne wished that she and George had a big jug that they could fill – it was such a nuisance to have to keep running to and fro with just a mug.

They had tea – biscuits, a sandwich each, and a bar of rather soft chocolate. George examined Timmy's ear for the hundredth time that day, and pronounced it very much better.

'Well, don't take off that collar yet,' said Anne. 'He'll only open the wound by scratching if you do.'

'I'm not *going* to take it off!' said George,

touchily. 'What shall we do now, Anne? Go for a walk?'

'Yes,' said Anne. 'Listen – you can hear those sharp, metallic noises again – that's the boy at work again, I expect. Funny boy he must be – coming to dig about all on his own with his comical little dog. I wish we could see what he's doing.'

'We promised we wouldn't,' said George. 'So I don't feel that we even ought to go and peep.'

'Of course not!' said Anne. 'Come on – let's go in the opposite direction, George – right away from the boy. I hope we shan't get lost!'

'Not while Timmy's with us, silly!' said George. 'You'd find your way home from the moon, wouldn't you, Tim?'

'Woof,' agreed Timmy.

'He always says yes to whatever you say, George,' said Anne. 'I say – isn't it a lovely evening? I wonder what Julian and Dick are doing?'

George immediately looked downcast. She

felt that her two cousins had no right to go rushing across France when she wanted them at Kirrin. Didn't they like Kirrin? Would they be having magnificent adventures abroad, and not want to spend even a week at Kirrin? She looked so lost in miserable thoughts that Anne laughed at her.

'Cheer up! At least *I* am here with you – though I agree that compared with Ju and Dick I'm very poor company, and not at all adventurous!'

They had a lovely walk, and sat down half-way to watch hordes of rabbits playing together. Timmy was very unhappy about this. Why *sit down* to watch silly rabbits? Rabbits were made to *chase*, weren't they? Why did George always put a restraining hand on his collar when she sat down to watch rabbits? He whined continually, as he watched with her.

'Shut up, Timmy, you ass,' said George. 'You'd only spoil the entertainment if you sent them to their holes.'

They watched for a long while and then got

up to go back to the camp. When they came near, they heard the sound of low whistling. Someone was about that evening, quite near their camp. Who was it?

They came round a big gorse bush, and almost bumped into a boy. He got out of their way politely, but said nothing.

'Why – it's *you*!' said George, in surprise. 'I don't know your name. What are you doing here? You said you wouldn't come near us.'

The boy stared, looking very surprised. His tousled hair fell right across his forehead, and he brushed it back.

'I said nothing of the sort,' he said.

'Oh, you *did*!' said Anne. 'You know you did. Well, if you break your promise, there's no reason for us to keep ours. We shall come and visit *your* camp.'

'I never made you any promise,' said the boy, looking quite startled. 'You're mad!'

'Don't be an idiot!' said George, getting cross. 'I suppose you'll be saying next that you didn't act like a hen, and a duck, and a horse this afternoon . . .'

'And a cat,' said Anne.

'Barmy!' said the boy, looking at them pityingly. 'Quite barmy.'

'Are you coming here again?' demanded George.

'If I want to,' said the boy. 'The water in this spring is better than the one over by my camp.'

'Then we shall come and explore *your* camp,' said George, firmly. 'If you don't keep your promise, we shan't keep ours.'

'By all means come if you want to,' said the boy. 'You seem quite mad, but I daresay you're harmless. But don't bring your dog. He might eat mine.'

'You know he wouldn't eat Jet!' said Anne. 'They're good friends.'

'I don't know anything of the sort,' said the boy, and went off, brushing his hair out of his eyes again.

'What do you make of *that*?' said George,

staring after him. 'Not a bit the same as he was this afternoon. Do you think he really *had* forgotten about his promise and everything?'

'I don't know,' said Anne, puzzled. 'He was so perky and jolly and full of fun before – grinning all the time – but just now he seemed quite serious – not a smile in him!'

'Oh well – perhaps he's a bit crazy,' said George. 'Are you sleepy, Anne? I am, though I can't think why!'

'Not very – but I'd like to lie down on this springy heather and watch the stars gradually come sparkling into the sky,' said Anne. 'I don't think I'll sleep in the tent, George. You'll want Timmy with you, and honestly there's so little room inside the tent that I'm quite sure Timmy would lie on my legs all night long.'

'I'll sleep in the open air as well,' said George. 'I only slept in the tent last night because it looked a bit like rain. Let's get some more heather and make a kind of mattress of it. We can put a rug on top of it, and lie on that.'

The two of them pulled a lot of heather and carried it to their 'bed'. Soon they had a fine pile, and Timmy went to lie on it.

'Hey – it's not for you!' cried George. 'Get off – you'll flatten it right down. Where's the rug, Anne?'

They laid the rug on the heather pile and then went to the spring to wash and clean their teeth. Timmy immediately got on to the heather bed again, and shut his eyes.

'You old fraud!' said George, lugging him off. 'You're not asleep. Keep off our bed! Look – there's a nice soft patch of grass for you. That's your bed!'

George lay down on the rug, and the heathery bed sank a little beneath her weight. 'Very comfortable!' said George. 'Shall we want a rug over us, Anne?'

'Well, I did bring one,' said Anne. 'But I don't think we'll want it, the night's so hot. Look – there is a star already!'

Soon there were six or seven – and then

gradually hundreds more pricked through the evening sky as the twilight deepened. It was a wonderful night.

'Don't the stars look big and bright?' said Anne, sleepily. 'They make me feel very small, they're such millions of miles away. George, are you asleep?'

There was no answer. George hadn't heard a word. She was fast asleep. Her hand fell down the side of the heather and rested on the ground below. Timmy moved a little nearer and gave it a small lick. Then he too fell asleep, and gave some small doggy snores.

The night darkened. There was no moon but the stars shone out well from the midnight sky. It was very quiet out there on the common, far away from streets and villages and towns. Not even an owl hooted.

Anne didn't quite know why she awoke. At first she had no idea where she was, and she lay gazing up at the stars in astonishment, thinking she must still be asleep.

She suddenly felt very thirsty. She groped about in the nearby tent for the mug, couldn't find it and gave it up.

'I'll drink from my cupped hands,' she thought, and set off for the little spring. Timmy wondered whether to follow her. No – he would stay with George. She wouldn't like it if she awoke and found him gone with Anne. So he settled his head down on his paws again and slept, leaving one ear open for Anne.

Anne found the little spring. Its tinkling gurgling sound guided her as soon as she heard it. She sat down on one of the stones nearby, and held out her cupped hands. How very cold the water was – and how delicious to drink on this hot night! She sipped thirstily, slopping some of the water down her front.

She got up to go back, and walked a few steps in the starlight. Then she stopped. Wait – was she going in the right direction? She wasn't sure.

'I *think* I am!' she decided, and went on,

carefully and quietly. Surely she must be near their little camp now?

Then all at once she stood still, and felt herself stiffen. She had suddenly seen a light. It had flashed and disappeared. Ah – there it was again! Whatever could it be?

Then, as her eyes strained through the starlit darkness, she suddenly saw that she *had* taken the wrong way – she had gone in the direction of the old ruined cottage, and not the camp – and the light had come from there!

She didn't dare go any nearer. She felt glued to the grass she was standing on! Now she could hear sounds – whispering sounds – and the noise of a football on the stone floor of the cottage – and then the flash of a light came again! Yes, it *was* from the old cottage!

Anne began to breathe fast. Who was it in the old cottage? She simply dared not go and see. She must go back to George, and to Timmy's protection. As fast and as silently as she could she found her way back to the spring – and then, almost stumbling now, made her way to where George was still lying peacefully asleep.

'Woof,' said Timmy, sleepily, and tried to lick her hand. Anne climbed on to the heathery bed beside George, her heart still beating fast.

'George!' she whispered. 'George, do wake up. I've something strange to tell you!'

[5]

That boy again!

George would not wake up. She grunted when Anne poked her and prodded her, and then she turned over, almost falling off the small heather bed.

'Oh George – *please* do wake!' begged Anne, in a whisper. She was afraid of speaking out loud in case anyone should hear her. Who knew what might happen if she drew attention to their little camp?

George awoke at last and was cross. 'Whatever is it, Anne?' she said, her voice sounding loud in the night.

'Sh!' said Anne. 'Sh!'

'Why? We're all alone here! We can make as much noise as we like!' said George, surprised.

'George, do listen! There's someone in that

old cottage!' said Anne, and at last George heard and understood. She sat up at once.

Anne told her the whole story – though it didn't really seem very much of a tale when she related it. George spoke to Timmy.

'Tim!' she said, keeping her voice low. 'We'll go and do a little exploring, shall we? Come on, then – and keep quiet!'

She slid off the rug and stood up. 'You stay here,' she said to Anne. 'Timmy and I will be very quiet and careful, and see what we can find out.'

'Oh no – I couldn't stay here *alone*!' said Anne in alarm, and got up hurriedly. 'I shall have to come too. I don't mind a bit now Timmy's with us. I wonder he didn't bark at the people in the old cottage, whoever they were.'

'He probably thought it was you messing about,' said George, and Anne nodded. Yes, of course, Timmy must have thought that any noises he heard had been made by her.

They took the path that led to the old cottage. George had Timmy well to heel. He knew
he must not push forward unless told to. His
ears were pricked now, and he was listening
hard.

They came cautiously to the cottage. They
could see its dark outline in the starlight, but
little else. There was no light flashing there. Nor
did there seem to be any noises at all.

All three stood still and quiet for about
five minutes. Then Timmy moved restlessly.
This was boring! Why wouldn't George let
him run forward and explore everywhere if
she wanted to know if intruders were
about?

'I don't think there's a soul here!' whispered
George into Anne's ear. 'They must have gone –
unless you dreamed it all, Anne!'

'I didn't!' whispered back Anne indignantly.
'Let's go forward a bit and send Timmy into the
cottage. He'll soon bark if there's anyone
there.'

George gave Timmy a little shove. 'Go on, then!' she said. 'Find, Timmy, find!'

Timmy gladly shot forward into the darkness. He trotted into the cottage, though it was impossible even to see him go to it. The two girls stood and listened, their heartbeats sounding very loud to them! There was not a sound to be heard, except occasionally the rattle of Timmy's strong claws on a stony slab.

'There can't be anyone there,' said George at last, 'else Timmy would have sniffed them out. You're an ass, Anne – you dreamt it all!'

'I did not!' said Anne, indignant again. 'I *know* there was someone there – in fact, more than one person, because I'm sure I heard whispering!'

George raised her voice. 'Timmy!' she called loudly, making Anne jump violently. 'Timmy! Come along. We've sent you on a silly wild goose chase – but now we'll go back to bed!'

Timmy came trotting out of the cottage and

went obediently to George. She heard him yawn as he stood beside her, and she laughed.

'Anne had a bad dream, that's all, Timmy,' she said.

Anne felt cross – very cross. She said no more and they left the old cottage and went back to their heather bed. Anne climbed on to her side and turned over with her back to George. All right – let George think it was a dream if she liked!

But when Anne awoke in the morning and remembered the happenings of the night before, she too began to wonder uneasily if she *had* dreamed what she had seen and heard in the old cottage.

'After all – Timmy would certainly have caught anyone who was there,' she thought. 'And he wasn't at all excited, so there can't have *been* anyone in the cottage. And anyway, why would they come? It's just silly!'

So, when George talked about Anne's dream-ing in the middle of the night, Anne did not defend herself. She really could *not* be sure that it had really happened. So she stuck out her tongue when George teased her, and said nothing.

'Let's go and see that boy and his camp,' George said when they had eaten a few rather stale sandwiches and some shortbread biscuits. 'I'm beginning to feel bored, aren't you? I wish Timmy's ear would quite heal up. I'd go back home like a shot then.'

They set off in the direction of the camp with Timmy. They heard a chip-chipping noise as they came near, and then something small and hairy shot out from a bush and rushed up, barking a welcome.

'Hallo, Jet!' said Anne. 'Don't you let Timmy have any more of your bones!'

The chipping noise had stopped. The two girls went on and came to a very messy piece of common. It had been well dug over, in some places very deeply. Surely that boy couldn't have done so much excavating by himself?

'Hey! Where are you?' called George. Then she saw the boy below her, examining something in a trench he had dug out. He jumped and looked upwards.

Then he scowled. 'Look – you promised not to come and disturb me!' he shouted. 'You're mean. Just like girls to break a promise.'

'Well! I like *that*!' said George amazed. 'It was *you* who broke yours! Who came messing round *our* camp yesterday evening I'd like to know?'

'Not me!' said the boy at once. 'I always keep my promises. Now go away and keep yours. Girls! Pooh!'

'Well, I can't say we think much of *you*,' said George, disgusted. 'We're going. *We* don't want to see anything of your silly digging. Good-bye!'

'Good-bye and good riddance!' called the boy rudely, and turned back to his work.

'I think he must be *quite* mad,' said Anne. 'First he makes a promise – then last evening he broke his promise and even said he hadn't made one – and now today he says he *did* make a promise and that he'd kept his and we'd broken ours. Idiotic!'

They went up a little rabbit path, and into a small copse of birch trees. Someone was sitting there reading. He looked up as they came.

The two girls stopped in amazement. It was that boy *again*! But how had he got here? They had just left him behind in a trench! Anne looked at the title of the book he was reading. Goodness – what a learned title – something about archaeology.

'Another little trick of yours, I suppose?' said George, sarcastically, stopping in front of him. 'You must be a jolly good runner, I must say, to have got here so quickly. Funny boy, aren't you – very very funny!'

'Good gracious – it's those potty girls again,' groaned the boy. 'Can't you leave me alone? You talked a lot of rubbish yesterday – and now you're talking it again.'

'How did you get here so quickly?' said Anne, puzzled.

'I didn't get here quickly. I came very slowly, reading my book as I went,' said the boy.

'Fibber!' said George. 'You must have run at top speed. Why do you pretend like this? It's only a minute or so ago that we saw you.'

'Now *you're* the fibber!' said the boy. 'I do think you two girls are awful. Go away and leave me alone and never let me see you again!'

Timmy didn't like the tone of the boy's voice and he growled. The boy scowled at him. 'And just you shut up too,' he said.

Anne pulled at George's sleeve. 'Come on,' she said, 'it's no good staying here arguing. The boy's crazy – mad – we'll never get any sense out of him!'

The two girls walked off together, Timmy following. The boy took absolutely no notice. His face was turned to his book and he was quite absorbed in it.

'I've never met anyone *quite* so mad before!' said Anne, rather puzzled. 'By the way, George – you don't suppose it could have been that idiotic boy last night in the cottage?'

'No. I tell you I think you dreamed it,' said George, firmly. 'Though that boy is quite idiot enough to explore an old cottage in the middle of the night. He would probably think it a very good time to do so. Oh Anne, look – there's a pool – in that hollow there. Do you think we could swim in it?'

It certainly shone very temptingly. They went down to have a closer look. 'Yes – we'll have a swim this afternoon,' said George. 'And then I really think, Anne, we ought to go back to Kirrin Cottage and get a few more provisions. The sandwiches we've got left are so dry that we really shan't enjoy eating them – and as Timmy's ear isn't healed, it looks as if we'll have to stay a bit longer.'

'Right!' said Anne, and they went on back to the camp. They changed into their swimsuits in the afternoon and went off to the little pool. It was fairly deep, very warm and quite clean. They spent a lovely hour swimming and basking and swimming again – then they reluctantly dressed and began to think of going off on the long journey to Kirrin Cottage.

George's mother was very surprised to see the two girls and Timmy. She said yes, of course they could have some more food, and sent them to ask Joanna for all she could spare.

'By the way, I've heard from Julian and Dick,' she said. 'They're back from France – and may be here in a day or two! Shall I tell them to join you or will you come back here?'

'Tell them to come and fetch us as soon as they get here!' said George, delighted. Her face shone. Ah – the Five would be together again. How wonderful!

'Leave me directions to give them so that they can find you,' said her mother. 'Then you can all come back – together. The boys can help to carry everything.'

What fun, what fun! Julian and Dick again, now things would be exciting, things would happen, as they always did. What FUN!

Storm in the night

It was fun to go back to their little camping place again. It was growing dark, as they had stayed to have a good meal at Kirrin Cottage, and Timmy had eaten a most enormous plate of meat, vegetables and gravy. Then he had sat down and sighed as if to say 'That was jolly good! I could do with some more!'

However, nobody took any notice of this, so he trotted off to have a good look round the garden to make sure it was just the same as when he had left it a day or two before. Then it was time to start back to the camping place, and Timmy heard George's whistle.

'Well, nobody laughed at Timmy this evening!' said Anne. 'Not even your father!'

'Oh, I expect Mother had told him not to,'

said George. 'Anyway, I *said* I would stay away till Tim's ear is better, and I mean to.'

'Well, I'm quite willing,' said Anne. 'The only thing I'm a bit worried about is – do you suppose there will be anyone snooping about in that old cottage again?'

'You dreamed it all!' said George. 'You admitted you did!'

'Well, yes, I did wonder if I *had* dreamed it,' said Anne, as they walked up the long Carters Lane to the moor. 'But now that it will soon be dark, I'm beginning to think I *didn't* dream it – and it isn't a very nice feeling.'

'Oh, don't be silly!' said George impatiently. 'You can't chop and change about like that. Anyway, we've got Timmy – no one would dare to upset Timmy! Would they, Tim?'

But Timmy was ahead, hoping against hope that he might for once in a while catch a rabbit. There were so many about on the common at this time of the evening, peeping at him here, making fun of him there, and showing their little white bobtails as soon as he moved in their direction.

The two girls got safely back to their camp. The tent was still up, their heather bed out in the open, covered with the old rug. They put down their loads thankfully, and went to the little spring for a drink.

George yawned. 'I'm tired. Let's get to bed at once, shall we? Or wait – perhaps it would be a good idea to have a look in at that cottage to make sure no one is there to disturb us tonight.'

'Oh no – I don't want to look,' said Anne. 'It's getting dark now.'

'All right – I'll go with Timmy,' said George, and off she went. She came back in about five minutes, her little torch shining in front of her, for it was now almost dark.

'Nothing to report,' she said. 'Nothing whatever – except one bat flying round that big room. Timmy nearly went mad when it flew down and almost touched his nose.'

'Oh. That's when he barked, I suppose,' said

Anne, who was now curled up on the heather bed. 'I heard him. Come on, George – I'm sleepy.'

'I must just look at Timmy's ear once more,' said George and shone her torch on it.

'Well, buck up, then,' said Anne. 'That's about the thousandth time today you've examined it.'

'It does seem much better,' said George, and she patted Timmy. 'I *shall* be glad when I can take this awful collar off him. I'm sure he hates it.'

'I don't believe he even *notices* it now,' said Anne. 'George, are you coming or not? I really can't keep awake one minute more.'

'I'm coming,' said George. 'No, Tim – you are *not* sleeping on our bed. I told you that last night. There's hardly enough room for Anne and me.'

She climbed carefully on to the heather bed, and lay looking up at the twinkling stars. 'I feel happy tonight,' she said, 'because Julian and

Dick are coming. I was down in the dumps when I thought they might not be coming at all these hols. When do you suppose they'll be here, Anne?'

There was no answer. Anne was asleep. George sighed. She would have liked to plan what they were going to do when the boys came. Timmy's ear would surely be all right in a day or two – and the boys could carry everything back from this little camp to Kirrin Cottage – and then long days of swimming and boating and fishing and all kinds of fun could begin – begin – begin – be . . .

And now George was asleep too! She didn't feel a small spider running over her hand, wondering whether or not to spin a web between her finger and thumb. She didn't hear the scramble of a hedgehog not far off – though Timmy did and pricked one ear. It was a very peaceful night indeed.

Next day the girls were very cheerful. They made a good breakfast of some of the food they had brought, and then spent some time getting more heather for their bed, which, under the weight of their two bodies, was now rather flat and uncomfortable.

'Now for a swim!' said George. They put on their swimsuits, threw cardigans over their shoulders and set off to the little pool. On the way they saw Jet, the little mongrel dog, in the distance, and the boy with him. Jet tore up to them and danced round Timmy excitedly.

The boy called to them. 'It's all right, don't worry, I'm not going near your place! I'm still keeping *my* promise! Jet – come here!'

The girls took no notice of the grinning boy, but couldn't resist patting the little one-eyed mongrel. Jet really was like a piece of quicksilver, darting in and out and round about. He shot back to the boy at once.

The girls went on to the pool – and stopped in dismay when they came near. Someone was already there, swimming vigorously!

'Who is it?' said Anne. 'Dear me, this lonely

common seems absolutely *crowded* with people!'

George was staring at the swimmer in utmost amazement. 'Anne – it's that boy!' she said. 'Look – tousled hair and everything! But – but . . .'

'But we've just met him going in the opposite direction!' said Anne, also amazed. 'How extraordinary! No, it *can't* be the boy!'

They went a little nearer. Yes – it *was* the boy. He called out to them. 'I'm just going out. I shan't be a minute!'

'How did you get here?' shouted George. 'We never saw you turn back and run.'

'I've been here for about ten minutes,' shouted back the boy.

'Fibber!' yelled back George at once.

'Ah – barmy as usual!' yelled the boy. 'Same as yesterday!'

He got out and walked off, dripping wet, in the direction of the trenches and pits which he was digging. George looked about for Jet, but she couldn't see him. 'Perhaps he's in the pool too,' she said. 'Come on, Anne – let's swim. I must say that that boy is extraordinary! I suppose he thinks it's funny to meet people, then double back and appear again!'

'He was nicer the first time of all that we saw him,' said Anne. 'I liked him then. I just don't understand him now. Ooooh – isn't this water lovely and warm!'

They had a long swim, got out and basked in the sun, lying on the heather, and then swam again. Then they began to feel hungry and went back to their little camping place.

The day passed quickly. They saw no more of the puzzling boy, or of Jet. They occasionally heard the sharp noise of metal on stone, or of chipping, from the place where the boy was presumably still digging in the old Roman camp.

'Or what he *hopes* is an old Roman camp,' said George. 'Personally I think he's so mad that I don't suppose he would know the difference between a Roman camp and a Boy Scouts' camp!'

They settled down on their heather bed that night but saw no stars twinkling above them this time. Instead there were rather heavy clouds, and it was not nearly so warm.

'Gosh – I hope it's not going to rain!' said George. 'Our tent wouldn't be much good against a real downpour! We could squeeze into it all right, but it's not a proper waterproof tent. Do you think it's going to rain, Anne?'

'No,' said Anne, sleepily. 'Anyway, I'm not getting up till I have to! I'm tired.'

She went to sleep, and so did George. Timmy didn't, though. He had heard the far-off growl of thunder, and he was uneasy. Timmy was not afraid of thunderstorms, but he didn't like them. They were things that growled like enormous dogs in the sky, and flashed angrily – but he never could get at them, or frighten them!

He closed both eyes, and put down one ear, leaving the other one up, listening.

Another thunder growl came, and one large and heavy drop of rain fell on Timmy's black nose. Then another fell on his cardboard collar and made a very loud noise indeed, startling him. He sat up, growling.

The rain came closer, and soon large drops, the size of ten-penny pieces, peppered the faces of the two sleeping girls. Then came such a crash of thunder that they both awoke in a fright.

'Blow! It's a thunderstorm!' said George. 'And pouring rain too. We shall be soaked.'

'Better get into the tent,' said Anne, as a flash of lightning forked down the sky and lit up everything with a quick brilliance.

'No good,' said George. 'It's soaked already. There's nothing for it but to get into the cottage, Anne. At least we'll have a roof over our heads or rather, a ceiling, for the roof's gone. Come on.'

Anne didn't in the least want to shelter in the old cottage, but there was absolutely nothing else to do. The girls grabbed their rug and ran through the rain, George flashing her torch to guide them. Timmy ran too, barking.

They came to the doorway of the cottage and went inside. What a relief to get out of the rain! The two girls huddled down into a corner, the rug round them – but soon they were too hot and threw it off.

The storm passed overhead with a few terrific crashes and much lightning. Gradually the rain grew less and soon stopped. One star came out, and then others followed as the thunderclouds swept away in the wind.

'We can't go back to the tent – we'll have to stay here,' said George. 'I'll go and get our bags for pillows. We can lie on the rug.'

Anne went with her, and carried a bag back too. Soon the girls were lying in a corner of the rug, their heads on the bags, and Timmy close beside them.

'Good night,' said Anne. 'We'll try to go to sleep again! Blow that storm!'

Soon they were both asleep – but Timmy wasn't. Timmy was uneasy. Very uneasy! And quite suddenly he broke into a volley of such loud barks that both girls woke up in a panic.

'Timmy! What's the matter? Oh Tim, what is it?' cried George. She clutched his leather collar and held on to him.

'Don't leave us! Timmy, what's scared you?'

[7]
Strange happenings

Timmy stopped barking and tried to get away from George's hand on his collar. But she would not let him. George was not easily frightened, but what with the thunderstorm, the strange old cottage and now Timmy's sudden excitement, she wanted him near her.

'What is it?' asked Anne, in a scared whisper.

'I don't know. I can't even imagine,' said George, also in a low voice. 'Perhaps it's nothing – just the thunderstorm that has upset him and made him nervous. We'll keep awake a bit, and see if we hear anything peculiar.'

They lay quietly in their corner, and George kept a firm hand on Timmy. He growled once or twice, but did not bark any more. George began to think it really must have been the storm that had upset him.

A rumble of thunder came again – the storm was returning, or else another one was blowing up!

George felt relieved. 'It's all right, Anne. It must have been the thunder and lightning in the distance that upset Timmy. You're silly, Timmy – scaring us like that!'

Crash – rumble – crash! Yes, certainly the storm was gathering force again! Timmy barked angrily.

'Be quiet! You make more noise than the thunder!' said George, crossly. 'No you can't go out into the rain, Timmy. It's begun again, as bad as before. You'd only get dripping wet – and then you'd want to come and sit as close to me as possible and make me wet too. I know you!'

'No – don't let him go, George,' said Anne. 'I like him here with us. My word – what a storm! I hope it won't strike this cottage.'

'Well, considering that it must have stood here for three or four hundred years, and have seen thousands of storms, I expect it will come safely through one more!' said George. 'Where are you going, Anne?'

'Just to look out of the window,' said Anne. 'Or out of the place where the window used to be! I like to see the countryside suddenly lit up for just one moment in a lightning flash – and then go back to darkness again.'

She went to stand at the window. There came the crash of thunder, not far away, and a brilliant flash of lightning. Anne stared over the countryside, which had suddenly become visible in the flash – and then disappeared like magic in a second!

Anne gave a sudden cry and stumbled back to George. 'George – George . . .'

'Whatever's the matter?' asked George, alarmed.

'There's someone out there – people!' said Anne, clutching George and making her jump.

'I saw them just for an instant, when the lightning flashed.'

'People? What sort of people?' said George,
astonished. 'How many?'

'I don't know. It was all so quick. I think
there were two – or maybe three. They were
standing some way off – quite still, out there in
the storm.'

'Anne, those are *trees*!' said George, scornfully. 'There are two or three small trees standing against the sky out there – I noticed them
the other day.'

'These weren't trees,' said Anne. 'I know they
weren't. What are people doing out there in this
storm? I'm frightened.'

George was absolutely certain that Anne had
seen the group of little trees that she knew were
there – they would look just like people, in a
quick flash of lightning. No sooner did you see
something in a storm than it was gone!

She comforted Anne. 'Don't worry, Anne!
it's the easiest thing in the world to imagine

seeing things in a lightning flash. Timmy would bark if there were people around. He would—'

'Well, he *did* bark, didn't he?' said Anne. 'He woke us both up with his barking.'

'Ah yes – but that was just because he heard the storm coming up again,' said George. 'And you know he gets angry when he hears the thunder growling.'

Just at that moment the thunder crashed again – then the lightning flashed its weird and brilliant light.

This time *both* the girls screamed, and Timmy gave an enormous bark, trying his hardest to get away from George.

'There! Did you see *that*?' said Anne, in a shaky voice.

'Yes. Yes, I did. Oh, Anne, you're right! Someone was looking in at the window! And if we saw him, he must have seen *us*! Whatever is he doing here in the middle of the night?'

'Well, I told you I saw two or three people,' said Anne, still shakily. 'I expect it was one of them. Maybe they saw the cottage in one of the lightning flashes, and thought they might shelter here – and sent one of their number to see.'

'Maybe. But what in the world is anyone *doing*, wandering about here at night?' said George. 'They can't possibly be up to any good. Let's go home tomorrow, Anne. I wish the boys were here! They'd know what to do, they would have some good plan!'

'The storm's going off again,' said Anne. 'Timmy has stopped barking too, thank goodness. Don't let him go, George. You never know – those people, whoever they are, might do him harm. Anyway, I feel safer when he's with us!'

'I wouldn't dream of letting him go,' said George. 'You're trembling, Anne! You needn't be as scared as that! Timmy won't let you come to any harm.'

'I know! But it wasn't very nice suddenly seeing somebody looking in at the window like that, outlined in a lightning flash!' said Anne. 'I can't possibly go to sleep again. Let's play some silly game to take our minds off it.'

So they played the Alphabet game with animals. Each had to think in turn of an animal beginning with A, and a mark went to the one who could keep it up longest! Then they went on to B and to C and to D.

They were doing the Es when they heard a loud and very comforting sound.

'Timmy's snoring,' said George. 'He's fast asleep. What an elephantine snore, Tim!'

'E for elephant,' said Anne, quickly.

'Cheat! That should have been *my* E!' said George. 'All right. E for Eland.'

'E for Egg-Eater,' said Anne, after a pause.

'Not allowed – you made that up!' said George. 'My mark!'

By the time they got to M, Anne was two marks ahead, and the dawn was breaking. It was a great relief to the two girls to see the silvering of the sky in the east and to know that soon the sun would be up. They immediately felt much better. George even stood up and went bravely to the window, where there was nothing to be seen but the quiet countryside outside, with its stretches of heather, gorse bushes and silver birches.

'We were silly to be so scared,' said George. 'I don't think we'll go back home today after all, Anne. I hate running away from anything. The boys would laugh at us.'

'I don't care if they do,' said Anne. 'I'm going back. If the boys were here, I'd stay – but goodness knows when they'll come – it might not be till next week! I'm just NOT staying here another night.'

'All right, all right,' said George. 'Do as you like – but for goodness' sake tell the boys it was *you* who wanted to run away, not me!'

'I will,' said Anne. 'Oh dear – now I feel sleepy all over again. I suppose it's because daylight is here and everything seems safe, so I know I can fall asleep.'

George felt the same! They cuddled down

together on the rug again and immediately fell asleep. They did not wake till quite late – and even then something woke them, or they might have slept on for hours, tired out with their broken night and the fright they had had.

They were awakened by something scuttling round them, making a very loud noise indeed. Then Timmy barked.

The girls awoke and sat up, rather dazed. 'Oh, it's *Jet*!' said Anne. 'Jet, have you come to see if we're all right, you dear, funny little one-eyed thing!'

'Wuff-wuff!' said Jet and rolled over on his back to be tickled, his long thin tail wagging all the time. Timmy leaped on him and pretended to eat him. Then a loud voice called to them.

They looked up. The boy was standing at the door, grinning widely.

'Hallo, sleepy-heads! I came to see if you were all right after that awful storm. I know I promised I wouldn't come here, but I felt a bit worried about you.'

'Oh. Well, that's nice of you,' said Anne, getting up and brushing the dust from her skirt. 'We're quite all right – but we had rather a peculiar night. We—'

She got a hard nudge from George and stopped suddenly. George was warning her not to say anything about the people they had seen – or the person at the window. Did she think they might have anything to do with this boy? Anne said no more and George spoke instead.

'Wasn't it a dreadful storm? How did you get on?'

'All right. I sleep down in a trench, and the rain can't get at me. Well – so long! Come on, Jet!'

The boy and the dog disappeared. 'That was nice of him,' said Anne. He doesn't seem crazy this morning, does he – quite normal! He didn't even contradict us. I think I quite like him after all.'

They went to their soaked tent and got a tin

of sardines out to eat with bread and butter. Just as they were opening it, they heard some-one whistling and looked up.

'Here comes that boy again!' said Anne.

'Good morning. I don't want to butt in – but I just wondered if you were all right after the storm,' said the boy, without even a smile. The girls stared at him in amazement.

'Look – don't start being crazy all over again!' said George. 'You know jolly well we're all right. We've already told you.'

'You haven't. And I *didn't* know!' said the boy. 'Well, I only came out of politeness. Sorry to see you are still barmy!'

And off he went. 'There!' said Anne, vexed. 'Just as we thought he was nice again, and not crazy, he starts all over again. I suppose he thinks it's funny. Silly ass!'

They set their things out to dry in the sun, and it was half past twelve before they were ready to pack and go back to Kirrin Cottage. George was rather cross about going, but Anne was quite firm. She was NOT going to spend another night on the common.

George was just strapping a package on her bicycle, when the two girls heard the sound of voices – and then Timmy went quite mad! He barked wildly, and set off down a path at top speed, his tail wagging nineteen to the dozen!

'Oh! It can't be – surely it can't be Julian and Dick!' shouted George, in sudden delight, and she shot off after Timmy.

It was! It *was* Julian and Dick! There they came, packs on their backs, grinning all over their faces! Hurrah! The Famous Five were all together once more!

[8]

All together again!

There was such excitement at the arrival of the boys that at first nobody could make themselves heard. Timmy barked at the top of his very loud voice and simply would *not* stop! George shouted, and Dick and Julian laughed. Anne hugged them, and felt proud of two such brown, good-looking brothers.

'Ju! We never guessed you'd come so soon!' said the delighted George. 'Gosh, I'm pleased to see you!'

'We got fed up with French food,' said Dick. 'I came out in spots and Julian was sick, and it was SO hot. Phew! Next time I go there I'll go when it's cooler.'

'And we kept on thinking of Kirrin and the bay, and you two girls and Timmy,' said Julian, giving George a friendly punch. 'I think we *really* got a bit homesick. So we packed up before we should, and flew home.'

'Flew?' said George. 'You lucky things! And then did you come straight down here?'

'We spent the night with Mother and Dad at home,' said Julian, 'and then caught the first train here that we possibly could this morning – only to find that you weren't at Kirrin!'

'So we packed camping-out things in smaller bags and came straight along to you!' said Dick. 'I say, George, old thing, do you think you could possibly make Timmy stop barking? I'm going a bit deaf!'

'Shut up, Tim,' ordered George. 'Let other people bark a bit. Do you notice his collar, Julian?'

'Can't help seeing it!' said Julian. 'He looks a scream in it, doesn't he? Ha ha! You're an Elizabethan dog with a ruff, Timmy – that's what Uncle Quentin told us – and that's what you look like, old fellow!'

'He looks most comical, I must say,' said Dick. 'Enough to make a cat laugh, hey, Timmy!'

Anne looked at George. Goodness, what would she say to hear *Julian and Dick* laughing at Timmy and making fun of him! Would she lose her temper at once?

But George only grinned. In fact she gave a little laugh herself. 'Yes – he does look funny, doesn't he? But he doesn't mind a bit!'

'You know, we came here to camp because George couldn't bear people laughing at—' began Anne, thinking that she wouldn't let George get away with this! But George gave her such a beseeching look, that she stopped at once. George could never bear to look small in front of Julian and Dick. She prided herself on being just like a boy – and she was suddenly certain that her two cousins would think she was 'just like a *girl*' if they heard the fuss she had made about people laughing at Timmy's collar.

'I say – you two seem to be packing up,' said Julian, looking at the package strapped to the back of George's bicycle. 'What's happened?'

'Well – it got a bit lonely and Anne was . . .' and then in her turn George caught a beseeching look from Anne! She knew what it meant. I didn't tell tales on *you* – so don't tell tales on *me* – *don't* say I was scared!

'Er – Anne was certain that there was something funny going on here,' went on George, who had quite meant to say that Anne was scared and insisted on going home. 'And we didn't feel that we could tackle it ourselves – though if you had been here we wouldn't have *dreamed* of going home, of course.'

'What do you mean – something funny?' asked Dick.

'Well – you see – it began like this,' said George, but Julian interrupted.

'If there's a tale to tell, let's have it over a meal, shall we? We've had nothing to eat since six o'clock this morning, Dick and I – and we're ravenous!'

'Yes. Good idea,' said Dick, and began to undo a big package which he took out of his bag. 'I've a picnic lunch here from your mother, George – a jolly good one, I can tell you. I think she was so relieved to think that she was going to get rid of us that she really surpassed herself! We've got a marvellous piece of boiled ham – look! It'll last us for ages – if we don't give bits to Timmy. Get away, Tim. This is *not* for you! Grrrrrr!'

George suddenly felt so happy that she could hardly speak. It had been fun camping with Anne – but what a difference the boys made! So confident of themselves, so merry, full of jokes, so idiotic, and yet so dependable. She felt that she wanted to sing at the top of her voice!

The sun had been hot again that morning and had dried the common beautifully. It wasn't long before the Five were sitting down in the heather with a very fine feast before them.

'I wouldn't sell anyone my hunger for a hundred pounds,' said Dick. 'Now then – who's going to carve this magnificent piece of gammon?'

There were no plates, so they had to make sandwiches of the ham. Dick had actually brought some mustard, and dabbed it generously over the slices of ham before George put them between pieces of bread. 'Aha, Tim – this is one way of making sure you won't get even a *bite* of these wonderful ham sandwiches!' said Dick. 'You can't bear mustard, can you? Ju, where's the meat we brought for Tim?'

'Here. Pooh – it smells a bit strong,' said Julian. 'Do you mind taking it to a nice secluded corner, Tim?'

Timmy immediately sat down close to Julian. 'Now – don't be so disobedient!' said Julian, and gave Timmy a friendly push.

'He doesn't understand the word "secluded",'

said George, with a grin. 'Tim – buzz off a bit!'

Timmy understood that and took his meat a little way away. Everyone took a ripe red tomato, and a little lettuce heart from a damp cloth brought by Julian, and settled down happily to munch sandwiches.

'Lovely!' said Anne, contentedly. 'Goodness gracious – I can hardly believe we had such a peculiar time last night!'

'Ah – tell us all about it!' said Dick.

So first Anne, then George related all that had happened. Anne told of the night she had seen a light in the old cottage and had heard whispers and footfalls inside.

'We did think I might have been dreaming,' she said, 'but now we don't think I was. We think I really did see and hear those things.'

'What next?' asked Julian, taking his third sandwich. 'This all sounds most interesting. Quite Famous Five-ish, in fact!'

George told of the storm in the night, and

how they had had to leave their heather bed and go to shelter in the old cottage – and how, in the flashes of lightning, Anne had seen two or three people standing outside – and then how they had *both* seen someone standing silently, looking in at the window.

'Strange,' said Julian, puzzled. 'Yes – something is up. I wonder what? I mean – there's absolutely nothing on this lonely bit of common that's at all interesting.'

'Well – there are the remains of an old Roman camp,' said Anne. 'And a boy there who is examining them to see if he can find anything old and interesting.'

'A completely *mad* boy,' said George. 'He doesn't seem to know what he says or doesn't say. Contradicts himself all the time – or to put it another way, tells the most idiotic fibs.'

'And he apparently thinks it's awfully funny to meet us somewhere, and then double round on his tracks and appear suddenly somewhere else,' said Anne. 'Sometimes I can't help liking him – other times he's too idiotic for words.'

'He's got a little one-eyed dog called Jet,' said George, and Timmy gave a sudden bark as he heard the name. 'You like Jet, don't you, Tim?'

'This all sounds most interesting,' said Dick. 'Pass me the tomato bag, Ju, before you eat the lot. Thanks. As I said, *most* interesting – a one-eyed dog, a mad boy, Roman remains – and people who come to an old ruined cottage in the dead of night and look into windows!'

'I wonder you two girls didn't pack up and go home,' said Julian. 'You must be braver without us than I thought possible!'

George caught Anne's eye and grinned mischievously, but said nothing. Anne owned up, red in the face.

'Well – I did tell George I was going home this very morning, I was so scared last night. George didn't want to, of course, but she was coming, all the same. But now you've turned up, things are different.'

'Ah – well, do we stay on, or don't we, Ju?' said Dick. 'Are we scared or are we not?'

Everyone laughed. 'Well – if you go back *I* shall stay on alone!' said Anne. 'Just to show you!'

'Good old Anne!' said Dick. 'We all stay, of course. It may be nothing – it may be something – we can't tell. But we'll certainly find out. And the first thing to do is to have a look at the Roman remains and the mad boy. I'm looking forward to meeting him, I must say! After that we'll tackle the ruined cottage!'

Timmy came up to see if he could get any tit-bits. Julian waved him away. 'You smell of too-strong meat, Timmy,' he said. 'Go and get a drink. By the way, *is* there anything to drink here, George?'

'Oh yes,' said George. 'A lovely spring. Not far off, either. Let's take the remains of our meal there, and the mug. We've only got one unfortunately, so it's no good getting water unless we all sit by the spring and take turns at the mug. Come on!'

The boys thought that the spring was a really splendid one. They grouped themselves around it and took turns at filling the mug and drinking from it. They were now eating slabs of Joanna's fruit cake and it was very good.

'Now, you girls unpack again,' said Dick, when they had finished their meal. 'Goodness, I did enjoy that! We'd better unpack too, Julian.'

'Right. Where shall we put our things?' asked Julian, looking around. 'I don't somehow like to leave everything under that little tent, with a mad boy about, and a one-eyed dog. I feel that both of them might like the rest of that ham.'

'Oh, it's too hot to leave ham out in this sun,' said George. 'We'll have to put it into the old cottage, on a shelf. We'll put *everything* there, shall we? Move in properly, in case it rains again at night. It's so tiresome to have to bundle everything indoors in the dark and the rain.'

'I agree,' said Dick. 'Right. We'll move into

the ruined cottage. What fun! Come on, every-one!'

They spent the next half-hour taking their things into the cottage and putting them in corners or on shelves. George found a dark corner behind the fireplace where she put the food, for she was half-afraid that Jet, nice little dog though he seemed, might perhaps smell the ham and gobble up most of their food.

'Now!' said Julian. 'Are we ready to go and see the Roman remains and the Mad Boy? Here we go, then – the Famous Five are off again, and who knows what will happen!'

[9]

A little exploration

The Five walked off together, Timmy at the back, delighted to have all his friends with him again. He kept nudging first one person's heels and then another, just to remind them that he was there.

As they came near the old camp, they saw a boy sitting beside a bush, reading.

'There's that boy we told you of!' said George. 'See?'

'He looks fairly ordinary,' said Dick. 'Very absorbed in his book, I must say. Determined to take no notice of us!'

'I'll speak to him,' said George. So, as they drew near, she called to the boy.

'Hallo! Where's Jet?'

The boy looked up, annoyed. 'How do I know?'

'Well, he was with you this morning,' said George.

'He was not,' said the boy. 'He's never with me! Please don't disturb me, I'm reading.'

'There you are!' said George to the others. 'He came to see us this morning with Jet – and now he says the little dog is never with him. Quite, quite mad!'

'Or plain rude,' said Dick. 'Not worth bothering about, anyway. Well, if he's not doing any excavating in his Roman camp, perhaps we can explore it without being ordered off!'

They walked on slowly and came to the camp, and at once heard a cheerful whistling going on, and the sound of someone digging. George looked over the top of the dug-out trench in surprise. She almost toppled in, she was so amazed at what she saw!

The boy was there, digging carefully, whistling as he did so! He brushed his tousled hair from his hot forehead and caught sight of

George and the others. He looked rather astonished.

'How on earth did you get down here so quickly?' said George. 'Do you have wings or something?'

'I've been down here all the afternoon,' said the boy. 'For at least an hour, I should think.'

'Fibber!' said George. The boy looked very angry, and shouted back at once.

'I'm tired of you two girls – and now you've brought your friends too, I suppose you think you can come and aggravate me even more!'

'Don't be an idiot,' said Dick, feeling as puzzled about this boy as George and Anne had been. How in the world had he run around them and got down in the trench so quickly? Did he enjoy playing tricks like that? He really didn't *look* mad!

'Is this your property, this old camp?' asked Julian.

'No. Of course not. Don't be daft!' said the boy. 'As if I could own a whole camp like this!

It was discovered by my father some time ago, and he gave me permission to work here for the hols. It's pretty exciting, I can tell you. See my finds?'

He pointed to a rough shelf where stood a broken pot, something that looked like an old brooch, a long pinlike thing, and part of a stone head. Julian was at once interested. He leapt down into the trench.

'I say – you've certainly got something there!' he said. 'Any coins too?'

'Yes – three,' said the boy and put his hand in his pocket. 'I found this one first – then these two close together yesterday. They must be hundreds and hundreds of years old.'

By this time all the others were down in the trench too. They looked about with much interest. Evidently the place had been well excavated by experts, and now the boy was working here and there on his own, hoping to find something that had been overlooked.

Dick went out of the trench and began to

clamber about over the great stones and rocks. A small animal suddenly caught his eye – a young rabbit.

It stared at him in fright and then disappeared behind a slab of stone. It peeped out at Dick again, and he was amused. He went cautiously over to the slab, and the little rabbit disappeared – but soon two or three whiskers poked out. Dick got down on hands and knees and looked behind the slab. A dark hole was there.

Dick pulled out his torch and flashed it into the hole, wondering if the small rabbit was hiding there, or whether it was the entrance to a burrow.

To his surprise there was a very big hole indeed – a hole that seemed to go down and down and down – his torch could make out no bottom to it.

'It's far too wide for a rabbit hole,' thought Dick. 'I wonder where it leads to. I'll ask that boy.'

He went back to where the boy was still showing his things to Julian, talking eagerly. 'I say,' began Dick, 'there's a most interesting hole behind one of the stone slabs over there – what is it?'

'Oh that – my father says it was explored and that it was only a place for storage – meat in hot weather, or loot, or something like that. Actually nothing whatever was found there – most uninteresting. As a matter of fact it may be nothing to do with the camp at all.'

'I say, look – here's another shelf with things on it,' said George, suddenly spying a little collection of things on a rough shelf in another part of the trench. 'Are these yours too?'

'Those? No,' said the boy. 'Nothing to do with me at all. Don't touch them, please.'

'Whose are they then?' asked George, curiously. The boy took no notice whatever of her question and went on talking to Julian. George took down a beautiful little round pot.

'Hey! I told you NOT to touch those!' yelled the boy, so suddenly and angrily that George almost dropped the pot. 'Put it back – and clear out if you can't do what you're told.'

'Easy, old man, easy!' said Julian. 'No need to yell at her like that. You scared that little dog of yours and made him jump almost out of his skin! We'd better go, I think.'

'Well – I don't like being disturbed too much,' said the boy. 'People always seem to be wandering around. I've turned off quite a lot.'

'People?' said Julian, remembering Anne's story of two or three figures standing outside the cottage the night before, and of someone looking in. 'What kind of people?'

'Oh – nosey ones – wanting to get down and explore – disturbing me – it's surprising how many idiots there are wandering about this lonely place,' said the boy, picking up a tool again and setting to work. He grinned suddenly. 'I don't mean you. You really *know* something about this kind of thing.'

'Was anyone about last night?' asked Julian.

'Well – I rather think so,' said the boy. 'Because Jet here barked like mad. But it might have been the storm that frightened him – not that he's *usually* frightened of storms.'

'What's your name?' asked Dick.

'Guy Lawdler,' said the boy, and Dick whistled.

'My word – is your father the famous explorer, Sir John Lawdler?' he asked. The boy nodded.

'Well, no wonder you're so keen on archae-ology!' said Dick. 'Your father's done pretty well in that line, hasn't he?'

'Come on, Dick!' said George. 'Let's go now. We might have time for a swim in the pool. We forgot to tell you about that.'

'Right,' said Dick. 'Come on, Julian. Good-bye, Guy!'

They left the rather desolate old camp and went back to the cottage to get their swimsuits and change. It wasn't long before they were running over the heather to the pool.

'Hallo – Guy's having a swim!' said Dick, in surprise. Sure enough, a boy was there, his hair falling over his forehead as usual.

'Hey, Guy!' shouted George. 'Have a swim with us!'

But the boy was already getting out of the water. Dick shouted. 'Wait a minute – don't go. We'd like to have a swim with you, Guy!'

But the boy turned defiantly. 'Don't be an ass!' he said. 'My name's not Guy!'

And, leaving four astonished people behind him, he ran lightly over the heather and disappeared.

'There you are – he's mad after all!' said Anne. 'Don't bother about him. Come on in – the water's lovely and warm.'

They lazed about afterwards and began to feel hungry. 'Though how *any* of us could feel hungry after eating about fifty sandwiches between us at lunch-time, I don't know!' said

Dick. 'Race you back to the cottage, Ju!'

They changed back into ordinary clothes and then had tea – fruit cake, shortbread biscuits and tinned pineapple on bread. They kept the juice and diluted it with cold spring water – it was simply delicious.

'Now let's explore the cottage,' said Dick.

'We already have, Anne and I,' said George. 'So I don't expect you'll find anything much.'

They went methodically through the old house, and even up the old stone stairway to the two rooms upstairs – though they could hardly be called rooms, for they had very little roof and not much wall!

'Nothing much here, that's certain,' said Dick, clattering down the stone stairway. 'Now let's go to the outbuildings – not that there's much left of them either!'

They examined everything, and came last of all to the old stables. It was dark inside, for the windows were very small, and it was some seconds before anyone could see properly.

'Old mangers,' said Dick, touching them. 'I wonder how long ago it is since they were used – and—'

'I say!' said George, suddenly. 'There's something funny here. Anne, look – this bit of floor was undisturbed yesterday, wasn't it?'

Anne looked down at the big white flagstone on which George was standing. It was quite obvious that it had been lifted, for the edges were not as green with moss as the others were, and the stone had been put back a little crookedly.

'Yes – someone's been interested in this stone – or in what is beneath it!' said Dick. 'I bet something is buried underneath!'

'Those men last night – that's what they came about!' said George. 'They went into these stables and lifted this stone. Why?'

'We'll soon find out!' said Julian. 'Come on, everyone, loosen it with your fingers – then we'll heave it up!'

[10]

What can be happening?

Forty fingers and thumbs were very hard at work trying to loosen the heavy stone. At last Julian got hold of a corner which could be held more easily than any other part of the stone. He tried to lift it and it came away a little.

'Help me this side, Dick,' said Julian, and Dick put his strong fingers there too. 'Heave-ho!' he said – and up came the stone.

It went over with a crash and Timmy barked loudly, jumping aside. Everyone peered down – and then looked exceedingly disappointed!

There was nothing there at all. Not even a hole! The black earth, hard as iron, lay under-neath, and nothing else.

They all stared down at the dry, hard earth, puzzled. George looked up at Julian.

'Well – that's strange, isn't it? Why should anyone lift up this heavy stone if there is nothing hidden underneath?'

'Well, it's clear that whoever was here didn't find anything – nor did he *hide* anything either,' said Julian. 'Dear me – why should anyone lift up a heavy store and put it back – just for nothing?

'He was obviously looking for something that wasn't here,' said Anne. 'The wrong stone, probably!'

'Yes. I think Anne's right,' said Dick. 'It's the wrong stone! Probably there is something very interesting under the *right* stone! But which one is it?'

They all sat and looked at one another, and Timmy sat too, wondering why all this fuss was made about a flat white stone. Julian thought hard.

'From what you've told me, Anne – about seeing a light in the cottage that first night you were here – and hearing voices – and then seeing those figures outside last night in the storm – it looks as if someone is urgently hunting for something round about here.'

'Yes – something under a stone. Treasure of some sort, do you think?' said George.

Julian shook his head. 'No. I hardly think that much treasure would be hidden anywhere about this old cottage – all the people who lived here must have been fairly poor. The most they would have hidden would have been a few pieces of gold, and that would have been found long ago.'

'Well – someone modern might have hidden something valuable here – even something stolen,' said Anne.

'Yes. We can't tell. It's obviously important and urgent to somebody,' said Dick. 'I wonder if the people that Guy said came bothering him were anything to do with this?'

'They may have been,' said Julian. 'But they have clearly decided that what they are looking for is here now, whatever it is. And they must have been most annoyed to find you and Anne here last night, George. That's why someone came and looked in at the window, I expect – to make sure you were asleep! And you weren't.'

'I don't know whether I want to stay on here or not now,' said Anne, alarmed. 'If they haven't found what they want, they'll probably come again – in the night too.'

'Who cares?' said Dick. 'We've got Timmy, haven't we? I'm not turning out of here because somebody's got a habit of turning up big stones!'

Julian laughed. 'Nor am I. Let's stay on! And I don't see why we shouldn't do a bit of pulling up of stones ourselves! We might come across something very interesting!'

'Right. It's decided that we stay on then, is it?' said Dick. 'What about you, Anne?'

'Oh yes – of course I'll stay,' said Anne, not wanting to in the least, but knowing that she simply could not bear not to be with the others.

The Five walked round and about the cottage for a while, trying to make out where the people that the girls had seen the night before had come from – from what direction did they come and where did they go?

'The figures I saw first in the lightning stood about there,' said Anne, pointing. 'Let's go and see if there are any footprints. It was pouring with rain and the ground must have been very muddy.'

'Good idea,' said Dick, and off they went to where Anne had pointed. But it was a heathery piece of ground, and difficult to tell even if anyone *had* trodden there, for the heather was thick and springy.

'Let's look just outside the window now – the one where Anne saw someone looking in,' said Dick. And there they had a find! Just in front of the window were two quite deeply printed footmarks. One was slightly blurred as if the maker of them had turned his foot sideways as he waited. The other was very clear indeed.

Dick got out a piece of paper. 'I rather think I'll measure these,' he said, 'and make a note of the pattern on the soles. They had rubber soles and heels – look at the markings – crêpe rubber I should think.'

He measured the prints. 'Size eight shoes,' he said. 'Same as yours, Ju.' Then he carefully drew an exact picture of the sole and heel markings.

'You're quite a detective, Dick,' said Anne, admiringly, and he laughed.

'Oh, anyone can copy footprints!' he said. 'The thing is to match them up with the owner!'

'I have a feeling it's getting on for supper-time – if anyone *wants* any supper,' said George. 'It's half past eight! Would you believe that the time could fly so fast?'

'I don't *really* feel very hungry,' said Dick. 'We've done pretty well today.'

'Well, don't waste our precious food if you don't feel hungry,' said George. 'We shall have to keep going home for more if we eat everything too quickly.'

Nobody felt terribly hungry. They made a cosy corner in the cottage and had a slice of cake and a biscuit each, with a drink of pineapple juice and spring-water. George had had the bright idea of filling the big empty pineapple tin, and they each filled a mug from it in turn, and drank.

'It's getting dark,' said Julian. 'Are we going to sleep inside the cottage or out?'

'In,' said Dick, promptly. 'We'll make things just as difficult for any night prowlers as possible!'

'Right,' said Julian. 'I bet they won't be pleased to find old Timmy here too. Shall we go out and get some heather for beds? I don't fancy sharing a thin rug between the four of us.'

Soon they were all dragging in armfuls of the springy heather. They laid it in the front room, in two corners, for the boys thought they would rather be in the same room as the girls, in case of danger.

'You need an awful lot of heather to make a *soft* bed,' said Dick, trying his. 'My bones seem to go right through the clumps and rub against the floor!'

'We can put our jackets over our heather,' said Julian. 'That will help. The girls can have the rug. We shan't need any covering, it's so hot.'

By the time they had finished, it was dark. George lay on her heather and yawned. 'I'm going to sleep,' she announced. 'We don't need to keep guard or anything like that, do we? Timmy will bark if anyone comes near.'

'You're right. I really don't think we need take turns at keeping awake,' said Julian. 'Move up, Dick – you've left me no room.'

Julian was the last to go to sleep. He lay awake puzzling over the lifted stone slab. It was clear that someone had expected to find something under it. How did they know it was that particular slab? Had they a map? If so, it must have shown the wrong stone – or perhaps the searchers read the map wrong?

Before he could work it out any further, he was asleep. Timmy was asleep too, happy because all the others were under his care. He had one ear open as usual, but not *very* much open!

It was enough to let him hear a small mouse of some kind run across the floor. It was even enough for him to hear a beetle scraping its way up the wall. After a while his ear dropped down and he didn't even hear a hedgehog outside.

But something caused his ear to listen again and it pricked up. A noise crept inside the cottage – a noise that got louder and louder – a weird and puzzling noise!

Timmy woke up and listened. He pawed at George, not knowing whether to bark or not. He knew he should not bark at owls, but this was not an owl. Perhaps George would know.

'Don't, Timmy,' said George sleepily, but Timmy went on pawing her. Then she too heard the noise and sat up in a hurry.

What a truly horrible sound! It was a whining and a wailing, rising and falling through the night. A sound of misery and woe, that went on and on.

'Julian! Dick! Wake up!' called George, her heart beating wildly. 'Something's happening.'

The boys awoke at once and so did Anne. They sat and listened to the weird noise. What in the world could it be? There it went again – wailing high in the air, and then dying away with a moan, only to begin again a few seconds later.

Dick felt the roots of his hair pricking. He leapt off the heather bed and ran to the window. 'Quick! Come and look at this!' he cried. 'What is it?'

They all crowded to the window, Timmy barking now as loudly as he could. In silence the others gazed at a very strange sight.

Blue and green lights were shining here and there, sometimes dimly, sometimes brightly. A curious round white light was travelling slowly in the air, and Anne clutched George, breathing fast.

'It won't come here,' she said. 'It won't, will it? I don't like it. What is happening, Julian?'

'I wish that awful wailing, whining noise would stop,' said Dick. 'It gets right inside my head. Do you make anything of all this, Julian?'

'Something very strange is going on,' said Julian. 'I'll go out with Timmy and see what I can find.' And before anyone could stop him, out he went, Timmy barking beside him.

'Oh Julian – come back!' called Anne, listening as his footsteps became distant. They all waited tensely at the window – and then suddenly the wailing noise stopped and the strange lights gradually began to fade.

Then they heard Julian's footsteps coming back firmly in the darkness.

'Ju! What was it?' called Dick, as his brother came in at the doorway.

'I don't know, Dick,' said Julian, sounding very puzzled. 'I simply – don't – know! Perhaps we can find out in the morning.'

[11]

Interesting discoveries –
and a plan

The four sat in the dark and talked over the horrible noises and the weird blue and green and white lights. Anne sat close to Julian. She really was frightened.

'I want to go back to Kirrin,' she said. 'Let's go tomorrow. I don't like this.'

'I didn't see a thing just now,' said Julian, puzzled, his arm close round Anne. 'I seemed to go quite close to those wailing sounds – and then they stopped as soon as I got fairly near. But although Timmy barked and ran around, there didn't seem to be anyone there.'

'Did you get near the lights?' asked Dick.

'Yes, fairly near. But the odd thing was that they seemed high up when I got near them – not near the ground as I expected. And *again* Timmy couldn't find anyone. You would have thought if there was anyone about, playing the fool, that Timmy would have found them. But he didn't.'

'Woof,' said Timmy, dolefully. He didn't like this funny business at all!

'Well, if *nobody's* making the noises and lights, it makes it even worse,' said Anne. 'Do let's go home, Julian. Tomorrow.'

'All right,' said Julian. 'I don't feel particularly thrilled about all this myself. But there is *one* idea I've got in my mind which I'd like to sort out tomorrow.'

'What's that?' said Dick.

'Well – it may quite well be that somebody very badly wants us out of here for some reason,' said Julian. 'And that somebody may want to come and lift other stones and have a thorough search all over the place – which he can't do with us around. So he's trying to frighten us out!'

'Yes, I believe you are right, Julian,' said Dick. 'Those noises – and lights – they would be enough to scare anyone out of a place. Too eerie for words! Well, let's have a good snoop round in the daylight, to see if we can find any trace of a trickster!'

'We will – but it's extremely odd that *Timmy* didn't find him,' said Julian. 'Timmy can smell anyone out of any hiding place! Yes – we'll have a very very good hunt round tomorrow.'

'And if you find nothing and nobody, we'll go home?' asked Anne.

'Yes, we will. I promise you,' said Julian, hugging Anne. 'Don't worry. You shan't have to stay here one night longer, unless you want to! Now, let's try and go to sleep again!'

It took the four a long time to go to sleep after all this excitement in the middle of the night. Anne kept listening for the wailing noises again, but none came. She kept her eyes shut tightly in case she should happen to see any more of the strange lights outside the window.

George and the boys lay awake too, puzzling out the problems of lights and noises which were not apparently caused by anyone! Julian especially was puzzled.

Only Timmy was unconcerned. He went to sleep before anyone else, though he kept one ear *wide* open – and up went the other one when George moved, or Dick whispered to Julian.

The excitement of the night made them all sleep late. Julian awoke first, and stared at the low ceiling in surprise. Now – where was he? In France? No. Ah, of course he was in the old ruined cottage!

He woke Dick, who yawned and stretched. 'Remember those strange lights and noises last night?' asked Dick. 'What a fright they gave us! It seems silly to think we were all so puzzled and scared, now that the sun is shining in at the window, and we can see the countryside around for miles!'

'I'm pretty certain someone is trying to scare

us away,' said Julian. 'We are in their way here
– they want to do some thorough explorations
and they can't, because of us! I've a good mind
to take the girls home, Dick, and come back
here with you.'

'Anne might go, but George wouldn't,' said
Dick. 'You know what old George is like – she
doesn't like to miss out. Let's not decide anything till we have had a look round this morning. I don't really believe there's anything
spooky about this at all – I agree with you that
it's just a few tricks to frighten us away.'

'Right,' said Julian. 'Let's wake the girls.
Hey, George! Anne! Sleepyheads! Get up and
get us breakfast!'

George sat up, looking furious, as Julian
intended. 'You jolly well get your own b—'
she began, and then laughed as she saw Julian's
amused face.

'I was only just striking a little match to set
you alight!' said Julian. 'Come on – let's all go
for a swim in the pool!'

They set off together happily in the warm sunshine, Timmy padding along, his tail waving vigorously. As soon as they got to the pool, they saw the boy there, floating lazily on his back.

'There's Guy!' said Anne.

'I wonder if he will admit to his name or not this morning!' said George. 'Remember how he told us his name was Guy – and then said it wasn't a little while after? Silly ass! I can't make out if he's quite mad, or just thinks it's funny to keep playing the fool!'

They came to the pool. The boy waved to them, grinning. 'Come on in – it's fine!'

'Is your name Guy this morning or not?' called George.

The boy looked surprised. 'Of course it's Guy!' he said. 'Don't be idiotic! Come on in and have a game.'

They had a fine swim and a mad one. Guy was like an eel, swimming under the water, catching their legs, splashing, swimming away fast, doubling round and going underwater just as they got up to him!

At last they all sat panting on the edge of the pond, the sun shining down warmly on them.

'I say, Guy – did you hear anything strange last night?' asked Dick. 'Or see anything?'

'I didn't *see* anything strange – but I thought I heard somebody wailing and crying in the distance,' said Guy. 'Just now and again when the wind brought the sound this way. Jet didn't like it at all – did you, Jet? He went and hid under my legs!'

'We heard it too – quite near us,' said Julian. 'And saw strange lights.'

They discussed the matter for some time, but Guy could not really help them, because he had not been near enough to the noises to hear them as clearly as the others had.

'I'm getting hungry,' said George, at last. 'I keep thinking of ham and tomatoes and cheese. Let's go back to the cottage.'

'Right,' said Julian. 'Good-bye, Guy – see

you sometime soon. Good-bye, Jet, you mad little thing.'

They went off together, their swimsuits almost dry already in the sun.

'Well, Guy was perfectly sensible this morning,' said Anne. 'Funny! I wonder why he's so silly sometimes.'

'See – isn't that him – running down the path there – to the right, look!' said George, suddenly. 'Now how did he get there so quickly? We left him by the pool!'

It certainly looked like Guy! They called to him, but he didn't even look round or wave, though he must have heard them. They went on, puzzled. How could one person be so different each time – and why? What was the point?

They had a good breakfast and then went out to look round and see if they could find anything to explain the strange happenings of the night before.

'The noises seemed to come from about here,

when I came out last night,' said Julian, stopping near the little group of trees. 'And the lights seemed to start about here too – but not near the ground – they were high up, above my head.'

'Above your head?' said Dick, puzzled. 'That seems odd.'

'It doesn't!' said Anne. 'Not a *bit* odd! What about those trees there? Couldn't somebody climb up them and do the wailing and whining there, with some strange instrument – and set off the weird lights?'

Julian stared up at the trees and then round at Anne. He grinned suddenly.

'Anne's got it! Clever girl! Of course someone was up there – or maybe two people – one doing the noises with some weird instrument and the other playing about with fireworks of some kind. Not the noisy kind – just coloured fire or balloons lit up from inside.'

'Yes! *That's* why the lights seemed to be so high up, when you came out!' said Dick. 'They were sent out by someone up in a tree!'

'And floated away to scare us,' said Anne. 'Golly – I *do* feel glad that it was silly tricks like that that frightened us so. They wouldn't frighten me *again*!'

'It explains something else too,' said George. 'It explains why Timmy didn't find anyone! They were safely up trees! I bet they hardly breathed when they knew Tim was down below.'

'Yes. Of course! That puzzled me too,' said Julian. 'It was too spooky for words when even old Tim couldn't find anyone real about – just noises and lights!'

'Here's something, look – a wrinkled little rubber-skin – pale green!' said Dick, picking something up from the ground. 'That's what those lights were – balloons lit up from inside in some way and sent floating away in the air.'

'Most ingenious,' said Julian. 'I expect they had quite a lot of funny tricks at their disposal last night. Yes – they certainly mean to scare us away!'

'Well, they won't,' said Anne, unexpectedly. '*I'm* not going, for one. I won't be scared away by stupid tricks!'

'Good old Anne!' said Julian, and clapped her on the back. 'Right – we'll all stay – but I've got an idea.'

'What?' asked everyone.

'We'll *pretend* to go!' said Julian. 'We'll pack up everything – remove our things from here – and go and camp somewhere else. But Dick and I will *hide* somewhere here tonight – and watch to see if anyone comes, and where they look for whatever it is they're hunting for, and why!'

'That's a fantastic plan,' said Dick, pleased. 'We'll do it! Roll on, tonight! Adventure is about – and we'll be ready for it!'

[12]
A good hiding place

The Five spent quite a pleasant day, but when late afternoon came, they decided that it was time to carry out their plan and pack as if they were leaving.

'I imagine someone is spying on our doings,' said Dick. 'And won't he be pleased to see us apparently on the point of leaving!'

'How can anyone be spying?' asked Anne, looking all round as if she expected to see someone behind a bush. 'Timmy would be sure to sniff out anyone in hiding.'

'Oh, he won't be near enough for Timmy to smell out,' said Dick. 'He'll be a long way off.'

'Then how can he possibly see us – or know that we're leaving?' asked Anne.

'Anne – I don't know if you've heard of field-glasses,' began Dick, solemnly. 'Well, they're things that can spot anything half a mile away . . .'

Anne went red and gave Dick a punch. 'Don't be an ass! Of course – that's it! Field-glasses used by someone on a hillside some-where – trained on the old cottage.'

'Actually I think I know where the someone is,' said Dick. 'I've caught sight of a little flash every now and again on the hill over there – the kind of flash that is made by the sun on glass – and I somehow think that our spy is sitting near the top of the hill, watching us carefully.'

Anne turned to look at the hill, but Julian at once spoke sharply. 'No – don't stand and stare up there, anyone. We don't want the watcher to know that *we* know we are being watched.'

They went on with their packing, and soon began to stagger out with their bundles. George was told to strap her things on her bicycle, and stand well out in the open as she did so, so that the watcher on the hill would be able to observe all her doings.

Julian was in the midst of carefully folding up his things to go into his knapsack, when Anne gave a sudden exclamation.

'Someone's coming!'

Everyone looked round, imagining that they would see a sinister-looking foreigner, or someone peculiar in some way.

But all they saw was a countrywoman hurrying along, a shawl over her head, and a basket under her arm. She wore glasses, had no make-up on, and her hair was pulled straight back under the shawl. She stopped when she saw the Five.

'Good afternoon,' said Julian, politely. 'Isn't it glorious weather!'

'Beautiful,' said the woman. 'Are you camping out – you've certainly chosen a very good time!'

'No – actually we're packing,' said Julian. 'We've been sleeping in the old cottage, but we've decided to move out. Is it very, very old?'

'Oh yes – and it's supposed to have strange things happening in it at nights,' said the woman.

'We know that!' said Julian. 'My word – we were pretty scared last night, I can tell you – weird noises and horrible, ghostly lights. We decided not to stay there any longer.'

'That's right,' said the woman. 'Don't you stay! You get as far from this place as you can! I can tell you, *I* wouldn't come by it at night. Where are you going?'

'Well, our home is at Kirrin,' said Julian, evading the question. 'You know – on Kirrin Bay.'

'Ah yes – a fine place,' said the woman. 'Well, don't you stay another night! Good-bye!'

She hurried off, and was soon lost to sight.

'Go on packing,' said Julian to the others. 'The watcher is still up in the hills. I caught sight of a flash again just then.'

'Julian, why did you tell all that to the woman?' asked Anne. 'You don't usually say so much when we are in the middle of something funny!'

'My dear, unsuspecting Anne – do you mean to say that you thought that woman was really what she pretended to be – a woman from a nearby farm?' said Julian.

'Well – wasn't she?' said Anne, surprised. 'She looked like one – no make-up – and that old shawl – and she knew all about the old cottage!'

'Anne – farm women don't have gold fillings in their teeth,' said Julian. 'Didn't you notice them when she smiled?'

'And her hair was dyed,' said George. 'I noticed it was blonde at the roots and black above.'

'*And* what about her hands?' said Dick. 'A farmer's wife does a great deal of hard, rough work, and her hands are never white and smooth – they are rough and brown. This woman's hands were as white as a princess's!'

'Well yes, I did notice them,' said Anne. 'And

I did notice too that she sometimes spoke with an accent and sometimes without.'

'Well, there you are!' said Julian. 'She's one of the unpleasant gang that tried to scare us last night – and when the watcher on the hill reported that we appeared to be packing up and going, she was told to go and make sure. So she pretended to be a countrywoman and came by – but unfortunately we weren't quite so stupid as she thought we would be!'

'You certainly fooled her!' said Dick, with a grin. 'The gang will be down here tonight, digging up all the big stones they can find. You and I will have a marvellous time, snooping round them.'

'You'll be careful they don't see you, won't you?' said Anne. 'Where will you hide?'

'We haven't planned that yet,' said Dick. 'Now come on and we'll make a new camp somewhere that won't be easily seen. You and George and Timmy can sleep there tonight, and Ju and I will come and watch here.'

'I want to come too,' said George at once. 'Anne will be all right with Timmy.'

'You aren't joining us this time, George,' said Ju. 'The fewer people watching the better. Sorry, old thing – but you'll have to stay with Anne.'

George scowled and looked sulky at once. Julian laughed and slapped her on the shoulder. 'What a *lovely* scowl! One of your best! I haven't seen it for quite a long time. Keep it up, George – go on, scowl a bit harder, it suits you!'

George grinned unwillingly, and pulled herself together. She hated being left out of anything, but she did see that it was no use having a crowd of people watching that night. All right, she would stay with Anne and keep her company.

It seemed as if the watcher on the hills must have gone, because there were no more sudden flashes such as came when he lifted his fieldglasses to watch the Five.

'That disguised countrywoman has con-
vinced the watcher that we're going! Any ideas,
anyone, where we can go? Not too far away –
but somewhere where the watcher can't follow
us with his glasses, if he's still up there.'

'I know a place,' said George. 'There's a
simply colossal gorse bush on the other side
of the spring. And underneath it is all hollow
and dry. It's almost like a kind of gorse cave.'

'Sounds all right,' said Julian. 'Let's go and
find it.'

George led the way, trying to remember
exactly where it was. Timmy followed, still
in his enormous cardboard collar, which was
now rather the worse for wear. George stopped
when they had gone a little way past the spring.

'It was somewhere here,' she said. 'I know I
could still hear the sound of the spring when I
found the hollow under the bush. Ah – there it
is!'

It certainly was a great bush, green and spiky
outside, with a few yellow blooms on it still.

Under it was a big hollow place, where the ground was soft and fine, scattered with dry old prickles.

The main trunk – for it was almost a trunk that supported the big bush – was not quite in the middle, so there was a good bit of room. Julian caught hold of the branches that hid the hollow, using a folded sheet of paper to hold them by, for the bush was very prickly.

'This is fine,' he said. 'Plenty of room for you two girls – and Timmy. My word, he'll have difficulty with his collar though, won't he – squeezing in and out!'

'Take it off!' said Dick. 'His ear really is practically healed now. Even if he scratches it, he can't do much damage. Dear old Timmy, we simply shan't *know* you without your collar.'

'Right,' said George. She took a quick look at the ear. It was still covered by a piece of elastoplast, but it was quite obvious that the ear was healthy. She cut the thread that bound the two ends of the circular collar and then bent it so that it came off.

They all stared at Timmy, who looked most surprised. He wagged his tail gently as if to say 'Well – so you've taken that thing off – I wonder why?'

'Oh Tim – you look sort of *undressed* without that collar now!' said Anne. 'It *is* nice to see you without it, though. Good old Tim! You'll guard me and George tonight, won't you? *You* know that we're in the Middle of Something again, don't you?'

'Woof,' said Timmy, wagging his tail violently. 'Woof!' Yes – he knew all right!

[13]

On watch in the cottage

It was getting dark – and under the gorse bush it was very dark indeed! All the Five had managed to squeeze in there, and Timmy too. One torch only was allowed to be used at a time, to save the batteries of the others.

The Five were having supper. The ham was now practically finished, but there were still a few tomatoes and plenty of cake.

Julian opened the last tin of sardines, and made some sandwiches for himself and Dick to take with them. He also wrapped up two enormous chunks of cake and pocketed two slabs of chocolate each.

'We shall need something to while away the time when we're on the watch tonight!' he said, with a grin. 'I don't know if the Weepies and

Wailies and Floating Lights will be along to give us a show – but I fear not. They would be wasted on an empty cottage!'

'I do hope you'll be careful,' said Anne.

'Anne – that's the seventh time you've said that,' said Dick. 'Don't be an ass. Don't you understand that Ju and I are going to *enjoy* ourselves? You'll be the one that has to be careful.'

'How?' asked Anne, surprised.

'Well – you'll have to be careful of that big black beetle squatting over there,' said Dick. 'And mind that a hedgehog doesn't sit down on your bare legs. And be careful in case a snake wants to share this nice safe warm place with you . . .'

'Now *you're* being an ass!' said Anne, giving him a punch. 'When will you be back?'

'We shall be back at exactly the moment you hear us squeezing under here,' said Julian. 'Now Dick – what about it? I think we might be going, don't you?'

'Right,' said Dick, and began to squeeze out carefully so as not to be pricked more than he could help. 'Oh – why are gorse bushes so horribly spiteful! Jab jab – anyone would think the bush was *trying* to prick me!'

The two girls sat quite still when the boys had gone from the bush. They tried to hear their footsteps, but they couldn't. Dick and Julian trod too softly on the wiry grass.

'I do so hope they'll be—' began Anne, and George groaned.

'If you say that again I shall slap you, Anne! Honestly I shall.'

'I *wasn't* saying it,' said Anne, 'I was only going to say that I hope they'll be *successful* tonight. I'd like to get back to Kirrin and have some fun swimming and boating, wouldn't you?'

'Yes. And some of Joanna's marvellous cooking,' said George. 'Sausages and mash – and tomatoes with it.'

'Yes. And fried plaice fresh from the sea with

Joanna's best chipped potatoes,' said Anne. 'I can almost smell it.'

'Woof,' said Timmy, sniffing hard.

'There! He thought I meant it!' said Anne. 'Isn't Timmy clever?'

They had a pleasant talk about how very very clever Timmy was, and Timmy listened and wagged his tail so hard that he made it quite dusty in the gorse hollow.

'Let's go to sleep,' said Anne. 'We can't talk all night – and keeping awake won't help the boys!'

They curled up on the rug they had brought and cuddled together – not so much for warmth, because it was a hot night, but because there was so little room! Anne put out her torch, and the little place immediately became black and dark. Timmy put his head on George's tummy. She groaned.

'Oh Tim – be careful, please! I had rather a lot of supper!'

Anne giggled and pulled Timmy's head close

to her. It was comforting to have old Timmy there. She agreed with George that he was the best dog in the whole world.

'I wonder what the boys are doing now,' she said, after a while. 'Do you suppose they are in the middle of something exciting? Perhaps they are!'

But they weren't! Julian and Dick were feeling extremely bored at that minute. They had gone cautiously to the cottage when they had left the girls, not using their torches at all, for fear of giving anyone warning that they were about. They had debated beforehand where would be the best place to hide, and had decided that it would be a good idea to climb up the little stone stair and hide in the roofless rooms above.

'There's no roof there – and hardly any walls,' said Dick. 'We can peep over any side to watch – and no one would guess that anyone was above them, spying down! It's a good thing it's such a starry night – once we get used to the dim light, we shall be able to see fairly well. Pity there's no moon.'

They had approached the cottage very cautiously indeed, stopping at every step and listening with bated breath for any sound. But there was none.

'Not even the light of somebody's torch, either,' said Dick in Julian's ear. 'I don't think anyone is here yet. Let's get into the cottage and up those stairs as soon as we can.'

They tiptoed into the cottage, not daring to put on their torches. They fumbled across to the little stone stairway, and climbed it with as little sound as they could. Holding their breath made their hearts thump loudly.

'Can you hear my heart thumping?' Dick whispered to Julian, as they at last stood on the floor of the roofless rooms above.

'No. Mine's just the same, thumping away! Well, we're safely here. Let's just shuffle to and fro and see if there are any loose stones we might fall over, and so give ourselves away!'

They cleared away a few loose stones, and then sat down silently on the low broken wall of the two ruined rooms. The wind blew gently but warmly. Everything was still except the rose-rambler climbing over the old house. It moved a little in the wind and made a faint scraping noise. Dick caught his hand on a thorn, and sucked his finger. The rambler was everywhere, across the floor, and over the walls and even up what was left of the little chimney.

The boys had been there for about three-quarters of an hour when Julian gave Dick a slight nudge.

'Here they come!' he whispered. 'See – over there!'

Dick looked round and about and then caught sight of a small, moving light, just a prick in the darkness. It cast a faint glow before it.

'A torch!' he whispered. 'And another – and another! Quite a procession! A slow one, too.'

The procession made very little noise. It made its way to the cottage, and then split up.

'Having a look to see if we really *are* gone,' whispered Julian. 'Hope they won't think of coming up here.'

'Let's get behind the chimney, in case,' whispered back Dick. So very quietly they rose and made their way to where the remains of the chimney stood, a dark shadow in the starry night. The chimney was quite big, though rather crumbly. The two boys crouched close to it, on the side farthest from where the stone stairway came up in the corner.

'Someone *is* coming up!' whispered Dick, his sharp ears catching the sound of someone's feet on the stone stairs. 'I hope he gets caught by the rambler – there's a big spray near the top!'

'Sh!' said Julian.

Someone came right up the stairway, and gave a sharp exclamation of annoyance near the top. 'Good!' thought Dick. 'He *has* got caught by the rambler!'

A torch shone out over the ruined rooms, the crumbling walls and the remains of the chimney. The boys held their breath, and stood like statues. The light of the torch played over the place for one second and then a voice called down the stairs.

'No one here. The kids have gone. We can get on with the job!'

The boys let out a long breath. Good – they were safe – for the time being at any rate! The visitors down below were no longer cautious – they spoke in ordinary voices and torches flashed all over the place. Then someone lit two lanterns, and the little cottage shone quite brightly.

'Where do we start?' said a voice. 'Here, Jess – where's that plan?'

'I've got it. I'll spread it on the floor,' said a voice that the boys recognised at once. It was the voice of the 'countrywoman' who had spoken to them that day! 'Not that it's much use. Paul's no good at drawing!'

Evidently the searchers were now leaning over the plan. Voices came up the stone stairway.

'All we know for certain is that we have to find that white stone slab – and we know the size. But we don't know the place, except that we think it *must* be here. After all – we've searched the old Roman camp, and there are no slabs there that size!'

Julian nudged Dick. So some of the visitors that Guy had complained of must have been these searchers! Whatever was it they were looking for, hidden behind a slab of stone?

He knew a minute later! A drawling voice said: 'If we have to get up every great slab in this neighbourhood, we will. I'm going to find that secret way if it's the last thing I do! If we don't find that, we don't find those blueprints – and if we don't find *them*, we might as well go into the poorhouse for the rest of our lives.'

'Or prison!' said someone.

'Not prison,' said the drawling voice. 'It'll be

Paul who goes to prison. *He* managed to steal them, we didn't!'

'Can't you get Paul to draw a better plan than this?' said the voice of the 'country-woman'. 'I can't understand half that's written here.'

'He's ill – almost off his head, too,' said someone. 'No good asking him. He had such a time escaping with those prints, he nearly died. No good asking him, I say.'

'I can't make out this word here,' said the woman.

' "W-A-D-E-R" – whatever does it mean?'

'I don't know – wait, though, I do! It might be W-A-T-E-R – water. T not D in the middle. Where's the well? Anywhere in this kitchen? That's it, that's it. *Water*! I bet there's a slab over the well. That's the way to the secret hiding place!'

Julian clutched Dick. He was as excited as the man down below. They listened eagerly, straining their ears.

'Here's the old sink – and this must be the remains of the pump. The well's underneath this slab – and see the stone is just about the right size. Get busy! Buck up, get busy!'

[14]

An exciting night – and a surprising morning

Soon there came the sound of loud breathing and grunts, as the searchers tried to prise up the stone by the pump. It was obviously very heavy, and very difficult to move, for it had become almost part of the floor itself, through the centuries!

'Drat the thing! It's tearing my hands to pieces!' said a voice. 'Lend me that jemmy, Tom – you don't seem to be doing much good with it!'

After a lot more struggling and panting the stone was loosened. 'Up she comes!' said a voice, and up came the stone so suddenly that it sounded as if most of those pulling at it had sat down very hard on the floor!

The two hidden boys were beside themselves with interest and excitement. How they wished they could go and watch! But it was impossible. They must just listen and try to make out what was happening from what the men said below them.

'Is it a well down there? Yes, it is! My, the water's pretty far down – and black as pitch too.'

There was a silence as the well was examined in the light of torches. Then an exasperated voice, the one with the drawl, said: '*This* is no secret way! Who's going to get through that water! It's just an ordinary small well, and nothing else. That word *can't* have meant Water.'

'All right, boss. What *does* it mean then?' said the woman. '*I* don't know. This isn't a plan, it's a riddle! Why couldn't Paul have made it clear where the stone slab is – he just goes and does a lot of scribble round it – and all we can make out is that it's on this common, somewhere near here – and the secret way is behind the slab!'

'And all we have to do is to go and look behind dozens of heavy slabs!' said someone else. 'I'm fed up. We've lifted slabs in that wretched camp – we've lifted some here – and we still don't know if we're anywhere near the right one.'

'Shut up,' said the voice of the drawler but now the voice was sharp and angry. 'If we have to pull this cottage down, if we have to lift every slab there is, if we have to take over that camp, I'll do it! I tell you, this makes all the difference between wealth and poverty! Anyone who wants to back out can do so – but he'd better be careful!'

'Now boss, now boss, don't you fly off the handle!' said the woman. 'We're all in this! We'll do all you say. Look, let's start by lifting a few more slabs. There are not so very many that are the size that Paul figured on this plan.'

Then began a boring time for the two hidden

boys, as slab after slab was lifted and put back. Nothing was found under any of them, apparently.

The men went to the outbuildings too, leaving the woman in the cottage. The boys thought she had gone as well, and Julian moved a little, feeling rather cramped after being still for so long. The woman's ears must have been sharp for she called out at once.

'Who's there? Is it you, Tom?'

The boys stiffened and stood like statues. The woman said no more. It was not long before the men came back, talking among themselves. It sounded as if there were three of them.

'No go,' said the drawler. 'I think we'll have to search that camp really well again.'

'That's going to be difficult with someone already there,' said the woman.

'We'll deal with him,' said a voice, grimly. Julian frowned. Did that mean that Guy was in danger? He had better warn him!

'I'm fed up with this place,' said the woman.

'Let's go. I don't think the slab is anywhere here! We're wasting our time!'

To the boys' great relief, the four searchers left the cottage and went off together. Julian and Dick leaned over the crumbling wall of the room they stood in, and watched the lights of the torches and lanterns getting dimmer and dimmer over the common. Good! Now they could go back to the girls!

'I'm stiff!' said Dick, stretching himself.

'Well, Ju – we know a lot more now, don't we? It's clear that someone called Paul had stolen some valuable blueprints of something – maybe a new plane, or battleship perhaps – and has hidden them in some secret place he knew of about here – and to get to it you have to lift a slab of stone of a certain size.'

'Yes. And we know the size because we've already seen the one they lifted in the old stables,' said Julian. 'I vote we go there and measure it – or measure the one by the sink. I should think that the right slab will be somewhere in the old camp. We'd better tell Guy and let him into the secret. He'll help us to search!'

'What a peculiar business this is to find ourselves mixed up in,' said Dick. 'All because George didn't like people laughing at old Timmy with a cardboard collar round his neck! Timmy's the cause of this!'

The boys went down the stone stairs, and, of course, Dick quite forgot about the rambler, which caught him neatly round the ankle and almost tripped him headlong down the stairs!

'Blow!' he said, clutching Julian and nearly making him topple too. 'Sorry. It was that rambler again. It's ripped my ankle all round. Put on the torch for goodness' sake.'

They carefully measured the stone slab by the sink and then made their way out of the cottage and up towards the spring, hoping that they would find the great gorse bush in the dark. They tried to get under the wrong one at first, but at last found the right one. They heard a small welcome bark from Timmy.

'Oh! Julian! Dick! Is it you?' said Anne's voice, as the boys squeezed through into the hollow middle. 'Oh, what AGES you've been! We haven't slept a wink. Keep still, Timmy, do – this place is too small for you to rampage about in!'

The boys settled down and torches were put on. Julian related the curious happenings to the two interested girls. George was thrilled.

'Oh I *say*! Fancy all this springing up out of the blue so suddenly! What are you going to do?'

'Warn Guy first thing in the morning – and then get in touch with the police, I think,' said Julian. 'We ourselves can't stop the men searching the camp, and as soon as they *do* find the slab they're looking for, they can easily get what they want and go off with it!'

'Well, it's really thrilling,' said George. 'I wish I'd been with you. I'll never go to sleep tonight!'

But they did manage to drop off to sleep, for

they were all very tired. After a few hours, just as dawn was breaking, Timmy lifted his head and growled. George awoke at once.

'What is it, Tim? I can't hear anything.'

But Timmy could, that was certain. George woke Julian, and made him listen to Timmy's continuous growling.

'What do you think he's growling at?' she asked. 'He keeps on and on. I can't hear a thing, can you?'

'No,' said Julian, listening. 'Well, it's no use my creeping out and going searching in the dark for whatever Timmy's growling at. It might be something silly like a weasel or a hedgehog or a stoat. Shut up, Tim. That's enough.'

Although it was as dark as night under the thick old gorse bush, outside it was just getting light. What *was* Timmy growling at? Were there people about again? Or was it just one of the hedgehogs he so heartily disliked?

He stopped growling at last and put his head

down on his paws, closing his eyes. George patted him.

'Well, whatever it was, it's gone. Are you comfy, Julian? It's very cramped in here – and hot too, isn't it?'

'Yes. We'll get up fairly early and go to warn Guy – then we'll have a swim,' said Julian, yawning. He switched off his torch and went to sleep again.

It was late when they awoke. Dick was the first, and he looked at his watch. He gave an exclamation.

'Gosh! It's half past eight! Hey, Ju – Anne – George wake up, it's almost afternoon!'

Everyone felt stiff and cramped, and they went off to have a swim and to warn Guy. As they came near the camp, they stopped in amazement.

Someone was howling down in the trench, howling so miserably and so broken-heartedly that the Five felt quite panic-stricken. Whatever in the world could have happened? They ran to the edge of the excavations and looked down into the trench.

The boy was there, lying on his face, sobbing. He kept lifting his head and howling, then putting it down again.

'Guy! GUY! Whatever's happened?' shouted Julian. He leapt down beside the boy. 'Are you hurt? Is Jet hurt? What's the matter?'

'It's Guy! He's gone! They've taken him,' howled the boy. 'And I was so awful to him. Now he's gone. He'll never come back, I know he won't!'

'Guy's gone? But – but *you're* Guy!' said Julian in astonishment. 'What do you mean?'

He felt sure that the boy really *was* mad now – quite mad – talking about himself like that. He patted him on the shoulder. 'Look, you're ill. You come along with us. You need a doctor.'

The boy sprang to his feet, his face swollen and stained. 'I'm not ill! I tell you Guy's gone. I'm *not* Guy. He's my twin. There are two of us.'

Everyone gasped. It took half a minute to think about this and get everything straight – and then, of course many things were clear! There was not one mad boy, there were two ordinary boys – but they were twins! There wasn't, as they had thought, just *one* boy who contradicted himself all the time, who seemed continually to appear suddenly and unexpectedly, and who was sometimes nice and sometimes not.

'Twins! Why on earth didn't we think of that before?' said Julian. 'We thought there was only one of you. You were never together.'

'No. We quarrelled – quarrelled bitterly,' said the boy, tears in his eyes again. 'And when twins quarrel, *really* quarrel, it's worse than any quarrel there is! We hated one another then – we really did! We wouldn't be with one another, we wouldn't eat together, or dig together, or sleep together. We've often quarrelled before, but not like this – not like this! I just pretended that he didn't exist – and he did the same with me!'

'What a to-do!' said Julian, astonished and worried. 'Well now, what's happened to make you so upset? Tell me!'

'Guy wanted to be friends with me again last night,' said the boy. 'And I wouldn't. I hit him and walked away. Then this morning I was sorry and went to find him and be friends – and – and . . .'

He stopped and howled again. Everyone felt very sad and uncomfortable. 'Go on, tell us,' said Julian, gently.

'I was just in time to see him fighting two men, and screaming at them, and kicking – then they hustled him away somewhere!' said the boy. 'I fell down in the trench and hurt my leg – and by the time I dragged myself up, Guy had gone – and so had everyone else!'

He turned away and wept again. 'I'll never forgive myself, never! If I'd made friends last night I could have helped him – and I didn't!'

[15]

Well done, George!

It was Anne who comforted the boy. She went to him and pulled him down on a stone beside her. 'Let me look at your leg,' she said. 'It's pretty bad, isn't it? Look, I'll bind it up for you. Don't be so upset – we'll help you. I think we know what's happened, don't we Julian?'

The boy looked at Anne gratefully, and sniffed hard. When she offered him her handkerchief, he took it and wiped his face. Dick gave Anne his big hanky to bind up the boy's cut and bruised leg. He must have fallen right into the trench in his fright at seeing his brother fighting and being taken away.

'How do *you* know what's happened?' he said to Julian. 'Can you get Guy back? Do say you can! I'll never forgive myself for this. My twin brother – and I wasn't there to fight by his side when he needed me!'

'Now don't soak my hanky all over again!' said Anne. He gave her a forlorn little smile and turned to Julian again.

'My name's Harry Lawdler, and Guy and I are mad on old camps and buildings and things. We spend almost all our holidays together, digging and finding all kinds of things, like these.' He nodded his head towards the little shelf of relics that the four had seen before.

'Yes, Guy told us,' said Dick. 'But he never said a word about you. We were often very puzzled – we thought you and he were one boy – not two, you see – and we couldn't understand a lot of things you both said. You're so very, very alike.'

'Well, I tell you, we each pretended that the other didn't even exist,' said Harry. 'We're like that. We love each other best in the world, and we hate each other worst – when we quarrel. We're simply *horrible* then!'

'Can you tell us a bit about the people that Guy was fighting?' asked Dick.

'Yes. They were some that came before, wanting Guy to clear out while they had a look round,' said Harry, wiping his face again. 'Guy was pretty rude to them. In fact I heard him say that if they messed about his camp he would throw stones at them – he's like that, you know, very fierce, when he's roused.'

'And you think these were the same people?' said Dick. 'Which way did they go with Guy?'

'That way,' said Harry, pointing. 'I've hunted the whole camp round, but they're gone – disappeared into thin air! It's extraordinary!'

'Let's have a hunt round,' said Julian. 'We might find something. But I imagine that the searchers have taken Guy off with them because he knew too much – perhaps they found here what they were looking for, and saw Guy watching.'

'Oh! Then we're too late!' said George, in deep disappointment. 'They've got what they want – and they'll disappear now and never be caught. I expect by now they are speeding away in a fast car – and have taken Guy with them to make sure he doesn't talk before they're safely in another country!'

'Oh no!' cried Harry. 'He's not kidnapped, is he? Don't say that!'

'Come on – let's have a hunt,' said Julian, and they all made their way among the various trenches and pits, looking for they hardly knew what.

They gave it up after a while. There were too many slabs and stones of all sizes! Besides, what good would it be even if they found the right one? The birds had flown – presumably with what they had come for! In fact, if Guy hadn't come along and seen the searchers, nobody would even have known that they had been in the camp and made a successful search!

'It's no good,' said Julian, at last. 'This is too big a place to know where to look for anything that might help us. Let's go back to the gorse bush and collect our things, return to Kirrin and go to the police. It's the only sensible thing left to do!'

'Come along, Harry,' said Anne, to the miserable twin. He was so full of remorse that her handkerchief was now soaked for the third time! 'You'd better come with us and tell all you know.'

'I'll come,' said Harry. 'I'll do anything to get Guy back. I'll never quarrel with him again. Never. To think that—'

'Now don't go all through that again,' said Anne. 'Look, you're upsetting Timmy so much that his tail is down all the time!'

Harry gave another forlorn little smile. They all left the camp and made their way back to the gorse bush. It was only when they got there, and began pulling out the tins of food, as well as the rug and other things, that they realised how extremely hungry they were!

'We've had no breakfast. We've been up for

ages, and it's very late. I'm simply starving!' said George.

'Well, if we finish up all the food, we shan't have to carry the tins!' said Dick. 'Let's have a meal. Ten minutes more here can't make much difference.'

They were thankful not to have to sit under the gorse bush again. They sat outside in the sun, and discussed everything.

'I believe when Timmy began to growl and growl about six o'clock this morning, it was because he could hear those people coming quietly by to go to search the camp,' said George.

'I think you're right,' said Julian. 'I bet they searched the camp well – till Guy woke and came on the scene and fought like fury. It's a pity I didn't squeeze out from under the bush and follow them, when Timmy growled.'

'Anyone want a drink?' said George. 'I'll go and fetch some water from the spring. Where's the pineapple tin?'

Anne passed it to her. George got up and took the little rabbit path that led to the spring. She could hear it gurgling and bubbling as she came near – a very pleasant noise.

'Water always sounds nice,' said George to herself. 'I love the sound of water.'

Water! Now why did that ring a bell in her mind just then? Who had been talking about water? Oh – Dick and Julian, of course, when they had come back from the old cottage last night. They had told Anne and herself about the word on the plan – the word that might have been WATER, not WADER.

'I wonder which it was,' said George to herself as she idly held the pineapple tin to the gurgling water. She gazed at the beautiful little spring, jutting up from the stony slabs – and then another bell rang loudly in the mind.

'Stone slabs! Water! Why – I wonder – I just wonder – if one of *these* slabs is the one! This one just here is about the right size!'

She stared at it. It was set firmly in a high

little bank at the back of the place where the spring gurgled up and then ran into the clean stony channel. *Did* it hide anything behind it?

George suddenly dropped the tin and ran back to the others at full speed. 'Julian! Julian! I believe I've found the slab! It's been staring us in the face the whole time!'

Julian was very startled. So were the others. They stared up at George in astonishment.

'What do you mean, George?' said Julian, jumping to his feet. 'Show me!'

Followed by everyone, George ran back to the spring. She pointed to the white slab behind the water. 'There!' she said. 'That's the right size, isn't it? And it's beside WATER – just as it said in the plan you told us about – only the people thought it was WADER.'

'Gosh, I wonder if you're right, George,' said Julian, excited. 'You might be – you never know. Sometimes springs come from underground passages – secret hidden ways into the earth.'

'Let's try and move it,' said Dick, his face red with sudden excitement. 'It looks pretty hefty to me.'

They began to struggle with the stone, getting extremely wet as they splashed about in the spring. But nobody minded that. This was too exciting for words. Harry helped too, heaving and tugging. He was very strong indeed.

The stone slab moved a little. It slid to one side and stuck. More tugging. More pulling. More panting and puffing!

'I believe we'll have to get help,' said Julian at last. 'It really is too heavy and well-embedded.'

'I'll go and get some of my tools,' said Harry. 'I'm used to heaving stones about with them. We can easily move it if we have the right tools.'

He flew off at top speed. The others sat down and mopped their streaming foreheads.

'Phew!' said Julian. 'What a job this is for a hot day! I'm glad Harry remembered his tools. Just what we want!'

'How funny that he and Guy are twins!' said George. 'I never even thought of such a thing!'

'Well, they behaved so idiotically,' said Julian. 'Always pretending there was just one of them, and neither of them even mentioning the other. I wonder where Guy has been taken to. I don't think he'll come to much harm – but it will be worrying for his family.'

'Here comes Harry,' said Anne, after a pause. 'One of us ought to have gone with him to help him. He's brought dozens of tools!'

The things he had fetched proved very useful indeed, especially a big jemmy-like tool. The stone soon began to move when this was applied by Julian and Harry!

'It's slipping – it's coming away – look out, it will fall right down into the spring!' cried Dick. 'Look out, you girls!'

The stone was prised right out, and fell into the stony channel where the water ran. The five children stared at the opening it left.

Julian leaned forward and looked into it.

'Yes – there's a big hole behind,' he said. 'Let me shine my torch in.'

In great excitement he flashed his torch into the opening. He turned round, his face glowing.

'Yes! I think we've got it! There's a tunnel behind, going down and down. It widens out behind this hole!'

Everyone was too thrilled for words. George gave Dick a punch, and Anne patted Timmy so hard that he whined. Harry beamed round, all his woes forgotten.

'Do we go down now?' asked Dick. 'We'll have to make the opening a bit wider. Earth and roots have narrowed it very much. Let's make it bigger.'

'Then we'll explore it!' said George, her eyes shining. 'A secret tunnel only known to us! Quick – let's explore it!'

[16]

The secret way

All the children were so excited that they got into each other's way. Julian pushed them back.

'Let's be sensible! We can't *all* make the opening wider – let Harry and me get at it with the tools – and we'll soon make it bigger!'

It took only a minute to hack away at the sides of the hole to make it big enough for even Julian to climb through. He stood there panting, smiling broadly.

'There – it's done! I'll get in first. Everyone got torches? We shall need them! It's going to be dark in there!'

He clambered up and into the hole. He had to crawl on hands and knees for a little way, and then the hole suddenly went downwards and became considerably bigger. Julian could walk in it, if he bent down, for at that point the tunnel was about three feet high.

He called back to the others. 'Follow me! Take hold of each other's shirts or jerseys and hang on. It's pitch black in here!'

George followed after Julian, then Anne, then Dick, then Harry. Timmy went with George, of course, pushing and shoving like all the rest. Everyone was excited, and nobody could talk in a normal voice. They all shouted!

'I'll give you a hand! One good shove and you're in!'

'I say – isn't it dark!'

'What a crawl! I feel like a fox going into its den!'

'Timmy, don't butt me from behind like that! I can't crawl any faster!'

'Ah – thank goodness I can stand up now! What size of rabbit do you think made *this* burrow!'

'It was made by water at some time perhaps. Don't *shove*, Timmy!'

'Water doesn't run uphill, ass! Hang on to my jersey, Harry. Don't get left behind.'

Julian, bent almost double at times, walked carefully along the narrow tunnel, which went steadily downwards. Soon it widened and became higher, and then it was easier to walk in comfort.

'Do you suppose this is the right secret way?' called George, after a time. 'We don't seem to be getting anywhere.'

'I can't tell. In fact we shan't know till we find something hidden somewhere – if we ever do!'

A sudden scuttering noise in front of him made Julian stop suddenly. Immediately everyone bumped into the one in front, and there were shouts at once.

'What's up, Ju?'

Julian's torch shone on to two pairs of bright, frightened eyes. He gave a laugh.

'It's all right – just a couple of rabbits using our burrow! There are small holes running out of the tunnel which, I imagine, are rabbit burrows. I bet we're giving the bunnies a shock!'

The tunnel wound about a good deal, and then suddenly the rather soft ground they were treading on turned to rock. The passage was now not so high, and the children had to bend down again. It was most uncomfortable.

Julian stopped once more. He had heard another sound. What was it?

'Water!' he said. 'There must be an underground stream here! How thrilling! Everyone all right?'

'Yes!' shouted those behind him. 'Get on, Julian – let's see the water!'

The tunnel suddenly ended, and Julian found himself in a big cave with a fairly high roof. Almost in the middle of it ran a stream – not a very big one, and not a very fast one. It gurgled along in a small channel of rock, which it had carved out for itself through hundreds of years.

Julian shone his torch on it. The water looked very black and glittered in the light of the torch. The others came one by one out of the tunnel and stared at the underground stream. It looked rather mysterious, slipping through the cave, gurgling quietly as it disappeared through a hole at one end.

'Strange,' said Dick.

'It's not unusual, this,' began Harry. 'In some parts of the country round about here, the ground below our feet is honeycombed with many little streams. Some come up as springs, of course, some join other streams when they come out into the open, others just run away goodness knows where!'

Julian was looking up round the cave. 'Does our tunnel end here?' he wondered. 'Is this where we have to look for whatever is hidden?'

'We'll have a look round the cave and see if there are any exits,' said Dick. Using their torches the five separated, Timmy keeping close to George, not seeming in the least surprised at this underground adventure.

'I've found another tunnel over here, leading

out of the cave!' called Dick. No sooner had he said that than Anne called out too.

'There's one here as well!'

'Now – which do we take?' said Julian. 'How annoying that there should be two!'

'Would the fellow – what's his name – Paul – have marked the correct underground way on his plan?' said George. 'I mean – I don't see how he could possibly expect either himself or anyone else to find what he had hidden, if there are numbers of passages to choose from down here!'

'You're right!' said Julian. 'Let's look about and see if we can find anything to help us.'

It wasn't long before Dick gave another shout. 'It's all right! This is the passage to take, over here – the one I found just now. There's an arrow drawn in white chalk on the wall.'

Everyone crowded over to Dick, stepping across the little stream as they did so. Dick held his torch up and they all saw the white arrow, drawn roughly on the wall.

Julian was pleased. 'Good. That helps a lot! It shows we're going the right way – and that this *is* the secret way that Paul chose. Come on!'

They entered the tunnel, left the little stream behind, and went on again. 'Anyone got any idea in which direction we're going?' called Dick. 'East, west, north, south?'

Harry had a compass. He looked at it. 'I think we're going rather in the direction of the old Roman camp,' he said.

'Ah – that's interesting,' said Julian. 'This tunnel was probably used in olden times.'

'Guy and I have seen the plan of the camp as it probably used to be,' said Harry. 'And there are plenty of tunnels and caves and holes shown on it – just roughed in, not a proper plan of them. Gosh, I never thought I'd be exploring one! My father warned me not to, in case of roof-falls and things like that.'

The tunnel suddenly forked into two. One passage was nice and wide, the other narrow. Julian took the wide one, thinking that the other was really too narrow to get through. But after a minute or two, he stopped, puzzled.

'There's a blank wall of rock here – the tunnel's ended! We'll have to turn back! I suppose we should have taken that very narrow opening.'

They went back, Harry leading the way now. Timmy suddenly took it into his head that *he* would like to lead, too, and made himself a real nuisance, pushing his way between everyone's legs!

They came back to the fork. Harry shone his torch in at the second opening, the very narrow one. There, clearly marked on the right hand wall, was a white arrow in chalk!

'We're idiots,' said Dick. 'We don't even look for the signposts! Lead the way, Julian!'

This tunnel was very narrow indeed, and had rough, jutting rocky sides. There were loud 'aahs!' and 'oohs!' as elbows and ankles were knocked against hard rock.

And then again there came a blank wall of

rock in front of Julian, and again he had to stop!

'Can't go this way either!' he said. 'There's a blank wall again – this is a blind alley too!'

There were cries of dismay at once.

'Blow! It can't be!'

'What's gone wrong? Look all round, Ju – flash your torch down at your feet and above your head!'

Julian shone his torch over his head, and gave an exclamation.

'There's a hole above my head!'

'Is there a white arrow anywhere?' called Harry.

'Yes! And it's pointing up, instead of forwards!' called back Julian. 'We're still all right – we've got to go upwards now – but how?'

George, who was just behind him, shone her torch on the side walls. 'Look!' she said. 'We can easily get up to the hole. There are rough, natural steps up – made by ledges of rock. Look, Julian!'

'Yes,' said Julian. 'We can manage to get up quite easily, I think. George, you go first – I'll give you a boost up.'

George was delighted to go first. She put her torch between her teeth, and began to climb up the ledges, Julian pushing her as best he could. She came to the hole and immediately saw that it would be quite easy to hoist herself through.

'One more boost and I'll be through!' she called to Julian. And with one last heave George was up, rolling on the floor of a small cave above! She called down in excitement to the others.

'I believe this is the place where those things are hidden! I can see something on a ledge. Oh, do buck up!'

The others followed eagerly. Dick slipped off the rocky ledges in his excitement and almost squashed poor Harry as he fell on him. However, everyone was up at last, even Timmy, who was the most difficult of all to heave through! He seemed to have far too many vigorous legs!

Harry found no difficulty at all. 'I'm used to this kind of thing,' he said. 'Guy and I have explored a whole lot of tunnels and caves in hills and other places.'

George was pointing her torch at a broad ledge of rock. On it was a brown leather bag, and beside it, marked on the rock, was a very large arrow indeed.

Julian was overjoyed. He picked up the bag at once. 'My word – I hope there's something in it!' he said. 'It feels jolly light – as if it's empty!'

'Open it!' cried everyone – but Julian couldn't. It was locked – and alas, there wasn't a key!

[17]

Full of surprises

It's locked – we can't open the bag,' said Julian, and shook it vigorously as if that might make it fly open and spill whatever contents it had!

'We don't know if it's got anything of value in it or not,' said Dick, in deep disappointment. 'I mean – it might be some trick on that fellow Paul's part – he might have taken the blueprints, or whatever they were he hid, for himself, and left the bag just to trick the others.'

'Can we cut it open?' asked George.

'No. I don't think so. It's made of really strong leather. We would need a special knife to cut through it – an ordinary penknife wouldn't be any use,' said Julian. 'I think we'll just have to assume that we've got the goods, and hope for the best. If they're not in here, it's just bad luck. Someone else has got them, if so.'

They all looked at the tantalising bag.

Now they would have to wait for ages before they found out whether their efforts had been successful or not!

'Well – what do we do now?' said George, feeling suddenly flat. 'Go back all through that long tunnel once more? I'll be glad to be in the open air again, won't you?'

'You bet!' said Julian. 'Well – I suppose we'd better get down through that hole again.'

'Wait!' said Anne, her sharp eyes catching sight of something. 'Look – what does all this mean?'

She shone her torch on to various signs on the wall. Again there were arrows drawn in white chalk – but very oddly, a line of them ran downwards across the wall of the little rocky room, right to the edge of the hole – and another line of arrows pointing the *other* way, ran horizontally across the wall!

'Well, do you suppose that's just meant to muddle people?' said Dick, puzzled. 'We know jolly well that the way out of this room is down that hole, because that's the way we came into it.'

'Perhaps the other line of arrows means that there's a second way out,' suggested George. They all looked round the little rocky room. There didn't seem any way out at all.

'Where's Timmy?' said Anne, suddenly, flashing her torch round. 'He's not here! Has he fallen down the hole? I never heard him yelp!'

At once there was a great to-do. 'Timmy, Timmy, Timmy! TIMMY! Where are you?'

George whistled shrilly, and the noise echoed round and round the little room. Then, from somewhere, there was a bark. How relieved everyone was.

'Where is he? Where did that bark come from?' said Dick. 'It didn't sound as if it came from below, down that hole!'

There came another welcome bark, and the sound of Timmy's feet. Then to everyone's amazement, he appeared in the little rocky room as if by magic – appearing straight out of the wall, it seemed!

'Timmy! Where were you? Where have you come from?' cried George, and ran to see. She came to a standstill and exclaimed loudly.

'Oh! What idiots we are! Why, just behind this big jutting-out piece of rock, there's another passage!'

So there was! A very, very narrow one, it is true – and completely hidden from the children because of the enormous slab of rock that jutted out from the wall that hid it! They stood and stared at it, shining their torches on the narrow way. The arrows ran round the wall to it.

'We never even looked properly!' said Dick. 'Still – it's a passage that would be extremely difficult to spot – hidden round the corner of that rock – and very narrow at that. Well, I do know one thing for certain about that man called Paul!'

'What?' asked Anne.

'He's thin – thin as a rake!' said Dick. 'No one but a skinny fellow could squeeze through *this* opening! I doubt if *you* can, Julian – you're the biggest of us.'

'Well, what about trying?' said George. 'What does everyone say? This might be an easier, shorter way out – or it might be a harder, longer one.'

'It won't be longer,' said Harry. 'By my reckoning we must be pretty well near the camp now. It's likely that the way leads straight there – though where it comes out I can't imagine. Guy and I have explored the camp pretty thoroughly.'

Dick suddenly thought of something he had noticed at the camp – the big hole behind the slab of stone, where he had seen the baby rabbit a day or two before! What had Guy said about that? He had said there was a great hole underground, which had been explored – but that it was probably just an ancient storage place for food or for loot! He turned eagerly to Harry.

'Harry, would this lead to that enormous hole underground – the one that Guy once told me had been explored, but was of no interest – probably just an old store place?'

'Let me see,' said Harry. 'Yes – yes, it *might* lead to that. Most of these underground ways are throughways – ways that led from one place to another. They don't as a rule stop suddenly, but have usually been of use as secret escape routes or something of that kind. I think you may be right, Dick – we're fairly near the camp, I'm sure, and we may quite well find that if we go on, instead of going back, we shall come into the camp itself – probably through that great hole!'

'Then come on,' said Julian. 'It will certainly be a shorter way!'

They tried to squeeze through the narrow opening that led out of the little rocky room.

Dick got through all right, and so did the others – but poor Julian found it very very difficult and almost gave up.

'You shouldn't eat so much,' said Dick, unkindly. 'Go on – one more try, Ju – I'll haul on your arm at the same time!'

Julian got through, groaning. 'I'm squashed flat!' he said. 'Now, if anyone makes any more jokes about too much breakfast, I'll pull his nose!'

The passage grew wider immediately, and everyone was thankful. It ran fairly straight, and then went steeply downwards, so that the five slithered about, and Timmy found himself suddenly running. Then it came to a stop – a complete stop! This time it was not a blank wall of rock that faced them – it was something else.

'A roof-fall!' groaned Dick. 'Look at that! Now we're done!'

It certainly looked most formidable. Earth, rocks and stones had fallen from the roof and blocked up the whole passageway. There was no use in going on – they would just have to turn and go back!

'Blow it!' said Dick, and kicked at the mass of earth. 'Well, there's no use staying here – we'd better turn back. My torch isn't too good now, and neither is yours, George. We don't want to lose any time – if our torches give out, we shall find things very difficult.'

They turned to go back, feeling very despondent. 'Come on, Timmy!' said George. But Timmy didn't come. He stood beside the roof-fall, looking very puzzled, his ears cocked and his head on one side. Then he suddenly gave a sharp bark.

It made everyone jump almost out of their skins, for the sound echoed round and about in a very strange way.

'Don't, Timmy!' said George, almost angrily. 'Whatever's the matter? Come along!'

But Timmy didn't come. He began to paw at the pile of earth and rocks in front of him, and barked without stopping. Wuff-wuff-wuff-wuff-wuff-WUFF!

'What's up?' said Julian, startled. 'Timmy, what on *earth's* the matter?'

Timmy took absolutely no notice, but went on feverishly scraping at the roof-fall, sending earth and stones flying all over the others.

'There's something he wants to get at – something behind this roof-fall,' said Dick. 'Or perhaps *somebody* – make him stop barking, George, and we'll listen ourselves and see if we can hear anything.'

George silenced Timmy with difficulty, and made him stand quiet and still. Then they all listened intently – and a sound came at once to their ears.

'Yap-yap-wuff-wuff-wuff!'

'It's Jet!' yelled Harry, making everyone jump violently again. 'Jet! Then Guy must be with him. He never leaves Guy! What's Guy doing here? He may be hurt. GUY! GUY! JET!'

Timmy began to bark wildly again and to scrape more furiously than ever. Julian shouted to the others above the barking.

'If we can hear Jet barking, this roof-fall can't be very big. We'd better try and get through it. Two of us can work in turn with Timmy. We can't all work at once, the passage is too narrow.'

Then began some very hard work – but it didn't last as long as Julian feared, because, quite suddenly, the mass of rubble and rock shifted as they worked, and a gap appeared at the top of the heap, between it and the roof.

Dick began to scramble up, but Julian called to him at once. 'Be careful, ass! The roof can't be too good here – it may come down again, and you'll be buried. Go carefully!'

But before Dick could go any further, a little figure appeared on the top of the rubble over their heads, and slid down to them yapping loudly, and waving a long wiry tail!

'Jet! Oh, Jet! Where's Guy?' cried Harry, as the little dog leapt into his arms and licked his face lavishly, barking joyfully in between the licks.

'GUY!' yelled Julian. 'Are you there?'

A weak voice came back. 'Yes! Who's that?' An absolute volley of voices answered him.

'It's us! And Harry! We're coming to you, we shan't be long!'

And it wasn't long, either, before the roof-fall was slowly and carefully climbed by each one – though Timmy, of course, scrambled up, over and down at top speed!

On the other side of the roof-fall was a passage, of course, the continuation of the one the children had come along. Guy was there, sitting down, looking very pale. Jet flung himself on him and licked him as if he hadn't seen him for a month, instead of just a minute or two before!

'Hallo!' said Guy, in a small voice. 'I'm all right. It's just my ankle, that's all. I'm jolly glad to—'

But before he could say a word more, Harry was beside him, his arms round him, his voice choking.

'Guy! Oh, Guy! I've been a beast. I wouldn't be friends! What happened to you? Are you really all right? Oh Guy, we *are* friends again, aren't we?'

'Look out Harry, old son,' said Julian gently. 'He's fainted. Now just let's be sensible and everything will come all right. Flap your hanky at him, Dick, and give him a little air. It's only the excitement!'

In half a minute Guy opened his eyes and smiled weakly. 'Sorry!' he said. 'I'm all right now. I only hope this isn't a dream, and that you really *are* here!'

'You bet we are!' said Dick. 'Have a bit of chocolate, then you'll know we're real!'

'Good idea!' said Julian. 'We'll all have some – and I've some biscuits in my pocket too. We'll eat and talk – and we'll make plans at the same time. Catch, Guy – here's a biscuit!'

[18]

The way out

Guy soon told his story. It was much as the others had imagined.

'I was fast asleep this morning, with Jet curled up to me,' he said. 'He began to bark and I wondered why, so I got up to see – and I saw four people in the camp.'

'The four we know!' said Dick, and Julian nodded. 'Go on, Guy.'

'They were looking all over the place,' said Guy, 'prising up rocks, messing about – so I yelled at them. But they only laughed. Then one of the men, who was trying to prise up a slab – the slab that covers that great hole underground, Harry – you remember it? – well, this man gave a yell and said "I've got it! This is the way in – down here, behind this slab!"'

Guy stopped, looking very angry. Jet licked him comfortingly. 'Well,' he went on. 'I set Jet on them, and they kicked him cruelly – so I went for them.'

'You're a plucky one, aren't you!' said Dick, admiringly. 'Did you knock them all out, by any chance?'

'No. Of course not,' said Guy. 'One of the men pretty well knocked *me* out though. He hit me on the head and I went down, dazed. I heard him say "Drat this kid – he'll be fetching help, and we shan't be able to get down and hunt for the goods." And then another man said "We'll take him with us then", and they got hold of me and dragged me through the opening.'

'But how did they get down into that great hole?' said Harry in wonder. 'There is such a steep drop into it. You need a rope.'

'Oh, they had a rope all right,' said Guy, munching his biscuit and chocolate and looking decidedly better. 'One of the men had one tied round and round his waist. They knotted it fast round a rock – that big one we can't move, Harry – and then they swung down on it. All except the woman. She said she'd stay at the top and keep watch. She hid behind a bush some way off.'

'I never saw her when I came along!' said Harry. 'I never thought of looking there! What about you? Did you get down too?'

'Yes. I screamed and shouted and kicked and howled, but it wasn't a bit of good. They made me swing down the rope – and I fell off halfway down and hurt my ankle. I howled at the top of my voice for help, and they hurried me along with them, shaking me like a rat.'

'The beasts!' said Harry, fervently. 'Oh, the beasts!'

'I heard one of them say that there should be a tunnel out of the hole somewhere, it was marked on Paul's plan – whatever that may be – and then I think I must have fainted – the pain of my ankle, you know. And when I came to myself again, we were all here, the three men and I – beside this roof-fall – though I really don't know how we got here. They must have dragged me along with them!'

'And that's all, is it?' asked Julian.

'Not quite. They were furious when they saw the roof-fall, but as soon as they began to scrabble in it a rock rolled down and hit one of the men quite a crack – and after that they were afraid to do anything. They stood and talked for a bit – and then they decided to go and get some tools, and come down again to see if they could remove all this stuff and get through it.'

'Good gracious!' said Julian, startled. 'Then they may be back at any moment!'

'I suppose so. They left me here because they couldn't think of anything else to do with me! They knew I couldn't walk, because of my ankle. I think it's broken. So of course I couldn't possibly find my way out myself! And here I've been waiting for those brutes to come back, and to hack through the rubble to go after whatever it is they want!'

Everyone began to feel rather uncomfortable at the thought that three violent men might be appearing at any moment. 'Is it very far to the opening you came down?' asked Julian. But Guy didn't know. He had fainted, as he had said, and he didn't even know what way they had come.

'It can't be far,' said Harry. 'I think it would be worth while trying to find the opening, see if the men have left the rope there, and get out that way. If Guy's ankle really is broken, he couldn't possibly manage to go back the long way we've come.'

'No. That's true,' said Julian, thoughtfully. 'Well, that's what we'll do then. But we'll go jolly cautiously, without a sound, because it might be just our luck to meet those fellows on their way back here!'

'Shall we start?' said George. 'What about Guy?'

Julian knelt down beside the boy, and gently examined his ankle. 'I've done my first aid training, like everybody else!' he said. 'And I *ought* to know if his ankle is broken or just sprained.'

He examined the swollen ankle carefully. 'It's not broken. I believe I could bandage it tightly with a couple of large hankies. Give me yours, Dick.'

The others watched admiringly as Julian deftly and confidently bandaged Guy's swollen ankle. 'There!' he said. 'You can perhaps hobble on it now, Guy. It may hurt, but I don't think it will damage it. Try. You'll have to go barefoot because your ankle is too swollen for your shoe to go on.'

Very gingerly Guy stood up, helped by Harry. He tried his hurt foot, and it certainly seemed all right to hobble on, though it was very painful. He grinned round at the others' anxious faces.

'It's fine!' he said. 'Come on, let's go! We don't want to bump into those fellows if we can help it. Thank goodness we've got Jet and Timmy.'

They set off down the passage, flashing their torches in front as usual, to show them the way. The tunnel was quite wide and high here, and in a very short time came out into an enormous pit underground.

'Ah – this is the hole I saw down behind the slab where the rabbit went,' said Dick. 'We weren't very far from the camp, as we thought. I'm surprised that when this pit was explored, the underground passages were not discovered, Guy.'

'I expect the men exploring it came to the roof-fall and thought there was nothing beyond,' said Guy. 'Or maybe they were afraid of going further in case of further falls. They can be very danger-ous, you know. Many a man has been buried under one and never heard of again.'

They looked round the enormous hole – it was really a huge round pit. Daylight showed in the roof at one place.

'That's the opening into it,' said Guy, ea-gerly. 'The one I came through, on the rope.'

He limped a few steps forward to look for the rope. Harry held him by the arm, thankful that the ankle was holding up so well. Guy pointed upwards.

'Yes. I can see the rope. The men have left it there, thank goodness. They must have been certain that I couldn't get to it!'

The rope hung down from the little opening high above their heads. Julian looked round at Anne.

'Can you manage to climb up the rope, Anne?' he said, doubtfully.

'Of course!' said Anne, scornfully. 'We do rope-climbing in the gym at school often enough. Don't we, George?'

'Yes, but our gym rope is a bit thicker!' said George.

'I'll go up first,' said Harry. 'We've got a much thicker rope, Guy and I, that we use when we want to haul on very heavy stones. I'll find it, and let it down.'

'Well, we can't afford to waste any time, in

case those fellows come back,' said Julian. 'I daresay the girls can manage all right. George, you go up first.'

George went up like a monkey, hand over hand, her legs twisted round the rope. She grinned down when she got to the top.

'Easy!' she said. 'Come on up next, Anne, and show the boys how to do it!'

Before the boys could leap to the rope, Anne was on it, pulling herself up lithely. Julian laughed. He called up to George.

'George! You might have a squint round and see if there's any sign of people about. If they were going to borrow *Guy's* tools, they would have been back long ago, so I think probably they've had to go to Kirrin or some farmhouse to borrow them.'

'They wouldn't get my tools,' said Guy, 'or Harry's. We had them stolen once, and now we always hide them where no one can possibly find them.'

'That settles it then,' said Julian. 'They've

had to go a good way, I expect, to get satisfactory tools to tackle that roof-fall. They probably imagine that it's a pretty *big* fall! All the same, keep a watch out, George, till we're all up.'

It was difficult to get Guy up, for he was feeling weak, but they managed it at last. The two dogs had to have the boys' shirts tied round them so that the rope would not cut them when they were hauled up. They didn't seem to mind at all. Timmy was very heavy to pull up because he appeared to think that he had to try and make his legs do a running action all the time – just to help! All that happened was that he began to spin round and round, as he went up!

Everyone was up in the open air at long last, hot and perspiring. Julian had the precious bag safely under his arm. Timmy sat down panting. Then he suddenly stopped panting, and pricked up his ears.

'Woof,' he said warningly, and stood up.

'Quiet, Tim, quiet, Jet,' said Julian, at once

aware that somebody must be about. 'Hide, everyone – quickly. It may be those fellows coming back!'

'Wuff,' began Jet, but Guy stopped him immediately. The six children separated and went into hiding at once, each choosing the best place he or she could see. There were plenty of hiding places in the old camp!

They heard voices coming near. Nobody dared to peep out and see who was coming – but Julian and Dick recognised the drawling voice of one of the men!

'What a time we've been!' said the man. 'Just chuck the spades and things down the hole – then we'll all climb down again. Buck up! We've wasted too much time already. Anyone might come on the scene at any moment!'

The spades and jemmies went hurtling down the hole. Then one by one the men went down the rope. The children could not hear the woman's voice. They thought she must have been left behind.

Julian gave a low whistle and all the others popped up their heads. 'We'll spring for it!' said Julian. 'Buck up!'

They all shot out of their hiding places at once and made off – except Julian. He stayed behind for a minute or two. What *could* he be doing?

Julian was doing something very simple indeed! He was hauling up the rope that dangled underground! He slipped it off the rock that held it and tied it round his waist, looking suddenly very bulky.

He grinned a very wide grin and went after the others. How very, very angry those men were going to be!

Back to Kirrin Cottage

Julian ran after the others. 'What were you doing?' said George. 'Calling rude names down to the men?'

'No. I hope they'll go and dig for hours if they want to!' said Julian. 'They'll soon find that when they've got through it, that roof-fall is nothing much, and they'll go on till they come to the little room – and what they'll say when they find that the bag is gone, I really don't know!'

'I wish I could be there!' said Dick.

'What are we going to do about Guy?' asked Harry. 'He really can't walk *very* far on that bad foot.'

'If he can walk as far as the gorse bush where we've left our things, I've got a bike there,' said

George. 'He could pedal with one foot, I should think.'

'Oh yes, I could easily do that,' said Guy, pleased. He had dreaded the thought of having to walk all the way to Kirrin – but neither did he want to be left behind!

He limped along, helped by Harry, who couldn't do enough for him. Jet ran along beside them, excited and happy at being with so many people. Timmy sometimes wuffed a little bark to him, which made Jet as proud as Punch. He thought the big Timmy was wonderful!

They came to the gorse bush, and found their things all safe. The bicycle was there, with its packages strapped to it. George unstrapped them, meaning to carry them herself, so that Guy would not have too heavy a weight to pedal with his one foot. They all started off together, Guy riding ahead on the bicycle.

'We will go to Kirrin, dump our things at the cottage, and get Aunt Fanny to ring the police and ask them if they'll come along and collect this bag from us,' said Julian. 'I don't want to leave it at the police station – I want to see it opened in front of us!'

'I do hope it won't be empty,' said Anne. 'It does feel terribly light!'

'Yes. It does,' said Julian, swinging it to and fro. 'I can't help fearing that Paul, who drew the plan that the men found so difficult to understand, may have double-crossed his friends – drawn a deliberately difficult plan – and then left the bag quite empty in the place he marked on the plan! It would be the kind of hoax that a trickster loves to play – and would give him time to get away in safety.'

'But they said he was ill,' said Dick. 'Still – perhaps he might have been pretending that too! It's a mystery!'

'How are you getting on, Guy?' called George, as they overtook the boy. He kept riding on by himself for a little way, and then resting, waiting for them to catch up with him before he pedalled on again with his one good foot.

'Very well indeed, thank you,' said Guy. 'This bike was a very good idea of yours. What a blessing you had it with you!'

'Your foot doesn't seem any more swollen,' said Anne. 'I expect you'll be able to walk on it properly in a day or two. Oh, dear – it does make me laugh when I think how puzzled we all were when we thought there was just one of you, not twins!'

'We met first one of you, then the other, and thought you were the same boy,' said George, with a chuckle. 'We were absolutely wild with you sometimes, you seemed so mad and contra-dictory!'

'Don't remind us of it,' said Harry. 'I can't bear thinking that if I'd only been with Guy, all this trouble of his would never have happened.'

'Oh well – it's an ill wind that blows nobody any good! said George. 'The bad and the good have fitted together very well this time, and made a most exciting adventure!'

'Here's Carters Lane at last,' said Anne.

'What a long walk it seemed over the common. It will be much easier for you to ride that bike when you're on a proper road, Guy. It won't go bumping over heather clumps now.'

They went down the long lane and came into Kirrin at last, realising that they were all very hungry indeed. 'It must be well past lunch-time,' said George, looking at her watch. 'Good gracious – it's a quarter to two! Would you believe it! I hope there's some lunch left over for us – Mother doesn't know we're coming.'

'We'll raid Joanna's larder!' said Dick. 'She never minds so long as she's there to grumble at us while we do it!'

They went in at the gate of Kirrin Cottage and up to the front door, which was open. George shouted.

'Mother! Where are you? We've come back!'

Nobody answered. George yelled again. 'Mother! We've come home!'

The door of the study opened and her father looked out, red in the face and frowning.

'George! How many times am I to tell you not to shout when I'm working? Oh, my goodness me, who are all these?'

'Hallo, Father!' said George, mildly. 'Surely you know Anne and Julian and Dick! *Don't* say you've forgotten them already!'

'Of course not! But who are these?' and George's father pointed to the startled twins. 'They're as like as peas. Where did *they* come from? I haven't seen them before, have I?'

'No, father. They're just friends of ours,' said George. 'Where's Mother? We've just had an adventure and we want to tell her. Oh, and we want to ring the police – and I think we ought to get a doctor to see to Guy's foot – and Father, look, Timmy's ear is healed!'

'Bless us all! There's never any peace when you are about, George,' said her father, groaning. 'Your mother's at the bottom of the garden, picking raspberries – or it might have been strawberries.'

'Oh no, Father – it's August, not June!' said George. 'You always—'

Julian thought he had better get his uncle safely back in his study before a row blew up between him and George. Uncle Quentin did *not* like being disturbed in his complicated work!

'Let's go and find Aunt Fanny,' he said, 'we can tell her everything out in the garden. Come on!'

'Wuff-wuff!' said Jet.

'Good gracious – that's not *another* dog, is it?' said George's father, scowling. 'How many times have I said that—'

'We won't disturb you any more, Uncle,' said Julian, hurriedly, seeing Guy's scared face. 'We'll go and find Aunt Fanny.'

They all went thankfully out in the garden, hearing the house echo to the slam of Uncle Quentin's study door. George shouted.

'Mother! Where are you?'

'Shut up, George – we don't want to make

your father leap out of the window after us!' said Dick. 'Ah – there's Aunt Fanny!'

His aunt was very surprised to see him and the others advancing on her. She went to greet them, a basket of raspberries on her arm.

'Well! I thought you wanted to stay away for longer than this!'

'We did – but an adventure descended on us!' said Dick. 'We'll tell you all about it in detail later on, Aunt Fanny.'

'But just now we want two things – can we ring the police – or will *you* – and ask them to come here?' said Julian, very grown-up all of a sudden. 'There's something that might be very important for them to know. And also do you think we should let a doctor see Guy's foot – he's sprained his ankle, I think?'

'Oh dear!' said Aunt Fanny, distressed to see the boy's swollen foot. 'Yes, he ought to have that seen to properly. Who is he? Dear me – there's another of them! Aren't they alike?'

'Twins,' said George. 'I don't know how I

shall be able to tell one from t'other when Guy's bad foot is better.'

'I'm going to ring the police,' said Julian, seeing that his aunt could now only think of Guy's swollen foot. He went off indoors, and they heard him speaking on the telephone. He put it down and came out again.

'The inspector himself is coming,' said Julian. 'Shall I ring the doctor now, Aunt Fanny?'

'Oh yes. His number is in the book,' said his aunt. 'How *did* you get such an ankle, Guy?'

'Mother, you don't seem at all interested in our adventure,' complained George.

'Oh, I am, dear,' said her mother. 'But you do have such a lot, you know. What have you been up to this time?'

But before George could do more than begin, a black police car drew up at the front gate, and the inspector of police got out and marched up to the front door. He knocked extremely loudly on the knocker.

Which, of course, had the immediate result of

bringing George's father hotfoot out of his study in another rage! He flung open the front door.

'Hammering at the door like that! What's the matter? I've a good mind to report you to the police! Oh – er – hm – good afternoon, Inspector. Do come in. Are we expecting you?'

Smiling broadly, the inspector came in. By this time Julian had come back in the house again and greeted him. His uncle went back into his study, rather red in the face, and actually closed the door quietly!

'You wanted me to come along at once, because of something important?' said the inspector. 'What is it?'

The others came into the room now, with Julian's aunt behind them. Julian nodded round at them. 'They're all in this – except my aunt, of course. We've brought something we think may be important. Quite a lot of people were looking for it – but we managed to get hold of it first!'

He put the brown bag on the table. The inspector's eyes went to it at once. 'What is it? What's inside? Stolen goods?'

'Yes – blueprints of some kind, I think. But I don't know what of, of course.'

'Open the bag, my boy! I'll examine them,' said the inspector.

'I can't open it,' said Julian. 'It's locked – and there's no key!'

'Well – we'll soon manage *that*!' said the inspector, and took out a small, strong-looking tool. He forced the lock, and the bag opened. Everyone leaned forward eagerly, even Timmy. What was in the bag?

There was nothing there! Absolutely nothing! Julian groaned in bitter disappointment.

'No wonder it felt so light. It's empty after all. Would you believe it!'

[20]

The adventure ends – as it began!

It was a moment of great disappointment for all the children. Although they had talked about the possibility of the bag being empty, everyone had secretly felt certain that something exciting would be inside.

The inspector was astonished. He looked round sharply. 'Where did you get this bag? What made you think it had stolen goods inside – and what kind of blueprints were they?'

'Well – it's rather a long story,' said Julian.

'I'm afraid you'll have to tell it to me,' said the inspector, taking out his notebook. 'Now – how did this all begin?'

'Well – it really began with Timmy hurting

his ear and having to wear a cardboard collar,' said George.

The inspector looked most surprised. He turned to Julian. '*You'd* better tell it,' he said. 'I don't want to waste time on cardboard collars!'

George went red and put on a scowl. Julian grinned at her, and began the story, making it as clear and short as he could.

The inspector became more and more interested. He laughed when Julian came to the weird noises and lights.

'They certainly wanted to get rid of you,' he said. 'You were plucky to stay on. Go on – there's something behind all this, that's certain!'

He jotted down the names 'Paul', 'Tom' and 'Jess', the name of the woman. He noted that one man had a drawl. 'Any other clues to them?' he asked.

'Only this,' said Julian and handed his drawing of the crêpe-soled shoe to the inspector.

This was carefully folded and put into the notebook too. 'Might be of use. Might not,' said the inspector. 'You never know!'

He listened intently to the tale of the underground passages, and picked up the bag again.

'I can't understand why it's empty,' he said. 'It isn't really like a crook deliberately to mislead his friends when they know quite well where he is and can get at him whenever they like.' He shook the bag hard. Then he began to examine it very very carefully.

Finally he took out a sharp knife and gently slit the lining at the bottom of the bag. He turned it back.

Something was there – under the lining! Something blue, folded very carefully. Something covered with thousands of minute figures, thousands of lines, thousands of strange little designs!

'Wheeeeeew!' whistled the inspector. 'So the bag's *not* empty, after all! Now what is this? It's a blueprint of some project – but what?'

'My father would know!' said George, at once. 'He's a scientist, you know, Inspector – one of the cleverest in the world. Shall I get him?'

'Yes,' said the inspector, laying out the blueprint on the table. 'Get him at once.'

George flew off and returned with her father, who didn't look very pleased.

'Good afternoon, once more. Sorry to disturb you,' said the inspector. 'But do you happen to know whether this document is of any importance?'

George's father took it up. He ran his eyes over it, and then gave a loud exclamation.

'Why – why – no, it's IMPOSSIBLE! Good heavens, it's – no, no, it can't be! Am I dreaming?'

Everyone gazed at him, surprised and anxious. What did he mean? What could it be, this blueprint?

'Er – it's important then?' said the inspector.

'Important? IMPORTANT? My dear fellow, there are only two of these prints in existence –

and at the moment I have the second one, which I am checking very carefully indeed. Where did this come from? Why – I simply can't believe it! Sir James Lawton-Harrison has the other. There isn't a third!'

'But – but – there must be if you have one here and Sir James has the other!' said the inspector. 'It's obvious there is a third!'

'You're wrong. It isn't obvious!' shouted George's father. 'What *is* obvious is that Sir James hasn't got his! I'll ring him up – this very minute. Astounding! Most disturbing! Bless us all, what will happen next?'

The children did not dare say a word. They were full of astonishment. To think that the blueprint was so important – and that George's father actually had the pair to this one. What was its importance?

They heard George's father shouting into the telephone, evidently angry and disturbed. He slammed it down and came back.

'Yes. Sir James's copy has been stolen – but

it's been kept very hush-hush because of its importance. Good heavens – they never even let *me* know! And to think I spilt a bottle of ink over mine yesterday – gross carelessness. Stolen! A thing like that – stolen out of his safe under his very nose. Now there's only my one copy left!'

'Two,' said the inspector, tapping the copy on the table. 'You're so upset to hear that Sir James's copy has gone that you've forgotten we have it here!'

'Bless us all! Thank goodness! Yes, I *had* forgotten for the moment!' said Uncle Quentin. 'My word, I even forgot to tell Sir James it was here.' He leapt up to go to the telephone again, but the inspector caught his arm.

'No. Don't telephone again. I think we should keep this as quiet as possible.'

'Father – what *is* this a blueprint of?' said George, voicing the thoughts of everyone there, the inspector included.

'This blueprint? I'm certainly not going to tell

you!' said her father. 'It's too big a thing even to speak of to you children – or the inspector either for that matter. It's one of the biggest secrets we have. Here, give it to me.'

The inspector placed his big hand on it at once. 'No. I think I must take it with me, and send a secret messenger to Sir James with it. It wouldn't do to have the only two copies in one place. Why, your house might catch fire and both prints might go up in flames!'

'Take it, then, take it! We can't possibly risk such a thing!' said George's father. He glared round at the children. 'I still don't understand how *you* came to possess it!' he said, looking suddenly amazed.

'Sit down, won't you, and listen to their tale,' said the inspector. 'They've done very well. They haven't finished their story.'

Julian went on with it. The inspector sat up straight when he heard where the three men were – down in the great pit below the Roman camp.

'You saw them go down into that pit?' he said. 'Watched them swing down on the rope? They may be there now!' He glanced at his watch. 'No, they won't. They'll be gone.'

He groaned loudly. 'And to think we might easily have caught three clever rogues. They've slipped through our hands again!'

'They haven't!' said Julian, his voice rising exultantly. 'They're still there!'

'How do you know?' said the inspector.

'Because I pulled up their rope and took it away – look, I've got it round me!' said Julian. 'They can't get out without a rope – and they won't know how to escape any other way. They're still there – waiting for you, Inspector!'

The inspector slapped the table so hard that everyone jumped and the two dogs barked.

'Good work!' he boomed. 'Magnificent! I must go at once and send some men out there. I'll let you know what happens!'

And out he went at a run, the precious blueprint buttoned safely in his pocket. He leapt into the driving seat and the police car roared away at top speed down the lane.

'Whew!' said Julian, flopping back into his chair. 'It's too exciting for words!'

Everyone felt the same, and began to talk at the tops of their voices. Poor Aunt Fanny couldn't make herself heard. But when Joanna came in and asked if anyone wanted anything to eat, they heard her at once!

The doctor came to see Guy's foot, and rebandaged it. 'Rest it for a day or two,' he said. 'It will soon be all right.'

'Well, you'll have to stay here with George and the others, Guy,' said George's mother. 'You can't go excavating in that camp of yours again yet. Harry can stay too. So can Jet.'

The twins beamed. They liked this jolly family, and the adventurous life they seemed to lead. It would be fun to stay with them for a while. They thought it would be even *more* fun, when Joanna arrived with a truly wonderful meal!

'Home-made veal-and-ham-pie! Stuffed to-matoes! And what a salad – what's in it, Joanna? Radishes, cucumber, carrot, beetroot, hard-boiled eggs, tomatoes, peas – Joanna, you're a marvel! What is the pudding?' George asked.

Soon they were all sitting down enjoying themselves, and talking over their adventure. Just as they were finishing, the telephone bell rang. Julian went to answer it. He came back looking thrilled.

'That was the inspector. They've got all three men! When they got to the pit, one of the men called up for help – said some idiot of a boy or some hoaxer must have taken their rope away. So the police – all in plain-clothes, so that of course the three men suspected nothing – the police let down a rope, and up came the men one by one . . .'

'And were arrested as soon as they popped out of the hole, I suppose!' said George, de-lighted. 'Oh, I wish I'd been there! What a joke!'

'The inspector's awfully pleased with us,' said Julian. 'And so is Sir James Lawton-Harrison too, apparently. We're to get a reward – very hush-hush, though. We mustn't say anything about it. There's to be something for each of us.'

'And for Timmy too?' said George at once.

Julian looked round at Timmy. 'Well, I can see what old Timmy ought to ask for,' he said. 'A new cardboard collar. He's scratching his ear to bits!'

George screamed and rushed to bend over Timmy. She lifted a woebegone face. 'Yes! He's scratched so hard he's made his ear bad again. Oh Timmy! You really are a stupid dog! Mother! Mother! Timmy's messed up his ear again!'

Her mother looked into the room. 'Oh George, what a pity! I *told* you not to take off that collar till his ear was absolutely healed!'

'It's maddening!' said George. 'Now everyone will laugh at him again.'

'Oh no they won't,' said Julian, and he smiled at George's scowling face. 'Cheer up – it's a very peculiar thing, George – this adventure *began* with Timmy and a cardboard collar – and bless me if it hasn't *ended* with Timmy and a cardboard collar. Three cheers for old Timmy!'

Yes – three cheers for old Timmy! Get your ear well before the next adventure, Tim – you really *can't* wear a cardboard collar again!